THE MARY RODGERS TREASURY

THREE MIND-BOGGLING NOVELS

WRITTEN BY MARY RODGERS

BARNES
&NOBLE
BOOKS
NEW YORK

HarperCollins*Publishers*

The Mary Rodgers Treasury

CONTENTS

❋ Freaky
Friday ❋

by

MARY RODGERS

📖 HarperCollins*Publishers*

For Nina, Kimmy, and Ma

❀ Freaky Friday ❀

One ❀

You are not going to believe me, nobody in their right minds could *possibly* believe me, but it's true, really it is!

When I woke up this morning, I found I'd turned into my mother. There I was, in my mother's bed, with my feet reaching all the way to the bottom, and my father sleeping in the other bed. I had on my mother's nightgown, and a ring on my left hand, I mean her left hand, and lumps and pins all over my head.

"I think that must be the rollers," I said to myself, "and if I have my mother's hair, I probably have her face, too."

I decided to take a look at myself in the bathroom mirror. After all, you don't turn into your mother every day of the week; maybe I was imagining it—or dreaming.

Well, I wasn't. What I saw in that mirror was absolutely my mother from top to toe, complete with no braces on the teeth. Now ordinarily, I don't bother to brush too often—it's a big nuisance with all those wires —but my mother's teeth looked like a fun job, and besides, if she was willing to do a terrific thing like turning her body over to me like that, the least I could do was take care of her teeth for *her*. Right? Right.

You see, I had reason to believe that she was responsible for this whole happening. Because last night, we had a sort of an argument about something and I told her one or two things that had been on my mind lately.

As a matter of fact, if it's OK with you, I think I'd better start back a little farther with some family history, or you won't know what I'm talking about or who (whom?).

My name is Annabel Andrews. (No middle name, I don't even have a nickname. I've been trying to get them to call me Bubbles at school, but it doesn't seem to catch on.) I'm thirteen; I have brown hair, brown eyes, and brown fingernails. (That's a joke—actually, I take a lot of baths.) I'm five feet; I don't remember what I weigh but I'm watching it, although my mother says it's ridiculous, and I'm not *completely* mature in

my figure yet. Maybe by the summer though.

My father is William Waring Andrews; he's called Bill; he's thirty-eight; he has brown hair which is a little too short, but I've seen worse, and blue eyes; he's six feet (well, five eleven and a half); and he's a fantastically cool person. He's an account executive at Joffert and Jennings, and last year his main account was Fosphree. If you're into the environment thing at all, you know what that is: no phosphates, low sudsing action, and, according to my mother, gray laundry. We had boxes of the stuff all over the kitchen. You couldn't *give* it away. This year, he has New Improved Fosphree (That's what they think!), plus something called Francie's Fortified Fish Fingers. *Barf* time! If there's anything more disgusting than fortified fish, I don't know what.

Oh yes, I do, I just thought of what's worse. My brother. He is I cannot begin to tell you how disgusting. It may not be a nice thing to say but, just between you and me, I *loathe* him. I'm not even going to bother to describe him—it's a waste of time. He looks like your average six-year-old with a few teeth out, except that, as my grandmother keeps saying, "Wouldn't you know it'd be the boy who gets the long eyelashes and the curly locks? It just doesn't seem fair." No, it certainly doesn't, but then what's fair? These days, not much. Which is exactly what I was trying to tell my

3

mother last night when we had the fight. I'll get to that in a minute, but first a few facts about Ma.

Her name is Ellen Jean Benjamin Andrews, she's thirty-five—which makes her one of the youngest mothers in my class—she has brown hair and *brown* eyes. (We're studying Mendel. I must be a hybrid brown. With one blue- and one brown-eyed parent you're supposed to get two brown-eyed kids and two blue-eyed kids. So far there are only two kids in our family, but look who's already gotten stuck with the brown eyes. Me. The sister of the only blue-eyed ape in captivity. That's what I call him. The blue-eyed ape. Ape Face for short. His real name is Ben.) Anyway, back to my mother. Brown hair, brown eyes, and, as I've already mentioned, nice straight teeth which I did *not* inherit, good figure, clothes a little on the square side; all in all, though, she's prettier than most mothers. But *stricter*.

That's the thing. I can't stand how strict she is. Take food, for instance. Do you know what she makes me eat for breakfast? Cereal, orange juice, toast, an egg, milk, and two Vitamin C's. She's going to turn me into a blimp. Then for lunch at school, you have one of two choices. You can bring your own bag lunch, with a jelly sandwich or a TV dinner (They're quite good cold.) and a Coke, or if you're me, you have to eat the hot meal the school gives you, which is not hot and I

4

wouldn't give it to a dog. Alpo is better. I know because our dog eats Alpo and I tried some once.

She's also very fussy about the way I keep my room. Her idea of neat isn't the same as mine, and besides, it's my room and I don't see why I can't keep it any way I want. She says it's so messy *nobody* can clean in there, but if that's true, how come it looks all right when I come home from school? When I asked her that last night, she just sighed.

A few other things we fight about are my hair—she wants me to have it trimmed but I'm not falling for that again (The last time it was "trimmed" they hacked six inches off it!)—and my nails which I bite.

But the biggest thing we fight about is freedom, because I'm old enough to be given more than I'm getting. I'm not allowed to walk home through the park even with a friend, because "New York is a very dangerous place and especially the park." Everybody else's mother lets them, "but I'm not everybody else's mother." You're telling me!

Tomorrow one of my best friends in school who lives in the Village is having a boy-girl party and she won't let me go because the last time that friend had a party they played kissing games. I told her the mother was there the whole time, staying out of the way in the bedroom, of course, and she said, "That's exactly what I mean."

What kind of an answer is that? I don't get it. I don't get any of it. All I know is I can't eat what I want, wear what I want, keep my hair and my nails the way I want, keep my room the way I want or go where I want. So last night we really had it out.

"Listen!" I screamed at her. "You are not letting me have any fun and I'm sick of it. You are always pushing me around and telling me what to do. How come nobody ever gets to tell *you* what to do, huh? Tell me that!"

She said, "Annabel, when you're grown-up, people don't tell you what to do; you have to tell yourself, which is sometimes much more difficult."

"Sounds like a picnic to me," I said bitterly. "You can tell yourself to go out to lunch with your friends, and watch television all day long, and eat marshmallows for breakfast and go to the movies at night..."

"And do the laundry and the shopping, and cook the food, and make things nice for Daddy and be responsible for Ben and you . . ."

"Why don't you just let me be responsible for myself?" I asked.

"You will be, soon enough," she said.

"Not soon enough to suit me," I snapped.

"Is that so!" she said. "Well, we'll just see about that!" and she marched out of the room.

6

Two ✿

All of which should explain why I wasn't as surprised as most people would be if they woke up in their mother's body.

I was a *little* surprised of course, but mostly I felt it was fantastically considerate of her. And imaginative. Instead of punishing me for rudeness, or crying phony tears like some mothers I know, she was just going to let me find out for myself. I could hardly wait. The whole day stretched out ahead of me. I was going to tell myself to do a whole bunch of fabulous things—as soon as the kids got off to school where—oh hey! oh wow!—I wasn't going to have to go! Not that I hate school. Actually, I like it, at least I like the people, but on the days when you haven't done all your assignments, Miss McGuirk (rhymes with work, shirk and *jerk*) gets mad, and this was going to be one of those days. I hadn't done any of it, not even the English composition I was supposed to hand in this week.

I flashed myself a radiant smile in the bathroom mirror and remembered that my first responsibility was to our teeth, which I brushed with great enthusiasm. Oh the smoothness of them all . . . a joy to the tongue! I rinsed and smiled again.

"Lovely. You're lovely. *I'm* lovely," I thought. I took the rollers out, fixed my hair, put on a silky bathrobe, and looked myself over again. Even lovelier. But a bit pale, maybe?

The next twenty minutes I spent mucking around with the moisturizer and the foundation and the translucent powder and the TV Touch (That's wrinkle hider and I wonder why she bothers with it. We certainly don't need it.), the rouge, and the three different eye shadows, the eyelash curler and finally the mascara. How did I know what I was doing? You may well ask! I've watched her do it a hundred and one thousand times when she was going out on a festive occasion. It's easy.

"Oh my!" I whispered to the mirror. "Aren't you something! Aren't you just something!"

Lately I'd been getting so fed up with my face and fed up with people saying how much I looked like my mother. My mother is always saying, "Her father and

8

I think Annabel looks like her very own self." You know why I think she says that? Because it's insulting to her to say I look like her. I guess I can't blame her. If I were Ma and had a daughter who looked like me, I wouldn't admit it either. Besides, I don't. Look like her, that is. I wish I did.

"Well, today I do, and it's a great improvement," I thought to myself, and slinked out of the bathroom and into the bedroom where Daddy was still sleeping. I gave him a little punch on the shoulder to wake him up.

"Hey," I said, "are you awake?"

"I am now," he said. "Was I dreaming or did you just punch me?" I guess grown-ups don't punch each other awake. He looked sort of annoyed.

"You must have been dreaming," I said. "Anyway, now that you're up, how do I look?"

"What makes you think I'm up?" he asked, closing his eyes again and rolling over. "I'm not at all up, I don't want to be up, and I don't know what *you're* doing up. As a matter of fact, what *are* you doing up? Is there something wrong?" He opened one eye.

"No, no, nothing," I said in a hurry. "I just wondered if you liked the way I look." He opened the other eye, leaned on one elbow and blinked at me.

"Ellen, what is going on with you this morning?" (Ellen, he really thinks I'm Ellen. Isn't this the most

9

marvelous, incredible . . .) "Of course I like the way you look. I always do. You look fine—a little fancy for this time of day, but fine."

"You mean my face, Bill?" I asked.

"Yes, I mean your face; you don't usually put all that stuff on before breakfast, but you look great. You have a great face, I love it. I love you. OK? Now can I go back to sleep?"

Just then the alarm went off. Daddy groaned and I slinked off to the kitchen to make breakfast before he could say anything else. Somehow, I had the feeling that until he'd had some coffee, anything else he said wouldn't be too friendly. And then I realized that after he'd had the coffee he might not be too friendly either because he was going to get instant. It was the only kind I knew how to make.

Three ✿

Breakfast went off not too badly, considering it was my first. Luckily, Daddy asked for fried (I learned how to do that a couple of years ago.) so I made fried, and toast. I also made a small mistake.

"Sorry about the instant, Daddy, but we're all out of regular," I said, giving him a nice friendly kiss on the cheek.

"*Daddy!* Since when did you start calling me Daddy? You never did that before," he said.

"No, and I won't again, Bill, dear," I said, relieved at least that he wasn't going to make a scene about the coffee. I ran back into the kitchen to find out what Ape Face wanted.

"What'll it be for you, lover boy?" I asked, crossing

my arms and giving him the hairy eyeball. Just watch him ask for scrambled!

"Could I have scrambled, Mommy, please?" What did I tell you!

"No, you can't," I said, very briskly. "I don't have time to wash two pans. It's fried or nothing."

"But I don't like fried," he said. (You know, she spoils him rotten, but not me!)

"Then eat cold cereal," I said, slapping down a box of Sugar Coated Snappy Krackles in front of him.

"But these are Annabel's. She bought them with her own money to eat when she watches television. She'll kill me if I eat up her cereal," he said anxiously. What a worrywart.

"Listen, Ben," I said very slowly and carefully. "Annabel *wants* you to eat her Sugar Coated Snappy Krackles. So eat 'em. NOW!" He jumped and started to eat.

Speaking of Annabel reminded me that I hadn't seen myself yet and she was going to be late for school if she didn't hurry. Me, she, I, her? I was getting very mixed up. I also wondered, as I stood outside the door to her room, what—who—I was going to find in there. Was it going to be Annabel's body with Annabel's mind in it, but I wouldn't know what the mind was thinking? Or was it going to be Annabel's body with

Ma's mind in it, which would certainly be a more tidy arrangement?

Whoever-it-was was lying on her stomach on the bed, waving her feet in the air and reading a comic book. It certainly looked like Annabel. It looked like her room, too. There were all kinds of clothes dribbling out of drawers and hanging around on the floor. And one sneaker hanging around on a lamp.

"Uh, hi there," I said cautiously.

"Phloomph," it said. It seemed to be eating something.

"How about a nice hot cup of instant?" I suggested.

With that, whoever-it-was sat up in a hurry, turned around, and stared at me with its mouth wide open. It had not swallowed what was in its mouth. A marshmallow. Since I have never in my entire life seen my mother eating a marshmallow, I began to have a sneaking hunch that this was not my mother. It gulped and swallowed.

"A nice hot cup of *instant*?" it repeated. "What are you? Crazy? You know I don't drink that stuff."

It was Annabel all right. No doubt about it. Outside of the fact that Ma doesn't eat marshmallows and I do, there is the fact that if it was really Ma, she wouldn't ask me if I was crazy because she'd know I was Annabel thinking she was Ma. But if *she* was really Annabel too, no wonder she thought I was crazy. Any mother who asks her daughter if she wants a nice hot cup of instant has to be crazy.

"I was talking about a nice hot cup of instant oatmeal," I said in my haughtiest voice, "and I'll thank you not to eat marshmallows before breakfast. It spoils your appetite."

"What appetite?" she said. "I never have any appetite for all that vomitizing stuff you pile into me. Besides, I'm full up on marshmallows." She patted her stomach.

I decided to give in because it was getting too late to argue.

"OK, Annabel, forget breakfast, just get yourself dressed."

"But I can't get dressed," she complained. "I can't get dressed 'til I find my blue tights and I don't see where they are." I didn't see where they were either but I found some red ones in between Book B and Book S of the Junior Britannica. (In my library, S comes after B and L follows that.)

"Why don't you wear red? Red would be nice," I suggested in Ma's most reasonable voice. I should have known better.

"No," she said, crossly, "I want blue." I looked around wildly, trying to remember where I'd put them last night. They were in the wastebasket.

"You are a living doll," she said, blowing me several ballerina kisses. "How can I possibly sank you for zis enormous favor you do for me?" She'd gone into her French routine. What a nut! At least she was in a good mood again. The thing about Annabel is that she usually changes her moods quickly and often. Today, I wasn't going to know what to expect, or when. What was going on in her head right now, I wondered. Maybe she was thinking about her homework and McGuirk the Jerk. If she wasn't, she should be!

"Annabel, what are you going to tell Miss McGuirk?" I asked.

"About what?" she said.

"About the English composition," I said.

"You mean the English composition I was behind on?" she asked.

"Uh-huh," I said.

"Oh, I handed that in early last week," she said, looking me right in the eye. You want somebody to believe you, you always look 'em right in the eye. It's a slick trick of mine . . . works every time.

"Good girl," I said, because that's what Ma would've said. And anyway, what did I care what went on in school? That was her problem, not mine.

Ape Face stood in the doorway, jacket on, earmuffs

on, and a big, gooney smile all over his dumb face.
Every day he's ready ahead of time, just to show me
up, the fink!

"I'm all ready, Mommy, and I walked Max," he
said in his dumb voice. "He did a big thing and two
little things. Annabel better hurry or we're going to
miss the bus."

"If we do, it's because you're standing in my way,"
she snarled. "Get out of here, Ape Face, and don't talk
to me."

"I wasn't."

"You are now! And don't!" she said, throwing on
the rest of her clothes.

"I'm not!" he said.

"Ape Face, *shut up!*" she said. To tell the truth,
both of them were getting on my nerves. I tried to remember what Ma did with us in the morning.

"All right, all right, all right, you two, that's
enough of that," I said, pushing them to the front door.
So far, so good.

"And Annabel, I've told you a million times, don't
call him Ape Face; his name is Ben." Even better! I
was beginning to sound more like Ma than Ma does.

"Bye-bye, darlings, have a nice day," I said, holding
the door open for them. But Ape Face just stood there.
What was he waiting for, I wondered? Then a grotesque thought came to me. He was waiting to be

16

kissed and I was going to have to do it. So I did—as quickly as possible. Actually, it wasn't too bad. He smelled kind of nice. But I hoped he didn't expect it again at lunchtime. Annabel didn't expect it at all, she never does. Just as well. I would have felt funny kissing myself good-bye.

Four ✽

Now that the kids were gone, the apartment was so quiet I could hear my own breathing. There were a few small noises: the sanitation truck grinding away down the street, Max lapping up water in the kitchen, Daddy clearing his throat and rustling the *Times* in the dining room; but they weren't noises I had to do anything about. It was what Ma calls a little peace and quiet to give her time to think. Ordinarily I hate peace and quiet; it's boring. But today . . .

Come to think of it, speaking of Ma, I'd been too busy to worry about it before (not that I was worried now, just curious) but if Annabel's mind was in Annabel's body, which it certainly seemed to be, and Annabel's mind was also in Ma's body, which it most

18

definitely was (me is me, no matter what I look like), then where did Ma's mind get to? Somebody else's body, I suppose—but whose? If I were Ma, who would I be? Queen Elizabeth? Jackie Onassis? Gloria Steinem, Willa Cather? Or is Willa Cather dead? Yeah, I think she's dead.

Oh well, whoever she was, I hoped she was enjoying it and I hoped she wasn't going to be back too soon. At least until after English was over—I couldn't think of anything more hairy than turning back into myself in front of McGuirk. "I hope she gives me a whole day," I thought to myself. A day and a night, so I can stay up late.

I looked in Ma's datebook to see if she had anything nice planned. It was rather disappointing. Under Morning, it said buy more scotch; under Afternoon, it said "2:30" with a box around it—two-thirty where? Who with? She must keep all those things in her head, and now she's gone off with her head, the inside of it anyway, so whatever is happening at two-thirty, I'm just going to have to miss it, unfortunately.

Under Evening, it was blank. How about that! My first chance to have a good time and we're not going out to someone's house for dinner, or to a festive occasion. Phooey! And as for buying more scotch, how much was more? I looked in Ma's purse—it had seven-

19

teen dollars in it. Was that enough? Daddy was still reading the paper in the dining room. I'd have to ask him.

"Hi, darling," he said. "Kids get off all right?"

"Oh sure," I said. "Listen, I was just wondering . . ."

"Hmmnn?" he said, still reading the paper.

"We seem to be out of scotch so I thought I'd get some more."

"Good idea," he said. "While you're at it, pick up a bourbon and two gin—we're always out of gin."

"Maybe I don't have enough money for all that," I said, doubtfully. Daddy put down the paper and looked at me for a minute. Then he sighed. Not a long, teed-off sigh, more of a short, soft grunt.

"Ellen," he said, "I gave you fifty dollars yesterday. Where did it all go?"

I was beginning to not like this conversation. How did I know what she spent her money on yesterday!

"I'm not sure," I said, "but I only have seventeen dollars left."

"Just think about it for a minute," he said, in the same voice he uses on me-Annabel when I can't do a math problem—patient/impatient.

"The butter and egg man? He gets paid on Thursday," I said hopefully.

"OK, that's about seven dollars. What else?"

"Five dollars for more vacuum cleaner bags?"

20

other twenty—two scotch, two gin, one bourbon, and is Mrs. Schmauss coming today?"

"Let's see. Today's Friday? Yes, why?"

"Don't let her touch my shirts. She may be a good cleaner but she's a crummy laundress. Be a good girl and you do them, though, because I'm almost out. Good-bye, I'm late, I love you," and out he went, slamming the front door behind him.

What a cute man!

Five ✿

Imagine letting that poor cute man run almost out of shirts! I decided the first thing to do, before I even turned on the boob tube or picked out my dress for tonight, was those shirts. I found them in our (their?) bathroom hamper along with some other stuff (you know, the usual—socks, a couple of sweaters, a bra, some panty hose, pajamas, a terry-cloth wrapper). When I carried it all into the kitchen, it seemed like a full load, but we have a great big machine. There was still room for more. Not wanting to waste electricity (*Our* generation *cares* about the environment.), I threw in a few other grimy goodies: P.F. Fliers belonging to Ape Face, my shirt from the Army & Navy Store, a shaggy rug belonging to Max. A cup and a half of New Improved Fosphree, three quaters of a cup of

26

Clorox, punch up the hot water dial, and away we go. Nothing to it.

I found a bowl of leftover macaroni in the fridge and I was just about to sit down and watch "The Little Rascals" when the doorbell rang. Not expecting anybody and not wishing to be robbed on this, the most splendid day of my life, I peeked through the burglar hole . . . and almost fainted dead away. On the other side of the door stood Boris Harris!

Boris Harris is fourteen, he has chestnut hair and hazel eyes. I don't know how tall he is but it's a good three inches more than I am, and whatever he weighs is just perfect. He lives in our building, he is beautiful, and I love him.

"And he is standing outside our door right this minute holding a spaghetti sieve, and how am I going to handle the situation?" I asked myself. "With charm and sophistication," I answered myself, and with that I hid the bowl of macaroni in a wastebasket, and flung open the door.

"Why, good morning, *Boris*!" I said, "What a lovely surp*rise*!"

"I cabe to returd your collader," said Boris.

"That's very sweet of you," I said.

"It was by buther's idea because it was by buther who borrowed it," said Boris.

"Ah well, yes, I see what you mean," I said, "but in

any case, why don't you come on in for a minute. The hall is no place to be standing in a negligee, don't you agree?"

"Doh, I guess dot," said Boris, stepping over the threshold (What *took* him so long?), "but I cad ohdly stay a biddit—by buther is expectig be hobe."

"Poor Boris, that's a perfectly dreadful cold you've got there. Do you ever take Vitamin C? Let me get you some Vitamin C."

"Please dohd bother, Brs. Adrews, I dohd . . ."

"It's no bother at all," I shouted over my shoulder as I galloped to the kitchen. "Why don't you sit down in the living room and make yourself comfortable? I'm coming right back."

I did come right back, but it took me a minute to find him because, dear God, do you know where he was? Standing in the doorway of my-Annabel's room, wide-eyed and slack-jawed. Slack-jawed could be due to the cold, but wide-eyed, I'm afraid, was due to something else.

"Who lives *there?*" he said, wrinkling his adorable red nose.

"My son, Ben," I said, closing the door firmly.

"With a cadopy bed ad a *doll* house?"

"Yes, with a canopy bed and a dollhouse," I said. "My son is a very peculiar little boy."

"I'll say," agreed Boris. "He is also a slob."

28

"Right on!" I said with enthusiasm. "Here, take your Vitamin C and then we can play a game or something. You want to?"

"Sure," said Boris, and we played Nok Hockey for twenty minutes on the floor of the living room. He beat, which was fine with me.

"You did very well for a lady, though. Whed was the last tibe you played?"

"Yesterday. As a matter of fact, I play every day with Annabel. If you think I'm good, you should see her. She's great. Not as good as you, of course, but she'd give you a run for your money. You ought to come down and play with Annabel sometime."

"I'd rather play with you," said Boris.

"She also plays gin rummy, Monopoly, Dirty Water —that's a pollution game; she's very into the environment thing, you know—and chess.

"*Plus*, it's all I can do to stop her from reading— everything from Willa Cather to Salinger to Ian Fleming—*plus* a super collection of records—everything from country and western . . ."

"I hate coudtry ad westerd," said Boris.

"—to mostly classical and one or two show albums. Actually, she only has one country and western. Some boy gave it to her.

"You know, Boris," I continued, "lately, Annabel has completely changed. She is no longer the same person who cut your scalp open with a tin shovel in the playground five years ago."

"Four," said Boris.

"OK, four," I conceded. "Anyway, if you saw her now, you wouldn't even recognize her."

"Does she still have braces?" he asked.

"Well—" I began.

"Because if she still has braces, I'd recognize her."

"However, she's much nicer now than she used to be," I said.

"I'm sure she is," said Boris amiably, "but Mrs. Andrews, to be perfectly frank, that's not saying much." Thud. Long silence.

"Mrs. Andrews," said Boris, "it's not your fault that Annabel is the way she is. She's probably what they call a bad seed."

I stared at him. Then he got to his feet. I got to my feet.

"I think I'd better be going now," he said, "but I want to thank you for a wonderful time."

"That's OK, Boris, you come on down and visit whenever you want. You don't even have to call. Just come. Maybe we'll play some Dirty Water."

"I'd like that," said Boris. "Most grown-ups don't want to play games. They're too busy or something. But then, you're not the same as most grown-ups. You're . . ." he looked at me carefully for a moment and then shrugged his shoulders and grinned.

"Anyway," he said, "thanks, and thanks for the Vitamin C. That must be very zappy stuff. Did you notice my cold is completely gone?" And with that, he opened the front door and left before I even had a chance to say I hadn't noticed. Which I hadn't. Oh, the pain of it all, the naked aching pain!

I fished the bowl of macaroni out of the wastebasket, and turned on the living-room television set. I was hoping to find a good cartoon, but it was after ten and I couldn't even find a bad cartoon. I suppose they figure all the kids are in school and grown-ups like to watch other kinds of shows. Not very thoughtful of them. What about a poor little sick kid who has to stay home, or a poor little kid who's changed into her mother for the day. Not even one "Road Runner"? No sir. One ladies' panel show, one sewing show, "Romper Room," one show that looked good but it was all in Spanish, and a show called "Swing and Sway with Jean Dupray, Physical Fitness the Real Fun Way." That seemed like the best of the bunch, but just as I was beginning to get the hang of the swinging and swaying (which was easier for old Jean than for me because she was wearing a tank suit over tights and I was wearing Ma's long silk thing), there was the most staggeringly horrible noise in the kitchen. Right away, I knew it had to be the washing machine, and it took all the guts I had to go in there and look. Not that there was much to see —just bubbles—but the clatter and bang was enough to make you deaf for life. I was just about to turn it off before it went into the spin cycle—because it was mad as a hornet now, but when it started spinning it would probably break loose and chase me around the room— when the phone rang.

"Hello," I said. Too late. The spin cycle had begun. Last year, our class took a trip to an automobile grave-yard—a big crane throws dead cars into a pile and then a compressor thing mashes them all together into one large, tutti-frutti mess. All I can tell you is that compared to the racket in the kitchen, a trip to an automobile graveyard is like a trip to Grant's Tomb (where we also went last year).

"Hello, hello, hello," I shouted. Couldn't hear a word. I put the phone down in the kitchen and picked it up in the hall. Couldn't hear a word there either because all the noise in the kitchen was coming through from one phone to the other. Stupid of me, wasn't it?

"Hello? Wait a minute, hang on, I gotta hang up in the kitchen," I said and ran back again, but now there were suds all over the floor; it was like Christmas in Vermont. And the machine was dead as a doornail.

"Couldn't you pick some other day to have a break-down?" I said, giving it a kick.

"I mean what was the matter with yesterday, when

32

my mother was around? If you were going to shake yourself to death, why didn't you do it then? You had to do it on her day off? Come on, now, shape up!" I said, giving it another kick and a hit. Sometimes if you hit a machine a couple of times you can get it going again, at least that's what I do with my record player. But this thing was a goner. I could tell.

"Thanks for nothing," I said. "And as for you," I said to Max, who was sampling the suds, "you lap up any more of that stuff and you're going to be good and sick."

I looked up the washing-machine-repair number and picked up the phone to call the place, and would you *believe* it? there was no dial tone! I hung up and picked it up again. Still no dial tone. On the third try, I picked it up in the middle of somebody saying hello. Crossed wires again. It happens all the time. I took a deep breath and then very slowly and distinctly, I said, "Madame, I think we have crossed wires. You are in on my line. If you will simply hang up and I will simply hang up you will be able to reach your party and I will be able to reach my party."

The other end cleared its throat, and then very slowly and distinctly said, "Five minutes ago you asked me to hang on. Now you want me to hang up. Have you gone absolutely out of your mind?"

"Oh, my goodness!" I said, "Are you the person I

was talking to before? Yes of course you are, I never hung up out there, did I? How idiotic of me. I'm *terribly* sorry! Listen, lemme just hang up in the hall and I'll be right . . ."

"Oh, no you don't!" screamed the voice. "That's what you said the last time. I'm not waiting one more minute. I have cream on my face and I've been waiting to get into the bathtub for over an hour!"

"Well, what's that got to do with me?" I said. "Who is this anyway?"

"Ellen Jean, this is your mother. Who in blue blazes did you think it was?"

Now that's what I call a lulu of a boo-boo, not to recognize your own grandmother (or mother, as the case may be).

"Oh, Mother," I said, "I do apologize, but it was so noisy in here on account of the machine. Anyway, how are you?"

"Oh, I'm all right, I suppose, but as you know, dear, I don't take my tub until after your call because it's so inconvenient to have to get *out* of the tub and chilly. So I do wish you'd remember to call me exactly at nine. Could you remember to do that, dear?"

"Sure, Mother, sure," I said.

"Thank you, dear," she said, "Oh, and Ellen Jean, do you and Bill have any plans for the Fourth of July weekend?"

34

"You want to know now, in February, what we're doing on the Fourth of July?" She's too much!

She said the reason she wanted to know *now* was that if we weren't coming (the house in Larchmont) she wanted to line up some other people because I knew how lonely it had been since Dad took sick and passed on. (If there's anything I can't stand, it's "took sick" and "passed on" or "passed away." What's the matter with just plain "died"?)

So I looked in Ma's date book which didn't have anything down for the Fourth of July, and then I got a brainstorm.

"Mother," I said, "Not only are we free for the weekend of the Fourth, but how would you like to have us for the whole month? That way, you wouldn't be lonely, and Bill and I could get out of the hot city . . ."

"I think that would be just wonderful," she said, "but what about the children? There are only two guest bedrooms, and surely Ben and Annabel are getting too old to share a room."

"Didn't I tell you?" I said gaily. "Annabel's going to camp this summer. There's plenty of room in your house and Bill will be thrilled."

"What accounts for his change of heart, I wonder? Ah well, ours not to question why, is it now?" I didn't have the faintest idea of what she was talking about but thought it best to agree with her anyway. Then I explained I had to get off the phone to call about the washing machine, and we both made kiss-kiss noises at each other and said good-bye.

Annabel Andrews, when you put your mind to it, you have a mind like a steel trap! Camp was saved; Daddy's July was saved; now if I could just figure out how to save the machine and the shirts, I'd be ahead of the game.

Six ✿

Would you be interested in knowing how long it took me to get the washing-machine-repair number to answer? Fifteen minutes. Might you also be interested in knowing how far I got with the man I finally talked to, after he kept me on hold for another five minutes?

I won't bore you with the whole conversation, just one or two highlights. First I gave him my name and address, and then I said, "My washing machine broke down this morning. I have six children, two in diapers, and I'm desperate. Please, could you come over and fix it—now?"

He said, "First I gotta get the particulars. What make machine?"

"It's a Miracle Maid."

"Miracle Maid. OK. Which type?"

"Top sider."

"Lady, you want a sneaker repaired, go to a shoe store. I'm a very busy man—no time for jokes. You don't mean top sider, you mean top loader. So *say* top loader."

"Top loader."

"Now we're getting somewhere. So how long you had this top loader?"

"Wait a minute, you're getting me all mixed up. I only said top loader because you said, 'Say top loader.' I don't have a top loader, I have a side loader. I mean front loader. A broken front loader which I desperately need you to come and fix, *today*."

You know what he said? He said, "I'll have a man up there a week from Wednesday, lady," and hung up. Zilch is how far I got.

I chewed off a couple of fingernails and then wandered into Ma's closet to try on a few things. I was just admiring myself in a black velvet pants suit (which looked very nice, I thought) when the doorbell rang. Could it possibly be beautiful Boris Harris coming back for another round of Nok Hockey? I peeked through the burglar peephole. No, it could not. It was Rose Schmauss, the cleaning lady. A dismal comedown.

Mrs. Schmauss I don't know very well. She usually arrives after I've gone to school and she's gone before I get home. Once in a while she baby-sits—I'd have to ask her about tonight. As far as looks go, let me put it to you this way: She's the next closest thing to a rhinoceros, with a voice that could shatter glass, and she smells funny.

"How *are* you, Mrs. Andrews? What a precious outfit. Going out to lunch, I imagine." Was she asking me or telling me? Maybe she knew something I didn't know. Maybe that's what two-thirty with a box around it meant. A late lunch date with somebody. But who?

"What's *your* guess Mrs. Schmauss?" I asked coyly.

"I'd guess you have a rawndyvoo with a secret lover, right?" she said, poking me in the ribs with her fat finger. The dirty bird!

"Wrong," said I, promptly. "I'm on my way to the liquor store."

"In *that* you're going to the liquor store? A ladies' luncheon maybe, but to go around the corner in?"

It's none of her business what I go around the corner in. I know just as well as she does people don't wear velvet with rhinestone buttons in the morning, but they do wear them in the evening and that's what I was dressed for. I don't see why grown-ups keep changing their clothes all day long. An old rag to do the breakfast dishes in (heck, I forgot to do the breakfast dishes; oh well, Mrs. Schmauss could) a skirt to go to the store in, a dress to go to lunch in, pants to go to the park in, and velvet and rhinestones to go to dinner in. If you count in and out of your nightgown twice, that makes six changes. What a bore! I like to get into one thing and stay in it.

"I'm quite comfortable the way I am," I said icily.

"Hon*ey*!" she said, pinching my cheek, "No offense intended. If it makes you happy, it makes me happy."

"I'm happy," I said.

"Good, great! That's what I like to hear," she boomed. "Now where do you want me to start today? In the kitchen, I'll bet."

"You bet absolutely right," I said happily, following her down the hall. "I have had a simply hideous morning. I haven't even gotten to the breakfast dishes."

"Oh?" she said, glaring at me over her fat shoulder, "How come?"

"Because the washing machine broke and there are suds all over the floor."

"That so," she said. By now we were in the kitchen.

"I don't see no suds," she said. I didn't see no suds either, just a little water on the floor. They must have melted.

"How do you know this machine is broke? It don't

look broke to me." She leaned down and squinted into it.

"Because it made this awful noise, and then it stopped altogether. And there *were* a lot of suds."

"It stopped because it was through," she said, pointing to the dial. "See? It says off. Off means through."

"No kidding," I said.

"Hon*ey*!" she said again, "No offense, I'm sure. Just trying to be helpful. Now let's take a look what's going on inside."

She opened the machine door and began unloading all the stuff into the laundry sink.

"Well, no *wonder*!" she said. "You're gonna cram your shirts *and* your rugs *and* your hose *and* your *sneakers,* and some little tin things—what are these little tin things? oh, they're jacks—*and* your jacks all in together, not to mention you used too much soap, and *that*," she said triumphantly, "*that* explains your noise and your suds."

"Yeah, I guess it might," I said. "That's what comes of letting Annabel help with the laundry. Those must be her jacks. Sweet thing was only trying to be helpful."

"A genuine first!" said Mrs. Schmauss, snorting through her sinuses. "Since when did she decide to be helpful? Or is today your birthday?" I decided to let that one pass.

"All right, Mrs. Schmauss," I said, "if you want to start finishing up the laundry now, please, but never mind doing the shirts today."

"Today? Whaddya mean *today*? I never did the shirts before, I should sunly stop doing them *now*?

"Lissen, honey," she said, waving her fat finger under my nose, "when I come to work for you what was it, two, three months ago?—we agreed on a couple things I don't do. Number one is *I don't do no men's shirts*."

"And number two is?" I could hardly wait to hear.

"Mrs. Andrews, we have to go into that again?"

"If it's not asking too much, Mrs. Schmauss, I demand to know—number two is *what*?"

"Don't holler on me, Missy, I'm not one of your colored!"

I blinked at her. "That is a disgusting thing to say," I shouted. "Hollering has nothing to do with coloring. And we don't call them colored, we call them . . ."

"Yah, yah, yah. All you liberals make me sick. I know what you call 'em; you call 'em black, right? Well *I* call 'em no-goodniks."

"And what do you call *you*?" I whispered. "You won't do this and you won't do that and you won't even tell me what you won't do. TELL ME WHAT IS THAT NUMBER TWO THING YOU WON'T DO!"

42

But Mrs. Schmauss was already halfway down the hall to the bedrooms.

"Come back here, where are you going?" I said.

"I don't have to tell you, I'll *show* you," said Mrs. Schmauss, turning the doorknob of Annabel's door and kicking the door with her foot.

"Holy Mother Of God, it's worse than usual!" she muttered.

"Number two is I do not pick up pigpens. That honor is reserved for the mother of the pig.

"Oh, beg pardon," she went on in this smarmy tone, "we don't call her a pig, do we? We call her 'a little thoughtless,' or 'a little forgetful.' Well I call her a little pig!

"Howdya like this?" she said, pointing to the red tights between Book B and Book S. "And this?"—she pointed to a marshmallow impaled on a magenta Mongol. "I suppose you can't call this a colored pencil, can you? And you can't call it a black pencil, so whaddya gonna call it? A Negro pencil? Ha!

"And how dya love this melted candle wax on your best bone china, and the apple core under the bed, and the underpanties under the bed . . ."

"They're perfectly clean underpants!" I said indignantly.

"But under the bed. Is that where they belong? Under the bed?

"Lemme tell you something, Mrs. Andrews. That kid's got no discipline, and a kid that's got no discipline is the fault of the mother and the father."

"Not necessarily," said I.

"Oh yes, oh *yes*. I've seen it time and again. You liberal folks are the ones turn out the troublemakers in this country. She'll be on drugs before you know it."

Rose Schmauss, you are one demented lady, I thought to myself. The whole conversation was so wild, I wasn't even mad anymore.

"Oh?" I said. "What makes you think so?"

"Well," she said, "remember Wednesday you asked me if I'd seen the half bottle of gin that was on the bar on Monday? That was probably your way of accusing me of drinking your liquor."

"It probably was," I said. No wonder she smells funny. People who don't smoke have a better sense of smell than people who smoke. Ma smokes like a chimney, but by Wednesday, even she must have wised up.

"That's what I thought," said Mrs. Schmauss smugly, "but now I'm going to tell you something." She leaned in toward me.

"I'm not saying I wouldn't take an occasional nip or two, but only my own hooch. I wouldn't touch nobody else's. She's never gonna admit it, but you know who's been drinking your gin?"

44

"Annabel," I said. My Lord. The woman was crazed!

"You said it; I didn't," said Mrs. Schmauss.

So then I did something that gave me such pleasure, I can't begin to tell you. In a grave and thoughtful voice, I said, "Mrs. Schmauss, honey, you're fired."

Seven ✿

What happened before I finally got her out of the apartment isn't worth describing in detail. Briefly, though, she asked me why I was firing her. I told her she was a liar and a drunk and prejudiced, which were not qualities I admired. She told me I was prejudiced —against Germans. I said I thought she was American. She said her grandfather was born in Germany. I said I had nothing against her grandfather. I didn't even know him. She said how could I know him, he was dead? I said I was sorry to hear it, was she very fond of him? She said she never knew him either, he died before she was born. In that case, I said, would she please give me the key to the apartment—which didn't have anything to do with anything but she was too far gone to notice. She gave me the key. I thanked her. She left.

The minute the twelve o'clock whistle blew, Max ran to the front door, ready to go out. Pavlov would have been delighted with him. Even I was kind of pleased; it gave me an excuse to get out of the apartment, and besides, I could buy the liquor at the same time.

For February, it was quite a nice day, and I took my time going to the corner. Had a friendly chat with the liquor store man, in which I warned him not to expect us to buy as much gin in the future, and told him about Mrs. Schmauss. He tsk-tsked a lot, gave me my change, and asked if I didn't want the bottles delivered—the boy could bring them right over. I said no thank you, I would just as soon carry them. If I'd had any idea what was going to happen next, I would have just as soon *not* carried them. I would, in fact, have been better off dead.

Up the block, across the street from our building, a crowd had collected. Also a police car. Now, she never lets me stop at accidents. I've told her a million times I only throw up at the sight of my *own* blood, but she hurries me along, saying, "Don't look, don't look!" This was my big chance.

Whoever said "curiosity killed the cat" must have had me in mind, because when I finally pushed my way to the center of the circle, me and the dog and the five bottles of liquor, what'd I see but the blue-eyed ape himself, screaming and crying at the top of his lungs for "Mommy." "I want my Mommy!" Ai-yi, I forgot to meet the bus!

You don't know how close I came to slipping quietly away again. After all, I wasn't his real mother anyway. Why not let the fuzz take him to the station house and feed him ice cream cones, and when she was ready to claim her own bod again (and give me back mine), she could go pick him up. Why not? I'll tell you why not. Because the little brat spotted me, that's why not.

"Oh Mommy, Mommy!" he sobbed, throwing his arms around my stomach, at the same time clobbering me in the small of the back with I don't know what—I couldn't see it.

"All right, I'm here, aren't I? Pipe down, cool it, that's en*ough*!" I snarled; but public opinion was running against me. People were saying things like, "Aw, the poor little fellow!" and "Vot kinda Mama is dot, I esk you?" and "That unfeeling woman should be reported to the ASPCA."

"C," I said, over my shoulder.

"Oh, a spic," said another voice. "She said *si*."

"We don't call them spics, we call them Puerto Ricans or Spanish-speaking Americans, and I said ASPC*C*."

"OK, Officer, report her to them," said the author of the unfeeling-woman line.

"Ladies, ladies, would you let me handle this, please?" said the cop. He unwrapped Ape Face's arms from around my middle (which, thank heavens, gave me a chance to set the five bottles down on the sidewalk—my arms were killing me), and then he kneeled down, saying, "Now, sonny, tell Officer Plonchik; is this your mother?"

"Of course I'm his mother. You heard him call me Mommy. Who else would I be?" Who else indeed? His sister, for one.

"Ma'am, please let him speak for himself. We have to have a positive identification. Once again, sonny, is this your mother?"

"Yes," said Ape Face.

The cop straightened up. "Well, Ma'am, it's a wise son that knows his own mother, as you might say."

"*You* might say it, I wouldn't," I said. "Can we go now?"

"In a minute. I'd like to ask you a few questions, if you don't mind. Have you ever abandoned this child before?"

"I didn't abandon him. I simply went to the liquor store and was late meeting the bus."

"Liquor is more important than your son, is that it?"

"Officer, I've never been late before. Ask him. Ask him if I've ever been late before." I poked the Ape.

"No," said Ape Face.

49

"Well, all right, then, but you're a very fortunate woman. He might have been killed crossing the street, or been abducted." (No such luck, I thought sourly.)

"So *ciao*, Officer, see you around," I said.

"Thank you for taking care of me, sir," said Mealy-mouth.

"You're old enough to take care of yourself," I said, as soon as we were out of earshot. "When you didn't see me there, why didn't you come on home alone?"

"And cross the street?" he squeaked. "You always told me if you didn't come, just to wait at the corner for you and *never* to cross the street."

"It's time you learned. Right now. Quick, tell me, what color does the light say now?" I wanted to make sure he wasn't color-blind.

"Green."

"Good. Now scram."

"Hold my helicopter, I don't want to cross with my hands full," he said and handed me his . . . helicopter? This is a helicopter? This is two hunks of nailed-together wood with three twisted pipe cleaners on top. This is also what clobbered me in the small of my back.

"Hey, Mom, I did it! I did it!" he shouted, jumping up and down on the other side of the street. "Did you see me?"

"Yes," I lied, and against the light, I raced across the

street, with the dog and the five bottles of liquor and the helicopter.

"You shouldn't do that. It's dangerous," he said.

"Grown-ups get to do it if they want to," I said. "And anyway, mind your own business."

He flashed me a quick look. "I'm sorry. Here, I can carry my own helicopter." He took it from me and didn't say another word until we were upstairs in the apartment.

I went right to the kitchen to start washing the soap out of Daddy's shirts and the rest of the stuff. It was ghastly work. Ape Face sat on a stool and watched me.

Finally, after about ten minutes, he said, "Aren't I going to get some lunch?"

"When I'm good and ready," I snapped. "I'm busy doing something. Can't you see?" From the look on his face, I think I had him pretty scared, but he squeezed his hands into fists, took a big, brave breath, and in a very little voice asked me where Mrs. Schmauss was.

"I fired her," I said, rinsing out a P.F. Flier.

"You mean she's not coming anymore? Not ever?" he whispered. Oh boy, if he starts crying again, I'll kill him! I thought to myself. I rinsed out the other sneaker.

"No," I said, calmly and firmly, "Not ever." There was a second of silence, and then behind my back there

51

was such an explosion of screaming and shouting and pounding on the counter, and the dog started barking, and when I turned around, that lunatic was tearing out the kitchen door, followed by the dog. Twice around the apartment they went, barking and shouting—for *joy,* mind you, for joy!—until they were both out of breath, and then the Ape sat right back down on the same kitchen stool and just grinned at me.

"I take it you didn't like her either," I said.

"Like her! Oh Ma, I hate her. She talks cross all the time and she smells bad, and mostly I hate her because she says Annabel is a spoiled brat and a pig . . ."

"I heard that once already, today. I don't have to hear it again." Mealymouthed hypocrite, I bet he loves repeating all those things about Ananbel.

"Well, anyway," he went on, "that's the mostly reason why I hate Mrs. Schmauss."

"Ooh, I'll just bet," I said, planting my hands on my hips and glaring at him with my eyebrows raised.

"I'll just bet!" I said again, and turned back to the sink to pick rug fuzz out of the drain.

"But it is," he insisted. "It honestly is." I heaved the gob of rug fuzz at the garbage (missed), dried my hands on the—whoops—on the velvet pants suit, and sat down opposite the Ape at the counter.

"Listen," I said, "lemme get something straight. The main reason you hate Mrs. Schmauss is because Mrs.

Schmauss hates Annabel, is that right?"

"Yes," he said. From the tone of his voice, you'd think I'd asked him if he was sure one and one made two.

"Look, stupid-o," I said. "You're not making any sense. You hate Mrs. Schmauss because Mrs. Schmauss hates Annabel; but Annabel hates *you,* so what do you care if Mrs. Schmauss hates her?"

"I just do," he said, twiddling the top of his hair with one finger—he does that when he gets embarrassed. When he was littler, he used to do it in his sleep and once he got his finger so snarled up in the hair, Ma had to cut the hair off to get the finger out. Stupidjerk!

"But it doesn't make any sense to hate somebody who hates somebody who hates you. I mean, if you want to hate Mrs. Schmauss for other reasons, OK, but the person you should really hate is Annabel."

"I know it," he said, twiddling away. "I try. But I just can't."

"Why not?" I asked.

"Dunno. Just can't," he said. Twiddle, twiddle, twiddle.

"Cut that out or you'll get your finger stuck again. Come on, now, tell me why not. If she's that great, what's so great about her? Tell me one thing. Just one."

"OK. Let's see. One thing. Uh . . . OK, yeah, I got one thing. Do you remember that time a long, long time ago when you and Daddy came home and said, 'What's all that white stuff out on the street? It looks like it's been hailing.' "

"You mean when you and Annabel threw the gobs of Kleenex and she said it was all your fault because it was your idea and besides you threw most of them, so you got punished and she didn't?"

"Yeah, that's the time," he said happily. "That was really great."

"You are a complete loon," I said. "It was Annabel's idea and Annabel threw most of them—you only threw two—so it was Annabel's fault and you got punished. What's so great about that, and what's so great about a person who pulls that kind of finky trick? That's not what I call great."

"Aw, Ma, you don't understand. I don't mind getting punished. It doesn't happen very often anyway" (that's for sure) "but we had such a good time doing it and I wouldn't of been able to reach where you keep the Kleenex by myself. I wouldn't of even thought of doing it by myself.

"See, Annabel gets these great ideas of things to do and I never get *any*. She is the smartest person I know." I wondered if he really meant it about the ideas or if he was just looking for a polite way to rat on me.

"What are some of her other ideas that you think are so terrific? What other bad things does she do?"

"Aren't I going to get some lunch soon?" he said, sliding off the stool and jiggling up and down. "I'm awful hungry because the graham crackers didn't go around twice. Also, I have to go to the bathroom." He ran out of the kitchen before I had a chance to ask him anything else, so I decided he might be a lot of other rotten things but he wasn't a rotten rat.

As I think I said before, I'm not much of a cook, so for the Ape's lunch, I took a bunch of stuff out of the fridge and put it on the counter for him to choose from. Plus the bowl of cold macaroni. When he came back from the bathroom, he looked at the macaroni and last night's damp salad and a couple of cold meatballs and half a thing of yogurt.

"Cleaning out the fridge?" he asked.

"This is a pick-up lunch. Pick up anything you want and throw the rest out," I said.

"No lamb chop or baked potato or string beans?" he asked.

"Not unless you want to cook it yourself."

"Nah, I hate hot lunches," he said. "They make me sick."

"Me, too," I said, and for a while nobody said anything. We ate the macaroni with our fingers out of the bowl. Then Ape Face asked if it was all right to put some grape jelly on the meat balls, they would taste nice that way, and I let him.

Then he said, "Another good thing about Annabel is she's very popular."

"Who with?" I asked.

"With everybody in my class," he said.

"Big deal," I said scornfully. "A whole mob of six year olds. Wowee!"

"She's also very popular with *her* class," he said.

"With the boys?" Maybe he knew something I didn't know.

"Oh, not the *boys* . . . just the girls," he said.

"Well, what's the matter with her? Why don't the boys like her? She's not bad looking." I leaned over and peered into his face. "Do you think she's bad looking?"

"I think she's beautiful," he said, "but I guess it's her braces. Not everybody likes braces. I don't know why. I love braces. When I get that old I hope I have them."

"With your luck, you won't need them," I said.

"That's what I'm afraid of," he said, "because then she's gonna hate me even more than she does now.

"Ma, why does she hate me so much?"

"Because you're a good little boy who never gets into any trouble, that's why. There is nothing more annoying in the whole entire world than a little blue-eyed saint with perfect teeth who is always on time and who never has a messy room!"

"Do you hate me, too?" asked Ape Face nervously.

"Oh, don't be a jackass! I'm just trying to explain why Annabel hates you. I mean I couldn't swear to it or anything, but if I was Annabel I wouldn't like having a brother who was cute-looking *and* neat."

"But I can't help those things! I can't help what I look like, I don't even care what I look like—and about being neat. I can't help that either.

"Listen!" he shouted. "Do you know something? If I thought she'd like me any better, I'd be messy. I've even tried being messy. Once I took all my piled-up blocks and the books in the shelves and the big bag of marbles and the Legos and flinged them all in the middle of the room so Annabel wouldn't be the only one getting in trouble, and you know what happened? That stinky Mrs. Schmauss said I was too young to know any better and picked everything up! So no matter what I do, Annabel keeps on hating me." His voice went into a wail and he hit the counter so hard the macaroni bowl jumped and his face was red and sweaty from yelling.

"Hey, hey, hey! Cool it. Calm down. Maybe you're exaggerating a little."

He calmed down all right, but he also started to cry.

"No," he said, in between sobs, "she really hates me."

Oh ook, oh cripes, oh crum, what to do now? I'd better make a joke. "Well then, why don't you just hate her right back?"

"I told you before," he said, "I try. But you can't hate someone and love them at the same time. Whoever heard of that?"

"Have a Kleenex," I said. "Your tears are getting in your mouth. Must taste lousy after grape jelly."

"Can you, Ma? Can you hate someone and love them at the same time?"

"I didn't used to think so, Ape Face, but I guess maybe you can." Maybe you can.

It's funny how little kids don't blow their noses very well. I helped him, and asked him if he was feeling better now. He said yes, thank you, he was. And then he said, "That's the first time you ever called me Ape Face." Another lulu of a boo-boo. I told him I was terribly sorry, it had just popped out of nowhere and he said—well you won't believe what *he* said!

He said, "You know, I love being called Ape Face. It's a real neat nickname. Nobody in my class has a nickname as good as that."

"You mean some of your friends call you that?"

"*All* my friends call me that," he said proudly. "See, the beginning of last year I told them that's what Annabel called me, and right away everybody did because . . ."

"Because they think Annabel is so terrific, right?"

"Yeah, right. But she won't call me it anymore if she thinks I like it, so don't tell her, OK?"

"You got yourself a deal, Ape Face," I said. Smart kid. Had me all figured out!

Eight ❀

It was two o'clock and I was just having a nice game of Crazy Eights with the Ape—actually, it's not the most interesting game in the world, but he picked it so what can you do?—when Daddy called.

"Oh good, I'm glad I caught you. I was afraid you'd already left," he said.

"Left for where?" I asked, jamming the phone between my ear and my shoulder and shuffling the cards.

"Wasn't today the day you had the big thing at the school with Dilk and McGuirk and the psychologist to discuss our little underachiever?" Two-thirty with a box around it. And I thought it was a late lunch. What a lovely surprise!

"Thanks for reminding me. I better get going or I'll never make it, it's after two now, talk to you la . . ."

"Ellen, hang in there a minute. You haven't even heard what I called up about in the first place. Look, did you get the sitter and everything lined up for tonight? Because if you did, cancel it, the whole thing's changed. We'll have to see 'Brucey and Betsy' some other night."

"Aw, why? I've been looking forward to it all day."

"I know, sweetheart, so've I, but Francie's Fortified Fish Fingers are in town and I had to invite them for dinner."

"Say that again?" I said, stupidly. My mind was boggling.

"OK, we'll take it from the top very slowly," he said. "The client and his wife, Mr. and Mrs. Philip Frampton, she calls him Philsie and he calls her Francie, and you've heard me talk about them a thousand times, are in town and I invited them for dinner."

"Here? You invited them *here*? You wouldn't! Not today! Invite them for tomorrow. Please Bill, how about tomorrow?" (Tomorrow—when maybe with a little luck, she'd be back.)

"No way, darling, they're only in town for one night. And they want to see the children so they're coming at six. I'll be home at five to change, did you do my shirts? And don't panic, you're one terrific cook." Male chauvinist pig!

"You're one terrific surprise after another," I

61

snapped into the phone, but it was too late. He'd already hung up.

"Ape Face, where are you? Come here, quick!" He scrambled to his feet and trotted into the hall.

"What's the matter, Mommy?"

"What's the matter is I completely forgot a meeting I have at school, with Mr. Dilk and Miss McGuirk and Dr. Artunian about that adorable sister of yours, in exactly twenty-five minutes and I don't have anybody to leave you with, so put on your Mighty-Mac and let's get moving."

"No," said Ape Face.

"Who do you think you're talking to, Benny-boy? This is your mother, remember me? Now get that Mighty-Mac and move it!"

"No," said Ape Face again. How do you like that? In my family there are not one but *two* male chauvinist pigs.

I took a deep breath, and in my most dripping-with-honey voice said, "Would you like to tell Mommy why you don't want to go with her or must Mommy try to read your horrible little mind?"

"Because I have been waiting for Paul to come over and play all year and every time he's going to come either he gets sick or I get sick and now he's finally coming and I'm not going!" The kid's got more guts than I gave him credit for.

"Ape Face, I admire your spirit and I appreciate your problem, but I cannot leave two little six-year-old boys alone in an apartment." He looked crushed. I felt sorry for him.

"Oh Ma, I hated Mrs. Schmauss the most of all of us, but couldn't you of waited 'til Monday to fire her? Don't you know any other sitters? Someone who could get here fast? Someone who . . ." Ai-yi, how could I be so stupid! The bluebird of happiness right in the building!

"Ape Face, I thought of someone. Quick, get the phone book."

"Harris residets, Boris speakig."

"This is Mrs. Andrews, Boris. What have you got on for the next hour or so?"

"The sabe thig I had odd this bordig, Brs. Adrews. Why?" Serves me right for being so grand.

"No, no, Boris, I mean what are you doing for the next hour or so? Are you busy?"

"Dot a bit. Would you like be to cub dowd ad play Dok Hockey?"

"Nok Hockey might be just the thing," I said, with a thoughtful eye on the Ape. "Come on down right now."

"Who's coming?" asked Ape Face.

"Boris Harris, the most beautiful boy in the building. At least Annabel thinks so. She's in love with him."

"Is he in love with her, too?"

"Not so's you'd notice," I said. "At least not yet. But anything we could do to help make Boris think more highly of Annabel we would certainly want to do, wouldn't you?"

"Sure," said Ape Face. "Like what?"

"I want you to let him think that your room is Annabel's room and Annabel's room is your room."

"Why?" he asked in a tone of whispery horror.

"Because that's what he already thinks anyway. When he was here playing Nok Hockey with me this morning, he happened to notice what a mess her room was, so . . ."

"So you told him it was *my* room? Aw, Ma!" I was about to remind him that it was all for Annabel when the doorbell rang and Ape Face vanished into thin air. Embarrassed, I guess.

"Hya, Boris, how's the champ? I can't tell you how glad I am to see you. How do you feel about baby-sitting?"

"Oh," he said, disappointed. "I thought you wadded be to play Dok Hockey."

"I do, I do," I said, "but not with me. With my son,

Ben." I explained all about the school meeting and Paul coming over and how desperate I was and how much I needed him, and finally he said, "Brs. Adrews, you doh I'd do eddythig for you, but could I please see your kid before I say yes?"

"Ben, darling," I called. "Come out, come out wherever you are and meet Boris Harris!"

The door to Annabel's room flew open and out stalked Tarzan. "Howdy, Boris," boomed Tarzan. "My mother calls me Ben but the guys at school call me Ape Face. Or just plain Ape. What do they call you in school?"

"Boris," said Boris to Tarzan. To me, he said, "I'll stay." Then he blew his nose and much to my amazement, all his m's and n's came back. "It's the oddest thing," he said. "I thought your Vitamin C fixed my cold, but upstairs in my apartment, the cold came right back, and down here it's gone again. Maybe I have a weirdo allergy to something.

"Oh well," he continued in a businesslike voice, "I know you're in a hurry so what are my instructions?"

"Just keep an eye on the boys, and answer the phone, and if you run out of things to do, you might whip up a smart dinner for four. My husband invited some clients home without any warning, and I just don't know *what* to *cook*."

"Don't give it another thought. I'd be glad to rustle up a little something for you. What time are your guests coming?"

"My mother was only kidding," said Ape Face.

"Boris was only kidding, too, weren't you Boris," I said.

"I wasn't kidding," said Boris, sounding rather hurt. "Mrs. Andrews, I'm an excellent cook. In fact, if I weren't I'd probably starve to death because I'm the only one in our house who can boil water."

"What about your mother?" I asked.

"Chinese, deli, or Chicken Delight—when she's in. Mostly she's out. When she's out, I cook."

"Isn't that sort of a girly thing to do?" asked Tarzan.

"Look who's talking! The slob who sleeps with the canopy bed and the doll house," retorted Boris. Ape Face opened his mouth to say something. I knew what he was going to say so I told him, "Shut up, I don't want to hear another word." Luckily he did what he was told.

"Never mind him anyway, Boris. He's just a male chauvinist pig."

"I'll say," agreed Boris, "but he's going to help me chop onions anyway, aren'tcha, ole pig, ole pal."

"Sure," said Ape Face, who is not one to hold a grudge, and when I left, they were both heading for the kitchen.

Nine ❀

The Barden School, on 75th between Park and Lex, is, as the crow flies, directly across the park from us. Not being a crow, and not having the time to take two up and down buses and one crosstown bus, I took a cab and arrived just as everybody was leaving. Have you ever tried to fight upstream through three hundred and fifty kids getting out of school on a Friday? Talk about your lemmings! I was practically knocked down by three of my best friends, Ginger, Jo-Jo, and Bambi.

"Hey Ginger, hey Jo-Jo, hey Bambi, how's every-thing?"

"Just fine, thank you, Mrs. Andrews."

"Anything happen in school today?" I asked.

"Nothing much," said Jo-Jo.

"How was English?"

"Fine," they all said.

"How's Annabel doing? She doing fine, too?" They all exchanged looks.

"Oh sure," said Jo-Jo. "Mrs. Andrews, please excuse us but we're in kind of a rush."

"And it's not too safe, standing in the middle of the door like that on a Friday afternoon. You might get knocked down," added Bambi.

"So we'll see you later, OK?" said Ginger.

Now ordinarily, I would have been extremely proud of my friends, because never rat to a parent no-matter-*what* is one of our first club rules. Today, though, I would have been grateful for one or two little scraps of gossip. About Annabel. About English. About McGuirk. About anything at all!

Funny about those kids, I thought to myself. They were in such a hurry to get going but they didn't seem to be going very far. In fact, they were standing still, halfway down the block, talking to each other and looking back toward me. Then, just as I was about to take the fatal plunge into the hallowed halls, Jo-Jo howled, "Mrs. Andrews, wait a sec; don't go in there yet! We gotta talk to you first."

In precisely a sec, they were all three at my side, panting and sniffling and yanking at their tights.

"Well, what is it, girls? I'm terribly late for a conference."

68

"That's what I thought," said Bambi.

"That's what I was afraid of," said Ginger.

"Who with?" asked my friend Jo-Jo, who never wastes a word in idle conversation. "Because if it's the one with Dilk and McGuirk about Annabel . . ."

"*Mr.* Dilk and *Miss* McGuirk," corrected Ginger. (When I get back into my own bod, I'm gonna drum that prig right out of the club!)

"Oh shut up, Virginia! She knows who I'm talking about. Anyway, is that who your conference is with?"

"Dilk and McGuirk and Artunian," I said. "Why?"

"Artunian, too? Chee!" said Jo-Jo, wiping imaginary sweat off her brow and shaking it to the pavement.

"Listen, ladies, what do the words 'I am already forty-five minutes late' mean to you? If you have something to say, I'd appreciate hearing it now."

"OK," sighed Jo-Jo. "I'm not sure how much you're going to like this, but here it is: Annabel was not in school today."

"Nonsense!" said I. "She left the house at eight fifteen with her brother. And *he* was in school. How did he get there if she didn't bring him?"

"Take him," corrected Ginger.

"Shut up, Virigina. Mrs. Andrews, after she saw he was inside the front door, she waited for us around the

69

corner. She said she didn't feel like going to school to-day on account of the English paper. She said she had better things to do and it was perfectly safe because the school never calls up to check on what's wrong with you the first day you're absent; they wait 'til the second day. She said she might see us this afternoon at the club meeting, all depending."

"All depending on what?"

"She didn't say. All she said was not to tell any-body, and of course we never would've, but then when we realized you were here for a conference, we wanted to warn you ahead of time so you wouldn't ask them how Annabel did in school today, or something ghastly like that."

"Ghastly is right," I said grimly. "When I get my mitts on that kid I'm gonna wring her neck!"

"Oh, Mrs. Andrews, it's the wildest thing how you and Annabel look like each other when you get an-gry."

"Shut up, Virginia!" I said and finally took the plunge inside the hallowed halls, which were by now deserted and gloomy and silent . . . except for one lone typewriter in the waiting room of Mr. Dilk's office. Behind the typewriter was the Secretary to the Prin-cipal, Mrs. Betty Parsons. How or why the Mrs., I sim-ply can't imagine. You'd have to be out of your skull to want to marry her. Old lemon-lips, old Brillo-hair, old

70

twinkle-tongue. She feels the same way about me, by the way, and judging from the reception I was getting from her now, she doesn't like my mother either.

"Well, better late than never," I said brightly. The response was zilch. She went right on typing.

"Yoo-hoo, hello, I'm finally here!" I said, putting my hands on her desk and leaning intimately into her darling face.

"I heard you the first time, Mrs. Andrews." She nodded her head toward Mr. Dilk's closed door (typing all the while, mind you) and said, "He has been waiting for you for over fifty minutes. Now, I fear, you will have to wait for him."

"Fair enough," I said and settled myself on one of those terrifically comfortable hard wood chairs, the kind with slats that get you right in the spine. Actually, I didn't mind waiting. There were a couple of things I wanted to figure out and this was as good a time as any to think about them. I folded my legs under me, Yoga style, rested my elbows on my knees and my head on my hands, which were over my ears to drown out the typewriter. And thought the following thoughts:

1) If I didn't go to school, where the heck did I go instead? Never having played hooky before, I had no idea where I might go. Maybe I went to a dirty movie on 42nd Street where I am not ever allowed to go be-

71

cause it's dangerous. Could I have gotten raped or strangled by a depraved killer in the dirty movie? or run over by a crosstown bus just as I came blinking out into the sunlight afterward?

My God, my bod! I never thought of it before, but I'm not all that careful with myself. Suppose right now I am lying stone cold dead in the city morgue, and then tomorrow, let's say, my mother wants her own bod back, where does that leave me? Or to be more exact, *what* does that leave me? I'll tell you one thing, possession is nine tenths of the law and if anything like that happens, I'm staying right in here where I am, whether I like it or not. After all, she's responsible for this mess, she can jolly well go back to whoever *she's* been all day—Queen Elizabeth or Jackie Onassis or somebody.

On the other hand, if I go on being Mrs. Andrews then I will have to explain to Daddy and Ape Face (who loves Annabel so much) and to all the teachers at Barden (who don't) how come I was careless enough to allow my little girl to play hooky from school and get crushed under a bus. Maybe it would be better to work out a trade with my mother and *I* could be Jackie Onassis.

Wait a minute! I've been assuming she was responsible, but what if she isn't? What if a third party

72

switched us all around and it's not her fault at all? If that's the case, I can't very well refuse to give her back her bod if she wants it. Annabel, old sock, wherever you are, I certainly hope you're being careful with yourself! Don't even walk through the park.

2) I'm being much too pessimistic. What about last night's fight, when she said, "We'll just see about that"? That's a threat if I ever heard one. Of *course* she's responsible. As a matter of fact, is there the tiniest chance that she really *is* in my body? If so, she's a better actress than I thought—all that marshmallow eating and stuff. And would she switch us around on the very day there's a big conference with the school about me? If so, she's stupider than I thought because she's putting me in a terrible spot. In other words, whatever I say about myself in the conference should depend on how long I'm going to go on being her. Which I don't know.

3) Maybe the best thing to do is sneak out right . . .

". . . now, Mrs. Andrews!" Mrs. Parsons was shrieking, but with my hands over my ears I hadn't heard her.

"Beg pardon?"

"I said Mr. Dilk will see you now, Mrs. Andrews." Have you ever seen someone jump from the lotus position to a standing position in one move? Not in velvet pajamas you haven't and you never will. It can't be done without falling down.

"Ups-a-daisy," I said, dusting myself off, and entered the chamber of horrors.

Arnold Dilk is what we call a super straight. (You know: the short hair, the three-piece suit, the string tie —I wonder where you go to get one of those, these days? Brooks Bros., I guess. He says poim instead of pome, and not an *r* in a carload. Clearah, finah, brightah, et ceterah.) It was no small surprise, therefore, to find him leaning back in his chair, feet on desk, cigarette in hand, and smile on face.

"Come on in, Mrs. Andrews; how've you been?"

"Well . . ." I started.

"Ah, you're not the only one. Everybody hates the hell out of February! But you *look grand*. Splendid! Have a seat while I get hold of Miss McGuirk and the good doctor."

Out of habit, I headed for one of the hard browns, but Dilk, while he was mumbling instructions into the phone, hissed at me to take the comfortable chair. I did. He drummed his fingers on the desk and smiled a knowing smile at me while nodding his head up and down.

"Relax, Mrs. Andrews. There's nothing to be

74

alarmed about. We'll get this business about your daughter all straightened out in no time.

"Of course, I haven't had the pleasure of teaching Annabel this year, but I'll tell you one thing: That little gal is a personality in her own right. She has a real mind of her own."

A fat lot you know about it, Silky Dilky!

"I guess that's true—most of the time," I said.

"You bet it is. And we, at the Barden, encourage that kind of spunk and zip. We *like* to see spunk and zip!" (Spunk and Zip, Spunk and Zip. It sounded like a book about two Swedish brothers. *The Adventures of Spunk and Zip. Spunk and Zip in the Frozen Fiord. Spunk and Zip in the Sunken Ship.* See Spunk zip. Good Lord, was I going mad?)

"I'm sorry," I said. "You were saying?"

". . . as long as it's accompanied by mature self-discipline and a sense of obligation to herself and her school." Jekyll to Hyde in midsentence! The feet were now on the floor, the cigarette had been stamped out viciously in the ashtray, the hands were clasped together with tapping index fingers (this is the church and this is the steeple, open the doors and kill all the people) and the smile had vanished completely. When do we get the long nails and the fangs, I wondered.

"Ah, Felicia, Cassandra, come in, come in. Mrs. Andrews, you know Miss McGuirk, of course, and this is our school psychologist, Dr. Artunian." Jekyll was back, a bundle of cheer, all of it directed toward the most beautiful creature I'd ever seen in my life. Not that I hadn't seen her before, you understand, but I thought she was a new kindergarten assistant—the kind that works for a year and then gets married.

"Well for heaven's sake! And here I'd been expecting the school ghoul," I said, and immediately wished I hadn't.

"Sorry to disappoint you," she said pleasantly.

"You're not, you're not!" I hastily assured her, "I'm delighted to meet you, and how are *you*, Miss McGuirk?"

"All right, ladies, let's get down to business, shall we?" said Dilk, eyeing the wall clock. "This meeting was a trifle late getting started, as you know," he flashed me one of those now-you-see-it-now-you-don't smiles.

"Sorry about that."

"—and we have a good deal to discuss. Felicia, perhaps you'll hand me Annabel's current report—I'd like to have a quick look-see before we all go over it together. As Annabel's homeroom teacher as well as her English teacher, Felicia—Miss McGuirk that is—has a slight edge over the rest of us, wouldn't you say so, Felicia?"

"If *you* say so, Mr. Dilk," said McGuirk. "At this

point, I really don't know what to say. I'm at my wits' end, as it were. Here. See for yourself." She passed the wretched thing over to Dilk.

"Yes. Let's see now. Winter report. Math, 72. 'Annabel has been having trouble mastering the techniques of long division. With more diligent application and attention to detail, however, we shall hope for a higher degree of accuracy in the future. Talks in class. H.M.' That's Harvey Mills."

"I know that," I said. A pox on Harvey Mills.

"French, 68. 'Although Annabel is developing a charming French accent, we would wish for more clarity in the written assignments. Her *Petit Cahier* is in deplorable condition and she cannot, or will not, comprehend the *plus-que-parfait*. Madame Murphy.' You know Madame Murphy, don't you, Mrs. Andrews?"

Boy, do I ever know Madame Murphy! To know her is to hate her. She's as American as I am with all the bad temper of a genuine French teacher.

"I understand she throws chalk," I said.

"All French teachers throw chalk," said Dr. Artunian.

"Even if they're American?"

"Mrs. Andrews, if Annabel had ever been seriously injured by flying chalk, I'm sure we would have heard about it from the school nurse. Do let's forge on, may we?

"Science. 80. 'D.R.' "

"Hey, that's quite a decent mark!" I said. "What's the comment?"

"There isn't any. Donald Rosenman never gives a comment," said Mr. Dilk. There is no justice in this world.

"American History and Current Events, 65." (Ook!) " 'Annabel can always be counted upon to make a lively and enthusiastic contribution to class discussion. Outspoken (sometimes to the point of belligerence) on such topics as our environment and the Women's Liberation Movement. She is occasionally inclined to be a touch intolerant of the other fellow's viewpoint. Nevertheless, she is to be commended for her passion!

" 'Unfortunately, Annabel's interest in our country's past is not commensurate with her concern for its future . . .' " Mr. Dilk looked up. "I do enjoy Sophie Benson's reports. She puts things so nicely, don't you think?"

"Let's give her a big fat A," I said sourly. "I know, I know, that was uncalled for, and I apologize, but honestly, listening to you guys say rotten things about Annabel is not my idea of how to spend a fun Friday afternoon."

McGuirk looked stunned. Dilk raised his eyebrows and sidled his eyes over to Artunian. Artunian looked

78

cool as a cucumber, and in a matching voice said, "Mrs. Andrews, we can all imagine how upsetting this must be for you, but in order to gain meaningful insight into your daughter's present inadequacies, we must examine, as objectively as possible . . ." She's a living vocabulary list!

"OK, I said I was sorry. Let's keep going."

"To continue where I left off," said Mr. Dilk, " 'past, blah, blah, blah, commensurate, blah, blah, future as is evidenced by the January test in which her confusion of the Annexation of Texas with the Louisiana Purchase resulted in a grade of zero on the essay question. If it weren't for this and several other errors of a similarly careless nature, Annabel could be one of the top students in my class. Regretfully, S.B.'

"Have you any comments or questions, Mrs. Andrews, before we go on?"

"Yes. What did she get in gym?"

"In *gym*? I hardly think that's . . ."

"Mr. Dilk, you asked me if I had any questions. If it's all the same to you, what did she get in gym?"

"95."

"Ah-*ha!*" I said, triumphant. "Read *that* comment, please."

As enthusiastically as a train conductor announcing the stops between New York and New Haven, Mr. Dilk did so.

" 'Annabel is a beautifully coordinated child, and a natural athlete. As far as team sports are concerned, her helpful and encouraging attitude toward less able playmates is a joy to behold. This year, her boundless energy has led her to investigate karate and wrestling, although I have repeatedly explained to her that the Barden does not permit coeducational contact sports at the present time, nor, in all probability, will it do so in the foreseeable future! W.H.' "

Good old Bill Hauk!

"I'm glad to hear *some*body likes her," I said, sitting a little taller in my chair.

"We *all* like her, Mrs. Andrews, truly we do," said McGuirk. (By the way, if you've wondered why I haven't given you any description of Miss McGuirk, it's because I swear to you there is nothing to describe. She isn't old and she isn't young—somewhere between thirty and fifty—she isn't fat and she isn't thin, she isn't tall and she isn't short, and so on. You get the picture.)

"All right, if you like her so much, what mark did you give her in English?" I folded my arms over my chest and waited. McGuirk looked a little uncomfortable.

"What mark did she give her in English, Mr. Dilk?"

With an icy smile, Mr. Dilk delivered the news. "37."

"But that's *flunking*," I said numbly.

"That's right," said McGuirk, sadly.

"You can't *do* that to me," I whispered. I felt a gentle hand on my arm. Nobody touches me when I'm angry, nobody! I pulled my arm away and the hand went back to Artunian's lap where it belonged.

"Mrs. Andrews," said Artunian softly, "Miss McGuirk didn't do anything to you."

"That's what you think," I said.

"And she didn't do anything to Annabel, either. Annabel did it to herself."

"But I've never heard of anybody getting a 37! *37?* How could you come up with a number like that? What about classwork? Doesn't she talk up in class?"

"All the time," said McGuirk.

"Well, doesn't that count for anything?"

"It counts for about 37," said McGuirk. "I tried every which way to give her a higher mark, but Mrs. Andrews, how could I? She begged for an independent project. I *gave* her an independent project. That project was the rest of her term grade and she never handed it in. Today was the final deadline, and as you know, she was home sick. I don't even know what the project is.

"I could absolutely kill her! If she were stupid, I could forgive her. An ordinary, pedestrian, untalented, unimaginative, boring student, I could feel sorry for

81

... and as long as such a student handed in her assignments, regardless of how ordinary, pedestrian, untalented, unimaginative, and boring they were, I would manage, somehow, to give her a passing grade.

"But when a fine mind, with an IQ of a hundred and fifty-five, whose verbal aptitude scores are higher than a freshman in college—yes, Mrs. Andrews, she scores *higher than the average college freshman!*—when a fine mind sits on its bottom—figuratively speaking, of course—and refuses to exert itself one little smidgen, well it's enough to make you SCREAM!"

"But I had simply no idea," I stammered. "I mean nobody told me any of that."

"Well, we're telling you now," said Artunian, the gentle moderator.

"So, Mrs. Andrews, perhaps you understand a little better about the 37," said Miss McGuirk.

"You know," she went on in a quivering voice, "one takes great pride in being a good teacher. One does one's...

"I don't know why I'm using the impersonal pronoun," she said, angrily interrupting herself. "It's stuffy and archaic—and an academic pretension."

(I am looking at Miss McGuirk through new eyes!)

"What I mean to say is *I* take great pride in being a good teacher and *I* do my best to infuse each pupil with a sense of self, to help him recognize and then develop his own potential, whatever that may be, and . . . and . . .

"Aah," she said disgustedly, interrupting herself once again. "That's a lot of garbage—straight out of teachers' college. What I'm trying to tell you, Mrs. Andrews, is I admire and love your little girl. She is the kind of child every teacher prays to discover in her classroom; only once or twice in a whole career (which is just about how often a child like that shows up) would be enough—but when you finally . . . But when *I* finally discover that child and then I can't get through to her, or be of any use to her at all, then I have to face the fact that Annabel may be doing 37 in English, but *I* am the failure. And Annabel, in more capable, or perhaps inspired, hands than mine, will learn to implement the extraordinary gifts God gave her; but I have no gift, I guess, and I've botched the only real opportunity ever to come my way."

And with that, she folded her hands and placed them carefully in her lap, opened her blue eyes very wide, and stared, quite deliberately, at nobody in the room. Every kid in the world knows *that* trick. It's to keep you from crying. It sometimes works and it sometimes doesn't, but it never works if you blink. She blinked.

"Oh, Miss McGuirk, *please* don't!" I was horrified.

"Here, Felicia," said Mr. Dilk, solicitously offering his handkerchief.

"Don't cry, please, Miss McGuirk. PLEASE!" I begged, in utter panic. But it was like monsoon season in the Ganges delta.

"Sh, sh, tears are the natural catharsis for natural grief," soothed Artunian. Sappy skull-scraper!

"Oh come on, now. Crying because your dog died or your grandmother—that's sensible, but crying over some rotten kid who isn't even dead (as far as we know anyway), that's just a waste of good grief!"

"Charlie Brown," added Mr. Dilk.

"Hey, that's pretty good!" I said, admiringly.

"Yes it is," said McGuirk, managing a faint smile.

"Rotten kid? *Rotten kid?*" repeated Artunian, "Mrs. Andrews, from what I have observed during the course of this interview, it would seem to me that in many instances, your behavior is inappropriate and your attitudes bizarre."

"Is that so?" I said. "Name one." Ladies unt chentlemen, ve haff here in our midst anuzza Zigmund Freud!

"Your visible discomfort at the sight of tears, for instance. To restrain yourself from crying is to deny yourself a perfectly legitimate and healthy emotional outlet. Children cry. Why shouldn't adults?"

84

"Children would rather *die* than cry!" I said through closed teeth.

"We won't argue about that now, however. Shall I go on?"

"Do," said I.

"Aside from the fact that you were almost an hour late for this meeting, which, unless you can satisfatorily explain it, would indicate a certain reluctance o your part to discuss your daughter's academic weak nesses, I find it revealing that when you finally did arrive, you demonstrated: one, marked hostility toward us for criticizing your daughter; and two, marked hostility toward your daughter for disappointing her teachers. Is it therefore possible that you harbor ambivalent and/or conflicting feelings about your child?"

"Absolutely possible," I said. "Doesn't everybody?"

"Are we talking about everybody's child in general, or Annabel in particular?"

"Listen, Dr. Artunian, it's my turn to ask questions. When I came in here and you three took pot shots at my daughter, my natural instinct was to defend her, right?"

"Right," said Dilk and McGuirk.

"And, in no uncertain terms and with no attempt to spare my maternal feelings, I was made aware of the fact that she was an underachiever, bossy, lazy, irresponsible, and a hideous source of disappointment to Miss McGuirk here. Right?"

"Right," said Artunian.

"So now that you have successfully convinced me that she is a rotten kid, not to mince words, and a stinker, you accuse me of being hostile toward her. Darn right I'm hostile! Why shouldn't I be?"

"Ladies, ladies!" said Dilk. "This conference is degenerating into a free-for-all. Now let's calm down, shall we?"

He lit a cigarette and then said, "Oh, I *am* sorry, that was pretty darn rude of me! Mrs. Andrews, do you smoke?"

"Certainly not," I said, and then remembered that only last week, in a homeroom rap session, Miss McGuirk had heard me give an impromptu speech on the dangers of smoking in which I cited my two-pack-a-day mother as a prime example of a person hell-bent on suicide.

"I mean, not anymore," I added.

"Oh, I was wondering," she said. "When did you stop?"

"I haven't had a cigarette all day," I said truthfully —and pridefully.

"Well, that explains a great deal," said Artunian. We were obviously friends again. "You're probably suffering from nicotine withdrawal."

"Gum?" asked Miss McGuirk, offering a stick. I took it gratefully, suddenly realizing that all I'd had to eat since breakfast was a few handfuls of cold macaroni.

"Ladies, could we please get back to business? In five minutes, the sun will be over the yardarm—" (Wha-at?) "—and I don't know about you, but I'd hate to miss the only reliable train to the Hamptons.

"Dr. Artunian, why don't you speak for all of us? Will that be hunky-dory with you, Mrs. Andrews?"

"As long as she promises to use short words and short sentences. No gobbledygook, just straight talk."

"I'll do my best."

"Terrific. OK, shoot."

"Mrs. Andrews, right up until this year, Annabel has been a model student, obviously a happy and well-adjusted little girl.

"But *this* year, we have all observed a marked change —for the worse. And what is the explanation for that change?

"Miss McGuirk feels she has failed Annabel as a teacher. Mr. Dilk feels . . ." She gestured gracefully to Mr. Dilk.

"That Annabel is totally lacking in mature self-discipline, and if she doesn't shape up fast, I'm going to kick her right out of the school, no matter how smart she is."

"And you, Mrs. Andrews, feel that she is, as you so

pungently put it, a 'rotten kid and a stinker.'

"Now with all due respect to the three of you, I must admit that, as a psychologist, I find your reactions simplistic, to say the least."

"What happened to the short words and the short sentences?"

"I think you are all reacting like simple-minded idiots, do you like that any better?!"

"Yes!" I snapped.

"I'm not sure," said McGuirk.

"*I* am a simple-minded idiot?" asked Dilk.

"You *especially*," said Artunian. "As the principal of a school, you should know better. When a child undergoes a sudden and inexplicable personality change, it's either a brain tumor . . ."

"That's really grotesque!" I said, viewing her with distaste.

"And highly unlikely. Anyway, it's either a brain tumor or we have to consider outside factors. The home environment, for instance. The emergence of a heretofore suppressed sibling rivalry, for example."

"Anh, anh, anh," I warned, waggling my finger at her.

"She has a younger brother, Mrs. Andrews. Is she jealous of him? Is there any reason why she *should* be jealous of him. Do you, by any chance, fall into the not

88

uncommon Oedipal pattern of favoring your son over your daughter?"

"No, I do not!"

"I understand he is a charming little boy. You are sure there is no resentment of this fact on the part of your daughter?"

"Positive. Any other suggestions?"

Never in a million years would you believe the things that old bat dreamed up to ask me! Was I an attentive mother? Yes. Was I an overly demanding mother? No, not really. Had there been any change in the quality of my mothering lately? A fraction more impatient, perhaps, but with ample cause. The quantity, then, because if I would forgive her for mentioning it, the outfit I had on was a bit unusual, shall we say. Had I been out to lunch or was I on my way out to dinner? Neither one. I was trying it on to see if it still fit from last year and was too busy to take it off again.

What about my husband? What about him? Were there any problems in the marriage? *No!* My husband was not, for instance, domineering or overbearing in his attitude toward me or the children?

"Dr. Artunian, you can ask me anything you want about myself or my daughter but it's none of your business how I get along with my father!"

"Oh, ho, *ho*! Mrs. Andrews! Did you hear what you just said?"

"Yeah, I called him my father instead of my husband. So what? A slip of the tongue."

"Rather revealing, don't you think?"

"No, I do not think! I have been here for an hour and a half, getting the once-over from you people, and if in all that time I only made one slip of the tongue, it's a bloody miracle. Look, everybody, I know you're only trying to help, and if I knew why Annabel's been acting this way, I'd be glad to tell you, but I don't think it has anything to do with her parents or her sibling or anything like that. Maybe she's just going through some stage or other. I'll bet that's all it is. So, Miss Mc-Guirk," I said, cheerfully patting her hand, "on Monday morning I'm sure you're going to see a completely new Annabel."

"Let's not get our hopes up too high," said Artunian. "We can't expect her to change overnight."

"Stranger things have happened," I said mysteriously.

"Well then, Mrs. Andrews, I suppose this concludes our little meeting." Mr. Dilk stood up and shook my hand. "And on Monday, we look forward to, if not a totally new Annabel, at least an older and wiser one."

"You bet."

"And you might tell her for me," said Miss Mc-

Guirk, "that if she will hand that paper in Monday, it's not too late to revise her grade."

"I'll tell her the minute I see her," I said, and truer words there never were! If I could only find her.

Ten ❁

Do you ever get a premonition about something? Like you've lost your bus pass and all of a sudden you get an insane sixth sense that it's mixed up in your science notebook so you look and there it is? Well, on my way home in the cab, I suddenly realized . . . I literally *knew* by some miraculous sixth sense that Annabel was home ahead of me! I tell you, it was an enormous relief.

Unfortunately, it was also an enormous mistake. An utterly, totally, disgustingly false premonition, based, I suppose, on wishful thinking. If you think *that's* bad, wait'll you hear the rest: although Annabel was not there, her whole howling mob, fifteen of them, were. They had rearranged all the living room furniture to make a commando course for themselves and

92

they were using a curtain rod for high jumping. The place looked terrific.

"What the bloody you-know-what do you think you're doing?" I screamed at them. "Where do you think you are—Parris Island? Fort Dix? This is a living room. To be more exact, this is *my* living room into which my husband and Francie's Fortified Fish Fingers are coming in less than an hour. Now you get every blooming stick of furniture back where it was and pick up your Coke cans and your apple cores. I want your ugly little bodies outta here in five minutes, d'ya hear?!"

Boy did I scare them! It was like running a cartoon backward and faster.

"We're awfully sorry, Mrs. Andrews," said Jo-Jo, "but when we saw you earlier, why didn't you tell us you didn't want the club to meet at your house?"

"Because I forgot it was supposed to meet at my house."

"Well, that's not *our* fault," said smarmy Virginia.

"SHUT UP, VIRGINIA," said fourteen girls.

"And anyway," I said, "You should have better manners than to hold a club meeting in the home of a member who has vanished into thin air, even if the meeting *was* originally scheduled to take place in that home."

"Gee, that's right," said Nina. "You must be wildly upset."

"And mad," added Liz.

"That, too," said Barbara.

"Oh, yes," said Bambi. "If I were her, I certainly wouldn't want to be her and come home and face you."

"Maybe she's never coming home. You know the way she crosses against the light and . . ."

"Shut up, Virginia," said Jo-Jo, giving her a poke.

"That's all right, Virginia, let's hear the rest of it."

"I just mean the way she crosses against the light and rides her bike down Seventh Avenue and everything, well maybe she's—you know."

"Dead," I announced flatly.

"Oh, Mrs. Andrews, that's a terrible thing to say. You mustn't let your imagination carry you away like that. Even if she *has* been hit by a car" (With her luck, it's a Number Seven bus.), "she's not necessarily dead. Maybe she's—she's only—uh—"

"Maimed and crippled for life?"

"Yes!" Virginia was relieved and delighted at the thought of Annabel's narrow escape from the great beyond.

Now I ask you: if you were my mother and you switched bodies with me and then got maimed and crippled for life by a bus, would you be content with your lot, or would you switch back to your old bod? That's what I think, too. After all, she may be a nice lady, but nobody's *that* self-sacrificing. Any moment now I could expect to find myself in some hospital, a total vegetable. I could just hear the club. "Come on, guys, it's our day to visit Annabel the Artichoke." "Oh, again?" Groan, groan. Eventually, I suppose, they'd stop coming—even your best friends aren't going to cut college classes to visit a vegetable. In the long run, there was probably only one person I could count on. The Ape would come, bless his loyal and reliable little heart. Which reminded me, where *was* the Ape?

"Where's Ben?"

"Ben?" They all looked at each other stupidly.

"Yes, Ben. Ben, my son. Ben. The Ape."

"We know who you mean, Mrs. Andrews. We haven't seen him, that's all." Steady now, Annabel. Get a firm grip.

"He was here when I left. I left him here with a baby-sitter. Boris, the boy from upstairs. If they weren't here, how did you get in?"

"Boris was here. Boris let us in. But we didn't see any Ape Face and he didn't mention him either. All he said was, 'Is Annabel with you?' and we said we were friends of hers but no, she wasn't with us, and he said, 'That's good.' Then he said he was going back to the kitchen to finish cooking . . ." A few of the girls nudged each other and giggled. I gave them the hairy eyeball. "Go on, Jo-Jo."

". . . to finish cooking. Which I guess he did, because a few minutes later he said good-bye, and left."

By now, I knew the number by heart.

"Harris residets, Boris speak . . ."

"What have you done with my son?"

"Brs. Adrews. I diddit do eddy . . ."

"You better get down here this minute and talk to me in my apartment where I can understand you!" Him and his neurotic adenoids!

"Right away, Brs. Adrews, ad idsidetally, it's tibe to put the beat loaf id the oved."

"Never mind that. Just get yourself down here fast."

The girls were already climbing into their coats and heading for the door. I couldn't blame them—after all, who wants to hang around a crazy lady!

Boris got off the same elevator the girls got on. Without a hello, even, I dragged him into the living room and sat him down on the couch.

"Now listen," I whispered, "I'm not angry. I'm not excited. I'm perfectly calm as you can see. I just want to know, *where is he?*"

Boris was apparently in shock. With someone in shock, you shake them. I shook him.

"I was chopping onions and parsley," he said.

"Go on."

"And the doorbell rang."

"Keep going."

"So the Ape said, 'I'll get it.' "

"And?"

"And then I heard him talking to someone."

"You didn't go out to see who the 'someone' was?"

"My hands were all gooky."

"Then what happened?"

"Then he yelled to me that he was going out and he'd be back in a while."

"And you never even went to see who he was going out *with*?"

"Of course I went to see!" he said indignantly. "Mrs. Andrews, you must think I'm completely irresponsible! He was going out with a beautiful chick."

"*Who* beautiful chick. *What* beautiful chick?"

"How would *I* know. I never saw her before!" He was getting quite agitated.

"You call that responsible? Letting a little boy be abducted out of the house with a total stranger he never saw before?"

"Mrs. Andrews, that isn't what I said. I said *I* never saw her before. He obviously knew who she was. He also obviously was very glad to see her and when he left, it was willingly—he was not ABDUCTED."

"All right, all right, all right, don't get so bubbled over. Shouting at me won't help."

"Sorry," he said meekly.

"Forget it. Now Boris, I want you to think very carefully. Did she say anything, anything at all, or did he say anything that might give me a clue as to her identity?"

"Let's see. She said thank you, young man, for taking care of him, she was going to buy him some ice cream, and I could run along now. That's positively all she said."

"Before she came, or after she left, you didn't receive any strange phone calls? Were there any phone calls at all?"

"Only the mother of his friend, Paul, to say Paul had a hundred and one and couldn't come over. Ape Face was very disappointed about that, so I thought going out for ice cream with that beautiful chick—boy, did she turn me on—would cheer him up."

By now, I was in what the movie mags call The Grip of Naked Terror. I always wondered what they meant when they said "her heart was in her mouth" and "her mind was in turmoil." Well, in case you're interested, a mouthful of heart is something like a mouthful of captured frog, and a mind in turmoil simply means all the blood in your body rushes around in your head, leaving you icy cold from the neck down. As for "butterflies in the stomach," there is no such thing. It's June bugs.

"Boris," I said, speaking slowly and distinctly so I could hear myself over the roar, "You are to be commended for your great taste in kidnappers. And now, if you will excuse me, I'm going into the bedroom. To make a phone call. To the police."

That really shook him up. He followed me all the way down the hall babbling about how if anything happened to Ape Face on account of him, he would kill himself (not if I get there first), and couldn't he please keep me company—maybe he could be of some assistance (I told him he'd already been of enough assistance, too much in fact.), couldn't he help me call the police . . .

"Boris," I said through the closed door, "do me a big fat favor and shut up!"

"Can I just say one more thing?" he asked.

"If you make it quick," I said, opening the door a crack.

"I love you," he whispered.

"Your timing stinks!" I said. "You should have told me that yesterday."

"I didn't know you yesterday," he protested.

"That's what you think," I said, and slammed the door in his face. So much for my love life. Onward and upward with the police department.

NEW YORK CITY OF—
POLICE DEPT—

Missing Persons, Missing Persons . . . persons . . . let your fingers do the walking (or the trembling), aha! here it is. What I wouldn't do for a push-button phone.

"Hello, Missing Persons? I am missing a person. In fact, I am missing two persons and maybe three."

"Madame, we are a statistical bureau only. For missing persons, dial your local precinct." I banged the phone down. Boris opened the door and poked his head in.

"I didn't mean to eavesdrop, but I heard you say you were missing two persons and maybe three. Who else besides Ape Face have you lost?"

"I've lost my mother and maybe my daughter. What's it to you?"

"Nothing, I guess. I mean, I wouldn't consider Annabel any great loss—" A headline flashed through my mind: INSANE MOTHER OF TWO STABS FOURTEEN-YEAR-OLD BABY-SITTER WITH BALL POINT PEN. "—and if your mother is anything like *my* mother, I wouldn't mind losing her either. But on the other hand, maybe you like your mother—some people do and anyway, I'm sorry I both-

100

ered you," he said, hastily, and backed out the door.

OK, back to work with the trembling fingers. Local precinct, huh? Fine and dandy—as long as you know which one you are. I didn't. There were over twenty listed. What was I going to do, try them all? Rats!

Then I came across a listing called Know Your Police Department. I called it and the cop who answered told me the precinct for where I lived was number twenty. I thanked him and was about to hang up when he said, "Wait a minute, lady. If you don't mind my asking, where'dja get this number?"

"In the phone book."

Listed under what, he wanted to know. I told him.

"Gee, I didn't know that," he said, very impressed.

I said I was missing two and maybe three persons, and I had to find them within fifteen minutes so I hoped he didn't think I was rude but I had to go now.

"Geez, that's tough," he said, sympathetically. "Have you tried Missing Persons?"

"Say, what else doesn't Know Your Police Department know?" I said. "Missing Persons is only a statistical bureau."

"Oh, *I* know that," he said.

"Then why'd you ask?"

"I didn't want you to waste your time calling them."

"That's very considerate of you. Are there any other numbers I shouldn't waste my time calling?"

101

"Oh, golly, yes! There's uh . . . lemme see, now . . ." I hung up. *Un*believable!

"Twentieth Precinct, Patrolman Plonchik." Annabel, you have finally lucked out, and it's about time!

"Officer Plonchik, do you by any chance happen to recall an incident that occurred at approximately twelve seventeen today on the corner of 71st and Central Park West, involving a darling little six-year-old boy whose mother was two minutes late meeting him at the school bus?"

"Yeah?" said Plonchik, by which he seemed to mean I should keep talking.

"Well, this is the mother speaking and I want to thank you very much for everything you did . . ."

"Tsawright," said Plonchik.

". . . and to ask for your help, because last time you only *thought* he was lost and he really wasn't, but this time he is definitely lost and I'm desperate!"

"Aw, come on, ma'am. On the level, now, you didn't just abandon him again and forget where? Try to retrace your steps. You already been to the liquor store. Maybe you left him at the cleaners? The drugstore?"

"Listen, that's enough of your dumb-dumb jokes. My son was kidnapped from our apartment while under the care of a reliable baby-sitter. As a matter of fact, the abductor was even *seen* by the baby-sitter. He says she was . . ."

102

"You mean *she* says *he* was . . ."

"No I do not mean that. I mean he says she was. *He* is the baby-sitter, a very reliable fourteen-year-old boy who lives upstairs, and *she* was apparently a beautiful chick who lured my son out for ice cream while *he* was making meatloaf in the kitchen and . . ." You know how people put their hands over the mouthpiece of the phone and think the person at the other end can't hear but they can? Plonchik made the same mistake. Rookie cop.

"Hey, Harve, listen in to this for a while, will ya? I can't figure out whether the dame is a fruitcake or for real."

I decided I didn't have time to get mad.

"Shall I repeat the first part for Harve?" I inquired politely.

"That won't be necessary, ma'am, just keep going. So the fourteen-year-old boy baby-sitter was making meatloaf in the kitchen . . ." Harve snorted.

"And apparently a beautiful chick lured my son away while I was at a school meeting concerning my daughter. I haven't seen him since. And she's missing too . . ." There was another snort of laughter. "Stop that, Harve, it's not funny. I'm not talking about the chick being missing, I'm talking about my daughter being missing."

"See if you can trace this," said Plonchik with his

103

hand over the phone, "I changed my mind. What we got here is either a nut or a child murderer."

"Murder*ess*," said a new voice.

"Thanks for the grammar lesson. That you, Stan?"

"No, it's me," said the voice.

"It's I," said I.

"Who is I?" asked Plonchik.

"Who *am* I," corrected the voice.

"Hey, goody, goody! We're going to play twenty questions," said Harve, the joker.

"OK, gang, cool it. I'm in charge here, and what I want to know is, the voice that said, 'It's me,' *who is me?*"

"You is Officer Plonchik and I is—am—the upstairs baby-sitter."

"Where are you now?" asked Plonchik suspiciously.

"Downstairs. Officer, I want to assure you that everything this lady says is absolutely true. I think you should listen to what she tells you instead of making fun of her and laughing and stuff. You ought to be ashamed."

"OK, then," said Plonchik, "but make it snappy. I haven't got all day."

"Neither have I," said I. "I've only got five minutes before my father comes home . . ."

"I thought your father had passed away," said Boris.

"*Dead,*" said I. "He is. I meant my husband. Anyway, here goes. Is everybody listening? I don't want to keep repeating things. Let's take a head check. Plonchik?"

"Here."

"Harve?"

"Here."

"Boris?"

"Here."

"Stan?"

Silence.

"So where's Stan? I don't want to start without Stan."

"Hey, Merve, tell Stan to pick up in the back, will ya?" I heard distant mumbling and then Plonchik got back on the phone.

"Stan can't come to the phone."

"Why not?"

"He's not here. He's been out sick all day."

"That's funny," said Harve. "I thought I heard him pick up before."

"No, that was me," said Boris.

"That was I," said I.

"How could it have been you, ma'am? You been *on* the phone the whole time."

"Forget it," I said. "Gimme Merve. I'll take Merve instead of Stan. You on there, Merve?"

"Yes, ma'am. I've been on since the beginning."

"Aren't *you* the sneaky one! At least I don't have to go back over the first part. OK, I'll take it from the top, quickly.

"My son, you know about. My daughter—she started out for school this morning with my son, but after she dropped him off, she played hooky. I don't know where she went. For all I know, she's lying under a Number Seven bus."

"Let's have a description of your daughter," said Merve.

"She's thirteen, about five feet three inches tall, brown eyes, brown hair . . ."

"Long, stringy brown hair, and a mouth full of braces. Real ugly kid," added Boris. Kill! Kill!

"But listen, guys, this is important. The point is I have also lost my mother."

There were a few seconds of silence and then Plonchik said, "I see. You have lost your son, your daughter, and your mother. Oksey-doksey. Let's have a description of your mother."

"She's thirty-five, brown hair . . ."

"Wait a minute, *wait a minute!* She's *thirty*-five? Your mother is thirty-five? So how old does that make you?"

All of a sudden, I was sick of the whole thing. Wearily, I said, "Thirteen. I am only thirteen. I am just a little girl who has been turned into her mother.

106

I mean I'm in my mother's body with *my* mind and I don't know if her mind is in my body or not because my body played hooky from school and hasn't been seen since early this morning. And maybe my mother isn't there anyway. She might have decided it would be more fun to be Jackie Onassis or Queen Elizabeth or who knows who she might want to turn into."

"How about Helena Troy?" suggested Harve.

"Shut up, Harve. It's a fruitcake. Never fool with a fruitcake. You don't know what they'll do."

"Gentlemen, please," I pleaded. "I'm not a fruitcake. I need your help."

"I don't think we can help you, lady," said Plonchik, sympathetically, "but we'd be glad to find you somebody who can. Just tell us your name and where you live." I heard a click.

"All right," I said obediently. "My name is Ann-a-aagh! Boris, what are you DOING? Gimme back that phone!"

"No way!" shouted Boris, slamming the phone down. "You think I'm going to let them come and cart you off?! Mrs. Andrews, are you out of your skull? You want to be locked up for life in a public funny farm? Some horrible home for nuts? If I hadn't hung up when I did, they would have traced that call—if you won't save yourself, *some*body's got to do it."

Poor thing was all out of breath and almost in tears.

I had plenty of breath, but I was almost in tears, too. He really did love me. What a pitiful waste.

"Darling Boris," I said, "I love you for trying to save me. As a matter of fact—and this is something I've been wanting to tell you for ages—I don't just love you for trying to save me . . . I love you period."

"You do?" said Boris, in tones of reverence. "That's more than I can say for my own mother, but actually, I don't think of you as a mother anyway."

"No? What do you think of me as?"

"I think of you as a beautiful human being who still remembers how to communicate with kids. I mean, how many mothers do you know who'll sit down on the floor and play Nok Hockey with a fourteen-year-old? Answer me that!"

"None, I guess."

"Darn right!" he said. He sighed. "If you were twenty years younger, I could marry you when I grew up."

"That'd make me older than you. How about twenty-two years younger."

"Mrs. Andrews, please don't start that again. I don't know why anyone wants to go back to their childhood—" he shuddered at the thought, "but it simply can't be done."

"Boris, you find it absolutely impossible to believe that I'm really Annabel, don't you?"

108

"Yes, I find it absolutely impossible to believe because it is absolutely impossible for such a thing to happen." He gazed at me steadily with his solemn hazel eyes. The moment of truth was upon us.

"If such a thing can't happen, then I've got to be crazy, right? Just like the cops said. So why don't we call them back and let them come and get me?" I reached for the phone.

"Because I don't think you're dangerously crazy," he said cautiously, removing the phone from my grasp. "And maybe you're just having a brief spell, so let's wait another couple of minutes. Your daddy'll be home very soon now, and you can tell him all about it." He was humoring me, and not very humorously, either.

"When my daddy comes home, he is not going to believe me any more than you do, and if you don't mind, I'd rather not be around when he finds out I've misplaced his two and only children. I'd rather have the police come and take me away first!"

The doorbell rang.

"Oh Lord, they traced the call," moaned Boris.

"Hurray for New York's finest!" I shouted triumphantly and sprinted for the door. Before opening it, I peeked through the burglar hole to see if they had a straitjacket with them. No straitjacket. Just a plain-clothes detective and a matron. I guess for crazy ladies, they send a matron.

"Hello, hello, hello!" I said. "You got here in record time. I didn't expect you quite so soon."

"Well, we didn't have too far to come," said the detective, modestly.

"And we would have called you to say when we were coming, in fact we tried to call you, but we had a little difficulty," added Matron.

"Oh, I know, I know," I murmured sympathetically. "But that wasn't entirely my fault." I allowed myself a quick smirk in the direction of Boris the phone grabber, the defender of maniacs.

"Is this the little boy we've heard so much about?" asked Matron. They certainly were handling me with kid gloves.

"This is the famous Boris Harris, the upstairs baby-sitter."

"Aw, golly," said the detective, "we're mighty glad to meet you, but where are you keeping your own little sprouts, Mrs. Andrews? I sure would hate for me and my wife to miss seeing them." Aren't they foxy, those two! I bet they think I'm a *homicidal* maniac, not just a regular maniac, and now they're going to nose around the place looking for a couple of corpses.

"Well, I'm afraid they're just not here," I said cheerily. "I mean you're welcome to look for yourselves, but..."

"Oh, we wouldn't want to intrude," said Matron.

"Golly, no," insisted the detective.

"Say, you people aren't very businesslike, are you? I mean, you're not at all what I expected."

"Shucks, hon, everybody meets us says the same thing. See, underneath it all, we're just plain home folks."

"I'm certainly relieved to hear that," said Boris with a comforting smile in my direction. "Could you tell us something about the home, though. Like how big a home it is, and what the daily routine is, and is it easy to get to? Because I definitely would enjoy visiting as soon as possible." Boris shot me another comforting smile. I shot *him* a smile that said, "Why don't you shut up, Boris, because there is something very peculiar going on here and you are going to make it worse!"

Unfortunately, it's hard to communicate all of that in one little smile, even one little smile through gritted teeth.

"Young man, we would be tickled pink for you to pay us a visit. Any time you're down Gulfport way, you just drop right on in, hear?"

"Gulfport? Gulfport where?" asked Boris.

"Gulfport, Loosiana. We got a real nice little house —real homey-like. See, my wife and me, we may be millionaires now, but like I said before, underneath it all, we're just home folks."

"Say, I guess I had you guys all wrong," said Boris,

delighted at this new turn of events. As for me, you would have been proud of me. I never missed a beat.

"Boris," I said, "Would you please entertain my husband's clients, Mr. and Mrs. Frampton, of Francie's Fortified Fish Finger fame, for a few minutes. Perhaps they'd like to see our kitchen on account of that's their specialty and all. Anyway, Boris, I'm going to ask you to be host because there's something I have to do in the bedroom."

Slitting my throat was what I had in mind, actually, but I couldn't find a decent weapon. Not even a letter opener. Instead, I just sat on her bed and had a mad monologue with her. Or at her. (Whichever makes more sense.) At any rate, it was mad in both senses of the word because by now I was feeling good and mad but also good and crazy.

Listen, I quit! I've had enough of this. That's what you wanted, isn't it? You wanted to teach me a terrific lesson? OK, I learned a terrific lesson. But you better get back here fast because things are all messed up and I can't fix them. And if you don't get back here fast, *you* won't be able to fix them either. Daddy's going to lose the Fish Finger account, and he doesn't have any shirts, and the cleaning woman's been fired. Although I suppose it doesn't matter whether there's a cleaning woman or not because what's left for her to do? Answer me that? Ape Face is gone. GONE!

Somebody came and stole him while you were out playing hooky or whatever you were doing. And Annabel's gone, too. Not that that's any great loss, but it's pretty hard to explain and if you think I'm going to be the one to explain it you've got another think coming, Ma. And when Daddy comes home any second now and finds out he's got no kids and a demented wife, he'll move straight to his club. (If he has a club. If not, he'll have to find one.) And then you want to know what's going to happen? I'm going right out that window. Splat on the pavement. You better get back in this bod fast, or you might not have a bod to get back into! Never thought of *that,* did you?! So if you know what's good for you, now's the time to show up. One, two, three, SHOW!

Where did that get me? Zilch. Maybe a slightly different approach:

All right, I won't go out the window. It's an ooky idea anyway. I'll just lie down on your bed here and close my eyes and count to ten, and you'll be back. OK, Ma? . . . nine, ten . . . Ma?

Oh Ma, please, please, where are you? Where did you go? I *need* you!

Ma?

MA?

MOMMY!

"Sh, sh, Annabel, darling. Not so much noise—

113

they'll hear you all the way in the kitchen."

Someone was sitting next to me on the bed. Stroking my hair. I was afraid to open my eyes and look, but it certainly sounded like her. I squirmed over to where the voice was coming from, put my arms around her middle and my head in her lap. A rhinestone button poked me in the cheek. Oh, wow!

"Sorry to cry all over your velvet pants suit," I said.

"Don't worry about it. It's already covered with carpet fluff, and at some point or other I think you wiped your wet hands on it, so a few tears won't make much difference—the poor thing's seen better days."

"So have I," I sniffed. She laughed.

"Ma?" I asked, "Did *you* do it?"

"Do what?" she said, all innocence.

"Did you turn me into you?"

"Yop," she said, sounding quite pleased with herself.

"And did you turn you into me?" She nodded, smugly.

"It wasn't very responsible of you to play hooky like that," I said, sternly. "I was worried out of my skull. All I could think of was you might have gotten hit by a bus, and how was I going to explain . . ." A hideous thought suddenly came to me, triggered, I suppose, by the word explain.

"Ma!" I shrieked, clutching at her.

"What? What's the matter now?" she said, alarmed.

114

"Oh Ma, a horrible, horrible thing has happened. This afternoon, when I was out, somebody kidnapped Ape Face. I mean Ben. Somebody came and took him away and we'll probably never see him again. It's all my fault. I should be shot!"

"Is that so?" said Ma, calmly. "I didn't know you cared."

"It just so happens I do," I said. "As a matter of fact, I care a whole lot. What's *your* problem all of a sudden? Don't you care? He's your kid!"

"Sure I care, but I'm not worried. Because I know something you don't know. *I* know where he is." Cat and mouse time.

"Where? I demand to know where."

"In the next room, playing with his Lego set. If you don't believe me, go see for yourself."

"I believe you, I believe you! I'm just so glad he's back." I wonder how he *got* back, though. Maybe the chick decided he wasn't worth the risk. In blue jeans and a Mighty-Mac he doesn't have much of a rich look. Oh well, who cares.

There was a faint tap-tapping on the door.

"Who is it?" said Ma.

"It's Boris," said guess who? (Boris.)

"Don't let him in, Ma. He thinks you're crazy and he hates me. I don't want to see him."

"Why does he hate you?" she whispered.

115

"Because I cut his head open with a shovel a few years ago."

"I suppose you can't blame him for that," she whispered, "but why does he think I'm crazy? I hardly know him—"

"You spent practically all of today with him, remember?"

"Oh, that's right," she hissed.

"He's in love with you, but he also thinks you're crazy."

The tap-tapping turned into rap-rapping, and then pound-pounding.

"Mrs. Andrews, are you all right in there?"

"Just fine, thank you, Boris."

"Then why are you talking to yourself? Your daddy is going to be home soon and you don't want him to hear you doing that, do you?"

"What's he talking about?" she whispered at me.

"No, I don't," she shouted at Boris.

"Never mind what he's talking about. I'll tell you later. Ask him what he's done with the Framptons."

"The *Framptons!* Are they in town?"

"Not only are they in town, they're in our kitchen. At least they were. Ask Boris."

"Boris, what've you done with the Framptons?"

"They left." Uh-oh. "They said they sure did enjoy seeing the kitchen and the children's rooms—" Ai-yi!

"—don't worry, Mrs. Andrews, Ape Face and I cleaned up his room this afternoon; we even washed the windows of the doll house . . ."

Ma started to snicker. "Annabel, what kind of nonsense were you pulling on that poor boy?"

"Too complicated to explain, now, tell you later."

"And," continued Boris, "they said since they'd come primarily to see the children and the children weren't home, they'd come back tomorrow because they're staying over an extra day anyhow. Frankly, I think they just didn't like the looks of my beatloaf."

"Beetloaf?" whispered Ma, wrinkling her nose.

"Naah, that's just the way he talks sometimes. Adenoids. Doesn't usually get them down here though. Oh well, he means meatloaf."

"I'm sure it's extremely tasty, Boris," said Ma tactfully.

"I did my best, Mrs. Andrews. Under the circs, maybe my best wasn't good enough, but I did try. I guess I'll be going on upstairs now, though, because there doesn't seem to be anything much for me to do here . . ."

Pause, pause. Ma and I looked at each other and shrugged.

"He sounds so forlorn," she said.

"I know, but what can you do?"

"Boris, dear, since you were kind enough to cook for

us, I think the least we could do is invite you to dinner. Why don't you run along now and come back at seven. We'll all eat together."

"Who all is we?" asked Boris.

"Mr. Andrews and me and the children."

I gave her a poke in the ribs. "You goofed it, Ma," I whispered.

"Mrs. Andrews, are you *sure* you're feeling yourself again? I mean all that hysteria about the children being missing and the calls to the police . . ." Ma raised her eyebrows at me, and I nodded yes, ". . . and now you seem to have entirely forgotten about it."

"I haven't forgotten, Boris, but I'm not unduly concerned about the children. And don't you be, either. Why, I'll bet when you come back at seven, they'll both be waiting for you."

"One would be plenty," muttered Boris. "The younger one."

"See?" I hissed. "I told you he hated me."

"You're going to find a big change in Annabel," said Ma soothingly.

"I've heard *that* one before! Well, OK then, Mrs. Andrews. I'll see you later."

"Aw, nuts!" I said to myself, but by mistake it was out loud.

"You really like that boy, don't you?" said Ma.

118

"Fat lot of good it does me. You heard him just now, didn't you? You heard him!"

"But you apparently got along wonderfully with him today. And he evidently cares a great deal about you. You said so yourself."

"Boris Harris cares a great deal about a thirty-five-year-old woman who is willing to play Nok Hockey on the floor with him."

"Carpet fluff," mused Mrs. Sherlock Holmes.

"And besides," I continued, "so what if he likes my personality? He doesn't even know it's mine—he thinks it's yours. And he hates the way *I* look. If he said it once, he said it thirty times today. He thinks I'm ugly. He only gets turned on by beautiful chicks. Come to think of it, if he didn't have such a thing about beautiful chicks, I wouldn't have spent half the afternoon on the phone with the police."

"Annabel, you're going too fast for me. Or else you're brighter than I am . . ." (You know, considering what Miss McGuirk says, I probably am. Poor dumb Mom! Darling but dumb.) ". . . so would you mind starting from the beginning, slowly?"

Anything to oblige. I had to start back in the dark ages of the morning because everything hinged on everything else. First of all, Mrs. Schmauss was prejudiced. Did Ma know that? Ma admitted she did know

119

that, but people were hard to get these days, so she'd tried to ignore it. That was embarrassing for Ma. Also, Mrs. Schmauss refused to iron Daddy's shirts. Did Ma know that? Of course Ma knew that—Ma was the one who had to iron them. But Daddy was under the impression that it was Mrs. Schmauss who ruined his shirts. Did Ma know that? Ma *did* know that Daddy didn't know who ironed his shirts, but she did *not* know he considered them ruined. That also was embarrassing for Ma. Did Ma know that Mrs. Schmauss absolutely refused to clean Annabel's room? Yes, and who could blame her? That was embarrassing for me.

"Well, then," I said, regaining my composure, "did you know that Mrs. Schmauss was secretly drinking our gin?"

"I was beginning to suspect her of that, but when you smoke, your sense of smell isn't as acute."

"You didn't have one cigarette all day today and your sense of smell was better than a bloodhound's. Mrs. Schmauss smelled like a brewery and at eleven-thirty this morning, you fired her. I hope you don't mind."

"The only part I mind," said Ma, "is that I would have relished that moment myself." I reminded her that it was her idea to switch us around, not mine. Didn't she think it was a touch greedy to expect all the fun at both ends? She conceded that point. Further-

more
ing l
she c
grate
"Y
tell r
happ
It w
only
then
at th
"I
of n
"I
wan
Sl
"

a lovely time earlier in the day, and ask
down and baby-sit. He reluctantly
"He seemed like a thorough
what's more, he offered to wh
which came as a great reli
cook.
"So then, what d
that grotesque
friends dive-b
body's seen
gone ho
"F
hi

edly. "Anyway, how *was* that meeting? Frankly, I've been dreading it for weeks."

"It was a bloodbath."

"Oh my," she said, "I'm glad I missed it."

"Not as glad as I am," said I.

"Anyway, to backtrack a little, with no Mrs. Schmauss for a baby-sitter, I was all set to drag Ben over to the school with me, but he refused to come because he thought his friend Paul was already on his way over to play. I called up Boris, with whom I'd had

ed him to come

greed.

reliable person, and
p up some dinner for us,
since as you know, I can't

I find when I come home from
eeting but fifteen of my own thug
mbing around the living room, but no-
me and nobody's seen Ben. And Boris has
me.

xtremely upset, I call Boris on the phone and tell
m to come back down here and explain what happened to Ben, and would you believe he told me he let a total stranger take that little kid out for ice cream because she was such a beautiful chick he thought it would cheer him up? It never once occurred to him that the beautiful chick who turned him on could be a beautiful kidnapper! Dumb stupid fathead ox! End of story."

"Very, very interesting," said Ma, looking thoughtful.

There was another tap-tapping on the door. Ape Face poked his head into the room.

"Is it OK if I come in?" he asked.

"Sure," I said. "I'd given you up for dead."

"Oh no," he said. "I was looking at a book in my

room and then I fell asleep by mistake. Otherwise, I would've come in before because I wanted to give this to you."

He held out the—helicopter?

"That's very nice of you, Ape Face. Thank you."

"Annabel, how many times have I asked you not to . . ."

"Mom, it's all right. I *like* being called Ape Face. Don't you remember I told you that at lunch?"

"You did?" She looked over at me. I nodded.

"Sure, Ma. He loves it. You're the only one who doesn't like it. He loves it, don'tcha, ole Ape, ole pal?" I put my arms around his shoulder.

"Well, if you're positive it doesn't bother you," she began. Ape Face ignored her altogether. He handed his creation to me again.

"I really want you to have it. I made it specially for you. It took me a whole week in shop."

"Looks it," I said.

"Can you guess what it is?" he asked anxiously.

"Guess?" I said, indignantly. "I don't have to guess. It's perfectly clear what it is."

"What?" said Ape Face breathlessly.

"A helicopter!" I said triumphantly.

"You guessed!" He was beside himself with excitement.

"You did a terrific job," I said, patting him on the

back, "and I'm proud to own it. Thank you very, very much."

"Oh, that's OK," he said. "Thank *you* for the ice cream."

I heard him wrong, obviously.

"For the what?"

"For the ice cream. For taking me out. It was great. Thank you."

I looked over at Ma. She had the faintest pleased smile on her lips. And she gave me the faintest small nod.

I think right then my whole brain went into the deep freeze. I could hear a clock ticking, but time slowed down. Stopped, for a second. Then, one by one, little green giant words began to defrost: *But if I took him out, then I am the . . .*

There were two more words to come, but they were frozen solid. Try again. *If I took him out, I am the . . .*

Annabel, you know what those words are. You're just afraid to think them.

Yes, because once you think a thought out loud—even if it's only out loud inside your own head—you can never take it back. That's not safe. That hurts. Because if the thought isn't true, it's already too late to pretend you don't want to be a beautiful chick. No!

Yes! Now say the whole sentence. Say it to her. She's waiting for you to say something anyway.

124

What if I'm wrong? She'll laugh.

Coward! Spineless! There's a full-length mirror on the closet door. Look in that then. See for yourself.

My clothes are all new. Nice.

And?

My hair. Shorter, cleaner, and out of my eyes. Hair pretty, eyes pretty!

And?

Nose is the same.

And?

Mouth is . . .

Mouth is what? Different? Better? Beautiful? A beautiful mouth has a beautiful smile, a beautiful smile has beautiful teeth, and beautiful teeth don't have braces on them *anymore,* do they?! Smile, Annabel. When you say those words, SMILE!

"I am the beautiful chick!"

"Yes, my darling, you are indeed."

"Why are Annabel's arms all over goosebumps, Mom?" Ape Face is right. I am shivering with cold, all of a sudden. But Ma's lap is warm, and a few more tears won't hurt the pants suit.

Eleven ❀

In our American history class when we've finished each chapter, Miss Benson makes up questions for us to "think about" and then answer in essay form. The answers to the questions aren't always in the chapter, but they're related *to* the chapter, and unless you're a total retard, you can usually figure out what you're supposed to say. (For instance, if the question is "How would you, as a British official, feel about the Boston Tea Party?" your essay might begin, "If I were a British official, I'd be pretty tea'd off." Then again you might not, because Miss Benson would give you a zero for being flip.)

Sometimes, though, you have to look the answers up in some other reference book, which is a bore—but

Miss Benson (You remember her, she's the one who "puts things so nicely," according to Dilk.) says, "The purpose of these assignments, children, is to correlate the facts you have already committed to memory" (ha!) "with newly acquired information in order to derive a deeper and more revelatory understanding of the material. Do I see a few blank faces? I believe I do. Well, then, I shall translate into your native tongue." (smirk, smirk) "The purpose of these assignments is to help you children 'get it all together,' as it were." (Hey, Miss Benson, you forgot to translate 'as it were'!)

Actually, when you come right down to it, I don't object to the assignments—I just object to Miss Benson and American History. When you get to the end of a chapter, her system for getting it all together is as good as any other, I suppose. Which is why I am about to use it.

You see, we have finally come to the end, or almost the end, of *my* chapter. But in order to derive a deeper and more revelatory understanding of the material, there are several questions to be raised and several answers to be given. Such as:

We all know how I spent my day, but how, exactly, did Ma spend hers?

The first three hours—six to nine—were pretty tricky because Ma had to pretend to me and Ape Face and Daddy that she was Annabel. She said she found this rather unpleasant because she loathes marshmallows and if she can't have her coffee and a cigarette in the morning, she gets wildly cranky. On the other hand, being cranky made it slightly easier for her to snarl at Ape Face, which she felt she had to do if she was going to be completely convincing. She sure fooled me.

As soon as she'd dropped Ape Face off at school, she headed for the nearest drugstore and ordered coffee and buttered toast. The counterman said, "Coffee might stunt your growth, little girl," to which she said, quite truthfully, "Oh, I always drink it at home." To which he said, "Oh, izzat so? I suppose you smoke home, too?" To which she also said yes and then realized she didn't have any cigarettes with her and when she tried to buy some, the counterman said it was illegal to sell them to her.

Anyway, when the stores opened at ten, she bopped from one to another for two solid hours buying sensational clothes for me. She had remembered to bring her charge plates with her, but she had to send almost everything home because, as one saleslady put it, "We have no way of knowing whether or not your mommy

128

would like you to purchase all these outfits." Or as another saleslady put it, "How do we know you're really your mommy's daughter? Maybe you're someone else." (Ma and I had a good giggle over that one.) Luckily, one saleslady knew me and let Ma wear the clothes right out of the store. What *she* said was, "Annabel, I'm sure your mother is going to approve of this dress. It's exactly the kind of thing she would have chosen herself." (tee-hee.) "And what would you like me to do with this—uh—garment or smock or—uh—whatever this is? I'm surprised your mother would let you out of the house in it."

"Burn it," said Ma.

After buying *The New York Times,* which she hadn't yet had a chance to read, Ma went to a little French restaurant she knew in the East Fifties.

"I ordered myself a nice lunch of Senegalese soup, tripe à la mode de Caen, tossed green salad, and more coffee, and read my *Times.* Or tried to read my *Times.* It was awfully hard to concentrate with half the restaurant whispering and snickering about me. Adults seem to be under the impression that children are deaf, dumb, blind, and utterly insensitive," she said with disgust.

"Not *all* adults," I said loyally. "Anyway, go on."

From two forty-five to four-thirty, she was at the

129

orthodontist, having the braces taken off my teeth. The *wonderful* part about that you already know, but the funny part is that if she hadn't switched us around, I wouldn't have had the braces taken off today because I wouldn't have remembered the appointment. Dr. Stein has an absolutely revolting personality and I forget as many appointments as I remember. When I asked her what she thought of Dr. Stein, she said he was harmless enough (Not when he's twisting those wires he isn't!), but had an irritating habit of asking things like, "Tell me, dear, how is Mother and how is baby brother?" when his hands were in her mouth and she couldn't possibly answer without biting him.

"Did you?" I asked.

"Only once," she said. What a howl! What a kicky lady!

"You have to admit he did a lovely job, though. Have another look at yourself." We both admired me in the bathroom mirror. (We were in the bathroom because Ma was getting changed for dinner before Daddy came home.)

"And now have a look at this," she said, producing the plaster cast of my old teeth taken two years ago.

"Yick! Where did you get that?" I said, backing off in horror. I didn't even want to touch the thing.

"Dr. Stein gave it to me. He wanted me to see

how much you'd improved."

"Gave it to which me? Me-Ma or me-Annabel? Because if its me-Annabel, I don't want it. It's revolting."

"It's for me-the-mother, so I can see where all our money went, and frankly, I don't want it either." She dropped it in the wastebasket and the whole malocculuded mess broke in a million pieces, buck teeth and all. Zap!

Anyway, to continue . . . After the dentist, Ma came home expecting to find me there (forgetting entirely that I might be at the school meeting), and when she found Ape Face in the highly capable (she was sure) but parsley-covered hands of Boris (whom she dimly remembered seeing with his mother . . . terrible woman, his mother, and always borrowing equipment) she decided to cheer up Ape Face by taking him out for ice cream.

So far, the story checked out, but there was one thing I was curious about.

"Ma, I have a question: if the change in me was so terrific that Boris didn't recognize me, how come Ape Face did?"

"Oh, that was easy," she said. "When he heard the front door, he came running out of your room. I said to him, 'Listen, Ape, if you broke anything of mine, I'll smash your Johnny Lightning cars,' and he knew me

131

right away. Wasn't that clever?"

"I couldn't have done it better myself," I said in admiration.

When Ma brought Ape Face home after the ice cream, she heard voices in the kitchen. She also heard a grown-up yelling "Mommy" in the bedroom, so she told Ape Face to play quietly in *his* room and went right into the bedroom, where she changed us back to ourselves again.

How did she do that?

I haven't the foggiest notion and she says she'll never tell me. Isn't that annoying!

What happened when Daddy came home?

I was in my room, straightening my tights and combing my hair when he arrived, but you could hear him all over the house anyway. He was howling about how he was late because he couldn't get off the phone —he'd tried to call for twenty solid minutes to warn us, but some idiot was on *our* phone. That was Annabel Idiot, chatting with Harve and Merve and Stan (No. Stan was out sick, remember?) and Plonchik and Company.

All right, then, where was a clean shirt? Ma explained about Mrs. Schmauss and how she'd been too busy to iron one for him but not to worry because the Framptons weren't coming until the next night anyway and she'd iron one for him by then.

And then I made my entrance. If I could repeat the dialogue for you, I would, but there's nothing much to repeat. Daddy kept saying "Hey!" over and over again. After about five minutes of that, he put out his arms and I got in them. I think he was very proud.

What happened when my grandmother called up?

Fooled you that time, didn't I? I'll bet you forgot all about my grandmother—the one with the house in Larchmont where they were going to spend the month of July while I was in camp? Well, she called up and my father answered the phone, and when he hung up he sat down opposite my mother in the living room and drummed his fingers on the coffee table.

"You've clearly gone mad," he said.

"What's the matter?" she asked. I snuck into the room and joined my mother on the couch.

"This is February Fools' Day, right? Any minute now you're going to tell me it's all a joke, that your mother made it up, right?"

"Bill, what did my mother say?"

"She said that you said that you and I and Ben would be delighted to spend the month of July with her in the house in Larchmont while Annabel was at camp." Ma looked definitely nervous.

"Oh Bill, I can't even remember the last time I talked to her . . ."

"This morning," I said.

"How would *you* know?" said Daddy.

"Because she talks to her mother every morning at nine, don't you, Ma?"

"I try. But that's beside the point. The point is, we always have so many things to talk about, it's hard to recall exactly what I said, but I'm sure I never said anything like that. I mean, why would I say a thing like that? I *know* how you hate Larchmont . . ."

"*I* never knew that!" I said. Ma glanced over at me, and suddenly she got the whole picture.

"Oh, Lord!" she said. "I'm terribly sorry."

"Too late for that now," said Daddy.

"Gee, I guess we're all going to have a rotten summer," I said.

"What's that supposed to mean?" asked Daddy.

"Well, you three are going to be stuck in Larchmont and I have to go to camp."

"HAVE to go to camp!" Twin voices, both shouting. "I thought you WANTED to go to camp. Nobody's MAKING you go," said Ma.

"You mean I don't have to? Oh! I'm so relieved!

Oh! What terrific news! Oh! I'm the happiest girl in the whole world! Thank you, thank you, both of you!" Oh! Am I one great actress! Although when you come right down to it, who wants to go to camp, an all-girl camp in Maine? Ook! I wonder why I ever thought I wanted to do that? I wonder where Boris spends the summer?

"Well, sweetie, of course you don't have to go if you don't want to," said Daddy. He had the look of someone who'd just found nine hundred dollars lying in the street.

Is my grandmother going to be mad or disappointed or anything?

No. She doesn't like little children particularly and she didn't want them for the whole month anyway—only for the July Fourth weekend.

What happened when Boris arrived, which he did, right after the camp discussion?

But first, I have to ask you a question: Have you been waiting for this? Have you been waiting for the moment when the chestnut-haired, hazel-eyed, three inches taller, champion Nok Hockey player, maker of meatloaves Boris finds out that the metal-mouthed killer ghoul of Central Park *is* no longer? That in her

135

place is Annabel the Beautiful? You *have* been waiting? Yeah, but not as long as I have. I've been waiting for three years.

Have you tried to imagine how it will all happen? After all, it could happen any number of ways. For instance:

1) When the doorbell rings, my parents are standing in the hall. I am standing shyly in the background.

My father says, "Boris, come in, come in. I'm Bill Andrews; I believe you've already met my wife, Ellen?"

Boris steps forward, says good evening without a trace of adenoids. Smiles at my mother. Notices me; is clearly devastated by the sight. With super effort, drags his eyes back to my parents.

"Glad to meet you, sir. Good to see you again, Mrs. Andrews." The super effort fails. The eyes zoom back to shy Annabel.

"But who is . . . ?"

"Boris, surely you've met our daughter, Annabel?"

Boris faints.

Oh come on, now. That's gross! Boris wouldn't faint. Let's run it again.

"Boris, surely you've met our daughter Annabel?"

Boris marches manfully over to me. Shakes my hand.

136

"I wouldn't have recognized you."

That's *dull!* Let's try something else altogether.

2) The doorbell rings. My parents are in the bedroom, and there's nobody else—oh yes, Ape Face. I could use Ape Face. Ape Face is in the hall and since I am on the phone talking to Robin (a boy called Robin—English exchange student, senior in my school), I say, in my lovely, musical voice, "Ben, be a love, will you, and answer the door?"

He does, and I'm still on the phone so I put my hand over the mouthpiece and say,

"Boris, old bean, how terrific to see you again! I'll be off the phone in a sec.

"Ah, Robin, that sounds slick, but I can't tonight. No, really I can't. An old, old friend of mine . . ." I wink at Boris. He realizes I am beautiful *and* a loyal, kind person—what more could anyone want?

I'm not going to bother finishing the conversation with Robin. (One of the good things about imagining: you get to cut out all the boring parts and go on with the juicy stuff.) I offer Boris a Coke. We're standing at the bar, smiling at each other and sipping Cokes when the phone rings again. It's Geoffrey. (Not Jeffrey, *Geoffrey*.) He has tickets for a sitar concert in Carnegie Hall for tomorrow. Would that be all right??

Sure, why not? Bye. Sitar. Sitar. Sitars in my eyes. My mind is wandering. Back to the telephone—which rings again. This time it's a black friend of mine called —let's see . . . called—uh—Gordon. Gordon wants to know if I'm working at Head Start on Tuesday because he is . . .

Now Boris knows I am beautiful, loyal, kind *and* a liberal. And always on the telephone. But I haven't imagined a conversation between Boris and me yet. I think it's too late. I don't like this one . . . it's sort of out of control.

3) My parents are in their bedroom, Ape Face is in his bedroom, I am on my way to the kitchen to get out the ice—because now that I am beautiful, I am also a helpful, domestic (still Women's Lib, though) person.

In the kitchen, I hear a noise. I am frightened! Who could be in there, a burglar? Am I finally going to be robbed on this, the most splendid day of my life? Just as I am peeking into the kitchen to see the burglar, I hear a loud bang. I gasp out loud. But it is only the oven door banging shut.

In the kitchen, I see the chestnut-haired, hazel-eyed, three inches taller, champion Nok-Hockey player and maker of meatloaves, Boris.

"I was just checking odd the beatloaf."

138

"How did you get in here, anyway? The doorbell didn't ring."

"Subuddy left the door opid," he said. He sniffed. In a minute, the m's and n's would be back.

"Hey!" he said, peering at me carefully. The great moment was happening.

"Hey!" he said again. "Aren't you the . . ."

"Aren't I the what?" I asked, leaning against the fridge, playing it cool.

"Aren't you the kidnapper who snatched that kid out of here this afternoon? Yes, you are!" he said, holding a two-pronged fork at my throat.

"OK, girlie, I gotcha now. What did you do with that kid?" He gave me a gentle jab—just enough to remind me that the fork was still there, I suppose. Richard Widmark couldn't have done it better.

"Listen, you dumb fathead," I said. "That kid is my brother and I have a perfect right to do anything I want to with him."

"*Now* what are you giving me?" he said with another jab at my throat.

"I'm giving you my name—which is Annabel Andrews."

"Prove it!" he snarled.

"How?"

"Show me your teeth." I did. He gave me another little jab.

"Nah, you're not Annabel Andrews. Now who are you and where's the kid, before I punch you full of holes?"

"Boris, leave her alone. It *is* my sister. She just looks different, that's all." Ape Face to the rescue. Boris put the fork in the dishwasher. (What's the matter with him? My neck is clean. Enough.)

"I certainly wish you'd told me that this afternoon when you left with her," said Boris. "Your mother and I were terribly worried." He stared at me in silence for a minute. Then another minute. It felt like a thousand minutes.

"She looks pretty, don't you think?" Oh, Ape Face! *You* are a loyal and kind person.

"Yes, she really does. You really do," he said.

I smiled at him and said thank you.

He smiled at me and said you're welcome.

And that, folks, is how it really happened. Not very glamorous, but who cares. At least it happened.

How did Boris's meatloaf turn out?

I'm glad you asked. Right after the thank you-you're welcome conversation, Ape Face went off somewhere or other and Boris and I sat around the kitchen having a nice time talking about all kinds of things. Then the timer went off, and he said, "Let's see how dinner is coming along. This stuff should be done by now."

"I've never made it," I admitted.

"Easy," he said, cutting into it with a knife. "It's not quite done but almost," he announced. To me, it looked positively raw.

"I don't like to argue with you, Boris, but it can't be. It's still bright red."

"What color did you have in mind?" he snapped. (Our first quarrel?)

"Meatloaf," I said with authority, "is supposed to be brown. Even *I* know that."

"Meatloaf is supposed to be brown, but beetloaf is supposed to be red. This is beetloaf," he said, with equal authority.

"Made out of *beets*? That's the most disgusting idea I ever heard in my life! It's to upchuck!"

"Listen, Princess, if you don't like it, you don't have to eat it." He slammed the knife down on the counter. "You know, you may *look* better than you did, but you don't *act* better. Where's the tin shovel? You got that hidden on you someplace?"

"I'm sorry," I said meekly. "It's just I never saw anything like it before."

"Neither did I. But your mother was in a panic about those people coming for dinner so I said I'd slap something together. Then she went barreling out of the house before I realized that there was nothing *in* the house to make dinner with. This is the best I could do."

"What's in it?"

"Onion, hard-boiled egg, celery, tomato paste, basil, tarragon, tuna fish and Crunchy Granola. And beets. I just hope it's good." He looked worried. Poor thing.

"I'm sure it's fantastically delicious," I said, very gung ho. "You've probably invented something. Beet-loaf by Boris. I wonder why I was so positive you'd said meatloaf."

"I know why," said Boris, wearily. "It's because when a person with adenoids says, 'Hello, by dabe is Boris add I've cub to bake you a beetloaf,' you automatically translate that into 'Hello, my name is Morris and I've come to make you a meatloaf.'"

"Hey, you're absolutely right. Aren't you smart! That's a brilliant theory. As a matter of fact, I bet a lot of people think your name is really Morris!" Boris was standing with folded arms, staring at me, smiling the way you smile at an idiot, and nodding his head up and down.

"Yes, they do. Because it is." ZONK!

How did Morris's beetloaf turn out?

Terrific, believe it or not. And my parents thought *he* was terrific and he told them *they* were terrific—in fact, he said he wished he had my mother for a mother because his father was dead and he didn't like his own mother at all.

142

"What's the matter with her?" asked Ape Face.

On his fingers, one by one, Morris began to list her faults.

"She's mean and selfish and she can't cook. All she cares about is buddy—she hates childred; id fact, she screabs at be all the tibe. If you wad to doh what I really thick, by buther is a crub!"

"Oh dear!" said Ma.

"Hmmn," said Daddy.

"*What* did he say?" said Ape Face.

"Morris, did it ever occur to you that your adenoids are fine—you simply have an allergy to your mother?" said I, beating Dr. Artunian at her own game.

Morris sniffed. "That sounds logical, but so what? I still have to spend about nine months out of the year with her."

"What about the other three?" I asked.

"In the summer, my mother goes to Europe, and I go stay with my grandfather in Stamford. That I like. He has a big old house on the water, there's a sailboat, and a made-over barn he rents out. When he rents to families with kids, I play with them."

"How big is that barn, would you say?" asked Daddy. (I don't have to go on with this, do I? The price was right, it was close enough to New York, it hadn't been rented yet, et cetera, et cetera, and sensational so forth.)

143

What happened after dinner?

After dinner, Morris and I played three games of Nok Hockey. He beat me two out of three—just the tactful amount, I think—and then he said he'd better be going home. My parents told him he was welcome to come back anytime, and he said how about tomorrow. We all said that would be swell. (Actually, my father said swell, my mother said lovely, and I said cool. Ape Face didn't say anything—he was already in bed.)

Then Daddy said to Ma, "Hey, what about the movie? I forgot all about it. I was going to take you to dinner and a movie tonight. You still game?"

"Sure, I guess so," said Ma, looking pleased. "What'll we see?"

"I thought you said you wanted to go to that flick around the corner. 'Brucey and Betsy.'"

"I might have said that," said Ma, "but I've changed my mind. Let's see something else. Or we could all just sit around and watch the boob tube."

"Not me," I said. "You guys go right ahead, but I have a long paper to write. Due Monday. I mean *over*-due Monday."

Was the paper finished in time?

You betcha! I worked day and night all weekend and Morris typed it for me. It was a hundred and forty-five pages and Miss McGuirk gave me an 88. I would have preferred 98, but she said she had to take *some*thing off for lateness. Also, she said I shouldn't call it fact when its "basic premise" was so utterly fantastic. Of course, that reaction didn't surprise me very much. After all, I predicted it, didn't I?

When did you do that?

Way back on page one, silly. You're not a very careful reader. Don't you remember page one? The story begins:

You are not going to believe me, nobody in their right minds could possibly believe me, but it's true, really it is.

And the story ends the same way.

Format by Kohar Alexanian
Set in 14 pt. Granjon

HarperCollins*Publishers*

"A deliciously original and consistently inventive story. Annabel, Boris, and Ben are a trio of brilliantly perspicacious and likeable characters."—*The Horn Book*

"The sprightly and articulate heroine of *Freaky Friday* reports another fantastic adventure that seems completely believable. Mary Rodgers has to a remarkable degree the ability to blend fantasy and realism. Spiced with humor and sophisticated dialogue, the story is a 'good read.'" (Recommended)—*Bulletin of the Center for Children's Books*

"Deft writing and timely humor."—ALA *The Booklist*

A Billion$ for Boris

An Ursula Nordstrom Book

A Billion $ for Boris

Mary Rodgers

HARPER & ROW, PUBLISHERS

This book is dedicated to my small sons,
Adam and Alec,
without whom I was finally able to finish it.

A Billion
for Boris

Barron University
Dept. of ESP and Parapsychology
Greensboro, N.C.

Dear Sirs:

Enclosed please find a detailed account of a most
unusual experience recently undergone by me, my
brother, and a friend of mine who lives upstairs in our
apartment building. This experience doesn't exactly
fall into the category of ESP, but it was definitely a
psychic phenomenon of some sort or other so I thought
you might like to have a record of it for your archives.
I also thought maybe you'd have a logical explanation
for the whole thing, but if you don't, I'll certainly
understand.

In any case, I'd appreciate hearing from you at your
earliest possible convenience.

Very sincerely yours,
Annabel Andrews

P.S. Rest assured that every word of the following
document is the *absolute verbatim truth*! I say this
only because I am a person to whom peculiar things
happen from time to time but nobody ever believes

me. Last year, for instance, there was a Friday in February when I woke up and found out I'd turned into my mother. It was a pretty freaky Friday, and not one I'd want to repeat—but that's not the point. The point is, when the going got rough and I needed help, I couldn't find anybody to believe me. I told three cops and my trusted (but not very trusting) friend who lives upstairs, and they all thought I was crazy. Granted, it was a rather bizarre occurrence, but compared to what you're about to read, it positively reeked with credibility. Anyway, I'm counting on the fact that you people *will* believe me, because if *you* don't, who will?

Very, *very* sincerely yours,
A.A.

Preliminary Information

Before I do anything else, I'd better list some basic facts about myself, my brother, and my friend.

BASIC FACTS ABOUT MYSELF

I am fourteen years old, five foot four and still growing (I hope). I have brown eyes, brown hair (mousy), and I weigh a hundred and fifteen pounds before breakfast. (If you don't want to be depressed, before breakfast is the only time to get on a scale.)

My parents, Ellen Jean Benjamin Andrews and William Waring Andrews, my brother Ape Face (on the birth certificate it says Benjamin but to me he's Ape Face), our dog Max, and I live in an apartment on Central Park West in New York City. I'm in the ninth grade at the Barden School where I do pretty well when I try and, according to my teachers, "surprisingly well" even when I don't. The subjects I try at are English, current events, history, and biology.

Home economics, which we have once a week, I

don't try at. I'm going to be a journalist when I grow up, and my husband will simply have to accept the fact that I don't cook, clean, or iron shirts. Not that there's anything demeaning about housework, but unlike my mother, I'm not the domestic type.

You know what she said to me the other day? She said, "Annabel, you are an incorrigible slob."

I said, "No, I'm not, Ma. You and I have different standards, that's all."

"Yes," she said. "Mine are higher."

Oh well, maybe now that she's started taking courses full-time at Columbia University, she'll be forced to lower hers. I hope so, because except for fights about my neatness, I would say we have an excellent relationship.

My father is an account executive at an advertising agency called Joffert and Jennings. Last year, he handled New Improved Fosphree; but then the EPA discovered it was killing all the fish in the Schoharie Reservoir, and the product was taken off the market. Just as well. The company used to send us a ton of the stuff free every month and it turned all the laundry gray. Personally, I was hoping he'd get assigned to a candy account—free chocolate bars every month would have been sensational—but instead he got Merrill Lynch which is a big brokerage firm and doesn't send you anything.

Generally speaking, I have an excellent relationship

4

with my father, too. The only trouble with him is he works too hard and worries about money too much. Other than that, he's a neat guy and fairly unsquare, considering his age. (Thirty-nine.)

BASIC FACTS ABOUT APE FACE

He is seven years old, four feet something-or-other and still growing (I assume). He has blue eyes, ash-blond hair (but in a couple of years it'll *turn* mousy, I'll bet), and I don't know what he weighs. All I know is he's one of those kids who eats everything that's put in front of him and then some and never gets fat. He must be shot with luck.

Incidentally, in case you're curious about his nickname, I started calling him that the day he came home from the hospital. I was six and a half, and at that age if you're planning on a sister and what you get instead is a male monkey, you're not inclined to mince words.

"It's got a face like an ape," I said, giving it a cautious poke. "What's it called?"

"Benjamin. Or Ben, if you like that better," said my mother, trying to be accommodating.

"I like Ape Face better."

"Well, he won't," said my mother firmly. "It'll only make him mad."

But it didn't. That's what's so funny. I only recently found out that all those years I was calling him Ape Face to make him mad, I was only making my mother

5

mad. Ape Face *loved* it. I think he feels it gives him a kind of macho authority. Sometimes he lopes around the apartment saying things like, "Annabel, you're not supposed to put your feet on the coffee table," and when I say, "Who says?" he says, "The Ape says," and pounds his chest like a twelve-foot gorilla. Other times, he just stands there embarrassing me in front of my friends by pushing his lower lip out with his tongue, scratching his ribs with his left paw, picking imaginary cooties out of his hair and eating them with the right paw, and grunting, *"Unh, unh, unh."* It's really disgusting. I should have stuck with the name Ben. Or Benjie. Actually, when I get mad enough, that's exactly what I do call him and it makes him furious. Shows what mothers know.

All in all, he's not too bad; I just wish he weren't so *tidy*. He's tidy about his clothes, tidy about toothpaste tubes (always squeezes from the bottom and puts the cap back on), and if you really want to see something, you should see his tiny, tidy room. It's only ten by twelve and in it he has managed to fit: twenty-seven stuffed animals, a fleet of Dinky cars, a toy chest full of assorted Lego pieces, a large Childcraft Work Bench, a toolbox of Baby Ben innards, and a pachinko set—tidily. My room is much bigger but it usually looks like the aftermath of a Macy's bargain-basement sale. I don't know how he does it.

In the old days, I used to think he did it just to show

me up; but now that I've gotten more tolerant, I've decided he can't help being the way he is. And anyway, he's improving; twice this week he's forgotten to wash out his bathtub ring.

BASIC FACTS ABOUT BORIS

Boris Harris is fifteen, five foot ten (definitely still growing—otherwise, why would his hands and feet be so enormous?), has hazel eyes, chestnut hair (beautiful), and probably weighs around one forty-five.

He lives upstairs in an apartment which until recently I'd never seen, with a mother I'd never met, even though I'd known him for umpteen years and been good friends with him for over a year. Can you *imagine*? His mother was a complete mystery. All I knew was that she was divorced from his father (who had then died when Boris was eight) and hated to cook—that much he'd told me. But I didn't know anything else because he didn't talk about her often. When he did, it wasn't very complimentary.

For instance, one night last year when he was having dinner in our apartment, my mother said, "Boris, I've never met your mother. Tell me, what's she like?"

Boris stared at his plate for a second and then flatly announced, "By buther is a crub," which translated loosely means "I don't like her much."

"I beg your pardon?" inquired my mother politely.

7

"Dever bide, Bisses Adrews. Forget I said it," said Boris.

It was then I finally realized why it was that whenever Boris came down from upstairs, he always sounded as though he had a cold for the first few minutes and then the symptoms cleared up. He was allergic to his mother! (I'm happy to report that he seems to have outgrown this; it almost never happens anymore.)

The same evening, I also realized that Boris's real name was actually Morris. But I went on calling him Boris anyway—because he was used to it by then, and so was I.

Other basic facts about Boris are: He's a grade ahead of himself in school and still gets all A's. He says his school is probably easier than mine but I doubt it. I think he's just incredibly smart. And modest.

He has a super sense of humor.

He wins almost every argument we have, and we have quite a few. It isn't that we don't get along or anything, we just like to argue for the fun of it.

But the most important basic fact about Boris is that I love him. And although he hasn't exactly said so, I think he loves me, too.

How It All Began

It was a Saturday afternoon in February. The weather was unbelievably repulsive; rain mixed with sleet, slippery sidewalks, icy wind that turned your umbrella inside out—the kind of day that makes you wish your dog was paper trained because he doesn't want to go out any more than you do. Especially a dog like our basset, Max, who's too lazy to go out even if it's a sunny morning in spring.

So anyway, that's the kind of afternoon it was. Boris and I were playing records in the living room, my mother was in the study doing her homework, my father was out to lunch with a client from Chicago, and Ape Face was being a pain in the neck. For about the eleventh time in the last half hour, he stood in the doorway of the living room.

"Annabel," he began.

"Are you here again? What do you want now?"

"Would you play me a game of Crazy Eights?"

"No."

"Boris, would you?"

"Thanks, anyway."

"Well, won't somebody play *some*thing with me? There's nothing to do around here."

"Watch television."

"I'm not allowed. Only *Sesame Street*, *The Electric Company*, or *Mr. Rogers' Neighborhood*, and they're not on."

"Get Mom to invite a friend over for you."

"She tried. Nobody's mother wants to go out in all this rain and stuff."

"I don't blame them. What about a friend in the building?"

"I don't *have* a friend in the building. My only friend was George and he moved to the country. *You* know that."

"As a matter of fact, I did not know that. Listen, I'm sorry your friend moved to the country and I'm sorry you're so bored, but there isn't a thing I can do about it. So if you wouldn't mind getting out of here and stop bothering us—*now*. Scram! Go amuse yourself. Take apart a Baby Ben clock or something."

I figured that should occupy him for at least an hour.

Ape Face sighed. "Okay," he said.

A hot ten minutes later, he was back again. I tried to control my temper.

"Finished already? My, that was speedy of you!" Much too speedy if you ask me. I shot Boris a look of despair. Boris took over.

10

"Ben, old boy, I have a great idea for you. Why don't you try putting the clock back together?"

"I already did."

"Oh," said Boris, nonplussed. "Congratulations."

"It was easy," said Ape Face. "I've done it a million times. There's nothing in my whole room I haven't done a million times. So Annabel, I was just wondering . . ." he said hesitantly.

"Wondering what?"

"Are you using your hair dryer right now?"

"Obviously not. Why?"

"I want to take it apart," Ape Face said.

"Oh you do, do you! Well, that's just altogether tough luck. It's a brand-new dryer and I'm not about to let you muck around with it. You'll wreck it up."

"Please?"

"*No!*" I shouted. "Now get out of here before I kill you!"

"Wait a minute," said Boris. "I think I have something that might interest you, Ape Face. In our apartment there's an old TV set. It's absolutely beyond repair—hasn't worked for years—but it has a lot of tubes and wires and parts you'd have fun fiddling around with. How does that sound?"

Ape Face was thrilled. "That sounds great!"

"I thought so. I'll tell you what: Seeing as it's no good to anyone but a mechanical nut like you, I'll sell it to you for a very low price."

"How much price?" asked Ape Face anxiously.

11

"Fifty cents."

Ape Face was crestfallen. "I don't have fifty cents. I spent all my money on Wacky Packs. Couldn't I go upstairs to your house and you just lend me the use of the set for a couple of hours?"

"No," said Boris firmly. "You going upstairs is not a good idea. But even if you don't have the money, I'd be happy to bring it down to you now anyway; and you could pay me later. Okay?"

"Okay," said Ape Face. "There's just one thing. I hope you're not going to get mad at me—but if the set's no good, why do I have to pay you fifty cents for it?" I must say, he had a point there. It did seem rather greedy.

Boris looked faintly annoyed. "The effort of lugging it down here is worth at least fifty cents. Besides, it's a seller's market. In other words, I've got what you want, and whether or not anyone else wants it is immaterial. You do want it, don't you?"

"Oh yes," said Ape Face.

"All right, then. It's a deal. Annabel, you're the witness."

"Fine by me," I said. "I just hope he doesn't electrocute himself."

"Oh, don't be silly," said Ape Face scornfully. "I know all about electricity. I know better than that. I wouldn't plug it in while I was working on it—only when it was all fixed up."

"That'll be the day," said Boris flippantly.

12

Friday, April 12

It was my fourteenth birthday. There was nothing particularly significant about it except that it was the nicest one I'd ever had. Its not being a school night, my parents took me and Boris to Gallagher's Steak House, and after that they let Boris take me alone to The Bitter End in the Village, where Boris finally presented me with the package he'd been lugging around all night. From the large size of it, I was prepared for the disappointing fact that it couldn't be anything personal like a ring or a bangle, but I was not prepared for anything as impersonal as a pair of walkie-talkies.

"Boy, Boris, that's got to be the most original present anybody ever gave anybody." I am nothing if not truthful.

"Useful, too," said Boris, obviously quite pleased with himself. Useful for what? I wondered.

"Oh, I'll bet. And even if they weren't, they're so attractive—those nice leather cases."

"Glad you like them," said Boris, putting one walkie-talkie back in the carton and shoving the other into the pocket of his parka.

"Hey!" I protested. "Where are you going with that? What am I going to do with *one* walkie-talkie?"

"One for you, one for me; these things'll transmit through steel, cement, carpets, the works—we'll use them instead of the telephone."

"But what's the matter with the telephone?"

"Too expensive," said Boris.

"Weren't the walkie-talkies expensive? They *look* expensive."

"Sure, but at the rate you and I talk to each other, I figure they'll amortize themselves in two and a half months."

"Since when did you get so economy-minded?"

"Since five days ago. My mother said if I didn't stop tying up her phone, she'd have my own phone installed and make me pay for it. This way is going to be a lot cheaper and we won't ever have to depend on the phone again."

When I got home and thought it all over, I decided Boris was a very practical person. I also decided that under certain circumstances, a walkie-talkie was more personal than a bangle. After all, bangles you could give to a thousand girls and none of them (including me) would be the wiser; but a walkie-talkie-for-two constituted a definite commitment to only one girl. And I was it. So I gave it a quick kiss, put it under my pillow, and went to sleep.

14

Saturday, April 13

BEEP, BEEP, BEEP. "Testing one two three four. This is Boris calling Annabel. Are you there, Annabel? If you are there, push the right-hand button and say something. Roger, over, and out."

I groped under the pillow for the walkie-talkie, pushed the right-hand button, and said, "What time is it?"

"You've got the wrong button, Annabel. I repeat: the *wrong button.* You've been pushing the signal button, which beeps." (You're telling me it beeps!) "The right-hand button is for talking, push the right-hand button. Roger, over, and out."

"I *am* pushing the right-hand button," I said grumpily. I wasn't, I was pushing the left-hand button—but it was too early to argue. Maybe his walkie-talkie was facing the other way.

"That's better. I hear you now. But not very well. You're coming through muffled." I took the walkie-talkie out of its leather case.

"Better now?" I inquired.

15

"Much," said Boris.

"Say, Boris," I yawned, "what time is it?"

"Seven thirty."

I pushed the talk button and groaned loudly.

"I didn't wake you, did I? I thought you were an early riser."

"Mondays through Fridays I'm an early riser. Out of necessity, not preference. Saturdays and Sundays I'm a late riser."

"Gee, Annabel, I'm sorry," said Boris. "I assumed you'd be up and if you weren't, you wouldn't hear the signal."

"Sleeping through beeping is a virtual impossibility. I could have heard it in Anchorage, Alaska. Anyway, never mind. What's it like out?" My room faces west on an alley and the rest of the apartment faces either west or north. The only way to find out what to wear is to get down on the street and sample the air. By that time, it's usually too late to go back up and change into something else. Boris's apartment faces south and east; if the sun was out, he'd know about it.

"Gorgeous. Not a cloud in the sky, warm—according to my thermometer, forty-eight degrees. You couldn't ask for a better day. Want to go biking in the park?"

"Can't. My mother's going to the library to do some research. She's paying me to baby-sit Ape Face."

"Bring him along and I'll split the fee with you. He knows how to bike, doesn't he?"

"Not too well. Besides, knowing him, he'll want to go to the zoo."

"To visit his friends, I suppose."

"What friends? What do you mean?"

"Chimps, orangutans, purple-bottomed baboons . . . forget it. I was just being funny."

"Oh, is that what you were being? I thought you were being stupid."

"Okay, Annabel. I obviously got you at a bad time. Check with you later. Roger, over, and out." When Boris is hurt he doesn't say much—he just turns off. For a scrappy person like me, it's a maddening technique, but when we talked about it once, he said it was his way of coping. He said he learned to do it years ago when his parents used to use him for a football in their fights.

I beeped him back. After three or four minutes, I decided he was either sulking or out of earshot.

"Yeah," he said finally.

"What took you so long? Couldn't you hear me? This is Annabel."

"No kidding. Of course I heard you. So did my mother. When you disturb *her* at seven thirty in the morning she's even more charming than you. If I don't get her some coffee fast, she'll throw something at me, so if you don't mind, I'll sign off now. Roger . . ."

"Wait a minute, Boris. I just wanted to say I was sorry for snapping at you."

17

"Better you than my mother. What does the word 'Good-bye' mean to you? Roger, over, and out."

I wanted like anything to ask Boris to go to the zoo with me and the Ape, but after what he said about his mother, I didn't dare beep him again.

Not a very auspicious beginning for a day.

By ten thirty, my mother had left for the library, my father had left for the office to take care of some odds and ends of paper work, and I started getting dressed to take Ape Face to the zoo. Forty-eight degrees and sunny? Good. I could wear my new boots (birthday present from my mother), my new turtleneck sweater (from my father), my new secondhand Eisenhower jacket (from my friend Virginia—she got it at the thrift shop across the street from school), and my most treasured, old, soft, threadbare pair of Cloroxed blue jeans.

"Hey, Ape Face," I yelled. "Come here a second."

Ape Face appeared, still in his pajamas.

"Ta-dah!" I said, spreading my arms out and turning around for inspection. "How do you like me?"

Ape Face didn't seem quite sure. He looked me up and down and then said, "Where are we going?"

"To the zoo. I thought you wanted to go to the zoo."

"I do. I love the zoo."

"Well, what's the matter then?" Ape Face looked me up and down some more.

"Are you going to be warm enough? No hat, no gloves or anything? It's going to snow, you know."

"Don't be ridiculous," I said. "It's forty-eight degrees out and sunny."

"But later it's going to snow."

"You're cuckoo. I never heard of such a cuckoo thing!"

Ape Face shrugged. "Are those the new boots Mom gave you?"

"Yes. Super, aren't they."

"Waterproof?"

"No, dummy. Waterproof boots are clumpy and cloddy. These are thin and delicate. Finest Italian leather."

"They're going to get roond in the snow."

"The word is *ru*-ined, not roond, and they're not; because it's *not going to snow!* Hurry up and get dressed and stop bugging me about the weather."

Ordinarily, Ape Face is a fairly snappy dresser (by which I mean *quick* snappy as opposed to groove snappy), but twenty minutes later, there was no sign of him.

"What's taking you so long?" I shouted. "I've been waiting for hours."

"Coming," he answered. He didn't have to tell me he was coming; I could hear him coming: An inexorable *schlup-schlup-schlup,* accompanied by *scrawk-*pause-*scrawk-*pause-*scrawk.* By now, I was prepared for practically anything. Which was fortunate, because what hove into view blew my mind. The Abominable Snowman himself, in Mighty-Mac, ski pants, scarf, mittens, galoshes (*schlup-schlup*), and a three-foot Flexible Flyer attached to a long rope (*scrawk*-pause-*scrawk*).

"Listen, you idiot fathead, if you think I'm going out on the street with you dressed like that on a day like this, you're out of your idiot fat head!"

The fact that I was absolutely incoherent with rage didn't seem to have the slightest effect on him. "You're getting paid a dollar twenty-five to baby-sit me to the zoo."

"Dragging a large sled over dry land all the way to Sixty-Fourth Street and back was not included in the bargain."

"I'll drag my own sled. Getting it home'll be easier anyway."

"You'll look like a horse's ass. Everybody'll laugh at you."

"Not when it snows, they won't. They'll laugh at *you*."

So down to the zoo we went, with Ape Face *schlup*ing and *scrawk*ing and me six paces behind pretending I'd never seen him before in my life.

At two forty-five, that selfsame Saturday afternoon, April 13th, a freak blizzard hit the tri-state area! Within an hour and a half, while Ape Face was serenely communing with his relatives in the house of large primates (and I was holding my nose and wondering how come more and more people kept leaving

20

until we were the only ones there), the temperature dropped twenty-five degrees, the wind velocity rose to near gale proportions, and six inches of snow covered the ground. Unbeknownst to me, of course. By four fifteen when we finally emerged, the entire zoo was totally deserted, and Central Park was a howling winter wonderland. Making our way home was going to be about as hazardous as marching across Antarctica.

I'll say one thing for my brother, though. He knows when to keep his mouth shut. Maybe it was only self-preservation—maybe he kept his mouth shut so the snow wouldn't blow in and drown him—but not once, in the whole hour it took us to get back, did he say, "I told you so." He did say, "I knew getting the sled home would be easier," but when I snarled, "Naturally it's easier. You're sitting on it and I'm pulling it across Sheep Meadow," he clammed up immediately.

Ape Face survived our little adventure unscathed. A slightly chapped chin where his wool scarf had rubbed, but otherwise toasty warm and contented. I, on the other hand, had to consign my beautiful new boots to the garbage and my frostbitten self to bed because I'd caught a revolting cold. In fact, two hours later, when I got around to beeping Boris to tell him what had happened, I already sounded so adenoidal he asked me if I was developing an allergy to *my* mother. Ha ha!

What he didn't ask me was how Ape Face could have known about the freak blizzard. I guess at the time it didn't seem significant. I was so glad to be home and warm, it didn't seem significant to me either. But it was—very. Because although we didn't know it at the time, IT had begun to happen.

Thursday, April 18

Five days later, my mother, needlessly consumed with guilt about going to college while I honked and snorted, had decided to stay home and look after me. I told her it was ridiculous; I was perfectly all right. I had my box of Kleenex Man-Sized Tissues, my nose spray, my vaporizer, the portable Sony—what more could I want?

"Suppose you get hungry?" she asked doubtfully.

"I won't. My taste buds are shot and I'm full up on phlegm."

My mother looked faintly ill. "Annabel, please." She's not as medically oriented as I am.

"Anyway, Ma, the cleaning lady comes today, doesn't she? If I need anything, I can ask Mattie. Go on, now. If you miss classes, you'll get behind."

"No," she said. "It would make me uncomfortable. I keep feeling if I'd stayed home yesterday and the day before, you'd be all better by now."

"Rot!"

"Nevertheless . . ." she said. "Call me if you need me. I'll be around." Either I was sicker than I thought (pneumonia? pleurisy?), or else she was simply looking for an excuse to cut school. Maybe that's it, I thought drowsily. Like daughter, like mother. With that, I drifted off to sleep.

Eight hours later I woke up. My mother was sitting in a chair near the window, reading a tome.

"That was quite some nap you had there. I was beginning to worry. How do you feel?"

"Terrific." I blew a quart of wonderfulness out of my nose and heaved the Kleenex at the wastebasket. Missed.

"Why is it," she said, retrieving the nasty thing with two dainty fingers, "why is it that you're on the first basketball team at school but you can't hit the broad side of a barn at home?"

"Maybe it's a question of incentive. At school you get points for making a basket." She laughed and moved the basket closer to the bed.

"There's Daddy," she said.

"Where?"

"I heard the door slam." (All mothers have phenomenal hearing.) "Now, he's making a drink. Make me one, too," she called. "Now he's on his way in." She took her glasses off.

"Hi there, sweetie, how are you feeling?" Dad leaned down to kiss me.

"Wouldn't, if I were you. You'll catch the plague."

"I'll take my chances," he said, planting one on my forehead and moving over to my mother.

"Now you're going to give it to her," I said.

"She'll take her chances, too, won't you?" he said, planting one on her mouth.

"Sure," she said. Not that she had any choice in the matter since he'd already done it.

Now that the evening greetings were over, my mother began what I call The Daily News Roundup. This always intrigues me because although my parents are crazy about each other—I'm positive of that— neither one seems terribly interested in what the other one is doing. But they always ask anyway—out of politeness, I guess.

"How was your day?" said my mother.

"Pretty good. I had a two-hour meeting with Marc Adams and Grantly Harding. If Cavendish buys it, we're going to get into the television bag. Then I had lunch at Nino's with Parks to discuss . . ."

"I don't know how you can discuss anything in that place. It's so noisy," said my mother.

"They know me there and the food's edible," said my father, happy to be sidetracked. His part of the recital was over; now it was her turn.

"And how was *your* day?"

"Fascinating," she said. Since there's obviously nothing fascinating about spending your day in the

25

company of a zonked-out kid, what she really meant was dull, but the irony eluded my father.

"That's good. Can I do anything for you? Get you anything?"

"No thanks." You know, it's interesting: If my mother offers to do something or get something, my father takes her up on it. If my father offers, my mother invariably says "No, thanks," and does it or gets it herself. Partly because it's easier—he never knows where anything is—and partly because her feminine consciousness hasn't been raised as much as mine has. When I grow up, Boris will have to know where things are; as a journalist who travels frequently, I may not always be around to show him.

"You could get me something, Daddy," I said brightly.

"I could?" His face was a study in incredulity.

"I'm starving." Which was true, as a matter of fact.

"Oh," he said. Now his face was a study in bewilderment and nervousness combined. "Well, uh . . ." He looked over at my mother.

"I'll do it, darling. What do you feel like eating, Annabel?"

"Just soup. Plain chicken noodle soup." My mother got to her feet. Dad put out a restraining hand. "Stay put," he said magnanimously. "I can make soup. Anybody can make soup. Pheasant under glass, no; soup, yes. I'll be back in a minute."

He was back in a minute, empty handed. Ma and I grinned at each other.

"I can't find any soup," he said helplessly. "Mattie must have switched all the cabinets around."

"No, she didn't," said Ma. "The soup's where it's always been: in the shallow cabinet by the kitchen door."

"It's not. I looked in there." Ma exhaled a sigh of irritation and wordlessly took off down the hall.

A minute later, she was back. "That's funny," she said sheepishly. "I can't find it either."

"Ha!" said Dad.

"Ha nothing," she said indignantly. "There were at least a dozen cans there yesterday. I put them there myself, *yesterday*. Because yesterday was the day I went to the A&P, remember, Annabel?"

"Yes, that's right."

"And they had a nice sale on Aunt Ethel's Quik 'n Easy Soup—twelve to a customer. I bought two mushroom, two tomato, two sorrel, and six chicken noodle for Annabel. Remember, Annabel? I fixed you some when I came home."

"Right. There should be eleven cans left."

"Good thinking!" said my father. He loves to tease me about my math. I stuck my tongue out at him. My mother wasn't in the mood for horseplay.

"Stop it, you two. I want to get to the bottom of this. What happened to those cans of soup?"

"Beats me," said Dad. "You don't suppose Mattie would . . ." he was too embarrassed to finish the sentence. I should hope so!

"She certainly wouldn't," I said. "She'd never take a thing out of this house unless we gave it to her. Ma, why don't you ask the Ape? Maybe he took them to school. At Thanksgiving, they ask us to donate canned goods for the poor and needy of St. James Parish."

"Annabel, this is not Thanksgiving, this is April," said my father.

"Maybe he forgot. And only just remembered," suggested Ma.

"Ape Face? He never forgets anything—a perfect person," I said acidly. "Anyway, why don't you ask him?"

"Yes, Ellen, why don't you? After all, twelve cans of soup don't just vanish into thin air."

"Eleven," I said tartly.

"Eleven," he conceded.

"Stop it, you two," said my mother. She went to the door of the room and yelled for Ape Face.

"Hi Mom, hi Dad, hi Annabel. Did you want me?"

"Ben," said my father. "This morning, did you, by any wild chance, take some cans of soup to school?"

"To school? No!" He sounded shocked.

"Did you," said Dad, drumming his fingers on my desk, "take eleven cans of soup, period?"

"Yes, but I didn't take them to school."

"What did you do with them?"

Ape Face looked distinctly uneasy. "Um," he said.

"That is not very informative," said Dad sternly. "Stop staring at your sneakers and give me a straight answer. *What did you do with them?*"

"I forget."

"You FORGET?!" Dad looked over at me. I shook my head. "I am told you never forget. Now, one more time: What . . . did . . . you . . ."

"Okay, okay," Ape Face said wearily. "I threw them away. In the outside garbage."

"You did *what*?!" said my parents in unison.

"Threw them away. So we wouldn't get sick."

"That's the most deranged thing I ever heard. Soup doesn't make you sick; soup is *good* for you," said Dad.

"Soup is especially good for you if you *are* sick, and now you've thrown mine out. Thanks a lump," I said, glaring at him.

He glared right back. "If you'd of eaten *that* soup you would of gotten dead."

"It just so happens I did eat some of that soup."

"You did?" said Ape Face in a shocked whisper.

"Yes, I did. And as you can see, I'm not a bit dead."

"Not yet. But soon maybe. That soup had a disease. A very bad disease."

"Oh yeah? Like what?"

"It's called botch . . . uh, botch, botchulum!" he finished triumphantly. "It kills you. Mom, if Annabel dies, can I move into her room? It's bigger than mine."

That shut us all up for a minute. Then Ma said, "Ben, darling, come here to me, will you?" She put out her arms and he slipped in. Brushing the hair off his face, she said gently, "Annabel is not going to die. All she has is a bad cold, so don't be afraid. As for what you call botchulum, the word is botulism. Botulism is extremely rare—canning companies are very, very careful about that. I don't think you need worry about it. Whatever put it into your head in the first place?"

"I dunno," said the Ape vaguely.

"It isn't as though the cans were dented or rusty or bulging."

"No . . . but . . ."

"But what?" prompted my father.

"Oh, nothing." Now, he was being not just vague but downright evasive. I can always tell. As they say, it takes one to know one.

"From where I sit, chucking out perfectly good cans of food is not nothing. There is no room in the budget for extravagant whims. Kindly bear that in mind, Sport, okay?"

"Okay," muttered the Ape, and fled from the room.

"The kid's a lunatic," said Dad.

"I think he must be going through some kind of hypochondriacal phase. Or else he's afraid of death.

30

I'll look it up in Spock," said my mother. I pronounced him just plain malicious. Ma accused me of being uncharitable, but when I pointed out it was my dinner he'd chucked out, not theirs, she relented and brought me Jell-O instead.

Friday, April 19

The next day, Ma went back to school and I spent the morning watching game shows and soap operas. By midafternoon, I was so lonely even Ape Face was a welcome sight; so although he's not supposed to watch television (except for the aforementioned *Sesame Street*, *The Electric Company*, and *Mr. Rogers*), I invited him in to see *Women's Prison* on Channel 9. He said *Abbott and Costello* was terrifically funny—why didn't we watch that? After a morning of soppy junk like John Loves Mary But Mary Loves Paul's Illegitimate Son, a little comic relief didn't sound like a bad idea, and at four o'clock we tuned in *Abbott and Costello* on Channel 11.

Okay, folks, are you ready for this? I wasn't:

At four ten, *Abbott and Costello* disappeared from the screen and a newscaster came on.

"We interrupt this program to bring you an important bulletin. Two cases of botulism have been reported in the Metropolitan area. . . ."

32

"See?!" exclaimed Ape Face vengefully.

"Shut up, I want to hear." I had a nasty pain in my stomach, suddenly.

". . . One victim, Charles Polistes of 320 East 73rd Street, Manhattan, is said to be in critical condition in New York Hospital; and the other, Mrs. Margaret Murphy of Dogwood Lane, Rye, is near death in the United Hospital in Port Chester. Both Polistes and Mrs. Murphy had apparently been drinking Aunt Ethel's Quik 'n Easy Sorrel Soup. . . ."

"See, see?! I told you," said Ape Face.

"*I* told *you* to shut up," I said, feeling sicker by the minute.

". . . Botulism is an extremely serious, frequently fatal disease. Symptoms of fatigue, dizziness, and shortness of breath generally occur within eighteen hours of ingesting the botulinus organism, and death usually occurs within eighteen to thirty-six hours." Thank God! It had been way over thirty-six hours since I'd ingested anything but Jell-O. My stomach felt better.

The announcement continued. "An investigation of the Aunt Ethel's Quik 'n Easy plant in Bayonne, New Jersey, is being conducted, and grocery-store managers have been alerted to remove all Aunt Ethel's Quik 'n Easy products from their shelves; but private citizens are urged to check their own shelves. We repeat: Check your shelves for Aunt Ethel's Quik 'n Easy products. They may be extremely dangerous."

Abbott and Costello reappeared.

"Turn it off," I commanded.

"Can't I wait 'til the part with the pecan pie?"

"I said TURN IT OFF!" I thundered, making a lunge at the controls. Ape hastily turned it off.

"Now," I said. "There are a couple of things I want to ask."

"Aren't you going to thank me for trying to save your life?"

"Thanks. Now in the first place . . ."

"You're welcome."

"Don't interrupt. Listen. About this botulism business. How did you know about it yesterday when nobody else did? And why didn't you tell us you knew and warn us, instead of just throwing the cans out and then when Ma and Dad asked you what you did with them, you just stood there like a jerk going buh-duh, buh-duh?"

"I didn't!"

"Yes, you did!"

"First I said buh-duh, buh-duh, but then I told them about the botchulum."

"Botul*ism*. Yes, but how did you *know*?"

"Uh . . ."

"Don't interrupt, I'm not finished. What about that snowstorm. If it took New York, New Jersey, and

Connecticut, not to mention me, by surprise, how come it didn't take you by surprise? What are you anyway—a midget clairvoyant? Where do you get your advance info from—God?"

"Television."

"You're lying." At the time, God seemed infinitely more plausible.

"Ben, do you think I'm a complete moron? That news about Aunt Ethel's Quik 'n Easy came over the air only five minutes ago. It was an emergency bulletin or they wouldn't have broken in on a program for it. It must have just happened because I've been watching for hours and there hasn't been a word about it. Besides, you've been in school all morning, nowhere near a television set, so when could you have heard it on television?"

"Yesterday I heard it!"

"Impossible! I keep telling you that's impossible. It only just happened."

Ape Face was unshakable. "I know it *sounds* weird," he began.

At last I was getting somewhere. "To put it mildly. So what's the real story?"

"That is the real story. Honestly. Yesterday afternoon I was watching *Abbott and Costello* and then the man said about the soup. I didn't want to tell Mom and Dad where I heard it because I'm not supposed to watch TV."

"What set were you watching, pray tell? The Sony was in here all day yesterday and the big set is out being fixed." Now I had him!

"Promise you won't rat?"

I nodded.

"I was watching mine."

"You mean that wrecked-up thing you bought from Boris?"

"It's not wrecked up anymore," he said proudly. "I fixed it. I fiddled around and fiddled around and then last Thursday I finally got it working great."

"That's unbelievable!"

"No, it's not. I'm good at fixing things."

"Ape Face, you're missing the point entirely. Getting the set to work isn't unbelievable—knowing you, anyway—but that it shows tomorrow's programs *is*! Don't you see that? It's like predicting the future. If what you say is true, that set has been predicting the *future*. Doesn't that sound odd to you? Odd, freaky, peculiar, scary, or anything?"

"It sounds like I didn't fix it quite right." Aargh! How could a person be so dense!

Ape Face continued, "I guess it doesn't matter, really. I don't care what day I watch a show on anyway. I mean a *Roadrunner* cartoon that's supposed to be on Wednesday is just as good on Tuesday. As long as the set works, that's all I care about. And it works."

In a pig's eye! Determined to put an end to this

once and for all, I leaped out of bed and climbed into my bathrobe.

"Show me," I demanded.

"Not unless you swear not to tell Mom. Do you?"

"I swear."

"Swear on the Bible."

"Find me a Bible."

"I don't know where one is."

"Neither do I." He folded his arms and waited. Stubborn little you-know-what.

"If I cross my heart and hope to die, would you buy that instead?"

"I guess so," he said reluctantly. "Lemme see you do it." I did it. What difference could it make? The kid was off his rocker anyway.

"Okay, now show me. Wait a sec—where's the *TV Guide*? I know it's around here someplace. I was using it this morning."

"What do you need it for?"

"So I can check out what's supposed to be on tomorrow and see if it's on today, dumb-dumb. Not that I believe you. Come on, help me look."

The first thing we found was the next week's issue, and then we finally located the current one: behind the bed, under a pile of Kleenex. Grabbing the *TV Guide*s in one hand and the Ape's skinny little arm in the other, I yanked him down the hall to his room.

"Close the door," he said. "I don't want Mattie to hear."

"Mattie's at the other end of the apartment. She can't hear anything."

"Even so," he said, and closed the door himself.

"All right. Now show me. Turn on . . . um . . ." I leafed through *TV Guide* 'til I got to Friday afternoon, four thirty. "Turn on Channel 11—*Superman*."

"Neat-o," he said with enthusiasm—which was replaced by instant dejection as soon as the set came to life.

"Aw, shoot, I forgot! That's not *Superman*—that's *I Love Lucy*. Who wants to see that?" With shaking fingers, I turned to the other issue: Saturday afternoon, four thirty, Channel 11. *I Love Lucy*. Who wants to see that is right!

"Ape Face, switch channels. Try 4."

". . . brings you the New York Mets–Cincinnati Reds Game, live from Shea Stadium."

"Great! I love the Mets, don't you?"

"Not today I don't," I said grimly, checking the *TV Guide* again. "They're not supposed to play the Reds 'til tomorrow. *The Courtship of Eddie's Father* is supposed to be on."

"Saw that yesterday," said Ape Face, completely immersed in the ball game. "It was pretty good."

Mind-boggling—absolutely mind-boggling! Even with a clear head it would have been mind-boggling, but with a head full of cold, and the thoughts inching their way like molasses from synapse to synapse, it was utterly beyond me. Pleading dizziness, I rushed to my room and beeped Boris seventeen times in a row.

"For God's sake, what's the matter with you, Annabel? I heard you the first time."

"Then why didn't you answer?"

"When you're signaling I can't transmit—remember?"

"Sorry. I forgot. Listen, Boris, can you come down?"

"Now? I'm in the middle of a current events paper. How about later?" Later wasn't soon enough to suit me.

"No, now," I insisted.

"Okay, but I can't stay long. Besides, you probably shouldn't have visitors; your cold sounds terrible."

"Oh no, it's much better," I assured him.

"Then why is your voice so hoarse?"

"Fear. Sheer animal terror."

"I'll be right there," he said promptly.

"Come down the back stairs and I'll let you in the kitchen door," I croaked.

"Right," he said.

By the time I got to the kitchen, he was already buzzing the back door.

"Are there more than one?" he asked.

"More than one what?"

"Burglars."

I stared at him blankly. "Burglars?"

"You said you were hoarse with fear, and then you told me to come in the back way. I figured burglars. What else could it be?"

"You'd be amazed," I said drily. "Anyway, it's not burglars."

"Then what did you get me down here for? I told you I was in the middle of a current events paper."

"Stick around 'til the six o'clock news and I might be able to be of service to you. Follow me."

Ape Face jumped up guiltily when we came in, and then, seeing it was only us, sat back down.

"Hiya, Boris. Look! I got your set to work."

"Good for you. I didn't think it could be done." To me, he said, "Is that what you dragged me down here for? To show me how he fixed the set? You could have told me that over the walkie-talkie."

"No, I couldn't have. You just wait."

"Hey Boris," said Ape Face. "The Mets are ahead two runs. Don't you want to watch?"

"No," said Boris crossly.

I said, "Yes you do, Boris. You most definitely do. First, read this." I pointed to the place in *TV Guide* where it said under Saturday: NY Mets–Cincinnati Reds, live, Shea Stadium.

"So?"

"So now look at the TV screen: The Mets and the Cincinnati Reds at Shea Stadium. The Mets are still playing the Montreal Expos today. Doesn't that strike you as odd?"

"So what? It's probably a rerun."

"No, it's live," said Ape Face happily.

"Tell him, Ape Face," I said. "Start at the beginning and tell him the whole thing."

Just then the phone rang. Mattie can't write messages down without her reading glasses so I ran to answer it. It was my mother. How was I? Fine. Cold better? Much. Ben? He was fine, too. Anybody call? No. Was everything all right? After a second's hesitation—yes. Did I feel well enough to feed Ben and put him to bed if she went directly from Columbia to the Brasserie to have dinner with Daddy? Sure. Three minutes worth of small talk to relieve her sense of guilt over not coming home to her chickies, then a lengthy farewell with Take-care's and I-love-you's, then Good-bye—good-bye.

When I returned, Ape Face was again looking at the ball game and Boris was looking speculatively off into space.

"Close the door," said Ape Face. A regular paranoia doll: Wind it up and it says "Close the door."

"Mattie's not around and Ma isn't coming home 'til after dinner. You can relax."

"Oh. Good. Could I see *TV Guide*?" I handed it to him.

"Boris, did he tell you?"

"Yes. Yes, he did," said Boris slowly.

"Well, what do you think? Don't you think it's spooky? Doesn't it just blow your mind?"

"Kind of," admitted Boris. "But I don't know what you were so frightened of."

"Spooky things frighten me. Ever since last year when I turned into . . ."

"Let's not go into *that* again," said Boris abruptly. (He never did believe me.) "This is different. This I can see with my own eyes. And this has some quite interesting possibilities. Listen, if it's okay with you, I think I'll take you up on your invitation to stick around for the six o'clock news."

Ape Face looked up from *TV Guide*. "Unh-unh," he said. "*The Mask of Dimitrios* is on at six."

"Why don't you watch it on the other set, tomorrow?" suggested Boris. "You'll see the same picture."

"Tomorrow's no good. Mom'll be home and she won't let me. Why don't you watch the news on the other set?"

"Because that's *not* the same. If I want to watch today's news, I can go back upstairs. I'd like to see tomorrow's news."

"Well, I wouldn't," said Ape Face flatly, "and it's my set. You sold it to me for fifty cents."

"Which you never paid me, right?"

"Ape Face!" I said, shocked to the core. "Is that true?"

"I haven't got it saved up yet, but I'm going to," he said desperately.

"Listen, squirt," said Boris, "when you buy something from a company on time—a stove, let's say—and you renege on the payments, the company repossesses your stove."

"TAKE THE STOVE!" shrieked Ape Face. "I hate eating anyway!"

"Hey, fellas, cool it, will you?" I said. "There's got to be a way to settle this." Ape Face put his hand on my arm. In a tone that would melt the heart of Hitler, he said, "Annabel, will you lend me fifty cents?"

"If you do," warned Boris, "I'll bust my half of the walkie-talkie and you'll never hear from me again."

"That is scummy emotional blackmail!"

"Call it what you will," said Boris defiantly.

"You mean to tell me you'd destroy our friendship for the sake of some dumb television set?"

Boris shrugged. "Annabel, I hope it doesn't come to that. But it's entirely up to you," he said. "Of course, if your brother wants to return what's rightfully mine . . ." His unfinished sentence hung in the air like a guillotine.

"But I don't want to," said Ape Face, his eyes filling up with tears.

"All right, Ape Face, turn off the waterworks and listen to me for a minute. Here's what *I* think: *I* think Boris is being extremely unreasonable and I don't know why that set is so important to him; but if he insists on having it back, you should return it to him."

"Aw, Annabel," moaned Ape Face, stabbed to the quick.

I shot him a pipe-down-I-have-it-all-under-control-look, and continued.

"Wait a minute, I haven't finished. I think you should return it to him—*in the exact condition in which you received it.*"

"You mean wrecked up?"

"Exactly. Where's your screwdriver?"

Boris was horrified. "You *wouldn't!*" he said in a strangled whisper.

"Oh, wouldn't I?" I said casually, as I rummaged around in the Ape's toolbox. "After all, Boris, you want to play legal eagle, look at it this way: Your stove company has the right to repossess the original merchandise, but a miracle stove that cooks tomorrow night's dinner? They have to pay more for that—let's say three hundred dollars which I happen to know you don't have. So . . ." I produced the screwdriver, and with a flourish handed it to Ape Face. "Go to it, kid."

"Okay, F. Lee Bailey," Boris said in a very ungracious tone. "You win. But with your kind permission, I'd like to ask your client a couple of questions."

"Certainly," I said. I instructed my client to turn off

the ball game, which had just finished anyway, and pay attention.

"Now tell me," said Boris, "what do you watch on television?"

"*Huckleberry Hound, The Beverly Hillbillies, The Match Game, Nanny and the Professor*, movies—"

"In other words, taped stuff or reruns, right?"

"Guess so," said Ape Face.

"No live stuff?" Boris was moving in for the kill. I could sense it, although I didn't know what he had in mind. Neither did Ape Face, who wanted to know what was "live stuff."

"News. Up-to-the-minute news—that's live stuff. You like that?"

"No," said Ape Face. "It's boring. Dead stuff is better—like *The Mask of Dimitrios*," he added balefully. "What time is it now? I don't want to miss it."

"Only ten of six. Don't worry." Ape Face looked dubious. Boris squatted down on his haunches so he was face-to-face with him.

"Listen, pal, I'm about to make you a terrific deal. I'll swap you this old pile of junk for my brand-new Motorola. You can watch all the dead stuff you want from morning to night in glorious living color instead of grainy black and white. How about it?"

Ape Face thought for a second. "Will I still owe you the fifty cents?"

"Naah," said Boris magnanimously. "What's a little

debt like that between friends? Do we have a deal?"

Ape Face thought for another second. Then he frowned and heaved a deep sigh. Uh-oh, I thought. Here it comes.

"I'm sorry," he said. Boris collapsed on the floor in dismay.

"What do you mean, sorry?"

"I think he means no," I said. Boris glared at me.

"Who asked you? This is between me and your client. When he wants advice from counsel he'll ask for it. Now listen, pal, what do you mean, sorry? How could you pass up a terrific deal like that; are you stupid or something? Give me one good reason."

"The reason is because when my mother is home and I want to watch television, all I have to do is just close the door and play 'Yellow Submarine' loud on the record player so she won't hear anything. She never comes in without knocking because I have this 'Don't come in without knocking first' sign on the door. When she knocks, I turn the set off fast."

"So why can't you play 'Yellow Submarine' and watch my color Motorola just as well?"

"I could. But what would happen when I was at school and she came in to put my socks away or something and saw a brand-new set? The old set she doesn't think works, so I'd rather keep it."

"If counsel could be permitted to make a suggestion," I began.

46

"My pleasure," said Boris sarcastically. "But it better be good. And it better be acceptable to both parties."

"Well," I said. "To begin with, I'm sure my client is most grateful for your kind offer of a Motorola color TV and regrets not being able to accept it; don't you, Ape?" Ape Face obediently manufactured a toothy smile of appreciation.

"What would he accept? My head on a platter, I suppose."

"Yich!" said Ape Face, turning away in disgust.

"My client is too young to understand literary or biblical references," I announced. "May I continue?"

Boris nodded curtly.

"Counsel would like to suggest that although a twenty-one inch Motorola would not be acceptable, my client might feel differently about one of those teensy-weensy battery-powered Sonys—small enough to be concealed in a toy chest underneath the Lego where the mother of the client never looks."

"Oh man, *I'd* like one of those, too!" said Ape Face enthusiastically.

"Evidently, your client is also too young to understand legal jargon."

"Yes, I don't," agreed Ape Face cheerfully.

"Okay, in plain English, Boris wants to know if you'd be satisfied with a teensy-weensy Sony? The latest model, of course." Nothing ventured, nothing gained.

"Boris also wants to know," said Boris, quivering with rage, "where Boris is going to lay his mitts on such an expensive item when he just blew his last remaining bucks on a birthday present for counsel!"

"I know where," said Ape Face. "The store where you got the Motorola. You take the set in there—tomorrow, maybe—and say to the store man, 'I'm about to make you a terrific deal. I'll swap you one of those dinky little Sonys for this brand-new Motorola I just bought from you. How about it?' He'll be glad to do it because a big set is better than a small set. Then, when you bring me the Sony, I'll be glad to swap you back your old pile of junk. Do we have a deal?"

Frankly, I was beginning to feel like a vestigial organ. I mean, what does a con artist need with a lawyer?

"So how about it, Boris. Do we have a deal or don't we?" Ape Face said again.

"I guess so," said Boris, "but on a contingency basis."

Even I didn't know what that meant. "Plain English, please. My client . . ."

"Your client is a pain in the neck! Your client has a deal contingent on my being able to watch the six o'clock news, *right here*, on *this set*, in precisely one minute."

"Annabel, can I take back my deal?"

"Let me think about that," I said.

48

Boris jumped up and switched on the set. "There is no time to think about that. I've had it to the eyeballs with both of you. If Ape Face is so damn determined to see that stupid-jerk movie, he is cordially invited to come to my house tomorrow at six o'clock and watch it there on my mother's set. He can even stay for dinner if he wants to."

"Me, too?" I wanted to know.

"Of course, you, too. You think I want to baby-sit that creep Shylock by myself?"

"Boris, I'm flabbergasted! You mean I'm finally going to get to see your house?"

"For what it's worth, yes."

"And meet your mother?" A staggering development! I could hardly believe my ears.

"She won't be there. She has a date or something." Nuts!

"Who's going to make dinner for us?" Ape Face asked. "Are you, Boris? Because if it's you, maybe I'll just stay for the movie." (Boris's cooking, which Ape Face and I had occasion to sample last year, is highly imaginative but a trifle exotic for a seven-year-old palate.)

"It just so happens the maid is coming tomorrow. She'll cook dinner. Will that suit Your Highness?"

"Sure," said Ape Face cheerfully. "I think I'll go ride my bike in the hall. You want to shake on the deal, first?"

"If I shook your hand now, I'd probably crunch it to bits," growled Boris, without lifting his eyes from the television screen. "Everybody shut up. Here comes the six o'clock news."

"Out, out!" I whispered to Ape Face. "I'll take care of your deal. As counsel, I'm empowered."

So for a solid hour, we watched the news to find out what goodies were going to go on in the world tomorrow. Boris, scribbling furiously in a lined composition book he found in the bookshelf, took voluminous notes on the U.S.–Russian grain deal, a Turkish military coup, the hijacking of a Japanese 747, a detailed report on the botulism bit (since the bulletin I'd seen, the man had died but the woman was still hanging in there), a rave review for a movie that opened at the Paris theater, the Mets–Cincinnati Reds game ("a triumph for Cincinnati and a sad Saturday for the home team"), the weather ("after yesterday's downpour, New Yorkers basked in sixty-two-degree sunshine. An estimated ten thousand people gathered in Sheep Meadow to fly kites, and bike paths were jammed"), and a couple of Metropolitan horror stories. ("The decapitated body of an unidentified male was discovered lodged behind the pins in a Bronx bowling alley, and a three-alarm flash fire gutted the Lullabye Lingerie factory at 43 Bleecker Street at four o'clock this afternoon. No lives were lost, although the watchman who was rescued from the fourth floor of the building told Chief Inspector Mullin that had the fire occurred on a weekday rather than today, thirty-seven employees might have perished in the inferno.") Finally, when the paper towel commercial began, I turned off the set.

"Well, what do you think?" I asked.

"Sh, I'm thinking," said Boris. For several minutes, he sat totally immersed in his notes, one hand absent-mindedly tugging at a hunk of his chestnut hair and the other twiddling a pencil between his upper and lower teeth. *Clickety-clickety-clickety.* Loathsome sound!

"Must you?" I complained.

"Must I what? Oh . . . sorry," he said, wiping the pencil off on his pants. "I forget I'm doing it."

"I know. You always do it when you're thinking. So what *are* you thinking?"

"I am thinking that this thing," he nodded toward the set, "is so incredible, I don't know *what* to think. It's supernatural. It can't happen, *how* can it happen?"

"Maybe it's like ESP. At Barron University they have lots of data on people who are clairvoyant."

"People maybe, but a *television* set?"

"No, I suppose not. Anyway, what's the good of wondering how it happened, Boris? The fact is, it did. Actually, it's going to come in quite handy. Take weather predictions, for instance. Half the time they stink. From now on, you'll be able to beep me on the beeper and say things like, 'There was a hailstorm tomorrow—wear boots.' Like that freak blizzard the Ape kept trying to tell me . . . What's the matter? Why do you have that terrible, supercilious sneer on your face?"

"Because I am stupefied by your total lack of imagination. Annabel, don't you realize that all this stuff I've written down—we are the only two people alive who know about it? And that that pile of junk we've been looking at has got to be the most extraordinary collection of atoms and molecules ever assembled by man or God?! Don't you understand the potential of a thing like this? To have a twenty-four-hour jump on the rest of the whole world and all you can think of to use it for is the WEATHER?!" Breathless, he brandished his notes under my nose and managed to cough out two final words of insult: "Earthbound idiot!"

"Listen, wise guy—" Sometimes Boris can be insufferable, "—if *you* were the one who could've not gotten a foul case of flu if only you hadn't not known about a big snowstorm, you'd think about the weather, too."

"My compliments on your exquisite syntax. Would you care to repeat that sentence?"

"No, I wouldn't," I retorted. "Furthermore, since I had to sit in stony silence for five minutes while you munched on an Eberhard Faber No. 2, I was under the impression that you were the self-appointed thinker around here. You want me to think? I'll think—gimme those notes." I snatched them out of his hand and began reading. The third item on the list gave me a sudden chill.

"Boris!" I gasped. "That Japan Airlines plane! We've got to *do* something about that. Warn them or something."

"How?"

"Call them up and warn them."

"And say what? 'Hello, I want to report a hijacking'?"

"Sure."

"So then they say, 'Can you give us any further details?' and you say, 'A 747 on the eight A.M. flight out of Tokyo en route to Paris was hijacked somewhere over Tibet and forced to land in Beirut.' Right?" I checked Boris's notes.

"Right."

"So then, after a lengthy pause, Japan Airlines says, kind of suspicious, 'We have not received any reports of this incident. When did it occur?' And *you* say?"

"Tomorrow. It occurred tomorrow," I answered sheepishly.

"Exactly. And then they will hang up on you because they think you are a nut."

"But wait a minute, Boris. What if I say the 747 is *going* to be hijacked tomorrow? Then they wouldn't think I was a nut."

"No, then they would think you were part of the hijacking gang, setting them up for blackmail. And if they could trace the call, which knowing how long you stay on the phone they could probably do, they'd come straight here and arrest you."

"We could tell them about the set, and show it to them. Then they'd believe us."

"They might, but then we wouldn't have it anymore. Word would get out, and the government would find some way to requisition it; then scientists would pull it apart and destroy it; either that or it might fall into the hands of unscrupulous people who wanted to make money out of it."

"How could they do that?"

"I don't know. I haven't figured it out myself yet. All I know is, I don't think a call to Japan Airlines is going to prevent that hijacking anyway, even if they do believe you."

"All those poor scared passengers and the little babies. Shouldn't we at least try? Couldn't I just run to the drugstore and talk fast in a phone booth?"

Boris smiled me a gentle, warm smile, and said, "You're good people, Annabel. Really good people. Look—sit down here next to me for a minute, and I'll try to put it into words. But it's sort of confusing, so give me a minute to think."

I sat down on the bed. Boris, his mind a million miles away, took my hand and began tracing his way up and down my fingers.

"All right," he said, about a minute later. "Listen carefully and see if you agree. This Thing, this miracle Box, oracle, mechanized prognosticator—whatever it is, is going to lead us into some very tricky areas. I don't know whether it has to do with metaphysics or philosophy or what, but when you're dealing with the future . . ." He broke off, snarled up in his thoughts, I guess.

"Go on."

"Well, I don't think the future can be changed. In other words, if our miracle Box shows us tomorrow's news, that news is definitely going to take place or we wouldn't be seeing it today. Because the Box does not *predict* events, it *shows* events that have actually taken place but will not come to pass until twenty-four hours later. Are you with me so far?" I nodded.

"Next point: We can't prevent events that have already happened in the future, but we can benefit from advance knowledge that they are going to."

"Like the botulism business. Or the blizzard."

"Yes. Or other things."

"Like what?"

"Well, staying home when you know there's going to be a blizzard is avoiding a bad thing. Like tomorrow I was going to ask you if you wanted to go bike riding, but the bike paths are going to be jammed so I won't."

"Thanks anyway."

"You're welcome. But what about taking advantage

of a good thing? If you already knew a mammoth surprise sale of records happened at Goody's tomorrow, wouldn't you get there first thing in the morning? And if I know, on Sunday, that the Mets are going to win on Monday, I can make a bet with my friend Chuckie Waterman Monday morning in school (and win, naturally). That's taking advantage of a good thing."

"That's taking advantage of a good friend. Doesn't sound too ethical to me."

"So okay, I'll bet Harvey Kuchel instead. He's a guy I hate."

"Is taking advantage of an enemy any better? More fun, but is it any better, ethically speaking?"

"When I want a spiritual advisor, I'll ask for one," said Boris impatiently. "Besides, I was only giving you a what-if. I might not do that at all. I'm only trying to explain to you, in theory, what a gold mine we've got here"—he patted the Box lovingly—"and how we'd be fools not to put it to work for us. Tomorrow," he said, smiling in happy anticipation, "I'm going to turn in the Motorola for the Sony, and tomorrow night when you and the Ape come up to watch the movie, you can bring this little baby with you. Then I'll study the whole situation more closely and come up with some plans."

"I don't know, Boris," I said uneasily. "Maybe I won't like your plans."

"Then maybe I won't tell you about them. Don't forget, it's my set."

"Not yet it isn't. We haven't made the deal yet, remember? And we're not going to, either, unless you agree to a few conditions of mine. Fine type you are —when I'm trying to save the lives of a hundred and forty hijack victims, you say 'Oh, no, because the set might fall into the hands of unscrupulous people who want to make money out of it.' What do you call you— *scru*pulous?!"

"Yes!" he said fiercely. "Yes, I am. But I also need money. I don't want to go into it now, but believe me, Annabel, I do. So I've just got to have the Box. Are you going to make the deal or not?"

"I guess so," I muttered. "But I sure hope I'm not making a mistake."

On his way out the door, Boris hastily and heartily assured me I wasn't—and ironically enough, he turned out to be right. A mistake, after all, is a little thing. You give a cab driver a five-dollar bill instead of a one; or you dial the wrong area code and get Anchorage, Alaska. Those are what I call mistakes. Chicken-feed folly. Consumating that deal between Boris and my brother was not, therefore, what you could call a mistake—it was what you could call a catastrophic, cataclysmic boo-boo.

Saturday, April 20

The next morning, the botulism thing was all over the front page of the *Times*. My father read the entire piece out loud to my mother at the breakfast table, and then said, "Ben, it seems we owe you an apology and a vote of thanks." The Ape grinned through a disgusting mouthful of scrambled eggs, and I lost my appetite altogether—partly from looking at him, but mostly from dread of what was coming next. I didn't have long to wait. My mother is no dummy.

"Benjie, wasn't it Thursday you threw out those cans?" He nodded and swallowed.

"Isn't that odd, Bill? You'd almost think he knew."

"Couldn't have, it only happened yesterday," said my father. "Anyway, don't ask me, ask him." Ape Face's mouth was empty now, and I was scared to death of what might come out of it in the way of words, so I asked him if he wanted his bacon—if not, could I have it? Being a real dog-in-the-manger type, he immediately stuffed all three strips in at once.

"Tell us your secret, Benjie," said my mother, teasingly. "How did you find out? Or was it just a lucky coincidence?"

"Coincidence," I said, kicking him under the table.

"Is your name Benjie?" said my father. "Let him speak for himself."

"With his *mouth* full?! You never let me do that." At this point, Ape Face mumbled something about having to go to the bathroom, and left the room. By the time he came back, I'd managed to steer the subject of conversation around to what we were all going to do on this beautiful sunny day. Ma and Dad and Ape Face decided to go biking in the park (good luck to them!) and I decided to go window-shopping in the Village with my friend Virginia. Ma wanted to know if I'd pick up some pork chops for dinner, which reminded me to tell her that Ape Face and I had been invited to Boris's for dinner if that was all right with her. It was.

At around twelve, they all three plowed out the door, swaddled in sweaters and mufflers up to their ears, poor things, and I was poking through my closet, looking for something suitable for sixty-two degrees, when Boris beeped me.

"Just thought you'd be interested in knowing that last night, after I left you, I got really worried about that plane. In fact, I was up half the night thinking about it. So at seven this morning, *I* went to the drug-store and made a quick call to Japan Airlines."

"How terrific of you. But why didn't you call from home?"

"I told you, my mother doesn't want me to use the phone."

"Even one little call? Boy, she must be an ogre."

"No comment. Also, I didn't want to take a chance on them tracing the call. Listen, do you want to hear what happened or don't you?"

"Yes indeedy. What happened?"

"I told them their eight A.M. 747 out of Tokyo en-route to Paris was going to be hijacked."

"Did they think you were a nut? Or a gangster?"

"No," said Boris, sounding rather bemused. "They thought I was a nuisance."

"A nuisance?! Why? I don't understand. What did they say?"

"I thought you'd never ask. They said, 'We already have that information, sir.'"

"That is utterly impossible. How could they have known at seven when the plane didn't take off 'til eight?"

"Exactly what I asked them. The explanation, my dear Good Samaritan, is so simple, it's funny." He began to chortle—just to prove how funny it was, I suppose. I was not amused.

"If it's so simple, let's have it."

60

"The time change!" he gurgled. "The eight A.M. 747 from Tokyo to Paris took off at *six* P.M. *last night*, New York time. Japan Airlines had known about the hijacking for hours. They were very polite and patient but they said I was the sixteenth call they'd received today from concerned citizens, and under the circumstances I could surely understand how busy they were; they thanked me for my concern and hung up. . . . Are you still there?"

"Yes. I'm trying to figure it out. Just as I think I've got it straight, it eludes me again."

"I know what you mean," he said. "The point is, we didn't watch the news until six o'clock last night, but if we'd watched earlier, on our set, we probably would have gotten the news in the morning. Or maybe even late the night before. Like all those other people who called up *this* morning."

"Aw, nuts! It's a real bummer, isn't it?"

"It's what you get when you mess around with the future, Annabel. I told you last night, I don't think it can be done. Frankly, that's why I made the call—to *see* if it could be done; but fate intervened."

"You want to call it fate, go ahead. I call it stupidity. One of us should have thought of the time change."

"*Even if we had, we still didn't turn the set on early enough to do anything about it.* That was fate, wasn't it? My God, you're the most stubborn person I ever met! I was up all night thinking about your problem;

61

then I got up at six thirty and ran to the corner to do something about your problem; and now I have to trundle a two-ton Motorola downtown for a trade-in to solve your brother's problem—which will be a big hassle—on no sleep. I don't want to talk anymore. I'll see you at six. Roger, over, and out."

"Roger, over, and out. And drop dead!"

If I'd known what kind of mood I was going to be in, I would never have made a date with Virginia. Virginia's a person who can drive you right up the wall unless you're in a tolerant frame of mind. She never used to be like that. As recently as two years ago she was a neat kid, but now she has Theatrical Aspirations and a lot of annoying habits. Like correcting your grammar. As it happens, I have an extremely good grasp of my native tongue and grades to prove it, but I don't bother to talk the way I write. Who does? Virginia does, that's who. If you say "Everybody's finished their assignment," she says, "His and her assignment." (Our school is coed.) If you say, "I know a boy you'd get along great with," she says "A boy with whom you'd get along beautifully." If you knock on the bathroom door and say, "It's only me," she says, "It's only I" (to which you are tempted to retort, "Never mind, I didn't really want to come in, anyway"). The colloquial use of the word "like" engenders in her such scorn that most of us have dropped the word from our vocabularies altogether.

Virginia used to be a fabulous basketball player, but now she gets out of gym at the drop of a hat. The excuses are varied and wondrous: sinus headaches, migraine headaches (pronounced meegraine), raging fevers (usually pronounced nonexistent by the school nurse), low blood sugar, fatigue, and when all else fails, her monthly Excuse which, if legitimate, she employs with such alarming frequency it's a miracle she hasn't died by now.

She also tends to dress nicely for school, which is her way of putting the rest of us down, I guess, because I can't think of a single other reason why she'd bother. None of the other kids do. ("Does," according to Virginia.)

Nevertheless, I still like her. I've known her ever since we were in nursery school together. That's going back a long time. We've got memories. For instance, in the fourth grade, she wanted to be class president and she made me her secret campaign manager. I did such a good job of being nice to people, they elected me instead. When we were ten, I slept over at her house one night and we spent a delightful couple of hours burning Kleenex in the toilet. Unfortunately, we also burned the bottom of the toilet seat in the process. This didn't go over too well with Virginia's mother, who deducted a usurious percentage from both our allowances for six weeks following. Oh yes, we've got memories, all right—and scars. In a towering rage over

I-no-longer-remember-what, I once threw my Indian-beaded belt at her, and accidentally cut her forehead open with the buckle. (Two stitches for her, remorse for me.)

After all these years, we've got a certain rapport going for us; we know each other so well we can catch each other's vibes from across a room. Right now, she's going through a stage I don't particularly admire, but if I could put up with a whole year of her thinking she was a five-gaited thoroughbred mare, I guess I can put up with this. At least now she talks. It's pretty fancy dialogue, but a vast improvement over whinnies and neighs. By next year, she'll probably be out of this stage and into something else. And anyway, she's an old friend.

When I got off the number thirty bus in front of Tiffany's, where Virginia and I had agreed to meet, she was already there, waiting for me. Correction: She was not waiting for me. She was admiring a gem in the window—the gem being herself, of course. It beats me why she bothers to window-shop at all. She could save a ton of shoe leather if she just stayed home all day in front of a full-length mirror.

"Hey, how's things?" I said.

"Hallo, luv," said Virginia. Who does she think she is today, I speculated—some English movie star?

She leaned over to give me a cool kiss on the cheek. I backed off.

"What's new?" I inquired.

"Not a bloody thing," she sighed. "Except, look at this, will you?" She sucked in her breath and patted her tiny tummy. "Bloat. Sheer bloat. It's *too* depressing!"

"You want to see bloat, get a load of this," I said, pulling up my turtleneck to display my own gorgeous gut. "If I get any fatter, I'm going to have an outsie belly button."

"Navel," gently chided Virginia. "If it bothers you so much, why don't you try some abdominal exercises?"

"It doesn't bother me *that* much," I said, yanking down my sweater before I was arrested for indecent exposure.

"It's up to you, darling girl," said Virginia blandly, "but if I were you, I'd keep an eye. What size are you?"

"Ten," I said defiantly.

"Are you *really*? In what—a caftan?"

That made me so mad I refused to talk to her all the way downtown on the Fifth Avenue bus. For forty-eight solid blocks, I sang "Parsley, Sage, Rosemary and Thyme" over and over again while Virginia pretended it wasn't driving her crazy.

By the time we had scrutinized both sides of Christopher Street, it was driving *me* crazy, so I switched to "I Don't Know How to Love Him" from *Jesus*

65

Christ Superstar, and Virginia counterattacked with "Row, Row, Row Your Boat." People were now beginning to look at us as though we were demented, which, considering what passes for normal in that neighborhood, should give you some idea of what we must have looked and sounded like.

Finally, in a hamburger joint on Greenwich Avenue, a détente was reached in the following manner.

Virginia said, "I'm positively famished, aren't you?"

I said, "Yeah."

"What are you going to eat?"

"A bacon cheeseburger with onion rings and French fries on the side. And a chocolate shake," I said, fixing her with a steely stare. "And you?"

"A lemon Tab," said Virginia with a martyred smile. Diet one-upmanship!

"I thought you were so famished."

"I am, but I'm taking you to lunch and I don't want to run out of money."

"In that case, *I'll* have the lemon Tab," I said politely.

"Oh no, please," she protested. "It's my treat. I want you to have whatever you want."

"I want a lemon Tab."

"Right you are. I think I'll have the bacon cheeseburger with onion rings and French fries on the side. Plus a vanilla shake. Plus a jelly doughnut," said Virginia, and the fight was over. Not because she paid for my lunch but because she allowed me the satisfaction of watching her gorge herself while I abstained. For a weight-watcher, this is the most generous gesture you can make.

For the next two hours, we thoroughly investigated practically every shop in the Village: handmade sandals, health food, reconditioned blue jeans, secondhand books, Navajo jewelry, Appalachian Mountain quilts—the works. Virginia, exercising exemplary self-control over her tendency to be a pretentious pain, managed to get on my nerves only once: After trying on a Mexican wedding dress—which she had no intention of buying, naturally—she said to the saleswoman, "I'm awfully afraid it's no go. My brahzeeaire would show through this transparent material."

Number one: The Mexican wedding dress was made of canvas tough enough to bury a man at sea in; you couldn't see through it with a fluoroscope.

Number two: Most people call it bra, some people call it a brazeer, but nobody (except my grandmother) calls it a brahzeeaire.

Number three: Virginia has a tiny top to match her tiny tummy. She never wears a bra at all.

Anyway, by a quarter to four, we'd covered everything but the newsstands, and in passing one of those, a headline about the hijacking caught my eye. I was suddenly reminded of something.

"Hey, Virginia, where's Bleecker Street, do you know?"

"Right over there, I believe. What's on Bleecker Street?"

"Let's go see."

"Right you are," said Virginia amiably.

I steered her past a row of quaint brownstones and a few nothing shops, coming to a halt in front of Number Forty-Three: Lullabye Lingerie, Inc. I sniffed the air carefully; no smell of smoke. Starting at the roof, I scanned the building from top to bottom, and then checked the alleys on both sides; no sign of smoke either.

"What are you *doing*?" asked Virginia.

"Admiring the architecture."

"What architecture? It's a perfectly ordinary, ugly, four-story building. It's boring. Come on, let's get a move on, shall we?"

"Virginia, I spent an hour and a half watching you climb in and out of stuff you weren't even planning to buy. The least you can do is give me—" I looked at my watch; it was five to four "—five minutes. What's boring to you isn't necessarily boring to me."

"You can say that again," she said grumpily.

"If you're still bored five minutes from now, we'll go," I promised.

Resigned, Virginia crossed the street and plunked herself down on someone's front stoop.

I simply couldn't fathom it. This time, there was no time change to contend with. Four P.M. uptown is four

P.M. downtown. How could there be an inferno at four if there wasn't even a wisp of smoke now? Had I gotten mixed up on the address and this was the wrong building? Then I remembered about the watchman. If it was the right building, there was a watchman who'd been rescued from the fourth floor. Maybe he'd been asleep up there and that's how the fire got started. If so, maybe I could prevent the fire by waking him up in time. Boris's metaphysical theories notwithstanding, I felt it was my humanitarian duty to try.

I rang the bell, loud, five times.

Ah-ha! A window opened on the top floor and a hard-hat head came out.

"Whaddya want."

"I want to buy a nightie."

"So whaddya bothering a guy now for? It's Satiddy. We're closed. Buyaself a nightie somewheres else. Crazy kid!" With that, he hurled an empty beer can and an obscene epithet at me. Stepping into the street for a better aim, I accurately and loudly returned them both.

It was perfect timing. The beer can had no sooner disappeared in the window than the six o'clock news came true. A good thing I was already in the street; if I hadn't been, I would have been blasted into it by a ferocious explosion.

"Holy crumb!" screamed Virginia. "What did you do?!"

"Are you still bored?" I shouted, over the roar of the flames and the already clanging fire engines. "Stick with me, kid, it's a laugh a minute! Beats Mexican wedding dresses any day!"

I joined her on the opposite side of the street—to get a better view and to get out of the way of the engines. Within minutes, all of the East Village had joined us, including a CBS camera crew and several reporters scribbling away. The fire chief was barking instructions over a loudspeaker, and I heard him say there was probably no one in the building but they'd better check anyway.

"You bet your boots they better," I remarked to the man next to me. "There's a watchman up there on the fourth floor."

"Is that so," said the man. Without bothering to look at me, he said "How do you know?"

"She was havin' a altercation widda guy whenda buildin' blew. Kid's gotta mout' onna like a sewa!" said a pimply-faced voice to my left. I ignored it, and so did the man. We were both watching the fireman who'd been assigned to the rescue operation. He climbed in the fourth-story window and immediately climbed out again, followed by my dear friend and epithet hurler, who was greeted by an enthusiastic cheer from the crowd. I, myself, felt like booing. Not that I'd want to see him fry or anything, but he certainly wasn't a cause for celebration.

Some lady behind me was speculating about

70

whether there was anybody else in there. I told her there wasn't, but it was a good thing it was Saturday; if it had been a weekday, thirty-seven people might have been in a lot of hot water, ha ha.

Now, the man next to me turned around and gave me a searching look.

"Just a joke," I said lamely. "I have a sick sense of humor. Black comedy, you might call it."

"You might. And then again, you might not. Tell me—you said thirty-seven people work there. How do you know that?" I was beginning to get a queasy feeling that maybe this man was more than just an interested bystander. I decided to play it dumb and casual.

"I don't *actually* know. It was a calculated guess— based on the size of the building and so forth. I mean, it wouldn't have to be thirty-seven—could be fifty, fifty-two . . . what do *you* think?" I asked.

"I think you know more than you're telling, young lady," said the man as he flashed his wallet under my nose. Detective Horgan. How do you like that? Two hundred people standing on the street, a hundred and ninety-nine of them innocent bystanders, and I strike up a conversation with a plainclothes cop!

"Yaah, yaah, baby doll, tell the nice policeman what you trun inna winda!" said the pimply-faced voice. (A hundred and ninety-*eight* interested bystanders, one cop, and one sadist.)

"Wait a *min*ute!" I began, but Pimples was grooving

71

on the whole scene now. There was no stopping him.

"Don't tell me you didn't trun nuttin' inna winda. I sore it. Prolly a bomb!"

"Both of you, come with me, please," said Detective Horgan. Protesting feebly, I was led, followed by the witness for the prosecution, to a cluster of uniformed fire officials and policemen who were conferring in the middle of the street.

"Chief," said Detective Horgan, "I think we got a live one here. And a witness, too."

"She trun a bomb inna winda," said Dan Diction. All the guys were staring at me.

"I did *not* trun a . . ." I took a deep breath and began again, enunciating carefully and clearly, and pausing between each and every word.

"I did not throw a bomb in the window. I threw a beer can. I was, in point of fact, returning the beer can to its rightful owner who had thrown it at *me*. Ask him yourself."

"We will. Mike, go get the guy and bring him over here."

"Now," said Detective Horgan, taking out a pencil and pad. "What's your name?"

"I'm not telling you. I didn't do anything wrong so I'm not telling you. I'm pleading the—um—Fifth. And the—uh Second, the Third, and the Fourth." Better to be safe than sorry, I always say.

"What about the First?" asked Detective Horgan.

"I'll take it," I said promptly. They all burst out laughing.

"Come on, kid. We got rights, too, you know, and one of them is you gotta tell us your name."

"Marvin the Torch," I snapped. This broke them up in a million little pieces which was all right with me. I loathe being laughed at, but being treated like a stand-up comic was better than being treated like a pyromaniac.

Mike showed up with the watchman. For someone who'd just emerged unscathed from a three-alarm fire, he was looking pretty good. Filthy but good. (He was probably filthy before the fire.)

"Chief, this is Mr. —?"

"Nickolik. Stanislaus Nickolik," said the watchman, ceremoniously shaking hands with everybody, including Detective Horgan, who immediately reached for a handkerchief and wiped himself off.

"Mr. Nickolik, meet Marvin the Torch," said the Chief with a grin.

"I already met Marva. You all right, kid? That was some blast, wasn't that some blast, huh, kid?" He threw a playful punch at me, which unfortunately landed with a grungy stain on my denim jacket.

"We were wondering if you could tell us about that," said Detective Horgan. "This gentleman here"—he indicated Pimples—"claims . . ."

"She trun a bomb!"

"A bomb?" Nickolik, who was beginning to worm his way into my heart, expressed great surprise. "—, —! She din't trow no bomb. She trew a beer can. To tell you the trute," he admitted, "she was trowin' it back after I trew it at her. Just a friendly little squabble, no harm done, right Marva?" He put his arm around me and gave me an affectionate squeeze. We were practically engaged.

"I wouldn't exactly call that no harm done," said Detective Horgan, nodding his head at the smoking ruins.

Nickolik was outraged. "She din't have nuttin' to do widdat! Inna first place, if she'd of trown a bomb into the fourt' floor, and I was on the fourt' floor which I was, you know where I'd be now? All over the fourt' floor—like raspberry jam. You could scoop me up with a spoon. And in the second place, I'll lay you five to one it was the furnace blew up."

"Oh?" said Horgan.

"Yeah. I been telling the boss and telling the boss— you don't get that furnace fixed, one of these days there's gonna be some conflagration. Confraglation. Anyway—some fire."

"Ah," they all murmured knowingly. Horgan chucked me under the chin. He should just try that again; I'll bite his finger off!

"Okay if I go now? I'm late for home," I said.

"Sure, sweetheart, run along," said Horgan. "Sorry

if I caused you any inconvenience. Just trying to do my job."

"Abso*lut*ely," I said, jaunty-jolly with relief. "Chief, guys, nice meeting you." I gave an enthusiastic salute, turned on my heel, and beat a hasty retreat down the block toward Broadway.

Halfway there, I realized someone was following me. Detective Horgan with another nosy question? A mugger? I ran faster. The person following me ran faster, too. I took a quick look over my shoulder: It was a carrot-haired man in a raincoat—clearly not Detective Horgan, but quite possibly a mugger. These days, anybody could be a mugger.

"Hey, Marvin! Marvin the Torch!" shouted the carrot-haired man.

"Leave me alone," I shouted breathlessly.

Long-distance running is not my forte. In a second, he'd caught up with me.

"Wait up!" he said, huffing and chuffing at my side. "I'm not going to hurt you—I only want to ask a couple of questions."

"I don't want to wait up. I'm late, I've got to get home, and I've answered enough questions for one day. Besides, I don't know you."

By now I was so exhausted I was reduced to a slow trot.

"Who are you anyway?"

"I'm a reporter. *Daily News*," he panted. "Do you want to see my card?"

I came to a full stop. "Not especially." Undaunted, he whipped out his notebook.

"Just a couple of quick questions? Detective Horgan said you were a witness to the explosion. Is that right?"

"That's right."

"Could you describe it for me?"

"A big bang," I said impatiently.

"Before the explosion occurred, did you notice anything unusual, anything that might lead you to believe the explosion was not accidental?"

"Why would anyone want to blow up a nightgown factory?"

"A nightgown factory could be a front for something else. Remember that house that blew up on Eleventh Street a few years ago? The Weathermen did it. Did you notice any suspicious-looking people on the block before the explosion?"

"No. The street was completely deserted."

"Then what were you doing there?"

"Trying to buy a nightie," I snapped. "Listen, you said quick questions. I'm in a hurry."

"Just one more—would you mind telling me your real name?"

"Ann Smith." I don't think it fooled him for a minute, but he wrote it down anyway. I also gave him a fake address and a fake age—eighteen.

"Well, Ann," he said pleasantly, "thank you for your time. I appreciate it." I thought this was quite forbearing of him, considering how unhelpful I'd been.

"You're welcome. Sorry I couldn't be of more use." He grinned at me. I noticed he had beautiful teeth and a cute nose and nice green eyes.

"I'm sure you did the best you could. But listen, if anything else does occur to you, I wish you'd call me. Here's my card—just in case."

I looked at it: Bartholomew Bacon, *Daily News*, 555–0176, ext. 421."

"Okay, Bartholomew. 'Bye now."

" 'Bye, *Ann*," he said with a knowing wink. I winked back and dashed down the subway steps.

Saturday, April 20, later

When I got home, I found a note from Ape Face Scotch-taped to the outside of the front door:

Dere Annabel, we had a awful time bikeing. it was to hot and my trainıng weels fell of. Dad got all most run over by a millyun poepul trying to fix them and then he got mad so we came home soon. They are takeing a nap. *sh*. Bariss called. He said he got delaid downtown but we should go upstairs anyway the maid would let us in. He said I could watch my movie in the den. if your not here befour 6, Im going alone.

LOVE
Ape Face.

PS you're frend called. she says to tell you your some frend. she is mad to.

What friend? Oh my God, Virginia! I completely forgot poor Virginia. Come to think of it, what do I mean "poor Virginia"? Where was she when I needed her? She could have come forth as a credible character witness, but instead she melts away—into an air-conditioned cab, no doubt—and abandons me to the hostile horde. Nuts to you, Virginia; some friend yourself!

In a rage, I crunched up the Ape's note, plunged into the dimly lit apartment—and immediately collided with a large lumpy something which was blocking my way. Whatever it was fell to the floor with a crash, and then I heard a stifled scream of anguish from my brother.

"I got it all the way from my room to here and now you knocked it off," he whispered. I turned on the entrance-hall light and surveyed the scene. What I saw was: item one, Ape Face, tear-streaked and sweat-drenched; item two, the large lumpy something which turned out to be the Box; and item three, a skateboard attached to a rope.

"What's with the skateboard?"

"I was trying to get the set upstairs to Boris's, but it's too heavy so I thought I could balance it on the skateboard, but it keeps falling off. Anyway, now you're here, can't you carry it? Because it's almost six and I'm going to be late for the movie."

I sighed. "Okay, just give me two secs to change my sweater. And you better do a job on your face. It's all smudged from . . ." I tactfully refrained from finishing the sentence, but he knew what I meant.

"I wasn't crying. It was just that thing keeping falling off made me so mad, I got prespired."

"Sure. Anyway, it was a good idea; I never would

79

have thought of it. Hurry up and get washed, and if you're done ahead of me, turn out the hall light and ring for the elevator."

"Gee, thanks, Annabel. I love you, Annabel," he said, cheerily trotting off to the bathroom. Doesn't take much to please him, thank heavens.

When I got back, the elevator was waiting and Ape Face was just stepping into it.

"No wonder you had trouble," I grumbled as I lurched in after him, staggering under the weight of our precious cargo.

"Say, what is this?" said Hector Wong, the afternoon man.

"What does it look like, a bunch of daisies? It's a television set," I gasped.

"That I could tell from looking. What I meant was what is this big traffic in TVs all of a sudden? Twelve o'clock I took your upstairs friend down with one, and now I'm taking you down with one."

"For one thing, it's none of your business, and for another, I don't want to go down, I want to go up."

"The kid buzzed the down," said Hector, reversing gears with stomach-sickening abruptness. "How was I to know?"

"The kid buzzed the down because he is a creature of habit and down is his usual route. However, we want up—to my upstairs friend's—and *quick*, por favor. It's heavy!"

Hector, being a Brooklyn-born Chinese Puerto Rican, is fluent in all three languages. When we're friends, which is most of the time, he's delighted to let me practice my Spanish on him, but today he seemed to be taking it as an ethnic slur.

"#%*@+!" he said darkly in inscrutable Mandarin, and brought the car to a deliberately inept crash landing at the ninth floor. I sank to my knees and had to let him help me up.

"Muchas gracias por nada," I retorted, staggering into the Harris's elevator hall.

"Are you going to ring the doorbell for me, Ape Face, or do you want me to ring it with my nose?"

Ape Face giggled. "Ring it with your no . . ."

"Ring that bell or I'll drop this on your head!" I commanded.

Ape Face rang the bell. Nobody came.

"Ring it again. I'm dying," I said.

He did. Still nobody came. Ape Face put his ear to the door.

"I think I hear the maid vacuuming in there. Maybe she can't notice us."

"She'll notice this," I said, heaving my full weight (approximately two hundred and twenty pounds) against the door. Because it was already open, it instantly gave way, and I landed in the middle of the entrance hall, where I deposited the set on the floor with a resounding *thunk*.

81

In the living room the Hoover was going full blast, but no one was attached to it.

"Where's the maid?" asked Ape Face.

"I don't know, but she's bound to be somewhere."

"Hey, look! What's that?" he shrieked, pointing to two legs sticking out from under the sofa.

"The maid, I guess."

"Is she dead?"

"Of course not, silly. Her legs are moving. She must be cleaning under there."

"Why doesn't she come out and say hello?"

"Because she doesn't know we're here."

"Let's tell her," said Ape Face, advancing cautiously toward the sofa. "I'll give her a little tap."

"Don't do that!" I said, grabbing him by the arm. "You'll give her a heart attack. We'll just say hello—loudly. Ready? One, two, three. HELL-O!"

"I think she heard," said Ape Face. "I can see more of her now than I could before."

We watched, fascinated, as first the bottom, then the middle and shoulders and arms, and finally the face appeared. It didn't seem too undone at the sight of us—just puzzled.

"Hi, there," I said jovially.

"What? Wait a minute," said the maid. She scrambled to her feet, dumped a handful of pistachio-nut shells into an ashtray, smoothed down her white uniform, and turned off the Hoover.

"There. That's better. Now—what did you say?"

"I said Hi, here we are."

"So I see," she said, looking us up and down. "How did you get in?"

"You left the front door open. You know, you really shouldn't do that," I said sternly. "Somebody might walk in and steal something."

"Somebody like you, you mean?"

"Certainly not," I said indignantly. "I'm Annabel Andrews and this is my brother, Ben. We're friends of Boris's."

She looked dubious.

"I mean Morris's. I always call him Boris. Didn't he tell you we were coming?"

"No, but that's all right. Make yourselves comfortable."

Ape Face was tugging at my sleeve. "Can I ask you a secret? Where's the den? *The Mask of Dimitrios* is going to start."

"What's he want—the bathroom?" asked the maid.

"No, the den. Boris said he could watch a movie on the TV in there."

"That way," said the maid, pointing.

"Thank you," said Ape Face, and sauntered off.

"Cute kid," remarked the maid. "Now what can I do for you? Can I get you anything?"

"Oh no, thanks," I said, plumping myself down on the sofa. "I'll just wait here for Boris. You just go on with whatever you were doing."

"I'm finished with whatever I was doing," she said,

plumping herself down on the sofa beside me. "Well, not *finished*, but finished—if you know what I mean."

A quick look around the living room and I knew exactly what she meant: Half the tables were covered with dust, the rug had flug on it, and every ashtray was filled with cigarette butts and pistachio-nut shells. And there sat the maid, pretty as you please, with her feet up on the coffee table! Maybe a tactful hint was in order.

"Are you sure I'm not interrupting you?" I asked.

"No, no," she said airily. "That's it for today. I hate housework, don't you?"

"Everybody hates housework," I said, trying not to sound sanctimonious, "but you shouldn't feel there's anything demeaning about it. After all, *somebody's* got to do it."

"I'd just as soon the somebody weren't me," she grumbled, and then abruptly changed the subject. "How about a drink?"

"I don't drink," I said stiffly, watching in horror as she drifted over to the bar and poured herself a Scotch. "And you shouldn't either," I blurted out. "It's not a good thing to do when you're working."

"Hell, no," she said in a bland tone. "But I've stopped working now, anyhow." Really, the woman was outrageous! I wondered if Boris and his mother had any idea what went on when they weren't there.

"Have you been working here long?" I asked.

"Only a couple of hours. The living room wasn't as bad as the kitchen."

"No, I mean have you been in this position long?"

"In this position long?" she repeated slowly, with a thoughtful frown.

Then, light suddenly dawned. "Oh, *now* I understand. You want to know if I've been in this *position* long." She hooted with laughter and sat down next to me on the sofa again.

"My dear, I've been in this position for ages. *Ages!* Does that surprise you?"

"Frankly, yes," I admitted. "Last year, we had a maid who drank. My mother fired her."

"Is that so?" She raised her eyebrows and looked at me owlishly. "Then it's a good thing I don't work for your mother, isn't it?"

"Darn right," I said in a steely tone.

There was an awkward silence. Then the maid said, "So you're a friend of Morris's. I'm glad to know he has one."

"He has plenty. He just never brings them home."

"So I've noticed. Why is that, do you suppose?"

Because thanks to you, his home is a disaster area, is what I was tempted to say. Instead, I said, "I don't know. Except maybe he doesn't want people to meet his mother. I get the impression he's not overly fond of her."

"I get that impression, too," she said, staring speculatively off into space.

"What's she like?" I asked curiously.

"Well, let's see now. How to describe her . . . ? I guess you could do it in one word." She chuckled. "Crazed."

"Dangerously crazed?" Poor Boris!

"Oh no, I wouldn't say so. Just eccentric. Most writers are, you know."

"I didn't know she was a writer. Boris never mentioned it. What kind of stuff does she write?"

"Oh—poetry, books, magazine articles. Poetry, mostly."

"Is it any good?"

"I wouldn't know how to judge that."

"No, I suppose you wouldn't," I said, thinking *True Confessions* was probably more up her alley.

"And she's a lousy mother, right?"

"I wouldn't know how to judge that either. I guess she's a lousy mother for someone like Morris. He's sensible, she's not."

"Well, what do you think of her as a *person*? Is she nice?"

"Hard to say. She tries to be nice. Sometimes I like her, sometimes I don't. But she's very easy to work for," she added with a mischievous grin. "Nobody else in the world would put up with me."

"Oh, I don't know about that," I said politely.

"You're not as conscientious as our maid, but you're quite interesting to pass the time of day with."

"Thank you. What time *is* it?" she said, glancing at her watch. "My God, I'm supposed to be somewhere by six thirty."

"But I thought you were staying to fix supper."

"Who me? Out of the question. If you get hungry, help yourself to whatever you want in the fridge. I'm going inside to change out of these rags."

While she was gone, I dusted off a few tables with my sleeve and emptied the ashtrays into a wastebasket. It was so messy in that room, even I couldn't stand it. I was just about to de-flug the rug when the maid reappeared, looking really quite attractive.

"What's it like out?" she asked, flinging open the hall closet door. "Too warm for fur?" *Now* what was she up to—borrowing Madame's clothes?!

"Much too warm for fur."

"Oh. Well, I'll wear this, then," she said, diving into a Bill Blass raincoat.

"Pardon me for asking, but is that yours?" I inquired.

"Yes," she said. "Pardon *me* for asking, but is *that* yours?" she said, pointing to the television set.

"Boris's. I'm returning it."

"I thought it looked familiar. When he comes back, tell him to move it out of the hall before somebody breaks a leg." Rather bossy of her, it seemed to me.

"Is there anything else you want me to tell Boris?"

"Yes. Tell him to invite you back again soon. His mother would enjoy talking to you."

"How do you know?"

"I know," she said, chucking me under the chin. "I've been in this position a long time, remember?"

And with that, she flew out the door.

Fifteen minutes later, with the Ape's new Sony in a box under his arm, Boris flew in. And I really mean flew; I'd never seen him so excited.

"Annabel!" he shouted. "It's going to work! It's going to *work*!"

"I should hope so. It's brand-new, isn't it? Anyway, where've you been, what took you so long, and why didn't you call? We've been waiting for hours."

Boris babbled on, "I'm not talking about the Sony, I'm talking about the whole thing. The whole thing's going to work. Whole new horizons have opened up, my life is going to change, I'm going to be a billionaire! I tell you, it's going to work—I knew it all along!"

"Boris," I said impatiently, "slow up and calm down. I don't know what you're talking about."

"Listen to me. Are you listening?"

"I'm listening."

"All right: What do you think this Sony cost? Take a rough guess."

"A hundred and fifty?"

"Wrong. A hundred and sixty-seven ninety-nine. They've gone up. Now, what do you think I got for my Motorola?"

"A hundred and *seventy*-seven ninety-nine."

"Wrong! A hundred and five," said Boris with a broad smile. Unless my arithmetic was worse than I thought, he'd just lost money on the deal. What was he so happy about?

"According to my calculations, you're out approximately sixty dollars."

"Wrong again," said Boris, beaming from ear to ear. With a flourish, he produced a wad of greasy bills from his pocket and waved them under my nose. "A hundred and thirty-seven dollars profit I made today! Aren't you going to guess how?"

"No, I'm not," I said. "I'm tired of guessing wrong and I'm tired of playing twenty questions. You tell me."

"I bet the guy! The guy in the TV store. See, we had the trade all worked out and then I asked him if Monday was okay to pay him the extra sixty-two ninety-nine because I didn't have it on me, and he said nothing doing. It looked like the transaction was falling through.

"Then I noticed he had all the sets in the store on—you know, to show how well they worked—and guess what was on? No, don't guess, I'll tell you: The Mets–Reds game. So, very casually, I got into a conversation with him about how I thought the Reds would win, easy. He told me I was off my rocker, so I bet him two hundred bucks. That's why I was late getting here; I had to wait 'til the game was over to collect. Boy, was he sore! Zowie!" he yelped with a final burst of enthusiasm, "Do I ever love this wrecked-up Box!"

"Charming," I said scornfully. "A charming display and a charming story. Taking advantage of a poor old man . . ."

"What poor old man? He was a middle-aged slob who would've taken advantage of *me* if I hadn't beat him to it! My Motorola was worth more than a hundred and five and he knew it. Come on, Annabel, help me carry the Box into my room; I want to catch the seven o'clock news."

"Two wrongs don't make a right. Carry it yourself. I lugged it up here, you can lug it the rest of the way."

Boris, still euphoric from his ill-gotten gains, said, "Fair enough." With a grunt, he hoisted it onto his shoulder, marched off with it, and returned, singing, "When I am a rich man, deedle, deedle, deedle, dydle, dydle, dah . . ."

"But Boris, it's not moral," I protested.

"I make it a rule," he said grandly, "never to discuss morals on an empty stomach. What time is the maid serving dinner?"

"She isn't. She left."

"Left! Rats! I'm starving. Why did she leave?"

"I dunno. She said she had to be somewhere at six thirty."

"I bet that's the last we see of her," he said gloomily. "Cranky old bat."

"She didn't strike me as cranky—just unreliable. As a matter of fact . . ." I was about to enlighten him further, but he was already on his way to the kitchen, muttering, "I guess I'll have to whip something up myself again."

"In that case, maybe I'd better call home and see if Ape Face can eat there." I reached for the kitchen phone.

Boris snatched it out of my hand. "I wouldn't do that if I were you."

"Why not? Your mother can't object to a guest making one quick call." I snatched it back.

"Proceed at your own risk," said Boris sourly.

I did. There was no dial tone.

"That's funny," I said. "It's out of order or something."

"Or something," said Boris, replacing the receiver in the cradle. "Too bad for Ape Face. I'll have to make do with whatever I find in the fridge—as usual. And I shudder to think what. Probably nothing but a desiccated lemon, a jar of pressed caviar, and a mystery mold in a covered dish. Am I right?"

I opened the fridge door. There was a ton of gorgeous-looking food.

"You're *wrong*, for a change."

Boris peered over my shoulder. "Where did all that come from? Oh, yeah—my mother had a party last night."

"I thought she didn't cook."

"She doesn't. She orders it in from Sardi's at ten dollars a head."

"But look how much is left! Wow, what a waste!"

"Here, hold the plates; I'll serve. Lasagne?"

"Thanks."

"Turkey?"

"Thanks."

"Ham? Chutney? Rye bread? Brie?"

"Thanks." Pretty soon I stopped saying thanks and just let him heap it on. We set a plate down in front of Ape Face, who was glued to his movie in the den. Then we made our way back to Boris's room with roughly four heads' worth on our own plates, which we managed to dispose of in fifteen minutes of uninterrupted gorging. We had to start with the peach tart because it was piled on top, and work our way down to the lasagne and salmon canapés at the bottom. I tell you, it was positively revolting.

"Well, now that we've got that over with," I said, stifling a mammoth burp, "let's talk."

"Let's not," said Boris, turning on the set. "We've missed half the news already. Just as long as I'm in time for the sports, though. . . ."

In enforced silence, while Boris scribbled in his notebook, I watched the results of Sunday's ball game (the Giants won), and a tennis match in Phoenix (Rosemary Casals won). I found it pretty stultifying; but then, unlike Boris, I wasn't out to rip off the world.

"Can I talk now?" I said acidly.

"Sure," he said, turning off the set. "What do you want to talk about?"

"Well, for one thing, I'd like to know who you're going to find to take advantage of tomorrow. It's Sunday; there won't be any unsuspecting shopkeepers around."

"Are you going to start that again?! I told you I didn't want to discuss it."

"You said you didn't want to discuss it on an empty stomach. Now you've got a full stomach. And so have I. So let's discuss it. I think you're a greedy, avaricious, mean, amoral miser!"

"That's some discussion! More like character assassination."

"Then defend yourself!"

"I can't."

"Just what I thought!" I said triumphantly.

"I mean I don't want to," said Boris. "Please, Annabel, *please*. I have reasons I don't want to go into—so please can't we change the subject?" He looked ashamed and miserable.

"All right," I said, relenting. "If I can think of what to change the subject *to*." My mind was a complete blank.

Finally I thought of something. "I know. Let's talk about your mother."

"Do we have to?" asked Boris uneasily. I glared at him. Resigned to his fate, he nodded. "What can I tell you?"

"Well, the maid said your mother was a writer. I never knew that."

Boris feigned nonchalance. "Oh yes. She's quite famous, old Sascha is."

"Sascha Harris? I've never heard of her "

"She uses the name Sascha Biegelman."

"Oh, Sascha *Biegelman.*"

"You've heard of her," said Boris delightedly.

"No, I haven't heard of her either." There's no point in lying about things like that; you always get caught.

"I thought from the way you said her name . . ." he trailed off, disappointed. "Biegelman is her pen name. She made it up," he added.

"Why Biegelman?"

"Would I know? She probably found it in the Yellow Pages under carpets. She found an analyst that way once."

"Under *carpets*?!"

"No, dummy. But she might just as well have, for all the good he did her. Three hours a week at forty-five dollars an hour for five years makes—let me see—approximately thirty-five thousand one hundred dollars down the drain."

"My Lord, Boris, you're a walking computer, aren't you! I had no idea you were so good at math."

"I have to be," he said grimly. "I didn't want to go into this—but as long as you've got me started— Would you like to see something?" He opened the bottom drawer of a file cabinet. "Look. Just look in there. You know what that is? Six years of bank statements and canceled checks. I've been balancing her checkbook ever since I was nine. And it's no picnic, let me tell you; she's overdrawn half the time, the ditz!"

He jerked open the middle drawer of the file cabinet. "You know what's in here? Monthly statements from the brokerage firm. A couple of years ago, she wanted to go on a thirty-seven-day Silk Screen and Ceramics tour of the Orient. When I reminded her she was into my school for twenty-five hundred and into the Feds for more than a thou for back taxes, she said, 'I can sell stock.' So I told her she didn't have any stock left to sell—which she believed because she's too sloppy to know what's what; and ever since then, I've been hiding her stock statements. I also hide her savings-account book. It's my hedge against bankruptcy."

"So she didn't get to go on the trip."

"Sure she did. A little problem like insufficient funds wouldn't stop Sascha. When I hit her with the good news about the stocks, she said, 'What the hell, Charley, you only live once, I'll sell the Picasso.' (My grandmother left her a Picasso.)

95

"The next day, she bopped into the Parke-Bernet gallery with the thing, made herself a deal, sent the big check to the Feds and half a dozen fairly big checks to charities; and a week later, she bopped off to the Land of the Rising Sun, leaving me to stare at an empty white rectangle on a dirty gray wall."

"Stupefying!" I said. "Simply stupefying!"

"Yeah, isn't it?" agreed Boris, mournfully. "And I loved that picture. It was a great picture. But that's not the worst. Wait'll you hear this: She never paid the school bill. Not that year, or this year either. They've been pretty nice about it, but they're not going to be much longer. In fact, they've already sent a letter saying they couldn't keep me next year 'unless,' et cetera, et cetera. From where I sit, 'unless' seems highly unlikely."

"My God, Boris, what will you do?"

"I don't know. I suppose I could go live with my uncle in California—the public schools are better out there than here—but I certainly wouldn't want to." Boris looked very morose, but not as morose as I felt. Boris in California? What a ghastly thought! Steady on, Annabel, it hasn't happened yet.

"Not that I don't like my uncle. He's an okay enough guy; in fact, a very okay guy. But I really couldn't move to California even if I did want to because . . ." He ran down, deep in dire thoughts of doom and gloom.

"Because?" Any reason for Boris not to go to California was a reason I was anxious to hear.

"Well, because, don't you see? She's so helpless. She's such a totally irresponsible . . . a child, that's what she is. The money hassles are a perfect example. Her father, my Connecticut grandfather, he's a typical Yankee; you'd think some of that penny-saved-is-a-penny-earned stuff would have rubbed off on her, but maybe it traumatized her instead. All I know is if I didn't keep an eye on her, she'd spend every dime she earned. As it is, she does pretty well in the spending department."

He paced up and down nervously for a minute or so, and then abruptly wheeled around to face me head-on. "Listen," he said in a choked-up voice, "You want to hear something really lovely? You want to hear the lovely latest?"

"I don't know if I do," I said. Boris's recital was unnerving me terribly.

"Well, you're going to, whether you like it or not. Serves you right for bugging me about wanting to make money.

"That present I gave you—the walkie-talkie—I said it was because Sascha wouldn't let me use the phone? Ha!" he sneered. "There *is* no phone. Not in operation, anyway, not right now. For the third time in two years, it's been cut off for nonpayment of bills. You know what you would've heard if you'd called up here in the last five days? 'I am sorry. The number you have reached is not in service at this time, or has been temporarily disconnected.' That's why I couldn't call you this afternoon. It's humiliating and horrible!"

He put his hands over his face and started to cry.

"Oh Boris, please Boris, don't! I can't bear it," I said, stricken.

"It's all right," he said. "I'll be all right in a second." He took a few deep breaths, and then straightened up and smiled wanly.

"That was dumb, wasn't it?"

"Not a bit," I assured him. "Furthermore, if I were in your shoes, I'd probably do the same thing."

"What else would you do if you were in my shoes? After six years of playing nursemaid to a nut, I'm getting pretty sick of my shoes."

"I can't say as I blame you."

"I mean it! What would *you* do?"

"I haven't the foggiest notion. It's a very complex problem, that much is obvious, and I couldn't come up with any quick answers. I haven't had enough time to think about it."

"Well, I have. Too much time. So last night, I made a little list." From his pocket, he produced a crumpled sheet of paper. "This is a list of things I've decided my mother needs in her life and doesn't have. I'd like to read it to you, and if you have any other suggestions, please make them, okay?"

98

"Shoot."

"One: a good shrink. That's the most important. Nothing from the Yellow Pages—she's got to have a sympathetic but well-qualified type who knows how to create order out of chaos. Two: a new accountant. The one she has only does her tax forms and charges a fortune; I do everything else and I don't want to do it anymore. Three: a lot of new furniture and a new paint job. This place is falling-down disgusting; nothing's been done to it since the day we moved in. Four: all new equipment for the kitchen. Five: a decent house-keeper to cook in the kitchen and clean the house; I'm sick of TV dinners and fuzz under the bed. Six: a secretary to answer the phones, type manuscripts, and paste rave reviews into nice leather scrapbooks. Seven: a whole new wardrobe for Sascha and one decent sports jacket for me. Eight: twenty thousand dollars to clean up past debts and another fifty thousand in case there are future ones. That sounds like a lot, but if the new shrink isn't more successful than his predecessor, she won't be able to pay him the thirty-five thousand he'll charge for helping her with her money neurosis unless I hold something in reserve. That's all I've come up with so far," concluded Boris. "What do you think?"

I was beginning to enjoy myself. Boris's list re-minded me of a game I used to play when I was a kid: If you found a million dollars lying in the gutter, how would you spend it?

"It's an extremely thorough list. You only forgot one item: a nice man."

"Oh, that. I didn't forget. But she had a nice man, once. My father. And she blew it—he left her. She'll probably never find another one," he added mournfully. "Unfortunately, it's something money can't buy. I wish it could."

"Never mind. I just thought there was no harm in mentioning it. After all, as long as we're in fantasy land, we might as well make it perfect."

"Who said anything about fantasy land?" he said indignantly. "This is a very real list to accommodate some very real needs." Dear God, he's going the way of his mother—stark, raving mad.

"Boris, you're on a trip. It may be a very real list, but it requires a heap of very real money. From whence, pray tell, are you going to get it?"

"From this whence right here," he said, patting the Box. "This same wonderful whence that brings you tomorrow's weather is going to bring me unlimited fortunes with which to pay for items one through eight."

"How? From betting on ball games with Chuckie Waterman, Charlie Kuchel, and innocent shopkeepers?"

"No. From betting on horses at OTB."

"Hey!" I said, admiringly. "I never thought of that. Aren't you the clever one. Like the Kentucky Derby—you could make a mint in one day." I was all excited.

"I don't want to make a mint in one day. Any time you win over six hundred dollars at once at OTB, it gets reported to the government and you have to pay income tax. It's better to make a mint in a lot of days—a little at a time. Like Aqueduct or Roosevelt, Monday through Saturday, month after month."

"Do they show the results of those races on television? I've never seen them."

"I vaguely remember they do. The trouble is I don't know when. It must be sometime in the afternoon or evening; I'll just have to keep switching channels 'til I catch it."

"Wouldn't it be easier to call OTB and ask them?"

Boris looked up in surprise. "It certainly would. Why didn't I think of that?"

I gave him a consolation pat on the shoulder. "Because you don't have a phone. Don't berate yourself. You can't be expected to think of everything."

"You know, Annabel," he said earnestly, "you could be a great help to me with all of this. I could really use you. Between us, we'd make a great team. If I promise not to take advantage of people like Chuckie Waterman and Harvey Kuchel (although if you knew Harvey Kuchel . . .)."

"Ah-ah-ah," I warned.

"All right, all right, forget Harvey Kuchel; he's penny-ante stuff anyway. But if I promise not to take advantage of people like that, will you help me?"

"How? You don't need me for betting. What else is there?"

"I don't know, offhand. But when I find out, will you help me?"

"If you'll help me," I said.

"Sure. But how?"

"Well," I said slowly, "this is going to sound kind of stupid . . ."

"That's nothing new," snickered Boris. He was back to his old self, I noted.

"Do you want me to help you or not?"

"Yes, I do. I'm sorry," he said promptly.

"Boris, remember when you made fun of me for not realizing the Box was good for more than just weather predictions? And then you explained how we couldn't prevent events from happening but we *could* benefit from advance information?

"Well, you want to benefit from advance information to change your mother's life—and yours, too. After what you've told me, I certainly don't blame you for that. But couldn't other people also benefit from advance information? I know this sounds sappy and idealistic, but take that freak blizzard, for instance. I'm built like a horse and being out in it didn't do me much harm; but suppose I had a little old frail grandmother who was going out for a walk that day. I'd want to warn her."

"Unless you gave the whole thing away, your little

102

old frail grandmother wouldn't believe you any more than you believed your brother."

"Probably not, but I could persuade her to stay indoors. I could play gin rummy with her until the blizzard began and she saw for herself. By using that advance information, I might actually be saving her life.

"Or take another for instance: We see on the Box that a woman in Queens has had quintuplets—over three pounds each and all of them healthy. But the poor lady is frantic with worry because the doctors have told her to expect multiple births and she doesn't know how many—or whether they'll survive. Wouldn't it be fun to tell her everything was going to be okay?"

"Why would *she* believe you? She'd figure if the doctors didn't know, why should you?"

"Oh Boris, don't take me literally—I'm just winging these examples. All I know is I'm sure there's a use for the Box *besides* making money.

"So I want you to promise you'll tell me everything that shows up on the Box whenever I want to know. Will you promise?"

"On one condition: that you never reveal your source."

"I absolutely never will."

"All right. I promise. And in return, you promise to help me?"

"I promise." He threw his arms around me joyfully and kissed me (on the cheek).

"Annabel, you are a super person! *I* thank you, and my *mother* thanks you . . ."

"That's ridiculous."

"Well, she would if she knew. Although maybe it's lucky she doesn't; she doesn't know what's good for her anyway, she's such a crazy lady."

"The maid said she wasn't crazy—just eccentric."

"Is that what the maid said? Flora the Fink said that? Some nerve! It's one thing for me to criticize my mother and quite another for her to."

"Don't get ruffled. She wasn't criticizing—just analyzing. You know something, Boris? From the way you talk now, I can't figure out: Do you like your mother or do you hate her?"

"What's your guess?" Shrewd of him, wasn't it—trying to get me to give him the answer.

"I simply don't know," I said.

"I simply don't either. Sometimes I like her, sometimes I don't."

"The maid said the same thing."

Boris gave me a queer look. "What else did the maid say?"

"Let me see, now. She said your mother was easy to work for—which is fortunate. She's a fiasco of a maid, you know."

"No, I didn't."

"Oh, yes, she's really frightful. *I'm* a better cleaner and that's not saying much."

"What else?" asked Boris curiously.

"Well, when I asked her if she thought your mother was a lousy mother, she said, 'Lousy for someone like Morris. He's sensible, she's not.'"

"She happens to be right; but how would she know a thing like that, I wonder."

"I suppose anybody who'd been around as long as she has could figure it out."

"Two weeks? I wouldn't call that long. Although, come to think of it, two weeks is *quite* a long time in our house. They usually leave sooner. Everything's so erratic, including the pay."

"Strange," I mused. "She gave me the feeling . . . No! She actually said, 'I've been in this position for ages.' And then she giggled."

"Tell me more," insisted Boris.

"I don't want to get her in trouble. She was very pleasant, really."

"More," he demanded.

"Well," I said hesitantly, "she drinks. Helped herself to a slug of Scotch."

"No kidding! Tsk, tsk, tsk!"

"Yes. And when she changed out of her uniform, she did it in the master bedroom. And then she put on a coat from the hall closet. I told her it was too warm for fur so she put on a good raincoat. I thought maybe it was your mother's and I asked her, but she said it was hers."

"I think I'm beginning to get the picture," said Boris. "Tell me, did the coat fit?"

"Perfectly. Why?"

"Was this maid about fifty-five years old and fat and spoke with a Spanish accent?"

"No! She was about forty years old, thin, and spoke plain English."

"Annabel," said Boris, howling with laughter, "that was no maid—that was my mother!"

I wanted to die on the spot. Since that wasn't possible, I did the next best thing: fled from it. It was like a Mack Sennett ballet. Without so much as a good-bye to Boris, I tore into the den, wrested my glassy-eyed brother away from *The Partridge Family*, stuffed the new Sony into a shopping bag (for purposes of concealment), rang the elevator bell, decided not to wait for the elevator, galloped down the back stairs to our apartment, dragged Ape Face to his room, hid the Sony in the toy chest under the Lego, shouted "Hello, we're back, I'm tired, good night" to my parents, ripped off my clothes, dived into bed, pulled the covers over my head—and nearly burned up with embarrassment. (*There's* an interesting headline for Bartholomew Bacon: GIRL'S FACE SETS SHEETS ON FIRE!)

Until nearly dawn, I tossed around looking for a

cool place on the pillow, and attempted to reconstruct the scene with Sascha. I must have sampled practically every emotion in the book: Rage—what a rotten trick, leading me on like that!; hope—maybe she never knew I thought she was the maid; despair—she knew. It was obvious I didn't think she was the mother. Who else would she be?; bafflement—if she knew, why didn't she stop me from making a fool of myself? Was she simply trying to spare my feelings?; panic—what about *her* feelings? That awful thing I said about Boris not liking his mother!; curiosity—but actually she didn't seem surprised. She even admitted she wasn't a good mother for him. Why *did* she admit that, she didn't have to?; admiration—because she's honest about herself; despair—she must think I'm an idiot. I bet she hates me; hope—wait a minute! When she left, she said to tell Boris to invite me back because his mother would enjoy talking to me; wonderment—she *doesn't* hate me. In spite of it all, she likes me. I like her, too; determination—I'm going to apologize the first chance I get; relief—I'm falling asle . . .

Sunday, April 21

BEEP, BEEP, BEEP

I opened one eye and looked at my watch. Nine o'clock. Too early for beeping. I ignored it. Then there was more beeping. In a stupor, I reached for the walkie-talkie and shoved it with my feet to the bottom of the bed. No dice; the covers muffled the sound but the vibrations were tickling my toes. I fished it back up again and punched the talk button.

"Whaddya want?" I croaked.

"Good morning. This is the butler speaking."

Har-de-har-har!

"Boris the Butler calling Annabel. Are you there, Annabel?"

"No." I clicked off and rolled over. On four hours' sleep, what I didn't need was a little light banter with Boris the Butler. What I needed was more sleep. I closed my eyes and tried for it; but waiting for the walkie-talkie to blast at me was like waiting for the other shoe to drop. When it didn't, I wondered why not, and the wondering kept me awake.

I beeped Boris impatiently, four or five times.

"Sh," he cautioned. "One of those is enough. The 'maid' is working on a sonnet. Or a novel. I forget which."

"Boris, if you have any sensitivity whatsoever, you will drop that extremely painful subject and never refer to it again."

"I don't know why you're so upset about it—I'm sure she isn't. But all right, *Sascha* is working on a sonnet or a novel, I forget which. Is that better?"

"Much," I said, mollified. "What did you beep me for?"

"To tell you I can't see you today. I'm working on my plan for Sascha—adding up the figures on that itemized list."

A Sunday without Boris? Unthinkable! My feelings were hurt.

"That's all right, Boris," I said stoically. "I'll make my own plans. Did you watch the late news last night?"

"Yes. Why?"

"Is anything interesting happening today?"

"Mmmn . . . they caught the hijackers."

"Where?"

"In Cairo." No good—too far away.

"Any local news—fires, murders, quintuplets?"

"A shoot-out on Lenox Avenue in Harlem."

"Lenox Avenue and where?"

"At 127th Street, I think. At two fifteen. Two dead

and one wounded. Let's see—what else? Sports you saw yesterday; the balmy weather turned blustery after lunch, and *Catch as Catch Can* opened at the Sutton Cinema; the critics loved it. What kind of good deed are you going to get out of all that?"

"I don't know yet, but I'll think of something. Goodbye."

I clicked off and went over today's events in my mind. The only thing that sounded promising was the shoot-out; but since I couldn't prevent it, what could I do with it?

Suddenly, for some reason (possibly having to do with his beautiful smile and his cute nose), a vision of Bartholomew Bacon popped into my head. A reporter could benefit from it.

With Bartholomew Bacon's card in my hand, I tiptoed to the kitchen phone. My parents were still asleep—but in case they woke up, I didn't want to be overheard.

The *Daily News* number rang eleven times and was finally answered by a grunt.

"Bartholomew Bacon, please," I said in a business-like tone.

"Snot innaday."

"Excuse me?"

"Bacon . . . snot . . . innaday," said the grunt, articulating carefully.

"Oh dear. It's vital that I get in touch with him.

110

Could you give me his home number? This is an emergency."

"Unh," grunted the grunt. "Hold on. Bacon, Bacon. 555–4382."

I thanked him, hung up, took a swig of orange juice from the carton in the fridge, and headed back for the phone. I could see it was going to be a long day.

Bacon's number rang only five times and was answered by a groan.

"Is this Bartholomew Bacon?"

"I think so. Check me around noon. I may know more by then. G'night."

"Wait a minute, don't hang up. This is Ann Smith. Remember me? Ann Smith? Marvin the Torch?"

"Oh, yes, sure. What's up—outside of me, that is?" He yawned loudly for my benefit. The nit—I can take a hint without sound effects!

"Should I call back later?"

"Nope. I'm up now. Once I'm up, I'm up. How did you get my number?"

"The paper. I told them it was an emergency. You said to call if something occurred to me. . . ." I heard Dad's voice in the hall. In a second, he'd be in the kitchen to start coffee.

"Listen, I can't talk now, but I do have some interesting information. Do you want to meet me for coffee in a couple of hours?"

"Make it one o'clock."

"Fine. Where? Just name the place."

"Three fifty-three West 52nd."

"What's way over there—a bar?"

"I live there. Fourth floor walk-up." Uh-oh. I didn't like the sound of that!

"Couldn't we meet at your corner drugstore?"

"Miss Smith, honey, today is my day of rest. I'm not stirring from my pad."

"But . . ."

"Morning, darling," said Dad. It was too late for buts.

"Okay, I'll be there. Good-bye. Morning, Dad. That was Virginia," I explained.

"Virginia. Is she the pretty one or the nasty one?" After all these years, he still can't keep my friends straight.

"Both. I have a date with her this afternoon." I didn't, of course, but I was going to have to manufacture one in order to account for my time; because although my parents are reasonably liberal, I had a feeling they wouldn't approve of me going to a strange man's pad on West 52nd Street.

When Dad left the kitchen, I called Virginia. She chewed me out royally for abandoning her on Bleecker Street, and when she'd finally wound down, I apologized meekly and profusely.

Then I said, "Virginia, will you do me a huge favor?"

"It depends," she said cagily.

"I'm going somewhere this afternoon I don't want my parents to know about. If I tell them I'm with you, will you cover for me?"

"Where are you going?" My mother walked into the kitchen and started frying bacon.

"I can't say. Wait a minute, I'll take it in the study." I picked up the phone in the study, hung up the phone in the kitchen, and ran back to pick up the phone in the study. By the time I got there. Dad had settled into the armchair with the Sunday *Times*.

"Virginia?"

"What kind of secret?"

"Juicy."

"But you won't tell me? Nuts to you, luv." I looked over at Dad. He seemed engrossed in the paper.

"Virginia," I whispered, "There is absolutely *no privacy* in this madhouse."

"Then pop on over here, sweets. Our flat's silent as a tomb." Virginia is the most persistent person in the whole entire world!

"All right. You win. I'll be over around eleven thirty."

"Right-i-o. I'll make us a nice pot of tea. Ta-ta, ducks."

Ta-ta, yourself!

To tell Virginia the truth was clearly impossible. The Box had to remain a secret. There was only one thing I could tell Virginia: a big fat lie. I didn't have one prepared, but I'm pretty good at fabricating on my feet; all I had to do was let her ask me a few leading questions and something would undoubtedly come to mind.

"Well, now, Annabel," she said, gracefully pouring me a cup of Constant Comment, "what's this all about?"

"You'll never guess," I said mysteriously.

"You're going to sneak into an X-rated movie?" Not a bad idea; unfortunately, I couldn't think of the name of a single one; if she asked me, I'd be stuck.

"No. Guess again."

"You're going to that funky coffeehouse we passed on Christopher Street yesterday—where the avant-garde poets hang out."

That wasn't a bad idea, either, but if I said yes she might decide to come with me.

"No. Keep going."

"You've got a date?"

Beautiful! Beautiful, and not altogether untrue. "That's it exactly."

"A date with a *man*?" she asked incredulously.

"Of course, what else?" I gazed serenely at her.

Virginia set her teacup down gently on the table and leaned toward me. In a hushed and solemn tone, she handed me my lie on a silver platter.

"Annabel, my dear, are you in love?" I lowered my eyes in becoming modesty and allowed a shy smile to

114

cross my face—you could've hung me in the Louvre alongside the *Mona Lisa.*

"Yes, Virginia," I murmured softly, "I am."

"Oh, Annabel," she squealed, "I'm *thrilled* for you! Absolutely thrilled. Look at you—you're blushing!"

I hate people who tell you're blushing. Unless you get up and inspect your face in the mirror there's no way to know whether it's true or not. Furthermore, I bet most of the time it isn't; it's just something people love to say.

"I'm not blushing."

"You are, you are," she insisted. "Annabel, I want to hear all about him. Have you known him long?"

"Not very. Only a couple of weeks. It's been sort of a whirlwind romance." Virginia moaned in ecstasy.

"What does he look like?" I told her. More moans.

"He sounds divine. Where does he go to school?"

"He doesn't. I mean he's out of school. He's older, you see."

Naturally, Virginia wanted to know how old. I told her twenty-four. She was very impressed. Then she wanted to know where I'd met him, which was rather a sticky wicket. Where *would* a fourteen-year-old girl meet a twenty-four-year-old man? I hadn't been to any dances or parties lately, I couldn't say I'd met him through my parents. . . . For lack of anything better, I decided to go with the truth.

"Actually, I met him on the street. We bumped into

each other and got to talking, and, well—that's how it all began. He's a newspaperman."

"A newspaperman?" Virginia curled her lip ever so slightly. "No wonder you don't want your parents to know."

"Not that kind of a newspaperman. He's a reporter. On the *Daily News*."

"Oh, what a relief! I'd hate to see you bumming around with a delivery boy."

"Virginia, you're a terrible snob."

I then proceeded to extol at great length the various virtues of Bartholomew Bacon—without giving his name, of course: honest, kind, humorous, intelligent, college graduate, fine old Yankee family, a sister married to a Presbyterian clergyman—the works.

When I got through, Virginia wanted to know why I had to keep him a secret from my parents if he was all that wonderful. Clever question. But I had a clever answer ready. "Because the difference in our ages would worry them," I said.

"It worries me, too," said Virginia, the mother hen. "Let me give you one good piece of advice: No matter how honorable you think his intentions are, don't let him get you alone in his apartment. Where are you meeting him this afternoon?"

I couldn't resist. "In his apartment."

"Well," she said with an exaggerated sigh, "I just hope you know what you're doing. Don't forget, as your sole confidante, which I trust I am . . ." she looked questioningly at me.

"Absolutely," I assured her. Virginia always wants an exclusive on secrets.

"That's good. It wouldn't do to have everybody and his aunt knowing about it. Anyway, as your sole confidante . . ."

"And cover," I added.

"As your sole confidante and cover, I'm carrying a grave responsibility. If anything bad ever happened, I'd feel awful."

"Don't worry, it won't," I said, getting up to leave.

"What'll I do if your mother calls?"

"Can't you go out? Then if she calls, she'll think we're both out. Which we will be. I'll tell you what: Go see that great new movie at the Sutton—*Catch as Catch Can*."

"Never heard of it."

"Go see it. By tomorrow, there'll be lines around the block. The critics . . . um—" Whoops! "—are going to love it—I feel it in my bones. And speaking of bones, wear a warm coat. It's nice out now, but it'll probably get colder." Two good deeds for Virginia.

"Right-i-o, pet," said Virginia, opening the front door for me. "And Annabel, I hope I didn't sound stuffy. I'm really very, very happy for you."

"Me, too," I said.

"By the way, what are you going to do about your boyfriend Boris?"

"Nothing. He's not my boyfriend anyway. I mean, I like him, but I don't love him," I said, crossing my fingers. It was the only lie I regretted telling.

Sunday, April 21, later

Bartholomew Bacon's brownstone was a dilapidated dump. Full of garbage and bad smells in the vestibule and peeling paint in the halls. Endless flights of sloping stairs (no elevator), and a bannister too splintery to touch. I began to have misgivings.

On the fourth floor, there were two apartments, neither of which seemed to be right, judging by the names under the doorbells. One said Krasny (Mrs. Helen), the other said Bacchante. Hm. Now what? Maybe I was on the wrong floor.

I stood around for a while, trying to screw up enough courage to ring one of the two doorbells and ask about Bacon. Then, I stood around some more, trying to figure out whose was the safer doorbell to ring. For all I knew both Krasny and Bacchante were murderers. Finally, I opted for Krasny, on the theory that a woman murderer would be easier to defend myself against, but she wasn't home. Bacchante was, though. I could hear music playing; so after offering up a silent prayer that Bacchante was also a woman, I pushed the bell and peered through the peephole. I couldn't see a thing, of course; you never can.

The music stopped, I heard footsteps come to the door, then—silence. Well, here we are, I thought giddily. Me and a potential murderer with nothing separating us but a one-inch slab of wood and two giant locks which will be unbolted any second.

I took a deep breath. "Hello?"

"Yeah," said a gruff male voice.

"Mr. Bacchante?"

"Yeah."

"I'm sorry to bother you, but could you tell me what floor Bartholomew Bacon lives on?"

"Sure thing," said a friendly, familiar voice. Were there two people there, or was it a case of Jekyll and Hyde?

After endless fumbling, clicking, turning, and twisting, the door opened a tiny crack, revealing one green eye, half a mouth, half a cute nose, and half a head of Bartholomew Bacon's carrot-red hair.

"Oh, it's you," he said, sounding relieved.

"You took the words right out of my mouth."

"Are you alone?"

"Yes. Are you?"

"Yes. Wait'll I undo the chain and the police lock."

"You were expecting me, weren't you? Why all the safety precautions?" I asked when he finally let me in.

"You never know. Can't be too careful around here; it's a rough neighborhood. But once I've got my barricade set up, it's not easy to break in here."

"It's also not easy to break out," I commented.

Bacon laughed. "That, too. Sometimes it takes me a good ten minutes to unscramble the locks. Have a seat. Sit anywhere."

It was a one-room apartment (bathtub in the kitchen type); my choice of anywhere was a chair with sprung springs or the bed. I chose the chair.

"Your voice sounded so funny at first. I thought I was in the wrong place."

"Nope. I talk like that to discourage unwelcome visitors."

"Is that why you have the wrong name under the doorbell, too?"

"That's not a wrong name. It's my name. Bartolomeo Bacchante," he said proudly. "I changed it to Bartholomew Bacon for purely professional reasons. Why did you change yours, Miss Smith?"

"I didn't," I stammered. "Ann Smith is my real name. Really."

"Okay," he said shrugging. "That's your story, you stick to it."

He reached for a pencil and pad from the desk and sat down at my feet.

"Now," he said briskly, "what's the rest of it?"

"The rest of what?"

121

"Your story. That's what you're here for, isn't it? To give me some dope on the Bleecker Street fire?" He waited expectantly, pencil poised.

"Uh . . . no, not exactly."

"No?! Then what *are* you here for? Gee whiz, you wake me up at the crack of dawn on my day off, get my hopes up about a hot lead—and I need one in the worst way—and then you haven't got anything to tell me?!" He scrambled to his feet and strode angrily to the window and back.

"I cleaned the place up for you and everything. Washed the cups, made coffee, made the bed. . . ." He glared at me. "Listen, Ann Smith. You're not Ann Smith. You're not eighteen years old. And that address you gave me is a phony, too. I checked it out."

"I thought you might. That's why I gave it to you. You struck me as being a very thorough person. I bet you're a good reporter."

"Flattery will get you nowhere. Yes, I'm a good reporter, but only when I have something to go on. At the rate I'm going now, I'll *never* get my own byline, let alone the Pulitzer Prize."

"Bart, I don't know anything more about the Bleecker Street fire than I've already told you; but I *do* know something that would make a sensational story for you. At two fifteen this afternoon, a vicious crime is going to be committed."

Bart looked nervous. "Are you involved in it?" Heavens, I hadn't thought of that!

"Oh no, not remotely." Thinking fast, I said, "I have ESP."

"Oh yeah? Prove it. Close your eyes." I did, dreading what was coming next. "I have a pack of cards in my hand. Now, I'm holding up one card. What suit is it?"

I opened my eyes. "I have a different kind of ESP. It doesn't work for cards."

"Nonsense. ESP is ESP. You've either got it or you don't. Close your eyes again. What suit am I holding up?"

I had a one-in-four chance of making it. "A spade."

"A heart. Now, I'm writing down a number between one and ten. What's the number?"

"Two?"

"Ten. You couldn't be farther away. Aah," he said disgustedly, "you don't have ESP. I wish you did. It would make a good story. Boy, do I need a good story. I haven't come up with anything decent in weeks; if I don't get something soon, they'll probably transfer me to the Women's Page—or fire me. One's almost as bad as the other. ESP my foot!"

"Then how did I know about that explosion on Bleecker Street? Because I did, you know. I had nothing to do with it whatsoever, but I was there ahead of time, waiting for it." Bacon's eyes widened in surprise. "I *knew* it was going to happen. I also *knew* the Mets were going to lose yesterday, and I know the Giants are going to win today. *And,*" I said, pausing for full dramatic effect, "I do know about something happening at two fifteen this afternoon which I'll be delighted to tell you about *if*."

"If what?"

"*If* you take me with you."

"Since you're the only one who knows where it is, I don't have much choice in the matter, do I?"

"Is your camera loaded?" He nodded. "Come on, then. If we hurry, we'll just make it."

We tumbled down the stairs, grabbed a cab, and arrived at 127th Street and Lenox at ten past two.

"I don't see anything," said Bart. "Everything looks normal."

"Wait," I said, crouching behind a mailbox. "Duck down. It'll be any minute now."

"I feel like a jerk," he complained.

"You won't in a minute. Better safe than sorry. Sh."

"I hope you're right. Hey, Ann," he whispered. "Why are you doing this for me?"

"I plan on being a journalist myself one day. I took pity on you." It was the only excuse I could think of. Besides, it was true.

"Oh."

"Get your camera ready."

"It is. But I don't know what to focus on." Neither did I. Boris hadn't given me any details.

Then I saw a couple of thuggy-looking guys sidle up to a drugstore, nod furtively to each other, and walk in.

124

"Over there," I pointed. "That must be it."

That was it all right. Bullets, screams, police cars, ambulance sirens—it was a crime reporter's dream and Bart caught it all—including a good clear shot of the escaping robber and several close-ups of the dead robber in the doorway. According to Boris, though, there were two dead and one wounded. Where were the others?

"Bart, see that cop sitting down, leaning against the side of the building—do you think he's hurt?"

"Cops don't usually lounge around in the middle of a gunfight. I suppose he must be."

"Why don't you ask him?"

"I'm going to. Maybe he'll give me an interview." We walked over to the cop.

"Hey, buddy, are you hurt?"

"Just a leg wound. Nothing serious." Two down and one to go.

"I'm from the *Daily News*. Feel like telling me what happened?"

"Nothing much to tell. Fairly routine stuff. Two junkies ripping off a drugstore."

I muttered to Bart, "Ask him if somebody else besides the junkie got killed."

"Why?"

"Because my ESP tells me there are two dead and one wounded. The body count doesn't add up right, yet."

"Whew," whistled Bart. "You're a regular ghoul, aren't you."

"I'm a budding professional. *Ask* him."

"Hey, buddy, were there any other casualties?"

"Yeah. The owner of the drugstore got shot." Three down and none to go.

The cop got to his feet and limped off to a nearby squad car. Obviously, he was only the wounded one.

Just then, two ambulance attendants came out of the drugstore carrying a man on a stretcher. A woman, his wife, I guess, was hurrying along beside them, sobbing.

"Take it easy, lady," said one of the attendants. "Your husband's going to be fine. He's got good blood pressure, he's fully conscious—see? He wants to say something to you."

They stopped walking to let her hear. "Belle? Don't worry, Belle. I'm going to make it."

"Is he?" she asked tearfully. "Is he really?"

"There's no reason why not," said the attendant. "The bullet just nicked him a little is all. They'll patch him up in the emergency room and he'll be home tonight, for sure."

Suddenly, it hit me how horrible it all was.

"They shouldn't *tell* her that!" I said fiercely, fighting back my own tears. "They shouldn't get her hopes up—it'll only make it harder."

"Annie, Annie, hang on there," Bart said. "The guy looked pretty healthy to me. Look at his wife *now*. Full of smiles. If she believes the men, why shouldn't you?"

"Because I *know:* two dead and one wounded. *I know!*"

"Maybe your ESP is wrong this time."

"It's not. I tell you it's not!" I shrieked at him. "That poor lady. She thinks everything's terrific; but she's going to get a phone call in the middle of the night and there won't be anybody with her to comfort her or keep her company. You've got to *do* something! I did something for you, now you do something for me!"

"I'll do anything you want if you'll just stop screaming," he said anxiously. "What do you want me to do?"

"I want you to go find someone to stay with that poor old lady."

"Right," he said obediently, and disappeared into the crowd.

"All done," he said when he returned.

He took my arm. "Annie, you may not want to give me your correct name or age, but you're going to have to give me your address because I'm taking you home, right now."

He hailed a cab and got in with me.

"One Fifteen Central Park West," I said sniffling.

He handed me his handkerchief. "You know, you're not a ghoul at all. You're a marshmallow. Soft and sweet." I eked out a feeble smile.

As the cab pulled up in front of my building, he said, "I guess it was pretty rough on you, but I'm awfully

127

grateful for this story. If you get any other flashes of ESP will you call me?"

"Sure. But I'm not coming with you to any more murders."

"I think that's a wise decision."

" 'Bye, Bart."

" 'Bye, Annie."

Monday, April 22

The next morning, before I left for school, I beeped
Boris.

"Well, at last," he grumbled. "Where *were* you all
afternoon?"

"Out. Out with Virginia. Where were you all evening?"

"Out with Virginia."

"You're kidding," I gasped.

"I called her to ask if she knew where you were; she
said you'd been by earlier but you'd left. I've always
thought she was snooty, but she was very friendly on
the phone, so I invited her to the movies. Or maybe she
invited me—I can't remember exactly who asked who."

Son of a gun! Talk about not letting the grass grow
under your feet!

"I hope you had a nice time," I said frostily.

Boris was casual. "It was okay. After spending most
of the day working over figures, it was at least a welcome diversion.

"Listen—I have two big things to report: First of all,

I found out which channel shows the racing results: Channel 5 on the ten P.M. news. Secondly, there's a sensational new development. Sascha is leaving for California on the eight o'clock plane tonight. She'll be gone a couple of weeks and maybe more. While she's away, I can get a great head start on the apartment—throw out all the old stuff, buy some new stuff, get the place painted. Which reminds me, do you know the name of a good painter?"

"No, but my mother keeps a list of people like that. I'll look it up for you. Boris, how are you going to pay for all this? You don't have any money yet."

"No problem. I told Sascha I needed some clothes and got her to give me all her credit cards plus a letter saying I have permission to charge. (Out of all those cards, her credit ought to be still good on one or two of them.) By the time the bills come in, I'll have made enough from OTB to pay them."

"Hmm," I said. "I hope you're right. Sounds risky to me."

"Don't be such a worrywart, Annabel. I'm very optimistic—in fact, I'm raring to go. Can you look up the name of the painter for me now?"

"I'll be late for school. How about this afternoon?"

"That'll do, I guess. Try me around five; before that, I'll be out. I'm going to take the money I won Saturday to the main office of the telephone company to get our phone out of hock which will probably take me the rest of the afternoon. And then tomorrow I'll go over to the OTB on 72nd and Broadway and bet whatever's left on whoever's going to win."

"Lotsa luck."

"Who needs luck?" he said gleefully. "Luck doesn't even enter into it. Roger, over, and out."

I collected my books and went to say good-bye to my parents. They were reading the *Times,* and Ape Face was sprawled on the floor, poring over "Dick Tracy."

"Hey, Ape Face, can I look at the *News* for a minute?"

"When I've finished the comics."

"That'll take all morning," I said, snatching it away from him. He howled in protest and Ma said, "Annabel, that's extremely rude. Give it right back to him."

"In a minute," I said, staring at the front page which had an electrifyingly graphic picture of the dead robber and a brief account of the holdup. Continued on page 5.

"Annabel, I said give it *back* to him! Now!"

"Wait, wait! I just want to see one quick thing."

I turned to page 5 and hastily scanned the article. The second-to-last paragraph told me what I didn't want to know—but knew already: "Harry Steinberg, owner of the drugstore, died of a heart attack on the way to the hospital. His wife, Belle . . ."

"Here, *take* your stupid paper!" I said, flinging it at Ape Face.

"Somebody got out on the wrong side of the bed this morning," Dad said archly.

"That's an original statement if ever I heard one. Ape Face, are you coming? Because I'm leaving."

As we went out the door, I heard Dad say, "What's her problem?"

"She's just a typical adolescent," sighed my mother. (They always blame *everything* on that; it makes me sick!)

"Buenos Días," said Hector.

"Morning." I jabbed Ape Face in the ribs. "Where's your manners? Say good morning." Ape Face obliged.

"The señorita is angry today?"

"At me," said Ape Face.

"Pobrecito." Hector clucked sympathetically.

"Hector, talk English, will you?"

"Pobrecito means poor little kid."

"I already know that, thank you."

"Just trying to be helpful," he said, opening the elevator door. Ape Face scampered down the hall.

"Well, you're not," I retorted. Hector closed the door in my face.

By the time I'd arrived at school, I was in a thoroughly foul temper: mad at the world because of Harry Steinberg, mad at Ape Face because I'd been mean to him, and mad at Hector because he'd *seen* me be mean to him; and as for my adorable friend, Virginia, mad wasn't the word. Kill was more like it. I

132

made a firm resolution not to talk to her unless I absolutely had to.

On the way home, I absolutely had to; there was no way to avoid it—we were on the same crosstown bus. She plunked herself down next to me and said, "Is anything wrong?"

I gazed out the window. "No, not at all."

"You've been avoiding me all day. You didn't even sit next to me in algebra." (I always sit next to her in algebra—she feeds me the answers. Today, I'd let her archenemy, Francine, feed me the answers.)

I shrugged. "Francine asked me first."

Virginia made another attempt. "How was your date?"

"Wonderful, thank you." I looked at her accusingly. "How was yours?"

The soul of innocence, she said, "Annabel, I'm thunderstruck! Is that why you're mad at me—because I went out with Boris? Why should you be mad at that?"

"Because you're my best friend—supposedly."

"But you're in love with another man! You spent an hour telling me how divine he was. And you also told me very specifically that Boris was not your boyfriend. How can you possibly object to my going out with him? Really, ducks, you're a dog in the manger."

"And you're an ambulance chaser! The body was

133

hardly cold in the grave before you couldn't wait to snatch it."

"That's unfair. Besides, I didn't call him—he called me."

"He called you to find out where *I* was," I pointed out.

"And where *were* you? Out with another man. Annabel, you're not being logical." She had me there.

"Maybe not," I admitted.

"If it's any comfort to you, Boris isn't even my type. I mean, he's very good-looking and all that—but he's too serious. Also, he's stingy; he made me pay for my own movie. So let's not talk about it anymore. Let's talk about something fun: How *was* your date?"

I was feeling better; it was time to let her off the hook. I rolled my eyes. "My date was super."

"Why don't you come home with me? There's chocolate cake. We can eat and you can tell me all about what's-his-name. Incidentally, what *is* his name?" That's what I need! I thought. Next thing I know, she'll be going out with him, too.

"What's-his-name will do nicely."

"You don't trust me?" she asked in an injured tone.

"Only as far as I can throw you," I said good-naturedly. "Listen, Virginia, I'd love to come home with you, but I have an errand to do." Which I did—look up the painter for Boris. "Here's my stop. I've got to get off." I decided to throw her a bone. "By the way, do you get the *Daily News?*"

"Yes."

"Read this morning's front-page story; what's-his-name wrote it and took all the pictures."

"How fabulous!" she exclaimed.

I blew her a kiss and jumped off the bus.

Boris didn't answer my beep at a quarter to five, or at five, or even at five fifteen. I hoped nothing had gone wrong with his plans. At five thirty, I wrote the painter's name and number down on a piece of paper and rang the elevator bell.

Patrick Sullivan, a big, fat, jolly guy, was on duty.

"Would you please deliver this envelope to Morris Harris?"

"I'll take it, Pat."

I nearly fainted dead away: Out from behind fat Pat stepped none other than Sascha Biegelman.

"Hello!" she said cordially. "Nice to see you again."

I was speechless.

"You are Annabel, aren't you? I'm—"

"I know," I said, bug-eyed with horror. "I know who you are—now."

"Well, do come in. I mean, come up. Come up and we'll have a drink. A Coke for you, a drink for me, 'Can't you see how happy we will be,' " she concluded musically.

I hesitated. Fat Pat was worried. "Will it be in or out, Miss? I have a call on ten."

"In," said Sascha decisively. I stepped in.

" 'Tea for two and two for tea,' " she sang on our way up in the elevator. "I forgot my key, do-dee," she sang in the elevator hall. "But the door's open anyway, unless Morris locked it when he left. Oh goody, he didn't."

I followed her into the apartment. She peered in the ice bucket. "Oh dear. No ice. It doesn't matter to me—I don't really want a drink; but I can get some out if you care. Do you?"

Wordlessly, I shook my head.

"Here you are, then," she said, handing me a warm can. "Come on in the bedroom and keep me company while I pack. I'm going to L.A. tonight—did Morris tell you?"

I nodded yes.

"You're a veritable Chatty Cathy today. Why so shy, all of a sudden?" She smiled at me encouragingly.

"Listen, Mrs. uh . . ." Harris? Biegelman? *Ms.* Biegelman?

"Sascha."

"I owe you an apology."

"Do you? What for?"

"You know what for. For thinking you were the maid."

She laughed. "A perfectly natural error. I was

dressed like one." That's right, she was. No wonder I was confused. If she'd been dressed like a mother, I would have known.

"It was very embarrassing. In fact, it still is. Why did you do it?"

"If you're going to scrub kitchen floors and go foraging under sofas for pistachio nuts, a nylon uniform is the most practical thing to wear. Besides, I'm a writer; writers need to know how other people live. So, when the maid didn't show up, I thought: What the hell, *I'll* be the maid and see what that feels like—maybe I'll learn something."

"Did you?"

"Yes. It's boring. It's the most unengrossing work in the world. But, as you said yourself, a job's a job; there's nothing demeaning about it. Didn't you say that?"

"Yes. Plus a whole lot of other things I wish I hadn't said. All those things about Boris." I gave an involuntary shudder. "I want to apologize for them, too."

Sascha began heaving clothes onto the bed. "Look, Annabel, you don't owe me any apologies. It was dirty pool—what I did to you. But by the time I realized, the joke had gone too far, I didn't know how to stop it without making you feel worse. Furthermore, there was nothing you said about Boris, I mean Morris—" She laughed. "Now you've got me doing it. Actually, why not? I think I like the name Boris. It has a nice

137

Russian sound to it. . . . Well, to continue, there was nothing you said about Boris I didn't already know. I know he can't stand me," she tossed a bunch of underwear and an armload of dresses and pants into a suitcase.

"I think that's overstating it a bit," I said judiciously.

"Well, his feelings are at best ambivalent, wouldn't you agree?" Next into the suitcase sailed a hair dryer, a cosmetics bag, two pairs of boots, and several pairs of shoes.

"I guess so," I conceded.

"He's ashamed of me, isn't he?" she said, jamming the suitcase closed. It was not a question I particularly wanted to answer.

"Aren't your dresses going to be all crunched up when you unpack at the other end?"

"They were all crunched up before I ever took them out of the closet," she said with a grin. "I imagine it's the kind of thing that makes Boris ashamed. But that's the way I am. Crazed! I just can't help myself." She threw her hands up in mock despair.

"So—I'm off to Lotus Land. Take care of Boris for me, not that he needs it. As a matter of fact, what he probably needs more than anything is a vacation from me. I hope he takes advantage of it—throws a few wild parties, invites all his friends over, has a swinging time. It'd be good for him."

"Boy," I said enviously, "I wish my mother had a little more of your attitude. It's funny: Boris is mad about *my* mother and I'm—" Suddenly I felt too self-conscious to say it. "—delighted we had a chance to talk," I finished lamely.

Sascha had a sort of disappointed look on her face. But taking her cue from me, she said politely, "I've enjoyed it, too, Annabel."

We shook hands, and then she picked up her suitcase and we walked to the front door.

I don't know what made me ask it—it must have been a premonition; but I said, "Do you have your ticket?"

"Oh my God, my ticket! I almost forgot." She rummaged through her purse. "I *did* forget. It's not in here and I've forgotten where I've put it. What did I do with it, where *is* it?!"

"Where did you see it last?" My mother always asks me that; sometimes it works.

"I can't remember ever seeing it. But I know I had a reservation."

"Then maybe it's at the reservation desk at the airport."

"Ai, of course! That's exactly where it is." She gave me a huge hug of gratitude.

"You know something, Sascha? You're *much* nicer than the maid said you were. That maid was a lousy judge of character."

She smiled at me wistfully. "I hope you're a better one."

Tuesday, April 23–Friday, April 26

Boris said the OTB place on 72nd Street was full of unshaven old bummy-looking men with racing sheets, unshaven middle-aged bummy-looking men with racing sheets, drunks, blacks, whites, Puerto Ricans—everybody poor and everybody standing around not talking to each other and looking as though they had no better place to be—even after they'd lost their last two dollars and had no more money to bet.

He said it was like a meeting place for the dregs of humanity—a club for creeps. They were so creepy-crawly he was afraid to ask any of them how to fill out the slip; so, in desperation, he finally asked the man at the window.

"I want to bet on Pace-o-Rama in the ninth at Roosevelt. How do I go about it?"

The man said, "How old are you, sonny?" and when Boris said nineteen, the man said, "Whaddya givin' me?" and threw him out.

He had to go to seven other OTBs before he found

one that was too busy to notice his voice hadn't
changed completely yet (or else they didn't care),
and then guess where *that* was? The Port Authority
Bus Terminal at 41st and Ninth. Hardly a convenient
location. Boris was furious. Even though he came
home with over a hundred dollars in his pocket, he was
still furious when he got there.

"It's sickening! If I have to go to the Port Authority
every day, I won't have time to do anything else.
Tomorrow, I want *you* to go to the 72nd Street OTB
and see if you make out any better."

"*Me?*" I squawked. "Why should I make out any
better?"

"Because your voice won't give you away. Get
dressed in your mother's clothes and go."

"Boris, I can't! I'd be terrified, don't ask me."

"I *am* asking you. That's all there is to it. Roger, over,
and out."

Wednesday, April 24

So the next day, after I came home from school, I
put on panty hose, my mother's black shoes with me-
dium heels, a black silk dress of hers with a black cash-
mere sweater with mink on the collar, and lipstick,
powder, rouge, eye shadow, and mascara.

On the way over to Broadway, three men tried to
pick me up. When I went to the window to place my

bet (Bite the Bullet in the ninth at Belmont), the man said, "Scram, sweetheart. G'wan home and play with your dollies." So I went straight to the Port Authority—where five more men tried to pick me up and one nice man showed me how to fill out the slip—and came back with over a hundred dollars in my mother's pocket-book. I was furious, too—at Boris.

"That's enough of that! From now on, you do the betting, I'll do something else. Roger, over, and—"

"How're you going to do something else if you won't even wait for me to tell you what to do?"

"I've got to get out of these clothes before my mother comes home from Columbia. Just give me my assignment and make it snappy."

"I can't think that fast."

"Then beep me later. Beep me after the evening news and tell me what's going on tomorrow besides horses which I'm tired of the subject of Roger, over, and out."

It turned out what he wanted me to do was meet the painter at his apartment the next day at five—he'd probably still be at the Port Authority but would get back as soon as he could. I should tell the painter to do whatever he thought necessary, regardless of cost, but he was to start immediately.

As far as news was concerned, there was going to be a strike at the Hunt's Point vegetable market; a gang of hoods would swipe a blind man's Seeing-Eye dog practically on the doorstep of the Lighthouse on 59th Street; the police would apprehend the alleged murderer in the Lenox Avenue holdup, thanks to the quick thinking of a young *Daily News* reporter, Bartholomew Bacon; the weather would be . . .

I told Boris to never mind the weather, clicked off, and called Bart.

"Hi-ya, Annie. How's my marshmallow?"

I giggled. "How's my Pulitzer Prize winner? Your story was terrific. Was the paper pleased?"

"Out of their skulls. So were the cops; because of my photo, they think they've got a lead on the guy who escaped."

"They'll get him within the next twenty-four hours."

"How do you know?"

"The same way I knew about Harry Steinberg, poor guy. Poor Belle. Anyway, if you don't believe me, watch Chris Borgen tomorrow night on CBS. There's a nice surprise in store for you—you're going to be a hero."

"No! Am I really?" He was delighted.

"Yes, really. Listen, Bart—do you want a human interest story? Hang around the Lighthouse on 59th, tomorrow—someone's going to swipe a blind man's Seeing-Eye dog. Can you use it?"

"Sure can. Does your ESP tell you when, though? Maybe I could get there in time to prevent it."

"But then you wouldn't get your story."

"The heck with that. I'd rather save the guy's dog."

"That's generous and nice of you, Bart—but take it from me, you wouldn't be able to. The dog's already been stolen. I mean it's definitely going to be, although I don't know exactly when."

"I think I'll give it a whirl anyway. Want to come along?"

I was sorely tempted—but business before pleasure. I had to see the painter. Maybe another time, I told him, and said good-bye.

Thursday, April 25

Julio María López, a tall, sad-eyed man with a face like a bloodhound, showed up on the dot of five. He lugubriously surveyed his immediate surroundings (hall, living room, and dining room), and pronounced them in very poor shape indeed.

"Very poor shape. Bad, terrible. How long since the last paint job? Don't tell me, I'll tell you." He picked off a piece of cracking paint by the front door, crumbled it in his fingers, and blew the dust out of his hand.

"Must be twenty years. Fifteen, anyway. Look at this here." He punched a bulging bubble of wall over the sideboard in the dining room and gloated with professional pride as three feet of dirty delft blue

144

dropped to the floor. He patted the plaster underneath.

"Damp. Must've been you had a leak. Is the rest of the residence in the same condition?"

I showed him around. In each room, he pointed out something awful and made it worse—like the den, where he ripped off a whole strip of wallpaper to prove how many layers were underneath (five), and then ripped them all off, too. I decided he either knew the job was his or he was making sure it would be.

"Well, what do you think?" I asked after we'd completed the grand tour. "I mean, how much is it going to cost?"

He took out a pad and pencil and began estimating.

"Let's see what we got here: Nine rooms, fifteen closets, four baths, seven or eight walls in need of canvassing—if you don't canvas, your paint'll peel again in six months on account of your damp—seventeen window frames in need of burning and scraping. . . . I'd say, give or take a little, four ought to cover it."

"Four coats of paint? That much?"

"Four thousand dollars."

"I *thought* four coats of paint sounded like a lot—" Then it hit me. "FOUR THOUSAND DOLLARS! That's highway robbery!"

The painter didn't bat an eye. "It'll take three men a minimum of five days at union scale, and don't forget two coats of paint throughout. At today's prices, a good

145

job like I'm going to do comes to five hundred bucks a room."

"How about skipping the closets?"

He didn't think much of that idea. "A saving of two hundred, merely. For the sake of two hundred you want to settle for dirty closets?"

I thought it was staggering, but Boris said regardless of cost. . . . So I told him to include the closets and start tomorrow. He said his men were on another job but he'd be there Monday with "three men 'n drop cloths." Then, he wanted to know what colors did I have in mind. White. All white, I told him. It seems there are a million shades of white: ivory white, cream white, white with a couple drops red, or with a couple drops brown—which did I want? *White* white, I told him. "Dead white? Okay, you're the boss. The usual finish—high gloss in the kitchen, semi on the woodwork, flat for the walls?" I told him high gloss all over—I liked things shiny. He said he'd give me anything I wanted—*he* didn't have to live there. Neither do I, I thought; and if Boris doesn't like my taste, he shouldn't have handed me the job in the first place.

Boris came home shortly after the painter had left, and I filled him in on the arrangements. He said he didn't care what color the place was, white, black, or burnt sienna, just as long as it got painted. The four-thousand-dollar tab didn't bother him either; he'd just won over four hundred on something called an Exacta and was giddy with power.

"When do they start?" was all he wanted to know.

"Jules said he and three men in drop cloths would come at eight on Monday. What's drop cloths—a new kind of coverall?"

"No, dummy. Drop cloths are what you drop over the furniture to protect it." He gazed at the living room in disgust. "Not that there's anything worth protecting. You know what we ought to do, Annabel? Get rid of the furniture before the painters start."

"All of it? That's a bit rash, don't you think?"

"Well, maybe not all of it, but a lot of it. It'll make the painters' work much easier. So you go downstairs now, and call the Salvation Army. Tell them to come tomorrow and to expect a full truckload. I'll stay here and tag what I want to throw out."

After a busy half hour on the phone I beeped Boris.

"What is it? I'm in the middle of the news, waiting for the sports to come on."

"The Salvation Army won't pick up 'til next week sometime. Goodwill Industries will pick up tomorrow but they've only got room for half a truckload. I called the super and asked if people were allowed to dump furniture on the street; he said you have to arrange it ahead with the Sanitation Department—sometimes weeks in advance and only on a pickup day, which tomorrow isn't. So what I want to know is this: Our housekeeper, Mattie, says her Granddaddy Clovis, who's deaf as a post and lives in a swamp in Georgia, just got burned out of his house. Is it all right if I give some of the stuff to her? Her brother could come for it tomorrow."

"I don't care what you do with it; just get it out of here before the weekend," he said impatiently. "It's your responsibility; you handle it."

"It's not my responsibility, it's your responsibility which you've bossily ordered me to assume. What am I getting out of this anyway? So far, it's been nothing but trouble and boring chores. When am I going to have some fun?"

"Saturday I'll take you shopping at Lord and Taylor. They're having a sale. We'll buy rugs, chairs, couches, lamps, and I'll let you buy a whole new wardrobe for Sascha, how's that?"

"That's more like it," I said, thinking of Sascha's closet full of crunched-up junk. I'd do anything for Sascha.

"Annabel, I know I've been bossy; but I'm so anxious to get it all together before my mother comes back, and there's so much to do."

One kind word and I melt like butter. "That's okay, Boris, I understand. It's just that we agreed that I'd help you use the Box to help your mother if you'd help *me* to use the Box to help other people. But lately, you haven't been keeping your end of the bargain."

"You're right," he admitted. "I've been so intent on the racing results, I haven't been on the lookout for your angle. But I will. I'll get on to something tomorrow, I promise."

Friday, April 26

At seven A.M. he called me. He was onto something.

"It's not much," he said apologetically, "but maybe it'll appeal to you. It's close by, too. There's a concert at the Mall this afternoon, and a little three-year-old kid called Gaylord gets separated from its mother. The mother finally shows up—that's the part I saw—but you might want to cruise the area and see if you can help the cops entertain the kid 'til the mother arrives."

"Boris, you're a prince. I'll try to be back in time for Operation Furniture Disposal."

"If you're not, don't worry. I'll manage."

Good old dependable Boris! When he says he'll be onto something, he's onto something.

Virginia was also onto something: What's-his-name's name! She'd heard it on the news and asked me at lunch if he was related to the Boston Bacons. I told her he was related to the Pittsburgh Bacons (who were distantly related to the Boston Bacons), and to please shut up before everybody at our table heard her.

So was my mother onto something: When I got home from school, she said Ape Face had been acting peculiarly lately. He spent most of his time in his room, listening to "Yellow Submarine."

"Sounds to me like he needs fresh air and exercise. Shall I take him to the park?" Mom thought that was a splendid suggestion.

On the way there, I told him to start playing some other record or he'd get caught with the Sony. He thanked me gratefully, and then asked if he could go to Boris's tomorrow to watch *The Phantom of the Opera* because on Sunday he had to go to a birthday party and would miss it. I told him sorry, but Boris and I were going to be out all day.

It wasn't a concert at the Mall; it was a concert at the Maul. People were pushing and shoving all over the lot; I didn't see how I was going to find one small kid in that mess. Actually, it was Ape Face who spotted him. He was sitting on the edge of the bandshell stage with his little overalled legs dangling down, and he was crying. A cop was hovering over him. I sat down next to him and said, "Aw, what's the matter? Lost your mommy, I'll bet."

"I didn't lose her; she lost me," he sobbed.

The cop turned to me in exasperation. "That's the only thing he's said for the last half hour—'I didn't lose her; she lost me.' I can't find out his name or his age or anything."

"He looks about three to me," I said. "Are you three?"

Gaylord stopped crying, nodded yes, and started crying again.

"You're doing better than I did," said the cop. "See what else you can find out."

"I know something," said Ape Face. "It's not a he, it's a she." A girl called Gaylord?

150

"You couldn't be more wrong," I said. "What makes you think so?"

"Short hair," said Ape Face. "A boy wouldn't have hair that short. Besides, it looks like a she." Gently, he prodded Gaylord's upper arm. "And it feels like a she. No muscles. It's a she."

"Okay, smarty, I'll ask. Are you a he or a she?"

"Yes," sobbed Gaylord.

"Maybe it doesn't know what it is," said the cop. At that, Gaylord stopped crying immediately.

"I do so. I'm a she."

"You're going great guns," said the cop admiringly. "See if you can find out her name."

It was an interesting challenge. I couldn't very well tell the cop I knew her name was Gaylord. Anyway, was it Somebody Gaylord, or Gaylord Somebody?

"What's your name?" I asked.

"My mommy lost me," said Gaylord.

"Crumb, we're back to that again," moaned the cop.

Wait a minute! Maybe her name was Gail Ord.

"I bet I can *guess* your name," I said to her. "Just tell me what letter it begins with."

"She's too little to know that," said Ape Face.

"Your kid brother's a live one, isn't he," said the cop. "Why don't you let him do the guessing?"

"Joan," said Ape Face.

"Betsy," I said. I didn't want to guess it too quickly.

"Ellen," said Ape Face.

"Debbie."

"Sidney."

"Sidney! That's a boy's name," I said scornfully. Chalk one up for me.

"There's a girl in my class called Sidney."

"Grace," I said, ignoring him.

"Barbara," said Ape Face.

I was getting bored. "Gail!" I said triumphantly. "It's Gail, isn't it?" I studied her face for confirmation. There was none, although she did look a little puzzled.

"Something *like* Gail?" I asked. She nodded happily. Gailord, Gaylord—ah-ha!

"Gay!" I said.

"Gay," she acknowledged, and jumped into my lap.

"Hurray," said the cop.

"Shoot," said Ape Face. "I wanted to be the guesser."

"Can't win 'em all, Junior," said the cop.

"Gay's mommy lost Gay," said Gay, snuggling up to me.

"But Gay's mommy is going to *find* Gay very soon, now. I have magic powers and I just know that."

"I wish I could say the same," grumbled the cop. "Else I got to drag her to the station house and stuff her with lollipops all afternoon."

"Mmn," said Gay. "Good."

There was a beep from the cop's walkie-talkie. "Officer Plonchik," he responded.

"Walt," squawked a voice, "This is Merve. I'm down

152

by Bethesda Fountain. Walt, we got a lady here by the name of Lord who says she's lost her little girl."

"See, Gay. I told you I had magic powers. They found your mommy. Isn't that nice?"

Gay burst into tears.

"Jesus, Mary, and Joseph, *now* what's wrong?" said the cop.

"I don't want my mommy. I want lollipops."

"Can't win 'em all, Officer. Come on, Ape Face, let's get going."

I was back in time for the tail end of Operation Furniture Disposal. Apparently, between Mattie's brother and Goodwill Industries, it had been going quite smoothly, on the whole. I witnessed only one hairy moment—when one of the Goodwill men pointed to the Box and said to Boris, "You want we should take this also?"

"Don't you TOUCH that!" he said, screaming like a banshee.

They must have thought he was nuts.

Saturday, April 27

Lord and Taylor was a trip and a half! Between ten thirty and one, under the solicitous guidance of a Mr. Hemphill, Boris bought: three rugs, two sofas, one love seat, one coffee table, one dining-room table, ten feet of sectional bookcases, six lamps, a digital clock, and an enormous desk for Sascha's workroom; all of it modern, and—as the conscientious Mr. Hemphill felt obliged to remind us—all of it on sale.

"You're quite sure about this merchandise, are you? Because it's nonreturnable, you know."

"Perfectly all right with me," said Boris, his eyes glistening with enthusiasm. "There's nothing I like more than a good bargain."

Mr. Hemphill wrote up the order and promised delivery within five days, which he said was only possible because the items we had purchased were floor samples and the department store wanted to clear out the old inventory to make way for the new. Boris couldn't have cared less what the reason was, as long as he got the stuff before Sascha came home.

"Now, it's your turn," he said amiably. "Let's see what's on sale in the way of clothes. You're about the same size as Sascha; you can even try everything on, if you like."

"What I'd like is lunch," I protested. "I'm too weak to stand up."

Boris fished a lint-covered Life Saver out of his pocket. "Here, eat this. It's quick sugar. If I'm going to get to OTB, we won't have time for lunch."

So from one 'til four, under the solicitous guidance of a Miss Fickett, I bought: two coats, six dresses, five pairs of slacks, one "very lovely gown, ideal for entertaining in the home," and one mink jacket, marked down from seventy-five hundred to a mere two thousand. It was too good to be true!

"What's wrong with it?" I asked suspiciously.

"Not a thing," said Miss Fickett. "It's a superb wrap and a wonderful bargain." So we bought that, too.

Somewhere in the dim recesses of my brain lurks the memory of my father gently chiding my mother for spending two hundred dollars at a January white sale. "A bargain is no bargain if you can't afford it in the first place" is what he said. He said a mouthful.

That night, when Boris and I added up what we'd blown at Lord and Taylor, it came to a grand total of eighty-three hundred and some odd dollars.

"Goodness," said Boris mildly. "That's quite a tab, isn't it?" The tone of his voice was calm enough, but he

155

gave himself away by twiddling a pencil between his upper and lower teeth. He never clickety-clicks like that unless there's something heavy on his mind.

"Quite a tab is right. It's absolutely horrendous. Between eighty-five hundred today and four thousand to the painter, you're in hock for over twelve thousand."

"I can add," he said.

"How much money have you made so far?"

"About two thousand. So I'm actually only in hock for ten, not twelve. And I would have had almost six hundred more—but I couldn't get to OTB yesterday because I had to stay home and supervise the furniture disposal. I'd been counting on you to do that, but I knew how much your good deed meant to you." That's what I call zinging it in. "I hope it was worth it," he added.

On the theory that he'd only feel worse if I told him he'd sacrificed almost six hundred dollars for the sake of Gay Lord and her lollipops, I decided to dress the story up a little.

"Wow, was it worth it! When I found that kid, she was crying so hysterically, she was on the verge of convulsions. I left her wreathed in smiles."

"You feel good, huh?" I felt rotten.

"Oh yes. It was a heartwarming experience."

He sighed. "Then it was worth it." I felt rottener.

"Boris, don't you think maybe you should call off the painter?"

"What—and have Sascha come home to brand-new furniture in the old slum surroundings, with musty old closets full of brand-new clothes? That'd be about as effective as I don't know what—hanging a silk purse on a sow's ear." He blinked at himself. "Well anyway, you know what I mean.

"No," he said, "I'll go ahead with the painter. If she doesn't come back too soon, I think I can make it. But from now on, I can't afford to miss a day of OTB."

"You also can't afford to spend another dime until you've made ten thousand dollars."

Clickety-click.

"Now what are you thinking?" I asked.

"About the new washer, dryer, stove, fridge, and dishwasher."

"Forget it. They'll have to wait."

"That's just it. They can't."

"Boris, you've gone around the bend! Why can't they?"

Sheepishly, he said, "Because yesterday, I gave the old ones to Mattie's brother. By now, they're on their way to Granddaddy Clovis's Georgia swamp."

"Dear God in heaven! You mean there's nothing in the kitchen but one-two-three-four-*five gaping holes*? Aside from everything else, how do you expect to live? What are you going to wear? What are you going to eat?"

"Life Savers, tuna fish, dried apricots. I'll manage. It's only 'til Monday."

"Monday." I stared stupidly at him.

"Monday the new stuff is coming. I bought it early this morning from a discount store on Broadway—for fifteen hundred."

"On sale, I suppose."

"Of course, on sale. It's not as though I'd want to return it—it's indispensable equipment. The five gaping holes, as you so picturesquely described them, have to be filled up with something."

"Boris, it's nitty-gritty time. How are you going to get that money before your mother comes back, and when *is* she coming back?"

"Well, let's see. She left Monday the 22nd, and said she'd be gone two weeks. Which would mean she'd be back on—uh . . . thirty days hath September, April, June, and November—she'd be back on Monday, May 6th. Except she's never yet been back when she's said she would—she's always at least a week late. So assuming she follows her usual pattern, that would give me—today's the 27th—that would give me twelve working days at just under six hundred a day which comes to—"

"Only just under seventy-two hundred dollars."

"Congratulations on learning your twelves tables."

"Don't change the subject, Boris. Seventy-two hundred dollars is not enough. What are you going to do?"

After an interminable period of clicking, his face lit up.

"There *is* something I can do. I can't win more than six hundred a day in any one *place*; but what's to stop me from going to two places a day? I could go to . . ." He snapped his fingers impatiently. "Think of another big OTB parlor where they won't notice my age."

"Penn Station? Grand Central?"

"Penn Station! Perfect! It's almost around the corner from the Port Authority. Don't worry about a thing— I've got it made! A billion for Boris coming right up!"

From that point on, things really began to move. In fact, the events were so numerous and happened so much on top of each other, I can hardly keep them straight. But I'll try.

Sunday, April 28–Thursday, May 2

Boris beeped me early; he was onto something for me: Bob Dylan was going to make a surprise appearance this afternoon in Sheep Meadow. Did I know somebody who could benefit from that advance information? "Can't you?" I asked him. He said he had to spend the day putting away knickknacky ornaments before the painters came on Monday.

So I called Bart (maybe he could get an exclusive interview); and I called my friend Leslie, who adores Bob Dylan, and gave her a strong hint. (P.S. The next day in school, she told me all about it. Bob Dylan had been wonderful, but her purse got ripped off. So much for *that* good deed.)

Boris won fifty dollars betting on a ball game with Harvey Kuchel. I was very angry with him and told him he was a rat fink. He agreed—said it was just that he couldn't bear to have a day go by without earning something—and promised never to do it again. At least he was honest with me.

Monday, April 29

Boris beeped me before breakfast with a list of murder, arson, rape, and robbery as long as your arm. (Good for Bart, but a little too gory for my taste.) And a spectacular item for me: Loretta Burke, daughter of Mr. and Mrs. John Burke of Manhattan, thought to have been abducted from her dormitory room at C. W. Post College over six months ago and presumed dead, turned up safe and sound in Burlington, Vermont with her boyfriend. According to the Burlington chief of police, it was a case of "*se*duction not *ab*duction." Very droll fellows, those Vermonters.

I called Bart before I left for school, gave him my ESP predictions for the day and learned, much to his gratification and mine, that his interview with Dylan would appear in next Sunday's magazine section, *with by-line*.

And when I got home from school, I called the Burkes. Do you know how many John Burkes there are in the Manhattan phone book? Eighteen. ("Hello, are you the Burkes with the missing daughter? No? Sorry, wrong Burkes, good-bye.")

When I finally located the right ones, and convinced them of the joyful news about Loretta in Vermont, Mrs. Burke said, "You better be wrong. Because if she did a thing like that to us, I don't ever want to see her again, do you, John?" And Mr. Burke said, "If she did a thing like that to us, I'd better never see her again because if I do, I'll wring her neck with my bare hands."

"Oh dear," I said, and hung up.

The only good deed I could have salvaged out of that situation would have been to find Loretta and warn her to stay in Vermont. Unfortunately, I didn't know how to do that.

Boris reported in, late that night.

"Boris the Billionaire speaking. My two-a-day plan worked brilliantly. I won eleven hundred and fifty-three dollars and twenty-four cents. How did you make out?"

"Only so-so. Listen, I can't talk. I'm in the middle of studying. We're having a monster bio quiz tomorrow."

"Don't bother. Save yourself the trouble. There's going to be a wildcat strike of school-building maintenance men; the schools'll all be closed. See? I did a good deed for *you* for a change."

"Super! What else is new?"

"The kitchen equipment is all in; and the painters have absolutely gutted the apartment. It looks like Pompeii. I hope they get through with this preparatory stage soon; I'm choking to death in the plaster."

"Poor Boris." I clucked sympathetically. "Just keep reminding yourself: It's all in a good cause."

"Right. Speaking of good causes, would you know

how I could line up a psychiatrist for Sascha for when she comes home? A new environment is only half the battle; she needs other kinds of help as well."

"Offhand, I can't think of any. Besides, even if I could, how do you know you can persuade her to go?"

"I don't. But I'd like to have a name or two up my sleeve, just in case I catch her in a receptive frame of mind some day."

I told him I'd do my best, and said good-bye. Then I put away my bio book and sat up half the night, rereading *Gone With The Wind*.

Tuesday, April 30

At seven thirty, Ma woke me. "Up, up, up, Annabel—you'll be late! What did you do, forget to set the alarm?"

"No school," I mumbled, and buried my face in the pillow.

"Nobody skips school in this house unless they're sick," she said firmly. "Now get up." She yanked the covers off me.

"There isn't any school," I said, yanking them back. "Something about a maintenance men's strike."

"Oh that," she said. "I just heard that on the news. It only applies to public schools. Your school is open and you're going to it."

"Meanie!" I said.

"Grouchy!" said Ma, and laughed.

She won't laugh when she sees my report card. I walked into bio totally unprepared and flunked the test cold. So much for *Boris's* good deed.

On the stairwell between classes, Virginia asked me how Bart was. I told her he was fine, why? She said that on Sunday she and James had had a frightful row —it was all over between them—so she was wondering if I'd mind if she invited Boris to the class dance. (!!!) I told her I'd mind very much because it was all over between me and Bart, too—I'd decided it was Boris I really loved—and *I* was going to invite him to the class dance.

At ten thirty that night, Boris beeped me, terribly upset.

"The Box isn't working! It's on, but there's nothing on the screen except grainy snow and a lot of staticky noise. It's as though all the channels were off the air."

"That's very odd," I said.

"It's worse than odd; it's a potential disaster. What if the Box is permanently on the blink? I'll be finished. Ruined!"

I told him not to panic; I'd get Ape Face up there first thing in the morning—maybe he could fix it.

At five after eleven, Boris beeped again.

"Never mind Ape Face. It's working now," he said somberly.

"But that's great," I said. "What are you so gloomy about?"

"Because I've just found out why it wasn't working before. Tomorrow there's going to be a total blackout in New York and Westchester, from five fourteen in the afternoon 'til eleven at night. Which means that not only did I miss today's OTB results because all the channels were off the air tomorrow, but I am also going to miss tomorrow's OTB results for Thursday because there won't be any electricity."

"Gee, that is a setback, isn't it? But you made something today, didn't you?"

"Eleven hundred and ninety dollars and forty-three cents. Still, I'm way behind schedule."

"What a shame you can't drag the Box to New Jersey and plug it in there. But I suppose that's not too practical a suggestion, is it?"

"Not too," he said witheringly. "Try again."

"Well . . . for the rest of the week, beginning Thursday, why don't you go to three OTB places? Port Authority, Penn Station, *and* Grand Central. That ought to do it."

"If I don't drop dead of exhaustion. Roger, over, and pray for me."

Wednesday, May 1

Before breakfast, I called Bart.

"What's the bad news for today, Annie old girl?" When I told him, he sounded rather disappointed.

"A blackout? That's all?"

165

"Isn't that enough?"

"It's all right, I guess, but it doesn't give me an advantage over any of the other reporters on the paper. We'll all be in the same boat—except that they'll be stumbling around in the dark and I'll be stumbling around in the dark with a flashlight."

"Bartholomew Bacon, you are becoming entirely too dependent on my ESP. See what you can do on your own, for once. Take your flashlight to the New York Foundling Hospital and entertain frightened children with hand shadows on the wall. That'd make a nice story. Or guide hysterical office workers out of the subway."

Subway! I suddenly realized that Dad always took the subway home. He'd be trapped himself!

"Anyway, Bart, my ESP tells me breakfast is getting cold. Good-bye."

Another good deed coming up!

"Dad, you're not eating eggs again, are you?"

"Why not? I love eggs."

"But they're full of cholesterol, and at your age . . . Dad, do you know the statistics on the number of men in their forties who drop dead of heart attacks? It's perfectly alarming. And the kind of men it happens to are men just like you: Men in your socioeconomic bracket, under a constant strain from high-pressure desk jobs, who don't get enough exercise."

I stared fixedly at his stomach. "I don't like to say

this, Dad, but you're getting flabby in the gut. You should get more exercise, shouldn't he, Ma?"

"He probably should, darling, but it's difficult, living in New York."

"He could walk home from work. Walking is wonderful exercise. Dad, why don't you walk home from work, starting tonight."

"I wouldn't dream of it," said Dad.

"Well, then," I intoned darkly, "don't blame me if you keel over at your desk some day. I just hope you have plenty of insurance to provide for your widow and your poor, fatherless, uneducated children."

"When is it going to happen?" asked Ape Face, his chin beginning to quiver.

"Now look what you've done!" whispered Ma angrily. She threw her napkin on the table and went over to comfort him.

"It's not, Ben, it's not." To me, she said, "Annabel, what is this morbid preoccupation with your father's death? It's very neurotic of you."

I decided to try to kill two birds with one stone.

"It isn't neurotic, Ma. Besides, if it were, I bet you wouldn't even know a good psychiatrist to send me to." Dad and Ma exchanged concerned glances.

"No, I don't. I'm happy to say no one in this family has ever needed one . . . so far." She looked at her watch. "Shake a leg, Annabel, or you and Ben will be late."

When I came home from school, I raced to the Japanese store to buy some fat candles for the apartment. (If Dad was going to be trapped in the subway, I could at least make the waiting a little brighter for Mom.) The Japanese store was fresh out of candles.

As predicted by Boris, the lights came back on at eleven. Dad slammed in the door half an hour later in a foul temper.

"Poor Bill," said Ma, oozing with empathy. "Was the subway a nightmare?"

"I wouldn't know," he said. "From what I hear, most people managed to get out of the subway fairly quickly—but I wasn't in it."

"Then where were you?" she said. "What happened to you?"

"What happened to me was I listened to *her*," he said, jerking his head venomously in my direction. "I got to thinking about what she'd said about exercise, and made up my mind to leave the office a little early and walk home. I have just spent the last six hours in a stalled elevator with a lot of overwrought office workers and Luther Parkhurst whom I loathe. Comparatively speaking, the subway would have been a festival of fun."

I was seized with an uncontrollable fit of giggling.

"For someone who displayed such filial concern for me this morning, you seem to be displaying an astonishing lack of it, now," Dad roared. "What's so funny about my being stuck in an elevator?"

"I can't explain."

"Then go to your room!"

BEEP, BEEP, BEEP. "Boris," I chortled. "You'll never guess what I've done!" I filled him in, and ended by saying, "The whole day was a total loss!"

"Mine wasn't," said Boris. "The painters are almost finished—they'll definitely be through by Friday, Lord and Taylor called to say they're definitely delivering the stuff Friday, and best of all, I made two hundred dollars."

"How did you manage that?"

"I bought out all the candles in the Japanese store and sold them to people in the building for two dollars apiece."

"You might have saved one for my mother," I said, and collapsed laughing all over again.

When I'd calmed down, I asked him what was on the Box for tomorrow. He said he hadn't bothered to watch since he'd missed the OTB results anyway; but he had listened to the radio and heard something sort of baffling. Apparently, during the blackout, burglars had made a clean sweep of the ground floor of Tiffany's—over two million dollars worth of precious gems. The police said it was almost as though the men who did it had known in advance that the burglar alarms would be inoperative. Didn't I think that was curious? Very curious indeed, I told him, and clicked off.

When Mom and Dad were safely asleep, I crept to the kitchen and called Bart.

"You know what my ESP tells me now?" I asked.

"Wha-?" he said drowsily.

"That you're a common thief!" Instantly awake, he demanded to know what I was talking about. The Tiffany robbery, I told him.

"I swear to you, Annie, on my mother's grave, I had nothing to do with it."

"Well, somebody knew—and knew in advance. *I* didn't tell anyone except you. Did *you* tell someone?"

"Only my neighbor, Mrs. Krasny. I didn't want her to be all alone in the dark in that crummy building of ours, so I gave her a flashlight and told her I'd heard that Con Ed was having trouble with Big Allis; that in all probability there would be a blackout later on in the day. She thanked me very kindly for the information."

"I'll bet she did. Bart, far be it from me to tell you how to further your own career, but if I were you, I'd investigate Mrs. Krasny."

"Is that what your ESP tells you?"

"No, that's what my common sense tells me."

The next morning, the paper was full of it. Bart and the police must have worked fast because the last edition of the *Daily News* goes to press at two thirty A.M.

> As the result of a tip from one of our own *Daily News* reporters, Bartholomew Bacon, police last night were able to recover an estimated two million dollars worth of Tiffany jewels, stolen during yesterday's blackout. The cache was found intact in the West 52nd Street apartment of Mrs. Helen Krasny, longtime girlfriend of gang leader Salvio (Lean Julian) Vizzini, and neighbor of Mr. Bacon. When apprehended, Mrs. Krasny spat at Bacon (see photo), and said, "Fine neighbor you turned out to be. Lean Julian'll get you for this!"

And to think I rang that woman's doorbell!

Since the gods seemed to be on my team, I thought I'd take another whack at finding a shrink for Sascha. In my free study period, I paid a call on the school psychologist, Dr. Vera Artunian.

"Dr. Artunian?" I said, peeking into her office.

She looked up, removed her reading glasses, and said, "It's Annabel Andrews, isn't it? Come in, my dear, come in. And close the door. We don't want the whole school to hear, do we?" She gestured toward a big leather chair opposite her desk. I sat down.

"Now," she said, "tell me what's on your mind. You have a little problem of some sort?"

"It's not my problem, it's my friend's problem. My friend, you see, has this mother . . ."

"Yes?" she said encouragingly.

"And the mother is crazy. Very nice—but irresponsible and crazy. Plumb nuts. She makes my friend very unhappy."

"I'm sorry to hear that." Artunian gazed at me thoughtfully and then, ever so casually, said, "Tell me more about your mother."

"*My* mother!" I gasped. "I'm not talking about *my* mother, I'm talking about my *friend's* mother."

In a warm and confiding tone, she said, "Annabel, when we have feelings that are difficult to express, we often find it easier to ascribe those feelings to someone other than ourselves. I can't tell you the number of patients who come to talk to me about a 'friend.'"

"But . . ." I began.

"But," she continued with a fanatical gleam in her eye, "it's such a transparent maneuver! I assure you, you can't fool me—although you *can* trust me."

"Dr. Artunian, I think you're crazier than my

friend's mother," I said, and fled from her office. The gods weren't on my team after all.

At home, Boris was having his own troubles.

"Listen," he said over the walkie-talkie, "I've just had a near miss. A short while ago, I came across one of the painters sprawled all over my room, watching the Box."

"Wow—that's dangerous! Do you think he caught on? What was he watching?"

"Only a game show, fortunately; but we've got to move that set to a safer place. I wouldn't want to take a chance on it happening again. Let's move it back down to the Ape's room."

I could see there was no point in arguing. "Okay," I sighed, "but you carry it."

At the sight of the Box, Ape Face was, at first, thoroughly bewildered. "But I like my Sony very much. You don't want to trade again, do you?"

When Boris assured him he didn't, he was delighted. "Great! Tomorrow I can watch *Torture Garden*, which I was going to have to miss on Saturday."

"Oh, no you don't, kiddo," snarled Boris. "That Box is still my property and don't you dare lay a hand on it. If your mother sees that it's working, the jig is up."

"Is someone taking my name in vain?" asked Ma, poking her head in the door. "Oh horrors, what's that great, hulking, no-good thing doing here again, Ben?

I thought you gave it back to Boris because you were tired of tinkering with it."

"But then you began to miss it, didn't you, Ben?" prompted Boris. Ape Face nodded.

"Ma," I whispered, "you said you'd been worried about him. Let him keep it—it's good therapy for him."

"All right," said Ma. "I just wish it didn't take up so much space. I keep barking my shins on it."

When she left, Boris said, "Don't forget, Ape, you're not to touch it. If you want to watch television, play the Sony."

"And another thing not to forget," I added, "is when you're watching the Sony, don't play 'Yellow Submarine,' play something else."

For the rest of the evening, all I heard coming out of his room was "Lucy in the Sky with Diamonds." My brother is a very literal-minded kid.

Friday, May 3

In retrospect, I find it hard to believe that so many grisly things could have happened in one twenty-four hour period. But they did.

When I got home from school, Hector said, "Are you going to be seeing your upstairs amigo?"

"I guess so; why?"

"Because this came for him." A telegram. "Shall I deliver it or if you're going to be seeing him, you can give it to him yourself."

"I'll give it to him," I said, stuffing it into my pocket. "Would you take me up there now, por favor?"

I rang the bell. (Boris, unlike Sascha, always keeps the door locked.) He let me in promptly, and with great pride showed me around the apartment. To describe it as dazzling would have been a gross understatement; in the high gloss *white* white, you could practically see your own reflection.

"Boris, it's ravishing!" I exclaimed. "But empty. Where's the furniture?"

"I'm waiting for it now. It'll be coming any minute."

"Speaking of coming," I produced the telegram, "this came for you. What do you suppose it is?"

He stared at it the way you'd stare at a hooded cobra—with fear and loathing.

"Nothing good," he croaked. "You open it. I'm afraid to look."

I ripped open the envelope, read the message—and felt the blood congealing in my veins. From my lips to the tips of my toes, I was numb all over.

I wanted to break it to him gently. "Boris," I whispered, "it's very bad."

"It's Sascha, isn't it? She's dead."

"Worse."

"What could be worse?"

"She's coming back—*soon*."

"That's definitely worse." He clutched his head. "How soon?"

I didn't have the guts to tell him. Wordlessly, I held out the telegram. He took it with trembling fingers.

" 'Home for Derby Day or before. Love Sascha.' Derby Day," he repeated dully. "My head doesn't seem to be functioning. When is it? *What* is it?"

"The Kentucky Derby. It's tomorrow."

Boris collapsed against the wall like Raggedy Andy and closed his eyes.

I grabbed him by the shoulders and shook him 'til he opened them again.

176

"Boris!" I shouted, "This is no time to go into a catatonic state! Your mother is coming home tomorrow or maybe even today. You've got to *do* something!"

"It's no use," he said faintly. "It's too late."

"It's *not* too late!" I said, punching him on the shoulder. "Pull yourself together and DO something!"

"All right, Annabel. Tell me what to do. Just tell me what to do and I'll do it."

"That's the spirit." Boris's mind may have been out to lunch, but mine was clicking along like an IBM computer. "First, how much money do you have?"

"Four thousand three hundred and forty-three dollars and sixty-seven cents. And I owe . . ."

"Never mind what you owe. You're going to take that money right now to OTB and bet it all on the Kentucky Derby."

"How can I? I don't know which horse."

I looked at my watch. "The race'll be starting in twenty minutes. By the time you've gotten to the Port Authority, I'll have seen the results on the Box, downstairs. Call me as soon as you get there and I'll tell you which horse."

"But suppose the furniture comes while you're downstairs? Who's going to sign for the furniture?"

"Aargh," I groaned. "Boris, you're the bleeding limit! Get your coat and your money. I'll run down and tell Ape Face to watch the Box. When you get to

177

Port Authority, you can call *him*. I'll wait here for the furniture."

"All right," he said. Putty in my hands, thank goodness.

I ran downstairs, gave Ape Face his instructions, made him repeat them to me twice to make sure he understood, and ran back up to Boris's.

"All set," I panted. "Now, GO! When that horse comes in first tomorrow, you'll make a fortune which, on Monday, you can deposit in Sascha's savings account. She'll never know the difference."

"I'll have to pay a huge income tax."

"Which is better? To pay a huge income tax on a huge amount of money, or be in *hock* for a huge amount of money? Don't be stupid. Now, get out of here!" I pushed him out the door.

Boris had no sooner left when Lord and Taylor arrived. Clothes first, I decided. I pushed all of Sascha's old, crummy stuff to the back of the closet and lovingly hung up the new collection in the front. The mink I hung in the hall closet where it put the other coats to shame.

Now for the furniture. After a few minutes of back-breaking (and fruitless) shoving and lugging, I realized I couldn't possibly manage it alone. Would Hector be willing to help me? For a slight fee, he would—and did.

"Gracias," I said when we were finished.

178

"De nada," he said. Five dollars of my own allowance was not what I called de nada—but oh, well, what can you do?

At five o'clock, having shifted from his catatonic mood to a manic one, Boris bounded in the door.

"It's Ticker Tape by half a length. I'm going to be rich, *rich*, RICH!" he hollered.

"How do you like where I put the furniture?" I asked.

"Perfection. Everything is perfection. *You* are perfection!" he said, swinging his jacket in circles over his head. "Let's sit on the new sofa and plan how we're going to spend all the leftover money."

The phone rang.

"Let's answer the phone, first."

"You answer it," he said nervously.

"Boy, Boris, I have to read your telegrams, answer your phones—what are you, chicken or something?"

"Yes," he said. "I'm so afraid our luck will run out."

I picked up the phone, listened for a moment, hung up, and said, "I think it just has. That was my mother. She sounds like a blast of wind from the North Pole and wants me to come home 'this instant.'"

"I'll come with you," said Boris manfully. "Just as long as it has to do with your mother; I'm not quite ready for my own, yet."

I don't think he could have been ready for mine, either. I know I wasn't. She was standing at the front door, waiting to pounce like a panther when I came in.

"Annabel Andrews," she said, ignoring Boris altogether. "You knew all about that set of Ben's, didn't you!"

Boris and I looked at each other and exchanged simultaneous telepathic messages: Which set is she talking about? Boris shook his head a millimeter of an inch. Don't ask that—you'll give it away, he was saying.

"You deliberately encouraged that child to do something he knew was strictly against my wishes."

"I didn't encourage him, Ma, I just didn't *dis*-courage him." That seemed noncommittal enough.

"As a responsible older sister, you *should* have."

"I'm sorry," I mumbled.

"Don't apologize to me—apologize to him. I've had to tell him he can't watch any television at all for a month."

Like two beaten dogs, Boris and I slunk down the hall to the Ape's room. "Our luck's running out. I knew it," muttered Boris.

"Think positive," I muttered back. "Maybe she only found the Sony."

Crossing our fingers, we opened the door and went in. The Ape was sitting cross-legged on the floor in the very spot where the Box had been.

"Hi," he said dejectedly.

"Hi," we said. I sat down on the bed. Boris closed the door and sat down next to me.

After casting a furtive glance behind him to make sure the door was really closed, Ape Face began burrowing feverishly in the toy chest. Like a mole, flipping pieces of multicolored Lego over his shoulder, he dug down to the bottom and came up with his precious Sony.

"For you," he said to Boris.

"Thanks, Ape, but you keep it. It's no good to me anyhow."

"Why not? It works great."

To me, Boris said, "Your brother doesn't seem to understand the significance of the Box."

"I don't think he ever did," I answered. "Ape Face, Boris appreciates the gesture, but he doesn't want your Sony. Put it away now, before Mom catches you."

With a vast sigh of relief, Ape Face replaced it in its bed of Lego.

"Say, Ape, when your mother took the Box away, do you know what she did with it?" That hadn't occurred to me. Maybe it was still in the back hall and we could reclaim it, secretly. Hope springs eternal!

"She gave it away." Hope, schmope.

The thought of somebody else benefiting from his Box was almost more than Boris could bear.

"Ugh," he groaned. "Who to?"

"To Mattie—for Granddaddy Clovis. Mattie said he was deaf as a post and wouldn't get much use out of the sound part, but he sure would enjoy looking at the pictures."

"At least it's not in the hands of an unscrupulous person," I pointed out.

"Yeah," said Boris. "Small comfort, though."

"I feel so bad," said Ape Face.

"Don't," said Boris. "We're the ones who made you watch the Derby."

"But that isn't when it happened," said Ape Face. Poor, guileless cretin.

Boris rose slowly to his feet. "Just what do you mean?" he asked.

"It happened after that. As soon as I saw it was Ticker Tape . . ." he got a glimpse of Boris's face and hesitated.

"Go on," said Boris. He looked like Jack the Ripper. Ape Face wiggled nearer to me.

"I switched to *Torture Garden*. And then the phone rang and I knew it would be you; so I left the room in a hurry and forgot to turn the set off and-that's-how-she-caught-me," he finished.

"That . . . is . . . exactly . . . what . . . I . . . told . . . you . . . never . . . to . . . do, isn't it?" said Boris.

Then he did something I would never have thought him capable of. Repeating, "Isn't that what I told you never to do, *isn't it?*" he shook Ape Face back and forth 'til I thought his teeth would fall out.

Next it was my turn to do something I never would have thought *I'd* be capable of. I hauled off and socked Boris in the chops—hard.

Then all three of us stood around—dumbstruck and miserable.

Finally, Ape Face said in tones of great awe, "Gee, Annabel, you're as tough as John Wayne!"

"I had it coming to me," said Boris, licking his swollen lip.

"And you *sound* like John Wayne," said Ape Face.

Boris and I looked at each other and grinned. Then I reached out and touched his cheek. Then he reached out and stroked the Ape's hair.

"Peace all around?" he asked.

"Peace," said my brother and I.

Saturday Morning, May 4

I was upstairs at Boris's, helping him put the finishing touches on the apartment. He was vacuuming and I was placing bunches of forsythia and pussy willows around the living room. We were in no particular hurry because unless Sascha had taken the Red Eye Express (which would have gotten her in early in the morning), she wouldn't be arriving 'til mid afternoon, at least. I felt strangely lighthearted.

"You know something, Boris?"

"What?" he shouted, over the roar of the Hoover.

"I feel as if a great load has been taken off my mind."

Boris turned off the Hoover. "You feel as if what?"

"As if a great load has been taken off my mind."

"How so?"

"Well—this may shock you, but I think I'm glad we don't have the Box anymore."

"Speak for yourself, John," he said glumly.

"Boris, how much money are you going to win on Ticker Tape?"

"I don't know exactly, but a lot. Around fifty thou, I guess."

"Right. So you've accomplished your mission, haven't you? The apartment is looking lovely, Sascha has a new wardrobe, and with the rest of the money, you'll be able to take care of the school bill, the back taxes, the housekeeper, the accountant, the psychiatrist—incidentally, I haven't gotten a lead on one, yet, but I'll keep trying."

"Please do," he said. "That's terribly important. Unless there's a fundamental change in her personality, all of this," he waved his arm at the living room, "won't amount to a hill of beans. Within a year, everything new will look old and cruddy again, and we'll be back in debt."

"*But*—on the assumption that a) I will find her a psychiatrist and b) you will persuade her to go to him (or her), you *have* accomplished your mission, have you not?"

"I guess so. Still . . ."

"Still what?"

"I still wish I had the Box."

"What for? So you can make more and more and more money? That's piggy of you. You don't *need* more money; and since money was the only thing you used the Box for, you no longer need the Box."

"I guess not," he reluctantly admitted. "But what about you? Aren't you going to miss it? You liked knowing about the future, didn't you?"

"No," I said slowly. "I think, actually, I hated it. To know about hijackings and fires and murders," I thought about Belle Steinberg, "and know people are going to suffer from things you can't prevent—that's not fun. It's very depressing."

"What about the things you could prevent, what about the good deeds? Playing gin rummy with your little, old, frail grandmother so she wouldn't get caught in the blizzard."

"Boris, I could spend the rest of my life doing things like that—but out of all the millions of opportunities that would present themselves, I'd be constantly having to decide which little old lady to save. I don't want that responsibility and I'm glad I don't have it.

"Furthermore, good deeds involve a great deal of work and aren't all that easy to do. Take my father, for example. I managed to keep him out of the subway, so what happened? He got stuck in an elevator instead.

"Come to think of it, all my good deeds were a complete washout—with one exception. . . ." Bart. But I had never told Boris about Bart and didn't plan to now, or ever.

"The little kid in the park?"

"Yes. That's the one I mean."

What *about* Bart? I suddenly thought. No more ESP for him! I'd better warn him.

"Boris, I have an errand to do. I'll be back in an hour, okay?"

"Sure. Take your time. While you're gone, I'll Windex the glass coffee table—it's covered with fingerprints."

In the lunchroom next door to the *Daily News*, while waiting for Bart, I prepared my pep talk to him. In fact, I prepared a whole scenario, which went roughly like this:

BART
[*enthusiastically*]
Hello. I came as soon as I could. Have you been waiting long?

ANNIE
No, no. Only a couple of minutes. How's everything going?

BART
So great, it's out of sight! You read Thursday's paper, didn't you? I'm a hero to the police department, a hero to my paper. By Sunday, I'll have my own by-line, and by the end of the week, I'll probably have a raise. And I owe it all to you. [*He clasps Annie's hands in gratitude.*]

ANNIE

[*modestly*]

Nonsense! That's a ridiculous thing to say.

BART

Where would I be today without you and your ESP, tell me that, huh?

ANNIE

[*earnestly and with conviction*]

Bart, I may have given you a few hot tips, but I didn't write your articles for you. You're a fine, fine writer. A talented writer. You do believe that about yourself, don't you?

BART

[*smiling shyly*]

I'm beginning to, I guess.

ANNIE

That's what I like to hear. You've got to develop more self-confidence. Because I know you have a fantastic future ahead of you.

BART

Tell me about it. Do I get the Pulitzer Prize?

ANNIE

[*fiddles with silverware, takes long drink
of chocolate float, averts eyes*]
I don't know.

BART

[*agitatedly*]
How can you not know?! What does your
ESP tell you?

ANNIE

That's the thing of it, Bart; it doesn't. You
see—[*She grips his hand to give him courage.*]
I don't have my ESP anymore. I've lost it.

BART

[*disbelieving*]
You mean it's *gone*?! Just like [*snaps fingers*] that, it's gone? Are you sure?

ANNIE

[*shakes head sadly*]
I'm afraid so. From now on, you'll have to
go it alone without my help.

BART

[*dismayed out of his skull*]
Oh no!

Just have confidence, and you'll be fine. I'm
sure you will. Someday. [*She rises, slips on
gloves, gracefully extends hand.*] I'll probably
read all about you winning that Pulitzer Prize,
and I'll think to myself, "I knew him, once."
[*She presses her gloved hand to his cheek.*]

BART

You mean I'm never going to see you again?
You mean this is—[*He chokes on the word. She
says it for him.*]

ANNIE

Good-bye.

"What about hello, first?" said Bart.

I jumped a mile high in the air. Bart was sitting
across the table from me.

"How long have you been there?" I asked.

"For about five minutes. I didn't want to interrupt
your reverie."

"Was I talking aloud all that time?" How embarrassing!

"No, good-bye was all I heard." Whew!

"Say, Bart, have they caught Lean Julian yet?"

"This morning. I wish you'd told me yesterday. I

could have been there and it would have made a fitting climax to the story."

I mumbled an apology, and then said, "How's everything?"

From there on in, the scenario went pretty much as I'd imagined it—with one small exception: the part about the gloves. I don't know why I put that in anyway. I *never* wear gloves for show, only for warmth. And one big exception: the ending.

Right after Bart said, "You mean I'm never going to see you again?" he said "Don't go—you mustn't, yet! There's something I want to tell you."

I sat down.

"What is it?" I asked.

"Annie," he took my hand in his and looked into my eyes. "Annie, I'm in love. I know there's an awfully big difference in our ages, but I'm sure that's not an insurmountable problem."

Even with*out* my ESP he felt that way! I don't mind admitting I was enormously touched and flattered. And sorry for him—because nice and adorable as he was, it was Boris I really loved. If only he'd told me earlier, I might have been able to head him off.

"You certainly kept your feelings a secret. How long have you known?"

"Since Wednesday night." Wednesday night. The night of the blackout. I was crashing around in the dark with my mother, and Bart was—?

"Where were you Wednesday night?"

"At home," he rhapsodized. "In the flickering candlelight, sharing a loaf of bread, a jug of wine . . ."
GIRL'S FACE SETS LUNCHROOM ON FIRE. How could I have *made* such a mistake!

"With whom," I asked. "I mean, what's her name?" As if I didn't know.

"Virginia. We met in the strangest way. It was as though it had been decreed by fate. I was on my way into the *Daily News* building, Tuesday afternoon—" That was the day I told Virginia it was all off between Bart and me. "—and she bumped into me and we got to talking and that's how it all began. She's the prettiest girl in the world. She has—"

"Honey-colored hair, blue eyes, a tiny top, and a tiny tummy, right?"

"Annie, were you lying to me before? It sounds as though you haven't lost your ESP at all."

"That wasn't ESP—it was just an educated guess." I rose, slipped on my blue-jean jacket, and gracefully extended my hand. He took it, and shook it cordially.

"*Am* I ever going to see you again? What's your educated guess on that?"

"My educated guess is yes." (At the class dance. I'll be with Boris and you'll be with Virginia-the-Body-Snatcher.)

"Good-bye, Bartholomew," I said.

How *about* that Virginia!

192

Saturday Afternoon, May 4

At five minutes to four, I was polishing Sascha's new dining-room table when Boris called to me.

"Annabel, put away the cleaning things and come here. I have a surprise for you."

"Where are you?"

"In the den," he shouted.

"What's the surprise? I don't see anything."

He pointed to the television set; it was on.

"You mean we're going to watch the Derby? That's not much of a surprise."

"No, but how about this?" From behind his back, he produced a chilled bottle of Dom Perignon and two chilled glasses.

"I thought a little celebration was in order."

He uncorked the champagne with a magnificent *pop*, and poured us each some bubbly.

"Here's to you and me and, most of all," he raised his glass high in the air, "to Ticker Tape!"

We clinked glasses and took a sip.

"Mmn," I said.

"How do you like it?" he asked.

"Not at all. How do you?"

"Not much," he admitted. "I guess it takes practice."

We both took another sip.

"You know what?" I said. "We forgot to toast Sascha, of all people."

"So we did. Better late than never, I always say. Here's to you and me and Ticker Tape and *Sascha*!"

We took another sip.

"And Ape Face." Sip.

"And your Mom and Dad." Sip.

"And Lord and Taylor, and OTB." Sip.

"And Virginia."

"Boris, I am not drinking to Virginia."

"No? I thought she was your best friend?"

"Was is correct."

"Oh well," he shrugged. "Here's to—uh—Hector." Sip.

"And Bart." Whoops!

"Who's that?"

"A cousin of mine from Duluth."

"I'm not drinking to people I don't know. If we start that, we'll finish the bottle before the race starts. Say, Annabel, do you feel anything?"

"Nope." I burped. "Nothing good, anyway. Do you?"

"Nope. Here's to our late, lamented Box." Sip.

"And to its new owner, Granddaddy Clovis who's deaf as a post," I giggled.

". . . and they're off!" shouted the announcer. "It's Gobbledygook way out in front with a fast start, followed by Super Stupidity, and Illiopolis, Bernie Busch is in the number four position . . . with Ticker Tape bringing up the rear."

Boris and I exchanged smug glances and sipped placidly at our Dom Perignon.

". . . And coming up fast on the outside is Cafe Noir, with Gobbledygook still in the lead, Bernie Busch has dropped back to seventh place, wait a minute! Ticker Tape is making a try for it; man, look at that little horse go. Ticker Tape is now in fourth place . . ."

"Come on, Ticker Tape, baby, come on!" screamed Boris.

"Boris, what are you screaming for, you know he's going to win anyway—COME ON TICKER TAPE—atta baby!"

". . . Gobbledygook has dropped back to fifth position, Super Stupidity, the odds-on favorite, is now in first, followed by Illiopolis, Ticker Tape third . . . Ticker Tape has just overtaken Illiopolis, coming into the home stretch now . . . Super Stupidity first, Ticker Tape half a length behind him and gaining . . ."

"Boris, stop jumping up and down on the bed—it's

195

a new bed, you'll bust the springs—COME ON, TICKER TAPE!"

". . . They're neck and neck now . . . Ticker Tape drawing ahead of Stuper Supidity . . . and it's TICKER TAPE! Winner by half a length! *Man*, what a *race* that *was!*"

Boris and I fell back onto the bed, exhausted and hoarse from screaming.

"I know it sounds silly," he said, "but I've never seen anything so exciting in my life."

"Nor me."

"Can you imagine anyone betting on a horse called Super Stupidity?"

". . . they'll be posting the official running time. Wa-it a minute, folks, there seems to be something . . . They're announcing something over the loud-speaker . . ."

"Boris!"

"Shut up and listen."

"Ladies and gentlemen, Eddie O'Rourke, Super Stupidity's jockey, has filed a complaint against Ticker Tape's jockey, Bud Balducci. He says Balducci whipped his horse—whipped Super Stupidity, that is —causing him to flinch and lose ground in the final seconds of the race. There will be a few minutes while the judges review the tapes to determine whether or not this was the case. Meanwhile, we bring you a brief message from our sponsor."

"Oh my God! Annabel!"

"I know," I said. "Feel my hands, they're like ice."

Boris's were, too. It's a miracle we didn't stick to each other.

"Ladies and gentlemen, the judges of the Kentucky Derby have come to a decision. Judge Marion Beaufort will make the announcement."

"We regret to inform you that it is our unanimous opinion, based on careful review of the tapes, that the charges lodged against Mr. Balducci were justified. Ticker Tape is, thereby, disqualified, and the official winner of this year's Kentucky Derby is Super Stupidity, ridden by jockey Eddie O'Rourke."

The announcer came back and droned on. "Super Stupidity's owner, Mrs. Tweetie Twombley, is now making her way to the winner's circle. . . ."

I turned off the set and looked at Boris. He was the color of pureed peas.

All he kept saying, over and over again, was, "I think I'm going to throw up. I think I'm going to throw up."

"It's the champagne."

"It's not the champagne and you know it. I think I'm going to throw up."

"Then stop talking about it and *do* it," I said. "But don't do it in here—you'll ruin the new rug."

He stumbled to the bathroom, closed the door, and stumbled right back again.

"Did you?" I asked.

"No. I couldn't. I'm going to do something else."

197

"What?"

"Kill myself." He lurched to the window and peered down. I yanked him away (he was weak as a puppy) and threw him into a chair.

I didn't know what to do with him. He seemed hell-bent on taking the plunge.

"Boris, I have an idea! Do you think there's the remotest possibility that OTB would give you your money back?"

"No," he said, and staggered to his feet. This time, I threw him back in the chair and planted a foot on his chest. Then I reached for the phone.

"You're wasting your time."

"I'm not calling OTB, I'm calling the police."

Quick as lightning, in a single, deft judo maneuver, he grabbed my foot, threw me off balance, and floored me.

"Sorry about that," he said, brushing his hands off, "but I had to stop you somehow. I'm going to my room."

"What for? So you can splash to your death right on Central Park West instead of in an empty court-yard? And possibly kill an innocent pedestrian as well as yourself?"

"I'm going to my room to pack. I'm running away."

I scrambled to my feet and followed him.

"That's the most cowardly thing I ever heard of. The least you could do is wait 'til Sascha comes back and tell her what you did and why you did it."

"I'd rather kill myself," he said, and began stuffing clothes into a Woolworth shopping bag.

"Here," he said, ripping a sheet of paper off his bulletin board. "Here's the itemized list I read to you—all nicely retyped. If you're so worried about Sascha, *you* tell her. Go over the list point by point. She probably won't know what you're talking about, but—"

"And what do I tell her when the bills come in? Boris, you can't do this to me."

As it turned out, he couldn't. Because just then, the doorbell rang.

"That's her!" I said.

"She," corrected Boris (about grammar, he's as bad as Virginia), and took a step toward the window. I blocked him. He sidestepped me. Once more, I blocked him. The doorbell rang again, longer and more persistently, this time, and was followed up by knocking and pounding.

"You answer it," he whispered. "While you're letting her in, I'll slip out the back door."

Out the window was more like it. I didn't dare leave him alone.

"No, Boris, I'm not taking any chances with you. Come on, we're both going to let her in."

I grabbed him by the arm and began dragging him to the front hall.

"Now listen, Boris. Put a good face on it. When we open the door, be smiling and happy to see her, and smiling and happy about how wonderful the place

199

looks. Then, we'll show her around the apartment and show her her new clothes and then . . ." I faltered.

"And then what?" said Boris.

"And then she'll be in a marvelous mood and we'll tell her the rest."

"Oh . . . oh," he moaned. "I really think I'm going to throw up."

"No, you're not, I said firmly, although I wasn't too sure. He was no longer the color of pureed peas. He looked more like pureed eggplant—gray and seedy. I'd have to put a good face on my own face—Boris's was obviously a lost cause.

Sascha was now banging on the door with some-thing hard—a shoe probably—and shouting, "Will somebody please let me in? I forgot my key!"

"Steady on, Boris, this is it."

With a radiant smile, I opened the door. Boris cow-ered behind it.

"Annabel!" she said, shifting her suitcase to the other hand and shaking mine. "What a delight!"

"Hello, Mrs. . . . Sascha. Come in."

She hesitated. "Only for a minute. I can't stay long."

Then, apparently baffled, she said, "I wonder why Hector let me off here?"

What is she talking about? Oh, now I see. Every-thing looks so different, she thinks she's in my apart-ment. This was going to be a lark. (The first part, anyway.)

"Because you live here," I said airily.

Sascha winked at me, and in a tone of mock wonderment said, "I *do*? Funny—it doesn't look at all the way it did when I left."

"Of course not. It's been done over. Welcome home."

Boris crept out from behind the door with his shopping bag. "Welcome home, Sascha," he echoed feebly.

"Hi there, friend. I didn't expect to see you here."

"I live here, too, remember?"

Sascha laughed. "Listen, fellas, the joke's over. I may be unobservant but I'm not that unobservant. I know my own home when I see it. . . . Boris, what are you doing with that shopping bag full of clothes?"

"I'm taking a trip," he said, inching toward the door.

She clearly didn't believe that either. "I can't say much for your luggage. To what unchic place are you going, might I ask?"

"No place," I said, blocking his way.

"Well, *I* am," said Sascha. "I'm going to *my* unchic place and take a hot bath."

I decided it was time to get the show on the road.

"Sascha, you're in it. You can take a bath right here. This *is* your home. It's not a joke."

She set her suitcase down and looked around. "No? What is it, then?"

"It's a surprise. While you were away, Boris had the apartment painted and we got new furniture and new clothes for you. . . ."

201

She turned to Boris. "True?" she asked. He managed a faint smile—actually, more of a grimace—and nodded.

"That's quite a surprise," she said expressionlessly.

"Come on, Boris," I said, pulling him away from the door. "Let's give her the Fifty-Cent Tour." An unfortunate phrase, but it was out of my mouth before I realized it.

The Fifty-Cent Tour was conducted entirely by me. Boris, an ambulatory zombie, contributed not one word and neither did Sascha. I felt like a showroom salesman with a couple of obdurate clients.

"Well," I said heartily, when we were back in the entrance hall, "how does it grab you?"

"I haven't decided yet," said Sascha.

Boris had finally found his voice—some of it, anyway. In a tentative croak, he said, "How about the paint job? Isn't it nice?"

"For a men's washroom, or an intensive care unit at Bellevue, very nice."

Then she pointed to the new white Naugahyde living-room sofa, and said, "Is it permitted to sit down on that? Because if so, I would like to sit there with both of you until I find out what this is all about."

We arranged ourselves, Sascha in the middle and Boris and me on either side. "All right," she said quietly, "what *is* it all about?"

"Well, Sascha." Boris had now recovered the rest

of his voice and it was coming out loud and clear and, I'm afraid, pompous. "For some time, now, I've been dissatisfied with the way things have been going around here."

"Indeed," she said. "Would you care to elucidate?"

Boris would. And for ten uninterrupted minutes, he did. It was as though years of pent-up indignation were finally exploding out of him. He told her what he thought of her as a housekeeper—rotten; as a manager of financial matters—careless and irresponsible; as a wife—a failure, obviously, or Pop wouldn't have left her; as a mother—inadequate; and as a human being—talented, but disorganized, self-destructive, unhappy, and badly in need of making a fresh start in life but utterly incapable of doing it on her own.

"So you've decided to help me, is that it, Boris?!"

"That's it," he said.

Aside from the whirring of the new digital clock, the silence in the room was deafening.

"And according to you, a fresh start in life begins with a fresh coat of paint."

"Yes. It's only a beginning, of course, but I felt there's nothing like new surroundings to turn a person's head around."

"You have definitely turned mine around. In fact, I'm amazed it's still attached to my neck," she said acidly. "This fresh start you're going to help me make— is it for me or is it for you?"

"For both of us, but primarily for you."

"In that case, don't you think you might have consulted me before you embarked on it? How do you know I want to make one?"

"I'm sure you don't," he said. "I don't mean to be rude, Sascha, but people like you always hate letting go of their hang-ups."

She smiled pleasantly at him; but I sensed something menacing underneath the smile. There was enough electricity in the room to light up Times Square, although Boris seemed blissfully unaware of it.

"I certainly hate letting go of my wonderful, battered old desk and my squooshy couch, my Peruvian rug, and all the other lares and penates you've seen fit to dispose of—if that's what you mean by hang-ups.

"But of course," she said sarcastically, "you know what's best for me, don't you, Boris? You know what will make me happy."

Boris shifted uncomfortably.

"Has it never passed through that conservative, Naugahyde-bound, mingy little mind of yours that I already *am* happy?"

Boris shifted again. "I think you *think* you're happy."

"Would you like to know what I think of what you think? Get a load of this, Mac!"

She picked up a brand-new brass lamp (seventy-five bucks) and threw it at the brand-new stainless-

steel-and-glass coffee table (three hundred bucks).
Smithereen time.

Boris winced. I winced. Sascha scornfully kicked
the shards out of her way and went on.

"You want to make me over in your own image,
don't you? What's best for Boris is best for Sascha,
right? WRONG! What's best for Boris is only best for
Boris. I *like* the way I am, and believe it or not, so do
quite a few other people. As a matter of fact even
your father liked me."

Boris looked startled.

"That shocks you, doesn't it? Judging by what you
said before, I knew it would. It seems you have been
laboring under a misapprehension, Mr. Fixit. Your
father left me only because after years of trying to
reconcile the basic differences in our personalities, *I*
was convinced that we were hopelessly mismatched,
and *I* finally persuaded him to go."

She paused for a moment, looked at Boris, and in a
gentler, more reflective tone, continued. "I am a rotten housekeeper—no doubt about it. I can't help it,
or else I don't want to help it, because those things
just aren't important to me. I spent my entire childhood with a mother to whom food and furnishings
mattered terribly, and I swore, when I grew up, that I
wouldn't let them matter to me. I never wanted the
kind of house where a kid couldn't climb on a couch.

"As for my lack of business acumen, Boris, that's
baloney. Since when haven't you had enough to eat?

205

Since when, enough to wear? Since when, a private school? We've always survived, haven't we? Maybe not your way—but your way is not my way.

"Now, let's talk about me as a mother."

"Let's not," said Boris in a quavering voice. On the verge of tears, he was pop-eyed from trying to hold them back.

Sascha ignored him. "Inadequate, you say. Well, if you say so, then it's true; because if that's how I seem to *you*, then that's what I am. And I'm truly sorry. We've always been on different wavelengths, I guess.

"But Boris, how about a little respect for someone else's wavelength? You happen to be clearheaded, disciplined, conventional, and extremely bright. I accept you the way you are. I, on the other hand, happen to be muddleheaded, self-indulgent, a confirmed nut, and a pretty good writer. Can't you accept me the way *I* am?"

"I *do*, Sasch." Boris was losing the battle of the tears.

"No, you don't," she said flatly. "I'm always aware of your disapproval. You don't bother to disguise it very well. Living with you is like living with a German governess. You know something? I've been afraid of you for years now. Isn't that ludicrous—for a mother to be afraid of her own son?!"

Boris was openly sobbing now.

"But Sasch, I'm afraid of you, too. You'll think it's stuffy and boring of me, but I never know what's coming next. I never know what you're going to do, where you're going to be—everything is always so uncertain."

"*Everything*, friend? At least you know I love you—you're not uncertain about that, are you?"

Boris evidently was. He looked up at her, his eyes full of tears and doubt.

"Because I do, baby, I do."

Then with a great shuddering sigh, he put his head in her lap.

"I love you, too, Sasch."

I started to leave.

Sascha said, "You don't have to go, Annabel. It's only fireworks. Good, healthy fireworks. We should have had them long ago."

"Sascha," whispered Boris, "I've done something awful. On this stupid apartment that doesn't even matter to you, I've spent over twelve thousand dollars of your money. I thought I was going to get it all back and more, betting on a horse, but the bloody horse lost. Now what are we going to do?"

She smoothed back his hair, and with the corner of her silk blouse wiped away the tears.

"Do? We're going to take some of the fifty thousand dollars Paramount just gave me for writing a movie script, and pay up—that's what we're going to do."

Boris was a new man. "Oh wow, what a relief!"

"Knowing you, I'm sure it is—but Boris, my angel, if I hadn't made that money, we would have survived anyway. We always do. When are you going to realize that?"

He blinked. You could almost see the light bulb going on in his head. "Right now!" he said joyfully. "And I'm never going to forget it."

"Oh yes you will," she said with a laugh. "That's the way you are—a born pessimist. Don't worry—I'm used to it. I forgive you in advance. However, there's just one thing . . ." She paused. "One thing I want to ask of you. If you wouldn't mind."

"Get the walls repainted."

"Hell no!" said Sascha. "Normal wear and tear around here will take care of the walls. They'll be gray in two months. No, it's . . ." she paused again. Whatever she wanted to say was apparently awkward.

"I'll do anything, Sascha, just name it."

"Okay, then, here it is: I wish you wouldn't call me Sascha. That's for everybody else to call me. (Except my father who still calls me Sarah.) But there's only one person in the whole world who can call me Mom."

She looked at him, kind of embarrassed. But Boris grinned at her, not a bit embarrassed. "Sure, Mom. Be glad to. I never liked the name Sascha anyway."

I do, I thought. I love the name Sascha because I love her. Just the way I love the name Boris (which is a dumb name really, even dumber than Morris) because I love him. More now than ever before. In fact, right now, I love everybody. Even Virginia!

This is not the end. Please turn the page and read carefully. Then decide what you think.

Barron University
Dept. of ESP and Parapsychology
Greensboro, N.C.

Ms. Annabel Andrews
115 C.P.W.
N.Y., N.Y., 10023

Dear Ms. Andrews,

This is to acknowledge receipt of your manuscript and to thank you for sending it. My colleagues and I found it extremely provocative; in fact, we wonder if there might be a way to document the account by means of concrete evidence. In other words, could you give us the exact name and address of your housekeeper's Granddaddy Clovis? Since he is hard of hearing, the Box cannot be of any significant value to him; surely a larger, more recent model would please him just as well. An exchange such as this would be beneficial to both parties; we are, therefore, anxious to communicate with Granddaddy Clovis as soon as possible.

As for your highly commendable concern that the Box not be misused for purposes of personal gain, I wish to alleviate any fears you may have regarding this: We, here at the University, are interested in the Box only insofar as it will aid us in our altruistic quest for knowledge. (Admittedly, we *would* like to know in advance how our report on the latest ESP findings will be received by the public when we present it next month, because a large grant rests on the outcome; but I promise you, we have no interest in horse racing.)

Looking forward to hearing from you soon, I remain

Yours very sincerely,
Oliver Elmswood.

P.S. My wife, who is a member of the English Department here, has also read your manuscript. Although I am convinced she is wrong, she tends to regard it as fiction and recommends that you send it to her old friend, Ursula Nordstrom, Senior Editor at Harper & Row. In the unlikely event that my wife's assessment of the manuscript is accurate, I am passing this information on to you; however, please note the enclosed stamped, self-addressed envelope, in which I fully expect to receive your information on the whereabouts of Granddaddy Clovis.

O. E.

SUMMER SWITCH

A CHARLOTTE ZOLOTOW BOOK

Also by Mary Rodgers

The Rotten Book

Freaky Friday

A Billion for Boris

MARY RODGERS

1 8 17

HARPER & ROW, PUBLISHERS

Cambridge, Philadelphia, San Francisco, London, Mexico City, São Paulo, Sydney

NEW YORK

For Hank & **For Tod**

1

I suppose, in a funny sort of way, I owe it all to Camp Soonawissakit, because if I hadn't told Dad I wanted to go there in the first place, I wouldn't have been in the Port Authority Bus Terminal on Departure Day (Thursday, June 30th), wishing to God I was somewhere else. Actually, wishing I was some*body* else—my father, to be exact, who was leaving that afternoon for Los Angeles on a business trip.

"I wish I was him," I remarked gloomily to my old friend from school, Duck Levine.

"Who?" said Duck, gazing at a gaggle of Soonawissakiddies, wondering, no doubt, which brawny no-brain I could possibly be envying.

I nodded in the direction of the men's room, where Dad had just disappeared. "My father," I said. "I would give anything to be him right now."

Well, you are not going to believe me, nobody in their right minds could *possibly* believe me, but the next thing I knew, *I* was in the men's room.

In the body of my father.

Standing at a urinal, looking down at . . .

OH WOW!!!

And then— No, wait. Before I go any further, I'd better give you some hard-nosed facts:

I am Benjamin "Ape Face" Andrews, aged twelve. The Ape Face is courtesy of my older sister, Annabel. She named me that when I was five days old, just out of the hospital. She was six and a half (years), and pretty ticked off at my mother for bringing home a brother who looked like a rhesus monkey minus the hair when what she had in mind was a sister who looked like a Barbie doll. I've been trying to make it up to her ever since, but it's only been in the last couple of years she's begun to find me even tolerable. I certainly hope it lasts, because I admire her a lot, I really do.

We live in New York (the we being me, my sister, my mother, my father, and Max the basset)—on 72nd and Central Park West. No, not the Dakota; across the street from the Dakota. Funny, whenever you tell people you live on 72nd and C.P.W., they always ask expectantly, "Oh, the Dakota?" and then when you say, "No, the Majestic, across the street," they say, "Oh."

That's all. Just "Oh." Thud. You'd think we lived in a slum dwelling or something, which the Majestic far from is.

I go to the Barden School, where I do pretty well. To be honest about it, except for being only a so-so athlete, I do very well . . . year after year my reports come home with grades in the high 90's and enthusiastic comments about my "extraordinary verbal ability" and about how I am "conscientious," "cooperative," "considerate of others," "a genuine pleasure to teach" . . . everybody thinks I'm perfect, it seems. Well, not quite everybody. There was one teacher, my third-grade homeroom teacher, Miss Moon (who moved the end of that year to Beverly Hills, California). She wrote, "Although Ben has maintained his usual high standard of academic excellence, I must admit to being somewhat disappointed in his performance in other areas. For an exceptionally bright child, he displays a perplexing tendency to 'lay back'—to accept unquestioningly the word of authority, whether it be in the schoolroom or the playground. It is my hope that if Ben is encouraged both at school and at home to become more outspokenly assertive, he may ultimately be able to realize his enormous potential as a leader in the Barden community. At the present time, however, he is entirely too agreeable for his own good."

You should have heard my father. He had a fit. "You just try being *dis*agreeable and see where that gets you!" he said, eyebrows raised.

"Tee-hee," went Annabel. She knew where it got

her. Time after time. As a matter of fact, Annabel was probably largely responsible for my being the way I was. Watching her get into trouble provided great incentive for staying out of it. If you're someone like me, anyway. (More about that later.)

Dad went on with his fit. "What kind of crazy teacher is she?" he grumbled to my mother. "If she keeps up, you know what we'll have on our hands? A rebel without a cause!"

"Not bloody likely," snorted Annabel.

Mom laughed and patted my cheek. "I doubt it, Willy. It's rather late in the game for this little leopard to change his spots."

"Spots where?" I said, anxiously checking my shirt for signs of ketchup. What a jerk I was in those days.

"I guess Mr. Clean doesn't know his Kipling," guffawed Annabel. I wanted to poke her one. Instead, I smiled and changed the subject.

"Don't worry, Dad. I'm going right on being agreeable no matter what Miss Moon says."

"At least that makes one of you," said Dad with a smirk in Annabel's direction. Undaunted, she smirked back and then stuck her tongue out at him. She's got guts!

Dad turned to me again. "Tell me something, Ben . . ."

Now what? Nervously, I balanced my right foot on the inside of my left knee.

"Stop standing stork," snapped Dad, "and tell me what you *really* think of this Miss Moon."

From his tone of voice, I knew what I was supposed to think of her. Down went my foot. "Oh," I said with a shrug, "she's all right, I guess."

Do you know, to this day I can't believe I said that. "She's all right, I guess"?? ALL RIGHT?! Miss Moon wasn't all right, Miss Moon was wonderful and I adored her. She was young, and round like her name, round from top to bottom like plump pillows—with a round, rowdy laugh. On the blackboard, even her a's and e's were round, and her brackets had a curve and a lilt I could never imitate in a million years. But the best thing about her was an ability to tell it like it is without hurting your feelings. Example: One day, when I was in the second grade (Miss Moon was assistant to Miss Milanowsky then), I was finishing up another painting of a stegosaurus—my eighth that year. It was turning out like the other seven—ugly. Ugly, runny, and unrecognizable. She came by, looked over my shoulder, and then, instead of making some dumb remark like "This is interesting work; tell me about it," which decoded simply means "What in heaven's name *is* that?" Miss Moon said, after a slight pause, "Okay, buddy, I give up."

"It's my usual," I explained.

Miss Moon looked amused. "You're just going to keep doing it till you get it right, is that it, pal?"

"Nobody lives to be a hundred and forty," I said, ripping the paper off the easel. I was about to crumple it up when she took it away from me, objecting, "Hey, hey, hey, where are you going with that?!"

She rolled it into a crinkly, crackly tube and handed it back. "Here. Take it home to your mom. She'll love it."

"That's what you think," I said rudely.

"Oh?" said Miss Moon, extremely surprised. With good reason. After all, Ben is "cooperative," "considerate of others," "a genuine pleasure to teach." Ben would never be *rude*. (More about that later.)

"Well, what do you think?" she asked, looking at me curiously, with her deep-blue eyes. So for the next twenty minutes, while the other kids were at recess on the roof, this is roughly what I told her:

In the past three years, aside from at least two paintings a week, I had also brought home several collages—one of spaghetti, macaroni, and pinto beans (uncooked, of course), my personal handprint in clay (except, due to a mix-up in school, I got Charley Kopple's and I assume he got mine), a wooden dog bed, a Christmas-tree ornament made out of a light bulb covered with red and silver glitter, homemade cranberry sauce, a Styrofoam necklace, and a pomander ball. With the following results: Some guest or other put a cigarette out on the handprint and when Mattie the cleaning lady put it in the dishwasher, it melted. The dog bed, Max absolutely refused to sleep in. Growled at me— *me*, his favorite!—when I tried to make him. Annabel hung the Christmas-tree ornament at the back of the tree where no one could admire it except the people at the Dakota. The cranberry sauce, my mother put in the back of the fridge and forgot all about until the Sunday after Thanksgiving, when there was no more turkey to eat it with, so she fed it to Max, who'll eat anything. Just to prove my point, Max also ate the Styrofoam necklace and got so sick it cost us a hundred dollars at the vet. And the pomander ball went bad because of a reason almost too embarrassing to go into. (The teacher told us to ask our mothers for an orange and a box of cloves, but I thought she said a box of *clothes.* So Mom, figuring the school was having a charity collection, gave me a bunch of Dad's old shirts and some of my outgrown cords. Of course, when I got to school, I instantly realized my mistake. Unfortunately, Brian Hitzigger, the rat who sat next to me, realized it, too. He also realized how anxious I was not to have the whole rest of the class realize it, and generously offered to sell me some of his cloves for *fifty cents a clove!* To make a long story short, a pomander ball with only eleven cloves in it goes bad just about as quickly as an ordinary untreated orange. Revolting!)

As for the paintings and collages, after being Scotch-taped to the fridge for a little while, they always mysteriously vanished, and when questioned about this, Mom would mumble vaguely about having put them away somewhere. Oh yeah? I'm no dummy . . . two paintings a week, times four and a half weeks in a month, times eight months in a school year, over a period of three years comes to two hundred and sixteen rolls of crinkly, crackly paper. There isn't a somewhere anywhere in our apartment big enough to accommodate all that! Somewhere like the garbage is more like it.

"Oh, *dear*," said Miss Moon when I'd finished. "That's quite a saga!"

"Yes," I agreed, tightening my grip on *Stegosaurus Number Eight*. "And since she's going to put this stupid thing in the garbage anyway, I might as well save her the trouble and do it now."

Again I started to crumple it up, and again Miss Moon came to its rescue.

"Ben," she said, palm outstretched, "don't do that. I'd love to keep it for myself."

Baffled but docile as ever, I gave it to her.

"Why? Is it any good?" I asked hopefully.

Miss Moon laughed. "To be perfectly honest, I suppose I've seen better. But it'll be a nice reminder of the first time you trusted me enough to say what you really felt about something. And considering what a strong, silent type you usually are, I'm very flattered indeed."

That's what I mean by telling it like it is without hurting your feelings. By the end of that recess period, Miss Moon had me thinking, "So what if I can't paint, and nobody at home wants the stuff I make. Sean Connery is probably lousy at arts and crafts, too!" I loved her for that. And I loved her for saying what she said about me in that third-grade report, because she was the only teacher in the whole darn school who didn't think I was perfect. And she was the only person in the whole *world* who had my real number—zero, a cipher. Or at least that's what she felt I was in danger of becoming if I didn't change.

Oh, Miss Moon, Miss Moon, how could I have done that to you, been so disloyal, told Dad you were "all right, I guess" when you were the only person with enough courage, and enough insight into Benjamin "Ape Face" Andrews to tell it like it was! More about that right now—I've put it off as long as I could:

I, Benjamin "Ape Face" Andrews, only son of Ellen Jean and William Waring Andrews, beloved of all elevator men and little old ladies on the street, star of the Barden School, the boy most likely to be invited for a sleep-over—I, the crowd pleaser, the yea-sayer, the boy with the ready smile on his face . . . was a coward. Yes, sirree, four feet eleven and a half inches of Yellow Jell-O. Would you like to know what was behind that ready smile of mine? *Another* ready smile. Ha-ha! Fooled you, didn't I, you thought I was going to say a snarl or something. Oh no, not me. I'd never snarled in my life, never lost my temper.

I had many friends. Many, many friends. It's easy. As long as you're born with a reasonable dose of looks and smarts, and are careful never to make people mad, everybody likes you, I guess. The hard part is figuring out who *you* like—because you're so grateful to people for liking you, it kind of colors your vision when you try to decide what you really think of them.

Who did I really like? I didn't know. Duck Levine, definitely. Annabel, definitely. And Miss Moon, indefinitely—meaning as long as I lived. Mom, sure. Dad . . . ?

Well, of course I liked Dad. Who wouldn't? A neat guy, with looks and smarts enough to burn, but unlike yours truly, forceful and unafraid. And successful— Vice President in Charge of East Coast Production, Galaxy Films. He used to be in advertising, but Galaxy meant more creative work and more money—which he always says we're in danger of running short if not completely out of, despite the fact that Mom contributes her salary from the Museum of Natural History. (She's a cultural anthropologist now. Until two years ago when she went back to Columbia, she was just a housewife, but if she heard me saying "just a housewife" she'd kill me. The way she calculates it, if Dad had to hire replacements for each of her various functions as Mother, Cook, Cleaning Lady, Social and Financial Secretary/Hostess, and Interior Decorator, it would cost him $54,060. Furthermore, since she's still doing all that stuff *and* contributing her salary, she says she's worth practically as much as he is.)

Anyway, absolutely, I liked Dad. The question was, did Dad like me? Oh, I knew he loved me, the way all parents usually love their kids (even Mr. and Mrs. Hitzigger probably love Brian, although it must be quite an effort); but we didn't seem to connect too well. For instance, every night when he came home, he'd say, "How was school?" and I'd say, "Fine, thanks." Then he'd say, "That's good." End of fascinating conversation. I kept having the feeling that if instead of

"Fine, thanks" I'd told him I'd accidentally sliced off the tip of my little finger in the jigsaw and fed it to the guinea pig, he'd have still said "That's good," because he hadn't heard me in the first place.

I had a feeling I bored him. I had a feeling that no matter how hard I tried to please him—me, the great crowd pleaser—he was the one person I was never going to please. But I kept working at it anyway—which explains why I told him I wanted to go to Soonawissakit. Soonawissakit, the toughest, the most jock-oriented, most Establishment establishment in the East, was Dad's old camp, and I hoped he'd appreciate my following in his footsteps—or trying to.

Well, in February, it had seemed like a good idea—especially since Duck had said he'd go if I'd go, and then Annabel got herself a job there as administrative assistant—but on June 30th, as I stood in the Port Authority terminal, surrounded by those lockjawed jocks in their dirty Adidas, I knew it had all been a terrible mistake.

I looked over at Dad, his arm around Mom's shoulder, having a merry old time with a bunch of other parents, and was disgusted with myself. Dad would never have said he'd go to a place he didn't want to go to, just to please another person.

I watched him gracefully excuse himself from the group and head for the men's room.

I silently wished to God I was somewhere else, some-*body* else—him, to be exact.

Then I said it out loud to Duck Levine. And it was

11

at this precise moment that I found myself at the urinal. Looking down at—as I've said before, oh, wow!

About half a minute went by.

Then on my right I heard, "Anything wrong, Andrews?"

Reluctantly tearing my eyes away, I looked up and over. The owner of the voice had just been introduced to me (Ape Face) outside: Captain Splasher Wilking, Camp Director.

Hastily, I zipped my summerweight flannel fly. Cautiously, I turned to check my reflection in the mirror just to make sure—but yes, it was Mr. Neat Guy, all right—forceful and unafraid . . . and leaving this afternoon for Los Angeles on a fun business trip while Mr. Nice Guy the Coward smiled through four horrible weeks in Moosehead Village, Maine. Hallelujah!

I winked at my wonderful, forceful face. So long, Yellow Jell-O. Hello, Bill!

"Wrong? No, nothing wrong," I said. Boomed, I mean, in a rich baritone. Enthralled by the sound of myself, I added, "I'm just fine, thanks, sir . . . uh . . . Captain," and finished with an involuntary giggle of delight. The giggle came out this melodious chuckle.

"Still the same old Andrews, huh, Andrews?" said the Captain, joining me in a chuckle of his own.

Together, we had this jolly chuckle while each of us tried to think of what to say next. On his way out the door, the Captain finally came up with something.

"You know what," he said, suddenly lapsing into

12

salty seafarin' talk, "I got me some great expectations for that little tadpole a yours."

At that very moment, the little tadpole himself made a jet-propelled entrance into the men's room, stopping short just in time to avoid a titanic collision with the Captain's belly. After several attempts to dodge around each other (that routine where you step to your right, then you step to your left, but the guy opposite does the same thing, so nobody moves off square one), Ape Face, with an uncharacteristically murderous glint in his eye, dove—get this! dove down on all fours and scrambled through the Captain's bowlegs, surfacing at the sink, where he proceeded to hippety-hop up and down in front of the mirror. Right away, I knew it was Dad.

The Captain stared at him suspiciously. "What's he doin'?"

I was nicely nonchalant. "Just trying to get a full-length view of himself, I guess."

"Well, that shouldn't be too difficult," he said, and with a jovial "Yo heave ho and away we go!" he hoisted my flabbergasted father high in the air for a better look.

"How's that, little feller?" he asked.

2

"Put me down," I squeaked, pummeling Wilking on the back with my puny fists. "Put me down—NOW!"

An indignant scowl replaced the grin on his venerable puss and he abruptly lowered me to the tile floor with a tooth-jolting thump.

"Just who do you think you're talking to, mate? Another outburst like that and I'll beat your butt till it's black and blue!" growled Wilking, exiting in high dudgeon.

"Why good heavens, Ben, what happened to your manners?" remonstrated my . . . father? . . . son? . . . *self?* Who? for Pete's sake!

As a kind of test, I fixed him with a beady stare and said, "Just you wait, Daddy-O, you'll get yours!"

Briefly, the eyes met mine, then fell away. Significant, but not one-hundred-percent conclusive. Then the sole of a Gucci-shod foot inched slowly up the other leg, coming to rest on the inner thigh. Ape Face! Indisputably Ape Face—standing stork. All righty, at least that much had been established. But how this grotesque ectoplasmic transmigration could possibly have happened in the first place was completely beyond me.

Mentally, I ran through the events directly preceding the switch: I went into the men's room to pee. I said hello to Splasher Wilking, who was obviously there for the same purpose. While standing next to one another, we exchanged some inane chit-chat about the good old days when I was at Soona and he was my canoeing instructor. He told me the camp was even better today than when I went there and much more rugged in approach. I said that sounded terrific and I was sure Ben would get a heckuva lot out of the summer . . . it would really put hair on his chest. (Little did I know!) Then he asked wasn't I just a smidgeon jealous of my son, who was about to embark on this wonderful experience, and I said . . . well, I can't remember exactly what I said (my mind was three thousand miles away on how glad I was my secretary Madeline had booked me into the Beverly Hills instead of the Bel Air), but I *think* I said something on the order of how I'd give anything to be in his shoes—which I didn't even mean, I was only being *gracious!* But then, without so much as a violin sting, or a ripple of ascending notes on an electronic synthesizer—without any warning *whatsoever*, I was in the main waiting room of the Port Authority, in my son's brand-new desert boots, to say nothing of his skin, eyeball to eyeball with a child I'd never seen before in my life. Or if I had, I didn't remember.

15

Time out for digression: It was next to impossible to keep track of Ape Face's friends, he had such a slew of them. Small wonder, actually. He was a great little kid—top grades in school, held his own reasonably well in sports, never gave us a moment's trouble at home—and his instinctive response to any situation was always so considerate and generous, it could make an ordinary person—me for instance—feel about one inch tall. Ironically enough, he seemed to worship the ground I walked on—trotted around after me being politely deferential as though I were a minor deity—which made communication between us somewhat sticky. After all, how do you rap with a saint who thinks you're one? Answer: You don't. But that's neither here nor there.

More to the point is how do you rap with a twelve-year-old son who is poaching on your corporeal preserve (and crushing your best lightweight trousers in the bargain)? Accuse him of interloping? Call him a rotten body snatcher? Treat him with sweet reasonableness?—"I say, old sport, let's make a deal: I'll give you back your body if you'll give me back mine." Out of the question, unfortunately. In the first place, judging by the fatuous smile on his (my) face, he was perfectly contented with things as they now stood. (Still on one foot, crushing my trousers.) And in the second place, since I had no idea how we'd gotten ourselves into this unbelievable predicament, I was equally in the dark as to how we were going to get out.

In the meantime, there was at least one thing I could do.

"Ape Face," I asked, "is that you?"

"Yes and no," he said coyly. For a forty-four-year-old man with a beard, coyly is not an appropriate way to respond.

"This is no time for tomfoolery," I told him, in a stern but squeaky voice. "Once again, is that you?"

"Yes."

"Then take my shoe off my best pants and stand properly!" I snapped.

"Whoops, sorry," he said, complying instantly. That was more like it!

"Come on, let's go somewhere where we can talk," I said, leading the way out of the men's room. "There's a coffee shop type place right here in the building."

"Okay," said Ape Face, striding after me. "But we'll have to talk fast—there isn't too much time."

With relish, he activated the dial on my $300 digital watch. "Nine-sixteen and thirty seconds. The bus leaves at nine-forty. You wouldn't want to miss it."

I stopped dead in my tracks. "Bus?! Are you kidding? You really think I'm going to climb on that Trailways torture chamber while you take off first class in a 747 for L.A.? What are you, crazy?!"

"No," he said, serene as a morning in May, "I'm not crazy, I'm you. And you"—pause, pause, pause—"are me."

So much for sainthood. The kid was getting more obnoxious by the minute. We walked the rest of the way in stony silence. Correction: The stony silence part is accurate. As for walking, neither of us walked. I trotted and sprinted, my puny legs pumping furiously to keep up with his long ones. And he? Well, first he hopped on one foot, then on the other; next, he hopped backward—into an old lady with an aluminum walker, which didn't faze him in the slightest (luckily, no damage done); then he skipped for a few yards; and for the fourth down, he gave

17

himself a good running start, and slid on my Gucci loafers right into the revolving door. Have you ever seen a grown man in a beard and business attire hopping, skipping, and sliding in the Port Authority terminal? It looks damn stupid.

"Sit down and behave yourself," I hissed under my breath as we reached the counter. "And don't twirl on your seat."

"Why not?"

"Because, dummy, you now weigh a hundred and fifty-five pounds, and if you get going too fast, the seat'll come off and spin you through the plate-glass window." A nasty thought occurred to me. "Leaving me locked in this fragile frame of yours forever." I shuddered.

Ape Face looked pensive. "Gee, that's right. Then you'd have to grow up all over again."

He pointed to a plastic-encased drink dispenser. "Can I have some of that red bubbly stuff and a jelly doughnut?"

"Miss!" I called out, rapping impatiently on the napkin box with a saltshaker.

The waitress turned around and glared at me. "Yes, *sir*," she said with elaborate sarcasm. "What can I *do* for you, sir?"

"One black coffee, one jelly doughnut, and one raspberry bilge from your fountain of perpetual poison." If she could get snarky, so could I.

"Coming right up," she said, slapping the coffee in front of Ape Face and the bilge and the doughnut in front of me.

"No, the other way around," said Ape Face. Hands on hips, disbelief on face, she watched while he switched beverages, taking care not to spill in the process, and helped himself to an obscenely large bite of doughnut. "I let my son have whatever he wants," he announced with his mouth full.

"I can see that," she said sourly. "Is there anything else your son wants? A cigar, perhaps? Or an Alka-Seltzer for his tiny dyspeptic tummy? Because if not, that'll be a dollar fifteen."

Accustomed to my grabbing the check, Ape Face just sat there.

"Pay the lady, will you, Ape?"

He fumbled around in my pocket, finally came up with a handful of loose change, and deposited a dollar fifteen on the counter.

"Tip!" I muttered under my breath.

"How much?" he muttered back.

"Twenty percent."

Ape Face added exactly twenty-three cents.

"Thanks *ever* so!" said the waitress, and in search of more remunerative quarry flounced off to another customer.

Alone at last! And not a minute too soon. According to the Timex on my (his) wrist, the bus left in ten minutes.

"Now, listen, Ape Face," I said to my son the father, "let's get one thing straight. I don't know how this happened, but you are to tell no one about it. *No one*, do you understand?"

"How come?" He seemed surprised.

"How come? Because the whole business is so utterly, outlandishly preposterous, people would think you were stark raving mad, that's how come. A hallucinating paranoid schizophrenic is what they'd figure you for, and the little men in the white coats would lock you up for life in the cookie jar. Is that what you want?"

"No!!" he gasped, paling under the beard.

"Well, then, not a word to a soul."

He sighed. "Not even Duck?"

"Not even *anyone*. . . . Who's Duck?"

"Duck is Duck Levine. My best friend."

"You have a best friend called Duck?!" Fascinating!

"That's not his real name. He's called Duck on account of he walks like one." More and more fascinating.

"Does he also quack like one?"

Ape Face shlurped the last of the raspberry bilge and shook his head. "Nope. Walks like a duck but sings like a bird. In choirs and operas and stuff. Last Christmas, he sang *Amahl and the Night Visitors* all over Long Island, and one performance in assembly at school. They call him the Jewish Nightingale."

"*Who* does?" I asked, aghast. Bigotry at Barden!

"His parents. It's okay, they're Jewish, too," he reassured me. Warming to the topic, he continued. "It's lucky he's in your bunk, because you're going to love Duck. He's very mature and sophisticated for his age."

That brought me up short. Bunk, shmunk!

"Ape Face . . ."

"Hmmn?" He was busy dropping water on a straw snake.

"Ben, pay attention!" That did it.

"What?"

I chose my words judiciously. "Ben, every little boy in the world wonders how it's going to feel to be all grown up like his father, with a deep voice, and hair on his chest, et cetera, et cetera . . ." Ape Face grinned sheepishly. Enough said about that. ". . . and I can easily imagine how uniquely exhilarating this . . . ah . . . switch, shall we call it, must be for you. Because now you *are* all grown up, right?"

He nodded happily.

"WRONG!" I shouted, pounding my fist on the counter for

20

emphasis. "You are *not* all grown up, you only *look* all grown up. You are only a little boy . . . with jelly in your beard!" I added contemptuously. With a wet paper napkin I scrubbed vigorously at his face—never mind what the waitress thought as long as she couldn't hear me; then I lowered my voice to a hoarse whisper, and continued. "You are a little boy in what amounts to a furnished sublet, in temporary possession of *my* body, *my* clothes, *my* watch, *my* money, and credit cards and checkbook, and as soon as I can figure out how to do it, I'm going to evict you and get on with my life. But in the meantime"— I hopped off the seat, Ape Face followed suit—"here's what's going to happen. We're going to find your mother and tell her that you have decided to take me with you to California because I've changed my mind, and I don't want to go to camp after all."

"But," said Ape Face, as hand in hand, we started walking back to our group, "I thought you loved camp."

"Ape Face," I sighed, "are you being dense on purpose, or dense because you're dense?! Let me tell you something. As a result of the recent takeover at Galaxy Films, Ty Donovan, President of Worldwide Production and the man responsible for my being where I am today, has resigned. In his place is a woman—"

"Oh, good," said Ape Face, "Mom'll approve of that."

". . . a woman," I continued doggedly, "who is known in the company as a shark in sheep's clothing."

"So?" said Ape Face.

"So you're an imaginative little chap. What kind of a person does that sound like to you?"

"Not exactly a pussycat," said Ape Face.

"Very perceptive," I snapped. "It just so happens, according to everything I hear, the new boss *is* a pussycat—on the surface, that is, and devastatingly attractive, too; but underneath, she's the coldest fish in filmdom. And since her opinion of me may well determine the outcome of my entire career, I'm sure you can understand why I'm just the teensiest bit reluctant to entrust *you*" (a long beat, accompanied by a disdainful stare) "with the sole responsibility of making that vitally important first impression. Like it or not, buddy, I am coming with you. Is that clear?"

"Okay, I guess" was the meek response. And that solved that. Or so I thought. . . .

At the farthermost fringe of the Soonawissakit cluster, we finally located Ellen, anxiously searching for a glimpse of her wayward menfolk.

Before I could stop him, Ape Face crept up behind her and put his hands over her eyes. "Betcha don't know who this is," he said, winking broadly at me.

"Betcha I do," she said in a bored tone. (Oh, yeah!?) "Where were you anyway? I was beginning to worry."

"Me, too," said a familiar voice to my left.

I turned, and once again found myself eyeball to eyeball with . . . ?; now, however, a furtive glance at . . . ?'s feet told me all I needed to know. They were resolutely in fifth position—Pavlova herself couldn't have done it better.

So delighted was I at having solved the mystery of his identity, I promptly forgot my own.

"Hey!" I crowed triumphantly. "You must be Duck!" A fishy stare from Duck and onward I plunged. "I'd like you to meet my dad. Dad, this is Duck, Duck, this is Dad."

"We've met," said Ape Face with another giant wink.

"We *have*?" said Duck. By now, he probably thought we were both crazy.

A counselor toward the front of the group blew a whistle and delivered preliminary embarkation instructions. The troops were clearly on the move—it was now or never.

I tugged at the sleeve of Ape Face's (my) blazer.

"Tell her," I urged. *"Now."*

"Tell me what, darling?" asked Ellen, an unsuspecting smile on her face.

"Um," said Ape Face, his eyes on mine, his left loafer inching up his right leg (oh, nuts—there goes the other side of my pants). "The thing is, I've changed my mind about wanting to go to camp—"

Dunderhead, fool, idiot, lamebrain—he couldn't remember who he was either!

I interrupted him with a dirty look and a cleverly ambiguous one-word hint: "Dad!"

He got the gist. "Hold it, hold it!" he demanded, lickety-split abandoning the stork stance. "Let me begin again."

"By all means, do," said Ellen.

This time he made it safely, though cautiously, through the whole speech, deliberately stressing each correct pronoun while simultaneously pointing to its rightful owner. To wit:

"*I* have decided to take *him* (Ben, that is), to California with *me* (his Dad), because *he* has changed his mind about wanting to go to camp. Haven't you, uh, Son." A nice but inaccurate final touch; I've never called him Son in my life.

"Oh, no!" wailed Duck, profoundly depressed at the prospect of an Ape-less four weeks. "You can't! You just can't!"

"That's right, he can't," agreed Ellen.

"Why can't I?" asked my son, the father.

"Because," said Ellen, "aside from the fact that it's utter lunacy for everything to be switched around at the last minute," you're telling me, dollface! "there are one or two practical considerations. Such as what are you going to do with him when you get back from California if I'm still in Window Rock, Arizona, with the Navajos—take him to the office with you every day?"

"Boy, that'd be neat!" exclaimed Ape Face.

"Funny, you've never thought so before, Bill," she said. "And another thing, I've already paid the camp—with *my* money, and it's too late to get a refund."

"Oh, well," I said with a blithe snap of the fingers, "easy come, easy go." It was a monstrous tactical error. Hell hath no fury like a feminist scorned.

She wheeled on me, ablaze with indignation. "Young man, I worked darn hard for that money, darn hard indeed. Don't you 'easy come, easy go' me!"

"No offense intended," I assured her. She dismissed me with a curt nod and renewed her attack on Ape Face.

"As for you, Bill, sweetheart, what on earth possessed you to make this half-baked, unilateral decision in the first place? I mean, instead of letting your son spend a nice, healthy, cool summer in Maine, with plenty of wholesome food and fresh air and exercise and sleep—"

At this juncture, to register my low opinion of the bucolic life, I interjected an inspired imitation of someone in a Grade B movie being strangled by a mobster. Ape Face snickered. My wife ignored both of us and, after a brief recap, plowed implacably on.

24

"Seriously, Bill, instead of a nice, cool camp in Maine, you want to drag that poor child all the way to California so he can choke to death on smog?! What kind of crummy summer is that for a twelve-year-old boy?!"

Traumatized by the onslaught, Mr. Nimble Wits chewed a hefty chunk out of the cuticle on my right thumb, and said, "Gee, Mom, I guess you're right."

Wrong, wrong, wrong! I screamed silently. Suddenly everything was going wrong, and now the head counselor—who looked for all the world like your run-of-the-mill, beer-bellied, pig-eyed, sadistic Kommandant from Bergen-Belsen—was shouting final embarkation instructions, and the hordes were moving forward, and my time was running out! And so was my luck! . . .

Decision: I would stage a scene. Improvement: a *S*cene. Further improvement: a SCENE.

With a Rumpelstiltskin-like stamp of my desert boot, I bellowed, "I don't wanna, I don't wanna, I'm not gonna, nobody can make me, no*body*, no *way!* I'd rather be dead of a fulminating brain tumor!"—crude but effective, I thought, and flung myself into Ellen's arms, sobbing piteously. "Please, Mom, pretty please, pretty Mommy, puleeze don't make me!"

It was a pyrotechnical display of unsurpassed brilliance; and Ellen, whose compliant younger child could usually be counted on to behave with suitable decorum, was aghast.

"Good Lord, Bill, what do I do now?" she asked Ape Face.

"You don't do anything, Ma'am, *we* do it," said Splasher Wilking.

What "we" did was the ultimate humiliation. "We" picked me up, slung me over his shoulder like a duffel bag of dirty laundry, and carried me, wailing and flailing and upside down, toward the Trailways departure gate.

"Wait, I have to kiss Daddy good-bye!" I screamed.

"Bull diddly!" said Wilking, purposefully accentuating his already nautical swagger. We were yawing and pitching like a dinghy on the high seas; in a second, I might vomit down his back. That'd teach him!

"Daddy, come say good-bye!"

Ape Face, ever obedient and fleet of foot, quickly caught up with us. Then, upon realizing that communication with a perilously bobbing, upturned human duffel would be next to impossible, he adroitly adjusted his posture to accommodate mine—by running backward alongside me with his head tilted at an angle I never knew anyone but a freak-show contortionist was capable of achieving.

"Good-bye," he said breathlessly. "I hope you have a terrifically good time."

Wilking flashed him a look of contempt, and tightened his grip on my ankles. "What's the matter, Andrews—no little last kiss for Junior Miss?"

Ape Face dutifully lurched sideways in the general direction of my forehead.

"Never mind *that*," I croaked. We were practically there. I had roughly thirty seconds in which to impart a ton of vital information. Obviously, selectivity was the name of the game.

"Listen, *call* me! Promise you'll call me as soon as you get to the Beverly Hills Hotel. That's the Bev-er-ly Hills. In Bev-er-ly Hills. Don't forget your credit cards and your briefcase, the ticket's in the briefcase—TWA, five-o'clock flight, Kennedy— and about driving, you know how they drive in California—like

26

maniacs! . . . So unless you want to get killed on the Santa Monica Freeway or lost halfway down the Baja Peninsula where a bunch of Mexican bandits will rob you blind, don't ever get behind the wheel of a car. I want your solemn word on that! Do I have your solemn word?''

It was just at this crucial point that Splasher Wilking reached the narrow doorway leading to the outside ramp. Without a moment's hesitation, he plunged through it, while Ape Face, also without a moment's hesitation, backed smack into the wall of the terminal.

As for the solemn word, I couldn't quite catch it, but I think it was "Awp!"

3

"Awp!" I said, caroming off the wall and pitching flat on my face on the floor.

In their mad rush to get on the bus, all kinds of campers stepped over and around me; one, a klutz in cleats (anyway, it felt like cleats), even stepped *on* me; and one—out of about fifty or so kids, one only!—bothered to help me up.

"Are you all right, sir?" asked good old Duck in a concerned voice.

"Absolutely, thank you, Duck." I managed a weak laugh. "That's what I get for not looking where I'm going, ha-ha-ha!" Ha-ha-ha! in your hat if you think there's anything funny about a mashed hand and a matching pair of bruised kneecaps.

"Well, okay then, if you're sure," said Duck, inching toward the door. "Because Ape Face and I agreed to sit together on the bus and I wouldn't want him to think I was a no-show, especially in the mood he's in, if you follow me."

"Duck, you're a good friend," I told him. "And don't worry, Ape Face is going to be just fine."

"Boy, I hope you're right. For my sake as well as his," he added uneasily. "You see, all along I've been kind of counting on him to keep my spirits up, but the way he's been acting today—all that screaming and yelling and nut stuff . . ." Perplexed, he combed his fingers through a hunk of long blond hair. "Gee, Mr. Andrews, do you think he's having a nervous breakdown?—because that's just not the Ape Face I know!"

I considered leveling with him ("Curious you should mention that, Duck. It just so happens he's in my body and I'm in his." "Golly! You must be a hallucinating paranoid schizophrenic! Wait right here; I'll go call the little men in the white coats."), then thought better of it.

"True," I admitted truthfully. "But cheer up, this can't last forever." How truthful was *that*? I wondered. Maybe it could. Would . . . wow! . . . weird . . .

Out of the corner of my eye, I saw a few final stragglers being herded through the door by Mr. Mallison, one of the counselors. (And was sinfully glad not to be one of them.)

"Well, I guess you'd better get going, Duck. Listen, if I get a chance on the Coast, I'll send you some long-life batteries for your transistor."

29

He looked around guiltily. Radios weren't allowed at Soonawissakit. He probably wondered how come I knew he was sneaking one in.

"Sh," he cautioned, finger to lips, then gave me a grateful hug and bolted for the bus.

"Don't worry," I shouted after him, "Ape Face is going to be just fine, absolutely terrifically fine. He will, I promise!"

Maybe it was just a case of saying is believing, but all of a sudden I was filled with this wonderful sense of pride and confidence in myself. And I don't mean my superficial Bill self (although it certainly doesn't hurt to be over six feet tall, dark, and handsome, with hair on your chest and other places, a deep, commanding voice, and money in your pocket), I mean my inner Ape Face self.

Suddenly I knew that I, Benjamin Ape Face Andrews, former Yellow Jell-O champion of the world, would inherit the earth, and the sky . . . and the entire West Coast office of Galaxy Films.

As for poor little piddling William Waring Andrews, "Well, too bad for you," I said to myself jubilantly, and marched off to find my mother—*wife*.

4

"He wanted me to tell you not to worry, everything was going to be just fine."

Oh, yeah? I turned my back and stared out the bus window. All those glum-faced people walking around free as air on Tenth Avenue, not appreciating their good fortune—it was enough to make you cry.

"And another thing he said, Ape Face . . . Ape Face, are you listening?"

"Unh?" I grunted, back still turned.

"He said he'd try to send me some transistor batteries when he got to the Coast. What Coast?"

"West Coast."

"What's he doing on the West Coast? I thought he was in

advertising in New York. On the Glamour Gums account."

"That was years ago. He's in films, now. Anyway, it's gams."

"What?"

"Gams," I corrected him irritably. "Not gums, gams . . .
Glamour *Gams.*" Jackass kid!

"Are you sure?" he persisted. "I always thought it was toothpaste. Are you sure it wasn't toothpaste? Or a dentifrice?"

"Panty hose!" I bellowed. "Glamour *Gams*, made out of
Clingalon, the fabulous new fashion fabric that conforms to
your figure and is guaranteed never to bag, wrinkle, or run,
is *panty hose,* and I ought to know!"

The entire bus erupted in raucous laughter. A red-faced, red-
haired, green-eyed, green-toothed slob leered over the back
of the seat in front of me and lisped, "Ith that tho!"

More raucous laughter, followed by several lewd whistles
and a foxtrot demonstration in the aisle, mincingly executed
and sung ("Yeth, Thir, That'th My Baby") by two fourteen-year-
old scions of the country-club set.

"Siddown and shuddup!" Splasher Wilking thundered at
them. "As for you," he said, wagging a menacing finger under
my nose, "if I hear another word out of you, another single
sissy syllable, I'll throw you off the bus in White Plains!"

Wonderful! Less than ten minutes into the summer and already everybody had my son pegged as a hotheaded homo
with a penchant for ladies' lingerie. Maybe getting thrown off
the bus wasn't such a bad idea.

"Is that a promise, Cap'n?" I asked hoping against hope.

Regrettably, it was merely an idle threat.

5

WHAT EVERY TWELVE-YEAR-OLD BOY MAS-
QUERADING AS A GROWN-UP OUGHT TO KNOW
ABOUT TRAVEL BUT SHOULDN'T ASK—unless he's
prepared to be taken for an imbecile.
This is a list of helpful hints, based on incidents that
occurred during the next few hours of my life. To anyone tempted to skip reading it—on the assumption
that he'll never find himself in the body of his father
anyway—all I can say is I think that's a pretty reckless
assumption. After all, I never thought it would happen
to me.

On Being Lost

If you can't find your wife/mother in the Port Authority Bus Terminal, what should you do?

a) Break out in a cold sweat because suddenly you're all alone?

b) Ask the man at the Information booth if he's seen your mother—an attractive, medium-tall, brown-eyed, brown-haired lady . . . about thirty-nine years old? (Completely forgetting that you look older than that yourself.)

c) Figure, after fifteen minutes of concerted searching, that she's gone home without you, and go home as fast as you can—in a taxi?

d) None of the above.

The answer is: None of the above. I did all of the above, except d), of course—and when Mom finally got home, twenty minutes after me, she was in a foul mood.

There are three lessons to be learned from all of this. The first is that when it comes to desertion in grubby public places, grown-ups don't react any better than kids.

"Thanks a lot," Mom said bitterly. "You should just try being a defenseless woman surrounded by nothing but hoods and harlots sometime, and see how you like it!" Thanks a lot yourself, lady, I've already got my hands full trying to be a middle-aged man.

"Sorry, babes"—Dad occasionally calls her babes. Whenever possible, emulate the speech patterns of your alter ego—it lends verisimilitude—"but I thought you'd left."

"Left! When did I ever?!"

Which brings me to the second lesson. A grown-up doesn't usually desert you without any warning; so even though the grown-up seems to have vanished into thin air, do not expect the worst. She is probably in the bathroom, fixing her lipstick. At least, that's where Mom was.

The third lesson has to do with cabdrivers and big bills. When a driver tells you he is not obliged by law to leave his cab to make change for you, and you are not permitted by law to leave his cab until you have paid him, "Therefore, if you don't got nothing smallern a twenny, you gotta gimme the twenny, irregardless," that driver is lying in his teeth. This is a perfect example of being taken for an imbecile. Also for a ride.

Packing

If you're going to be away for two weeks, don't forget to take a suitcase with some stuff, or your wife/mother will think you're a real oddball. I know mine did.

"Bill, your plane leaves in an hour and a half. Hadn't you better get started?"

"If you say so, my love," I said, giving her a peck on the cheek and heading for the front door. "Goodbye, see you on Soonawissavisitors' Day—July sixteenth, isn't it?"

"I mean get started packing," she said, looking at me strangely.

"Good Lord!" I slapped my forehead with the palm of my hand. "It slipped my mind altogether."

"Maybe your mind is slipping altogether," she suggested dryly. Not slipping, merely on the move, I was tempted to say. (Attention: Resist all such temptations; they do not lend verisimilitude.)

Okay, now for the packing itself. This can be a somewhat tricky business. You may not know which stuff your Dad would want to take or where it is, or even where the suitcase is, and you also may not know how to do the actual packing because your mother has always done it for you. The safest stratagem is to let her do it for you again—although, these days, that takes a certain amount of manipulating.

"Honey, if you're not too busy, how would you like to throw a few things in a bag for me?"

A quizzical look, followed by, "What am I—your slave?"

A stricken look, followed by "Golly, Ellen, how insensitive can a fellow get! You must think I have some nerve, asking a favor like that of you!"

An incredulous look, followed by a burst of good-natured laughter, followed by, "Oh come on now, Willy, it's hardly a federal offense!" followed by the rapid selection of an appropriate California wardrobe, followed by the deft placing of same in a hanging garment bag and a medium-large piece of Samsonite . . . and ta-da, what do you know—that was that in no time flat!

Finally, if, at the last minute, you decide you can't live without your collection of *Lampoons*, your *Find the Hidden Words* paperback puzzle book, and the pink plush hippo you've kept your pajamas in ever

36

since Uncle Burt gave it to you for your sixth birthday, that's okay. Just make sure you hide these things at the bottom of the suitcase where your wife won't see them when she goes to put in the toenail clippers she forgot; because if she does see them she'll probably ask scornfully, "What in heaven's name is all this?" and you won't know what to answer.

For me, that particular problem never came up; I hid everything in my briefcase. For some reason or other, women never open men's briefcases. I guess they think it's rude.

Departures

You may be edgy about getting there on your own, but don't invite your wife to come with you to the airport; you'll discover she hasn't done this in years. "It's not that I don't love you, Bill darling, but I've seen an airport. Besides, I have my own packing to do." If you're lucky, you'll find some other tenant (in my case, a Mrs. Herman Wormser from 11F) waiting in front of your building for a cab to Kennedy, and dying to share it with you. If not, relax; the cabdriver will know a million ways to get there. One of them, according to Mrs. Wormser, a seasoned traveler, is via Westchester County, takes over two hours, and costs fifty-two bucks, minus tip. Needless to say, this is not the best route. The Triborough Bridge is the best route, because when you say to the driver in an authoritative tone, "Kennedy Airport, take the Triborough," he figures you know where you're going and doesn't dare mess around. Anyway, that's what Mrs. Wormser did, and it worked.

At the Airport

TWA, on a Saturday, is a very busy place. The clerk behind the check-in counter and all the people behind you in line won't like to be kept waiting while you fumble in six different pockets for the plane ticket— or, if you're me, surreptitiously rummage around for it under the pink hippo in your briefcase. And when asked whether you prefer smoking or nonsmoking, try to refrain from hooting with mirth; remember, adults consider this a perfectly sensible question. In other words, A.Y.A.*!

On the Plane

First class is different from tourist. As soon as you sit down they offer you stuff: newspapers and magazines—they won't have *Penthouse*, so don't bother to ask; free headsets—if it's one of those Disney flicks about a talking woodchuck at Michigan State, A.Y.A. and don't accept—you'd be the only one watching; they'll also offer you a free preflight champagne cocktail. Don't accept that either—it'll go to your head and loosen your tongue—next thing you know you'll be yackety-yacketing with your seatmate.

Her name was Peggotty Horn. Fiftyish, fattish, and friendly. Tan leather bag, tan leather shoes, tan leather skin, hair of honey and a voice to match.

* Act Your Age

38

"So you're with Galaxy Films, Mr. Andrews," she enthused mellifluously during hors d'oeuvres. "I hear they've had quite a shake-up over there. Care to tell me about it?"

"Wuh, ashually . . ." Due to something rubbery and disgusting in my mouth, I was coming through muffled. Swallow first, talk later, I figured. "Nuhshing mushatell."

"Excuse me?" she inquired.

Chomp, chomp, chomp—the stuff just wouldn't go down. "Whash *izh*-ish?!" I said desperately, pointing at my plate.

"Come again?" said Peggotty.

"Mediterranean Fruits de Mer," said a passing flight attendant, who understood perfectly. "Mussels, clams, scallops, and squid in a flavorful garlic—"

"Urghh!" I moaned. The flight attendant understood that, too.

"Here, sir," she said, hastily handing me a glass of water. Gulp, gulp, gulp, the day was saved. I thanked her, and turned back to Peggotty.

"You were saying?" she prompted. What *was* I saying? Between the champagne and the Fruits de Mer, I'd kind of lost track.

"About the shake-up."

"Ah, yes. Well, let me see now. Ty Donovan resigned—"

"Resigned? Oh, come off it, baby cakes, what're you giving me?" she purred. "Ty Donovan didn't resign, Ty Donovan was canned; otherwise, how come that item about him ankling to Indie Prod, right, baby cakes?" She kiss-kissed at me and continued the inquest. "Now what about Stephanie Marshak—" Stephanie Marshak? Indie Prod? Who *were* all these people!

"You tell me," I suggested cleverly.

"Listen, I didn't meet her yet, but anyone who goes from lowly script girl to first female president of a film company in five short years," oh, *her!* "is either very smart or very, *very*"—she gazed knowingly at me—"alluring, if you know what I mean."

"Both. Definitely both," I assured her. And then, between forkfuls of Tender Prime Ribs of Beef au Jus and Potatoes Anna (the Broccoli Mornay, I passed up), I verbatimed what Dad had said about the devastatingly attractive shark in sheep's clothing, pussycat on the surface, coldest fish in filmdom, et cetera, et cetera, blah-blah-blah, ending up with an inspired invention of my own.

"And you'll never guess what her nickname is."

"Tell, *tell!*" begged Peggotty, all agog.

At that point we were interrupted by a flight attendant with the dessert cart asking what we wanted on our sundaes. I said everything; Peggotty, impatient to get on with it, said nothing, just plain vanilla.

"So what *do* they call her, baby cakes? I'm dying of suspense!"

A nice long pause while I loaded up my spoon with a huge gob of butterscotch, tilted my head back, and dribbled it into my mouth from above.

"Strictly off the record," pleaded Peggotty.

"The Killer Cream Puff!" I announced. "Isn't that great?!"

"Fabulous!" she gurgled. "Simply fabulous. Who's responsible for that one, I wonder."

"Me," I said smugly, licking butterscotch remnants off the back of my spoon.

"Well, *you*," she said, "are nothing short of di*vine!*" Then she curled up against the window and went to sleep. Which reminds me: In first class, you can get seconds on dessert, so instead of letting the flight attendant catch you stealing your seatmate's dish of melting vanilla, just ask for another butterscotch sundae. She'll be happy to oblige. Also, don't forget to use your napkin or some kid on his way back from the bathroom will stop by your seat to tell you you have nuts in your mustache.

Other helpful don'ts are: Don't practice your father's signature in public unless you've prepared a logical explanation for this. I told the man across the aisle I was trying to get the ink flowing in my ball-point, but when he noticed the American Express card I was copying from, it made him kind of suspicious, I think.

Finally, don't fall asleep reading the Galaxy production "book" containing thirty or so pages of highly confidential info about present and future film projects. Because when you wake up just in time to prevent Peggotty Horn from ever so gently slipping it off your lap and onto her own, you'll be too dumb to worry about what if she'd succeeded. That's because you're too dumb to know who she is. (More about that later.)

41

6

"God bless our home away from home
And help us do our bit
To cherish every stick and stone
Of Soonawissakit,"

warbled the Soonawissakiddies as they eagerly tumbled out of the bus.

Duck and I, last off, stood to one side in a desolate huddle. Up ahead, someone with a clipboard and a bullhorn was barking instructions we were too nervous to listen to, much less assimilate.

"How's it look to you?" whispered Duck.

"I'd hoped for better. . . ." Any other camp would have

made a few improvements in thirty years—enlarged the dining hall, bulldozed the rocks out of the ballfield, upgraded the washroom facilities, or at least painted the dock a different color——

"But it's exactly the same," I observed.

"As what?" asked Duck.

"As it always was," I said, reminiscing gloomily. "Ice-cold showers, moldy tents, black flies, spiders, bloodsuckers . . . *bats! . . .*" suddenly it was all coming back with horrendous clarity, "not to mention the kid who snored, the kid who wet his bed every night and had to sleep in garbage bags . . . and the constant rain—it must've rained thirty out of the forty-nine da—"

Duck clutched my arm. "Ape Face, if your dad told you all that," but I hadn't, of course, having only just remembered it, "why are we here? Why did you want to come?"

Good question. All I ever said to Ape Face was if he wanted to go to my old camp, that was fine with me—hardly a rave review.

"Good question," I said.

Duck grabbed me by the neck of my Soonawissakiteeshirt. "Listen, scum, you told me he said it was wonderful!"

"Obviously, *he** was lying!"

"Shaddup!" growled a voice from behind. "I'm trying to hear what cabin I'm in, so just shaddup!" A sharp blow between the shoulder blades knocked me into the guy in front, who without bothering to turn around retaliated with an elbow gouge in my ribs.

"Charming chap," I muttered to Duck, sneaking a peek at

---

* The Ambiguous He, a device akin to the Editorial We, but much more useful to someone in my predicament.

the guy in back. To my no great surprise, it was the same red-haired, green-eyed, green-toothed slob who'd made fun of me on the bus.

"What do you expect from Hitzigger? He hates you." Does he now?

"Why is that?" I asked.

"I don't know. He's always hated you." Duck continued bitterly, "Listen, count your blessings, he's the only one. A lot of people hate me."

"De Menocal, Swensen, Biddle, Beaty, and King will be quartered in High Ledge with Snorkel Bains," bellowed the bullhorn. "And with Mr. Mallison in Mount Olympus," a misnomer if I ever heard one; Mount Olympus is a damp dump, "Murdock, Andrews, Levine, Von Volkening, and Hitzigger."

"Ke-ristmas! Gimme a break!" yelped Hitzigger. "If my old man knew I was rooming with a singing faggot and a panty-hose queen, he'd have me home in no time."

"That'd be hunky-dory with us," retorted Duck, whereupon Hitzigger promptly knocked him to the ground, and I, committing the ultimate betrayal, played the role of a disinterested bystander. (Not that I wanted to, you understand. My natural inclination was to clobber the Bejeezus out of Hitzigger, but trapped as I was in the body of my noncombative son, there was a good chance Hitzigger would clobber me instead, thus contributing yet another black mark to Ape Face's already besmirched reputation which he/I could ill afford.)

"Here," I said, offering Duck a hand up.

"It's okay," said Duck, rising unassisted to his splayed feet. "Not that I expected you to defend me physically or anything," was this a mild rebuke or wasn't it? "but the next time it happens,

44

maybe you could shout one of your usual *No! No!*s or *Don't DO that!*s. It might've helped.''

"The next time it happens, it won't happen," I declared, "because just let him lift one little finger at either of us, I'm gonna bust that s.o.b. right in the chops!"

"That'll be the day," said Duck with a tolerant smile. "That'll really be the day."

7

Question: What's big and pink and sprawls all over?
Answer: The Beverly Hills Hotel.

According to Dad, the Bev Hills is beyond compare.
Well maybe, but according to me, you could compare
it with a HoJo's and the latter would win hands down—
except for outside appearances. (All HoJo's look the
same—if you hate one orange roof, you hate them all.
On the other hand, pink is a really dumb color for a
hotel, so I guess you could call it a tie.)

Here's what goes on at the Bev Hills: If your plane
arrives at 7:40 (10:40 in New York), by the time the
cab gets you to the hotel, it's almost nine. Then you
check in at the desk, nervous about having to put your

46

not-quite-perfected William W. Andrews signature on the registration card. Luckily, the reception guy says, "Charge it to the company, Mr. Andrews?" so that's no problem. What's slightly a problem is his handing you the key to your "Same old room, sir, the boy will be right along with the bags," because you don't even know your way to the elevator, let alone where to go when you get off it (assuming the room is not on the ground floor). This is solved by waiting for the "boy"— who's no more of a boy than I am (ha-ha!), he's a middle-aged man with a paunch—to lead you there. (Fourth floor, go right when you get out of the elevator down a long hall, left down another long hall, then right again, and into a fantastically huge corner room with a king-sized bed, wraparound terrace, color TV, flowers, and a basket of fruit from Richard de Virgilio. Who? Some friend of Dad's, probably.)

Now for another small problem. The "boy" won't leave. Hangs around doing stupid things like closing the curtains, adjusting the air-conditioning, turning on the lights in the closet and the bathroom, showing you how the television works (I *know* how a television works!), telling you there's a swimming pool and three tennis courts . . .

"Thank you, that's terrific," you say, tactfully opening the door for him.

"Thank *you* sir," he says, slamming the door behind him. Where have you heard that super-nice-on-the-surface, nasty-underneath voice before? you wonder. The waitress in the Port Authority coffee shop, you remember. *Tip!* you remember, and fish out a quarter—but it's too late. He's already out of sight. Oh well, you can give it to him tomorrow.

Here's a bigger problem. It's now about 9:45 (12:45 in New York) and you should be tired but you're not. After sampling two grapes and half a pink-and-slimy something-or-other (mango? papaya?), you realize you're not hungry either. What you are is bored.

You open the briefcase and take a look at the Week-at-a-Glance datebook under Thurs., June 30; maybe there's a big Hollywood party you're supposed to go to. There isn't. TV's no good either—nothing but reruns.

You might as well unpack. Flat stuff in the drawers, hanging stuff in the closet, the pants you've been wearing (and storking on) in a ball on the floor—they need pressing anyway. Then you take your pajamas out of the pink hippo and start to get into them, but surprise, surprise! they don't fit because they're not yours, idiot, they're *his.* So you put the hippo back in the briefcase, wondering where are yours, then?

Standing in your nude, searching one drawer after another, you decide Mom forgot to pack them. Either that or Dad doesn't wear any (woo-hoo! pretty racy for an old guy!). Possibly he sleeps in swimming trunks—not as fun a theory but more plausible, considering the two pairs of trunks in the bottom drawer. Hold it! you think, could be he *swims* in swimming trunks! That's what you'll do, that's exactly what you feel like doing! So you climb into the blue ones with the red stripe down the side, grab a towel, and head quick-o for the pool. You can hardly wait.

It's at about this point, folks, that you* . . . that *I* began to get disgusted with the good old Bev Hills that's so beyond compare, because the entrance to the pool was locked. A mistake, obviously.

Up the stairs to the lobby I sprinted (pant, pant, puff, puff; boy, Dad's in rotten shape—in my own body I could beat him in a race, easy!), and made my modest request to a lady busy shuffling papers behind the reception desk. "Listen, would somebody please do me a great favor and let me into the pool area, if it's not too much trouble?"

It was as polite as I knew how to make it, but in Hollywood, politeness is not the way to go, evidently. The lady didn't even bother to look up.

"Sorry, sir, the pool is closed," she said, flat out.

"What for?" Polluted?

"For the night."

"Aw, come on," I wheedled, "I'm all ready to go in!"

That got to her. She immediately stopped shuffling and frowned up at me.

"Well you shouldn't be," she said sternly. "The management doesn't consider swimming attire appropriate for the lobby. As you can see." She gestured toward gobs of people milling around, all of them very dressed up (on their way to those parties I wasn't invited to, no doubt), and several of them staring at me.

* I don't know why I keep saying you, I don't mean you, I mean me.

49

Uncomfortable but determined, I stood stork and stood my ground. "Management is dead right. Swimming attire would be much more appropriate in a swimming pool. So how about—"

"Sir," she said through clenched teeth, "The management *does not permit swimming attire in this lobby is that clear!*"

"Want me to take it off?" I threatened. Kidding, of course, but if politeness isn't the way to go in Hollywood, neither is funnyness. She signaled with alarmed eyes to someone in back of me who smarmily inquired, "What seems to be the difficulty, Miss Vondermuhl?"

Uh-oh, here comes trouble, how would Dad handle it? With authority—cool and firm. FIRM. *Both* feet on the ground.

"That's what I'd like to know," I said, destorking and turning. Once again, I was face to face with a face that knew mine but I didn't know his.

"Why it's Mr. Andrews, welcome back!"

"Not so's you'd notice," I said coolly.

He looked me up and down, mostly down. Inadvertently, I storked (firm, *firm*, you fool!) then destorked.

"Your room is not satisfactory, sir?" Must be the manager.

"My room," I said with an impatient flick of the towel, "is perfectly fine. What's not so fine is your pool rule. *And* your dress code," I added for Vondermuhl's benefit.

"Mr. Andrews," he reasoned, "please don't be child-

50

ish." (Yuk-yuk!) "If we let you wander around like that, we'd have to let everybody."

"Then couldn't you change your pool rule and I'll wander around in the water? What's the pool doing closed for the night for anyway?"

Not unaware of the small crowd of busybodies we were beginning to attract, he plowed pleasantly on. "Well for one thing, it gets cold in the evening and most of our guests don't care for swimming so late." Neither would I if I had a party to go to.

"It's colder and later in New York and we all swim there—I even swam in a HoJo's pool at midnight once, in Keene, New Hampshire. That was really cold!"

"Besides, we have no lifeguard on duty now," he added.

"So what, so *what*?!" I squealed. "I've got a Red Cross Advanced *Swimmers*, for crumb sake! Would you be happier if I wore a Styrofoam bubble?! Okay," I shouted, "who here wants to lend me their Styrofoam bubble?"

Apprehensively, the crowd backed off a few feet— you'd've thought I was the Hillside Strangler. To be fair, you could hardly blame them. I don't know how I look when I get mad because it happens so rarely and I'm never in front of a mirror when it does (who is?), but I know how Dad looks. Demented! This was no time for demented.

I adjusted the towel around my shoulders. "Couldn't we continue our discussion in a more private location?" I inquired loftily.

51

"Perhaps my office, sir" was his prompt suggestion.

"As you wish," I replied, and allowed myself to be deftly steered to a room behind the cashier's cubicle, where I settled myself cross-legged in an easy chair in front of the desk, and he perched on it (desk, not chair). Frankly, I was relieved to be off the hook.

So, apparently, was he. "I really do apologize," he said with an ingratiating smile, "but they're not my rules, you know."

"Yeah, I know," I conceded grudgingly, picking my left big toenail (a little habit I caught from Annabel which she recently broke herself of—to save the nail polish, I guess). "The thing is, what do you *do* around here?"

"Me? I work," he said wryly.

"No, no, not you, *me*. What do *I* do around here? Swimming is out, what else is there?"

He was puzzled. I elaborated. "Don't you have a game room—with a Space Invaders in it?" He shook his head. "Asteroids, then? Or Galaxia—it's not so good, but—" More head shaking, continuing throughout the next. "Pinball? . . . A pool table? No pool table? . . . *Darts!* . . . No?! Not even darts, well what *do* you have in your game room, nothing but cards, I'll bet," I said scornfully, "for silly old ladies to play bridge. Well, okay, you want to play me a game of Crazy Eights? I'll win, I usually do, maybe you'd rather play Double Solitaire?"

In a minute he was going to have himself a fat case

of Inner Ear Disturbance from too much head shaking.

"What does *this* mean," I said, shaking my own head, "No, you don't want to play Crazy Eights or no, you don't want to play Double Solitaire? Or"—an incredible thought occurred to me—"no, you don't have any cards in there, either?"

One final shake, followed by a "you got it" nod of affirmation.

"You're kidding!" Outraged, I began a negative countdown. "No Space Invaders, no Asteroids, no Galaxia, no pool table, no pinball, no darts—"

"No game room."

"No cards, no— What did you say?! No *game* room?" Unbelievable!

Now it was his turn for a negative countdown. "That's correct," he said blandly. "No game room, and no Boom Boom room, and no discotheque—as a matter of fact, we don't even have a jukebox on the premises—"

"Well what am I supposed to do around here all night?" I demanded angrily. "Sit in my room smelling flowers and munching funny fruit sent by some total utter stranger?"

"Mr. Andrews," he protested, "we may not be bosom buddies, but I wouldn't exactly call me a total stranger."

A quick look at the i.d. sign on his desk confirmed it. Richard de Virgilio, Mgr. At the thought of hurting his feelings, I instantly reverted to type. (Yellow Jell-O.) "Heck, no, heck, *no!*" I heartily assured him.

53

"And thank you so much. It was extremely generous of you."

"No, it wasn't," he said rather ungraciously. "The management pays and we send it to everyone." Thud.

After a weary sigh, he continued in a friendlier but baffled tone. "Mr. Andrews, what's gotten *into* you this trip?" (Wouldn't *you* like to know!) "You've been here many times before, you're familiar with us, you know which services we offer and which ones we don't. . . . Mr. Andrews, putting it very bluntly, we are not a Howard Johnson's."

"You said it, I didn't," I told him. "In my opinion, you are absolutely beyond compare!" He beamed complacently. I stood up, and on exiting, added, "With the possible exception of a morgue."

Thus endeth the Gospel According to Ape Face on the subject of HoJo versus the boring Beverly Hills Hotel. The rest of the night was less boring only because I slept through it in my king-sized bed—until five A.M. (eight A.M. in New York, also in Maine), when the phone rang.

8

"C'mon, 'mon, 'mon, answer the phone, why don't you!" I begged.

"Because he's asleep, creep," said Annabel.

"Eight o'clock, any right-thinkin' person's risin' and shinin'," grumbled Splasher Wilking.

The three of us were in the admin office above the dining room, where I had ingested a seven-hundred-and-fifty-calorie carbohydrate festival of o-juice, oatmeal, pancakes, sausages, and cocoa. (Under duress, you understand—a plea for "just plain toast and coffee, I can't eat all this" having elicited a short laugh from the counselor and "Eat it now when it's hot, or for lunch when it's not" in singsong unison from my fellow campers.)

"I'm sorry, sir, there seems to be no an—"

"Keep ringing," I told the operator. "Up, *up!*" I said into the phone.

"Face it, kid, your old man's the same city slugabed he always was."

"But Captain Wilking," said Annabel, hotly defending dear old Dad, "he's in California, where it's a lot earlier." She flashed me a dirty look.

"Unh," groaned Ape Face, at last.

"Daddy," I began, "I'm sorry to wake you—"

"You're not waking me," mumbled Ape Face—which was confirmed instantly by the sound of heavy breathing.

"Hey!" I said.

"California!" Wilking poked me in the chest with his finger. "I want time and charges on this one, squirt!"

"Considering the thousand-dollar tab, I should think Soona-wissakit could pop for one long-distance call," I told him.

"Ape Face!" Annabel was shocked.

"Aren't you kinda forgettin' yourself, young feller!" warned Wilking.

"Right." I shrugged apologetically and went back to the phone. "Ben!" I shouted. Wrong! A quick fix: "This is *Ben.* Your son Ben."

"Hi, Ben," murmured Ape Face. *Ben?* He knew perfectly well I wasn't Ben! Either he was extremely sleepy or . . .

"Is there someone in the room with you?" I asked, not realizing how peculiar this was going to sound.

"At five in the morning and Mom's in the desert?!" said Annabel, aghast. Wilking concentrated on filling his pipe.

"I just wondered," I said, opting for wide-eyed innocence—

after all, what would a twelve-year-old child know about marital infidelity anyway?—"are you having a sleep-over or something?"

"Dad!" said Ape Face. More than I thought. Well at least he was awake.

"Please, Daddy, this is important," I pleaded. "You've got to get me out of here. Because I need you, and *you . . . need . . . me*, believe me you do!"

"Oh, he does *not!*" said Annabel, thoroughly disgusted.

Wilking grabbed the phone out of my hand.

"But Daddy," said the phone on the way to Wilking's ear. We all three heard it. Two of us blinked. I winced.

"What's goin' on here anyhow?" Wilking asked me. "You call him Daddy, he calls *you* Daddy, hell's bells, let's all call him Daddy.

"Hey there, Daddy," he said into the phone, "this is Cap'n Splasher Wilking. Your youngun here's takin' himself a sorry spell a I dunno what, homesicketyness, most likely—says he didn't sleep a wink all night, and then this mornin' made such a ruckus at breakfast just now over wantin' to get you on the phone, his sister had to leave her own breakfast and drag him up here to do that."

He listened for a second. Then, in response to a seemingly irrelevant question, he looked at Annabel. "Is she mad? I dunno. Ask her yourself." He passed her the phone.

"I am not mad," said Annabel. "I am apoplectic with rage and humiliation. Dad, he's been a complete maniac ever since he got off the bus."

Wilking reclaimed the phone. "Shoulda seen him *on* the bus," he added. "And before. Hoo-ie!" Another brief listen, then,

"Yup, I forgot, you did see him before, didn't you, Daddy. Well then, you know what I'm talkin' about." Chuckle, chuckle. "But never you mind, we'll shape him up in no time. Meanwhile, anythin' in partikler you want me to tell him?"

He listened, then repeated to me, "Don't worry . . . everythin's fine . . . the hotel's fine . . . the plane ride was fine . . . he sat next to a nice lady called Peggotty Horn. . . ."

Peggotty Horn! I made an adrenalin-fueled leap to Wilking's ear and grabbed the phone back. "You didn't talk to her, did you?"

"Sure I talked to her. It would've been rude not to. She was talking to me."

"No, no, no, what I mean is you didn't quote me on anything, did you—about business things, for instance?"

"Why?" said Ape Face cautiously.

"Because Peggotty Horn is the new show-biz gossip reporter on the *Today* show, that's why." Dunce! Clod!

"Ape Face, Dad knows how to take care of himself," said Annabel.

"*Did* you?" I repeated menacingly.

Silence from the phone. Flat on his back in bed, storking horizontally, I'll bet—and about to tell me a big fat lie.

"Uh, no, not really," said Ape Face. A big fat lie, I could hear it in his voice. By now, I was probably out of a job.

"Listen, you listen to me," I shouted. "Either you tell Captain Wilking to put me on the next available flight to the coast or I'll throw myself off a mountaintop and it'll be all your fault!" I thrust the phone at Wilking.

"Kid's talkin' hogwash, sir," drawled Wilking in a voice that would lull a lion. "Forty years Soonawissakit's been runnin', we never had a suicide yet and we're not fixin' to have one now. So you can go on back to sleep with a clear conscience."

A look of disbelief, followed by "Nighty-night to you, too, sir," concluded the conversation.

Gently, he replaced the phone in the cradle, then, not so gently, gave me a knuckle rap on the head.

"I got one or two things to say to you, young feller. Thing one is your daddy, and me, and Sis, here, all agree . . ." without even knowing what she was agreeing to, "Sis, here," alias my daughter the fink, nodded heartily, "that you are stayin' in this camp whether you like it or no. Thing two is before you can throw yourself off a mountain, you gotta learn how to climb one."

He glanced at his watch. "The Outward Bound program—includin' rock scalin' and the like, begins in four minutes. See that he gets there," he barked to Annabel, and stomped out of the room.

Trapped. Helpless and trapped. Helpless, *job*less, and trapped—with a wife and two children to support. Or an inaccessible mother, an unsympathetic sister, and a twelve-year-old father to depend on. Either way, it stank.

It's enough to make you cry! I said to myself. Out loud, apparently.

"Go ahead," said Annabel, with an unexpectedly sympathetic smile. "It wouldn't be the first time."

To tell the truth, I would have rather liked to, but after thirty or so years, I was out of practice. The best I could produce was a heavy sigh.

Annabel put her hand on my shoulder. "Do yourself a favor, stop worrying about Dad, will you, Ape?"

"Easy for you to say," I answered.

"Since when have you cornered the market on filial affection? Come on, you're going to be late," she said, leading me to the door. "I love him as much as you do, you know."

"Probably more," I said, trailing behind her. "But how much would you love him if he couldn't pay the rent, couldn't pay the tuitions, couldn't pay the food bills"—words were now tumbling out of my mouth faster than I was tumbling down the stairs—"no more fancy restaurants, or vacations, no more Health and Racquet Club, not even a park permit for tennis . . . how much will* you love him when your little pals ask you what he does for a living and you have to say, 'Nothing. His wife and kids left him, he lives all alone in a burned-out section of the South Bronx, sitting around in his undershirt all day, drinking beer out of a can, watching game shows, and waiting for the phone to ring, which it won't.' How much will you love him then!"

"Wha-at?!" Annabel came to a dead stop on the stairs—I nearly crashed into her. "What kind of lurid X-rated scenario is that!" she said, turning around to face me.

"Anybody who blabs company business to Peggotty Horn is going to get fired, Annabel. It has to be."

"But you don't even know what he said to Peggotty Horn."

"I can imagine, though," I said grimly.

"Imagine, imagine! That's the trouble with you. This whole thing is nothing but pure conjecture and gross hyperbole, which means—"

"I know what it means," I said irritably—one year at Yale, the girl was a walking thesaurus, "but seriously, Annabel, let's say your dad did get—"

* Please note change of tense in midstream of thought from *would* to *will*.

"He's your dad, too."

"Yes, well, if Dad did get fired, how *would* you feel? Seriously."

"Seriously?" She was on the verge of answering when Terry Mallison, my counselor, appeared, breathless, at the foot of the stairs behind her.

"Ben Andrews, they're waiting for you in Outward Bound."

"In a minute," I said. "Go on, Annabel." Too late. She was already turning her back on me—literally and figuratively.

"*Now*, Ben," said Terry, "Captain Wilking wants you *now*. He sent me to get you, spit-spot, on the double."

"Terrific," I said. "What are you, his Punctual Flunky?"

Annabel tittered girlishly. Oh-ho! I thought to myself, what's going on here? I hadn't heard that sound since Boris Harris—with whom she was madly in love five years ago—kissed her in the front hall. I was eavesdropping in the front-hall closet. (No apology; she was only fourteen, don't forget, and any responsible parent—oh, never mind.)

"Hello, Terry," she said. "Remember me?"

"That can't be *you*, is it, Annabel?" said Terry, evidently knowing full well it could be and was.

"None other," she said with a second titter and a toss of her tawny mane.

"You two know each other?" I asked.

"From the orthodontist," said Annabel, without bothering to look at me.

"Astonishing what can happen in just two years," murmured Terry, sizing her up and down . . . and up—and suddenly, ZAP! there was eye contact between them that would burn a hole through your hand.

"Your teeth look wonderful," he ogled.

"Thank you," purred Annabel. "So do yours." They exchanged winsome, well-occluded smiles.

"I'm in my last year at Harvard. You?"

"Yale. Sophomore. It was a wild winter, I can't wait to relax." A flutter and a sigh.

"How about relaxing with me tonight after taps?" A wink and a half smile.

"How about getting me to Outward Bound before Wilking chews me up?" As long as I was stuck in the godawful place, the least I could do was try to make a go of it.

"In a minute," they said together.

"What happened to spit-spot on the double?" I inquired acidly.

The not-so-Punctual Flunky broke eye contact with the Tawny Titterer just long enough to ask me what my hurry was, then turned to her again.

"There's a place called Lookout Point you can row to on the other side of the lake where you catch a great view of the open sky. Shall we?"

"Sounds good, Terry, but I'm not off until Monday. . . ."

On and on and on they went, with the winks, and the titters, and the burbles, and the flutters, and the ogles, and the gurgles and the murmurs and the sighs—let me tell you, I could have dropped dead without their noticing!

I'll tell you something else: In the end, I found my own way to Outward Bound; it was plenty rough. But being a possessive father incarcerated in the body of his twelve-year-old son, unable to prevent an assignation between his nineteen-year-old daughter and her slimy, sleazy new boyfriend, is a whole lot rougher, I promise you.

9

The first spoonful of Frosted Flakes was on the way to my mouth when I was struck by an overwhelming urge to add a bunch more sugar to the bowl—making up, I guess, for all Mom's breakfasts of shredded beaverboard which she calls fiber and good for you.

I had no sooner satisfied the urge when another one struck. This urge, equally overwhelming but a lot harder to account for, was to turn on the *Today* show.

Why? I wondered. Why do I want to do that? I never do at home. The only person who ever watches the *Today* show at home is— Oh, NO, I remember something!. . . No, wait, maybe I dreamed it, please, *please*, I dreamed the whole phone call and Peggotty Horn is just some fat nobody from nowhere I'll never see again in my life. . . .

Until I turned on the *Today* show and there she was, running off at the mouth for five agonizing minutes about people and projects I'd never heard of; but then winding up with "And for those of you dying to know the inside scoop on that Galaxy takeover, one of the execs 'way up there' in the company told me confidentially last night that ex-Prez Ty Donovan, who insisted to this reporter he was *voluntarily* ankling to Indie Prod, was definitely axed. I also learned that his replacement, beauteous Stephanie Marshak, filmland's first female studio head, is known around Galaxy as the Killer Cream Puff. Beauty is as beauty does, Stephanie!"

So that was that. It was all over. Unless—a ray of hope—unless there are so many high-level execs at Galaxy, they won't know who to pin it on. . . .

The phone must've rung five or six times before I was aware of it, then three or four more times before I screwed up the courage to answer it.

"Hello," I finally whispered into the mouthpiece.

"Is this the Galaxy exec who's 'way up there'?" asked a male voice.

"Not any longer, obviously." Oh Dad, I'm so sorry! "Boy, you're mighty swift with the executions around here, aren't you? Ready, aim, fired before a guy's even finished breakfast." A bitter afterthought. "Who needs breakfast?" I pushed the tray away.

"Hold on, Andrews. How can I fire you, I just got

fired myself—according to you," he added pointedly.

It was "axed" Ty Donovan; axed and angry.

"Ty, I never said that. Peggotty Horn put words in my mouth."

"Funny, it's usually the other way around," he said wryly. "Aah, what's the difference, nobody ever believes that myth about independent production anyway. All I can say to you, fella, is you've got more guts than I thought. Just as well—after this morning, you're going to need them. Killer Cream Puff, my eye!" He ha-ha-ed mirthlessly and hung up.

So Indie Prod meant independent production. That was one mystery solved. But what did "you've got more guts than I thought" mean? If anybody had guts it was Dad—oh Jeeze Louise, the phone again. Was *this* the firing squad?

No, this was only the message operator to say while I'd been talking, Mavis Ohler had called to remind me about the Galaxy story meeting at ten o'clock in Mr. Weller's office.

What time was it now? I asked her. Eight-fifty-nine. And how long did it take from here to there? Beverly Hills to Burbank this time of day, I should allow a good forty minutes, she told me. I told her to order me a cab, please, I'd be down in fifteen.

Which I was. Unshowered but otherwise presentable—in tie and jacket, with teeth brushed, beard brushed, mustache brushed, *loafers* brushed, and I even remembered the briefcase.

But they hadn't ordered the cab.

"Why not?" I said to the doorman. "I asked for one."

"We assumed you'd forgotten about the prearranged rental, Mr. Andrews, and the operator had no way of knowing about it. That's Our Department."

With a proud flourish, he opened the door of a spanking-new Ford sedan. "The keys are on the dashboard, sir. Have a nice day."

It was very tempting. In fact, I was halfway in and about to ask the way to Burbank when a hysterical voice from the past screamed, "Don't ever get behind the wheel of a car. I want your solemn word on that! Do I have your solemn word?"

Did he or didn't he? I couldn't recall, but if he did . . .

Old Yellow Jell-O stepped back out.

"Anything the matter, sir?"

"Is this what my secretary requested? I'm sure I told her a Mercedes," I said, perplexed. (Well, I had to make up *some*thing, didn't I?)

"Oh, sir, I'm terribly sorry," said the doorman, hailing me a cab.

"Perfectly all right, I just don't want to be late for my ten-o'clock meeting," I said graciously, tipping him a dollar and climbing in.

"You won't be, sir. Get Mr. Andrews to Galaxy in Burbank before ten, will you, good buddy?" he said to the driver.

"No problem," said the driver.

He went like a bat out of hell and got me there at one minute of, so by the time I found Mr. Weller's office, I was still only five minutes late. Not that it mattered. I could have missed the whole thing, for all they cared.

"Morning," I said cheerily, and to Tony Crane, the one person I recognized from having come for dinner once in New York, "Hi, Tony."

They—a couple of youngish women in slacks and, including Tony, four men about Dad's age wearing open shirts—looked up from the blue papers they were all studying and studied me instead. Briefly, but long enough to see something they didn't like. My clothes, I hoped.

"I haven't unpacked yet," I explained, loosening my tie and removing my blazer.

"Really? We heard you came in last night on the five," said toneless Tony. Without so much as a "have a seat, Bill," he and the others went back to their blue papers. The problem was clearly deeper than clothes.

Have you ever been to a shunning? A Puritan shunning where nobody talks to the sinner or takes notice of anything he does—even when he opens his briefcase upside down, nervously looking for his own blue papers—and one *Lampoon*, two *Penthouse*s, and a pink hippo fall out on the floor? No? You haven't lived.

In the anteroom after the meeting, I made a final stab at détente. "Anyone for lunch?"

Coincidentally enough, every single one of them had other plans. Even I did, according to Mavis Ohler, Mr. Weller's secretary.

"Mr. Andrews, don't forget lunch in the commissary with Ray Ewald."

"Good old Ray Ewald!" Another friend of Dad's I'd met in New York; it was nice to know there was at least one person, other than Mavis Ohler, willing to communicate with me.

"And your appointment with Miss Marshak is at two," said Mavis, "but I guess you don't need reminding about that, do you." She sucked in her breath, crossed both sets of fingers on both hands, and added in a whisper, "Oh, gosh, good luck, we're all praying for you!"

Mavis Ohler may have looked like a prune in a polyester pants suit, but she was rapidly becoming my best friend.

"Thanks. Thanks a lot," I said gratefully, and kissed her good-bye on the cheek.

Finding the commissary—which I did by simply following a horde of people all headed for the same stucco building (at 1:00, where else would they be going?)— was easier than finding Ray Ewald. I checked the entire room, table by table, and the cafeteria line; he was nowhere to be seen.

To be seen were:

four Roman gladiators in breastplates and plumed helmets

a bevy of identically costumed show girls from one of those 40's movies (good-looking girls)

68

an enormous fat man, a bearded lady (real beard, I think), three clowns, and two midgets, all eating at the same table, the midgets sitting on those baby seats that fit on regular chairs—must be a circus movie

three surgeons in green coveralls, an operating-room nurse, and a lady bandaged from top to toe, one arm in a cast—a hospital movie

some grease-streaked G.I.'s in camouflage jumpsuits

one werewolf

a seven-foot gorilla taking off his head in order to eat a fruit-salad platter brought to him by his five-and-a-half-foot gorilla girl friend (I guess it was a girl—she had a dainty way of walking)

some regular people in work clothes (unless they were actors in a movie about regular people who worked)

and me, who was too hungry to wait any longer for Ray Ewald—word travels fast out here; by now he was probably captain of the shunning team.

The bandaged lady, just behind me in the cafeteria line, needed help with her tray, so I carried hers and mine to a big table where, among G.I.'s, Romans, and show girls, I'd spotted two empty places.

"Here we go," I said, unloading tuna fish and chocolate milk for me, conch chowder and rice pudding for her—blech!

"How can you eat that stuff!"

She pointed to her wired jaw, and rolled her eyes. "No choice."

Boy, if that's what you go through being an actor, it's not worth it.

"How long is that thing on for?" I asked sympathetically.

She put up ten fingers.

"Ten days?"

With her hands, she indicated longer.

"Ten *weeks*?" Ten weeks, she must be the star of the picture. That might be worth it.

"What are you in?"

"What am *I* in?" she croaked. "A lot of pain. From a car accident." She shook her head in amazement. "It never occurs to you people there are other professions in this world besides acting, does it?"

For someone in a lot of pain, she was remarkably chatty, I thought.

"Sorry, it was dumb of me," I said.

"All actors are dumb," she announced. "What are you in, a remake of *The Man in the Gray Flannel Suit*?"

"This is the way we dress on the East Coast," I said aloofly.

One of the Romans picked up his ears. "I hear there's some East Coast Galaxy dude got canned this morning by the Killer Cream Puff herself."

"Says who?" My beard was standing on end.

"Says everyone. It's all over the lot."

Astonishing! Eight-thirty this morning Peggotty Horn goes on the air, by lunchtime the whole studio

70

knows Marshak's nickname and my fate. Who needs lunch! Besides, it was almost two o'clock.

I pushed the tuna fish away and hastily excused myself from the table.

As I headed for the door, one of the show girls, referring to me, said, "What's he in?"

"Trouble, I think," said the Roman thoughtfully.

All actors are not dumb. . . .

I wonder how it's going to happen and how you're supposed to behave.

With dignity?: "Miss Marshak, I guess there's nothing I can possibly say—"

"I think you've said quite enough already, Mr. Andrews."

"Or do," I persist.

"Do?" She studies her blood-red talons for a moment, then smiles a Mona Lisa smile. "Yes, there is something you can do." Quick as lightning, a cruel forefinger points to the door. "Out!" she rasps. "Get out, now!"

With restrained outrage?: "Miss Marshak, firing me is your privilege, of course, but you might have done me the courtesy of informing me before you informed everybody else."

"*You* are accusing *me* of informing?! Ho-ho, that's rich!" A malevolent cackle, followed by "Out! Get out, now!"

She's got a point there. Scratch that one.

Unrestrained outrage?: "If you think I'm sorry I

called you a Killer Cream Puff, you're right—it's too good a compliment for anyone as mean and horrible as you!"

No, too babyish.

Guile, maybe? "I never called you a Killer Cream Puff. It was Ty Donovan."

"Tainting your best friend with libel and slander, that's attractive, I must say!" she sneers. "Out!" she points. "Don't bother opening the door, just slither right under it, you contemptible worm!"

Scratch that one, too. I'm ashamed I even thought of it.

Candor. How about candor?: "Miss Marshak, if you fire me, you may well be destroying the career of an innocent man."

"Are you trying to tell me you did *not* discuss Galaxy affairs last night on the plane with Peggotty Horn? Mr. Andrews, really!"

"No, I'm not, yes, I did, but my *dad didn't!*"

She leans forward, a flicker of interest in her beady little eyes. Now we're getting somewhere!

"I fail to see the connection . . ."

With relish, I connect her, beginning with the body exchange in the Port Authority terminal, ending with "So what you see before you, Miss Marshak, is only a twelve-year-old boy," here's where I start to cry, "who's very scared and homesick and Mom is in the desert with the Navajos," here's where I notice her blood-red talon pressing a button on the office intercom machine. "Hey, what are you doing that for?" and

72

here's where she whispers into it, "This man is a hallucinating paranoid schizophrenic! I want you to call the little men in the white coats and tell them to get him out of here, *now!*"

"Okay, okay, I'll go," I moan, "but if Dad and I change bodies again while I'm in the cookie jar, will you give him his old job back?"

Tears are now cascading down my cheeks, my beard is sopping wet and dripping on my briefcase . . .

"Mr. Andrews?" What, *what*, who said that, where *am* I?! "Would you like a tissue, Mr. Andrews?"

Reality returned. I was in the waiting room of Stephanie Marshak's office. Waiting for my two-o'clock hour of judgment. Waiting, and crying—in front of Betty Lou Bienenstock, Stephanie Marshak's secretary.

I helped myself to several tissues, blew my nose, wiped my eyes, and blotted my beard.

"Rose fever," I explained.

"I understand," she said tactfully. "Look, this is none of my business, but whatever you do, don't do anything foolish."

"Like what?" What's left!

"Oh, like get on your high horse and say, 'You don't fire me, I quit!' or something like that."

"Sounds good to me. Why not?"

"Because you'll lose all your stock options and severance pay." She peered at me over the rims of her half glasses. "Forgive me for being personal—"

A buzzer sounded. Like a klaxon, it sounded. I jumped a foot.

"I'm afraid that's it, hon."

I rose, straightened my shoulders, strode manfully to the door—that was the easy part—and hesitated.

"Go on in," urged Betty Lou gently. "She's expecting you."

I opened the door.

Seated at the desk, head down, too engrossed in paperwork to acknowledge my presence, was the Killer Cream Puff. No red talons, I noticed. Just plain ordinary hands—but plenty capable-looking. Capable of signing a company death warrant, which was probably what she was doing right now. Aw, nuts, I might as well get it over with.

With my fingers, I beat a timid tattoo on the doorjamb.

She lifted her head. What I could see of her—the part that wasn't obscured by black aviator glasses—was, as Dad had described, devastatingly attractive on the surface—blond hair (natural), good nose, great mouth, but the coldest fish in filmdom underneath, I reminded myself.

"I don't quit, you fire me," I declared resolutely.

At that, she whipped off her aviator glasses and I nearly fainted dead away—partly from lack of breakfast and lunch, but mostly from shock.

Because gazing at me with those enormous deep-blue eyes of hers was my own beloved Miss Moon.

10

Wouldn't you know it, Hitzigger snores. And when Hitzigger snores, the whole tent shakes, including—especially including—the double-decker bunk he and I share. (For bed assignment the cabin drew lots. I drew Hitzigger; shot with luck, I am.)

Some people sleep through Hitzigger; I am not one of them, and between Thursday and tonight (Monday), I'd had approximately eight fitful hours of shut-eye—hardly enough for a growing boy. I could just see Ape Face at twenty, still only 4'11". ("Hey, shorty, what's the matter with you you're so short?" "It's called Hitzigger's Syndrome.")

Oh well, I grew to 6'1" myself; Ape Face should be genetically programmed to follow suit. . . . He'd better do it, too! I sat bolt upright in bed—adolescence was bad enough the first time, if I had to go through it twice . . . Crikey, Hitzigger, shut up! I pounded the sagging bedsprings under his butt.

We will now have a minute of silence in which to pray for ten more. Nothing doing; Mount Vesuvius is at it again.

From my neighboring bottom bunk, I enviously watched the serene rise and fall of Duck's chest and hissed what I thought was a rhetorical question at him.

"How can you sleep through that!"

"What?"

I repeated the question, louder this time.

"Ravel? I love it—it *puts* me to sleep. Here, have a try."

"Thank you," said Mallison, intercepting the transistor on its way from Duck to me.

We heard the click of the lock on Mallison's Confiscated Articles strongbox, then the creak of bedsprings as he lay back down again. And then I heard . . . ?

"Duck," I whispered, "are you crying?!"

He answered with a couple of snuffles and a sniff.

"Aw, come on, Duck, you'll get it back at the end of the summer."

"I can't get *through* the summer without music, you know that."

"Aren't you two asleep yet? One more squawk and I'll have to give you each a demerit," warned Mallison.

After five minutes of relative silence (Hitzigger notwithstanding), Mallison creaked to a sitting position and checked the cabin for signs of life. Finding none, he quickly dressed himself and crept stealthily out of the cabin.

"Where's he going? He's supposed to be on duty," said Duck.

76

"To meet my daugh-um-sister at Lookout Point, the slimy sleaze bag. Some nerve he's got cracking down on us when he's breaking rules himself!"

No response.

"Are you asleep?" I asked.

"Of course not. I've just been thinking. About rules. I've read the rule book: three demerits equals one black mark; three black marks and they send you home. Well, if they hand out demerits for talking after taps, we could get ourselves kicked out of here in no time—I mean a demerit for talking, think what we'd get for swearing—"

"—or fighting. I could punch out Hitzigger!"

"That's no good. You'd lose and I wouldn't get a demerit. How about we both punch out Hitzigger?"

"You're on. How about we both streak in Sunday church service—hand in hand." I was beginning to enjoy this.

So was he. "Duck Levine and the panty-hose queen, together again!" he giggled. "But that's almost a whole week away, though. I don't want to wait that long, do you?"

"I *can't* wait that long," I said, thinking of Ape Face and Stephanie Marshak. "But you know something?" A brilliant idea had just popped into my head. "We don't have to. Listen, you know those enormous music books you keep under the bed?"

"My orchestral scores—what about them?"

"Grab a couple of really fat ones and get dressed. We're leaving now!"

Not until all the cabins and the admin building were safely behind us, and the road to freedom lay a few tantalizing feet ahead, did we finally stop to catch our breath.

"Ape, this is crazy," panted Duck. "We'll never make it—especially lugging nine Beethoven symphonies. What do we need them for?"

"You'll see."

"But yesterday we barely made it around the lake, and Moosehead Village is a ten-mile hike from here."

"Who said anything about hike? Pipe down and follow me."

I led him to a bunch of outbuildings where the camp van, a green Chevy number known as the Reluctant Dragon, was parked under an open shed.

I opened the door on the driver's side and climbed in. As anticipated, due to Hitzigger's Syndrome, I had an unobstructed view of the steering wheel.

"The Beethovens, please," I commanded.

Speechless, Duck passed them over and I slipped them under. A vast improvement, I thought smugly. I'm wonderful, I think of everything!

I leaned over and opened the door on the passenger side. "Hop in."

He hesitated.

"What are you waiting for—Mallison to chauffeur us to town personally? Hop in and close the door quietly."

He did. "But—" he began.

"Don't worry, I know how. I've known how for years. Now let's see"—I felt over the sun visor—"keys, keys, if you were the keys, where would you be?"

"Under Wilking's pillow," said Duck.

"You're a natural-born pessimist," I said, locating them under the rubber floor mat. "All righty"—I turned on the ignition—"one, two, three, and away we go!"

"Lights!" he howled. "You forgot lights!"

"Duck, old sock," I said, nose to the windshield, "you can either have lights and get caught, or no lights—"

"—and get killed."

"Nonsense, I know these roads like the back of my hand."

"Then how come you're going in the wrong direction? The front gate's back there."

"So is Wilking's house. The back way is up here. Or used to be."

And still was, I noted with satisfaction.

"See?" I crowed triumphantly as I made a left onto Route 42. "Now do you believe me?"

"So far so good," he conceded. "What I want to know is, how did you know—about the back way?" I'm not the only one who thinks of everything.

"Oh," I said, ad-libbing airily, "Dad described it to me."

I was getting pretty good at this dissembling game. In fact, instead of spending endless days in a South Bronx tenement with beer and television, I could probably be circling the globe as a double agent—assuming I repossess myself sometime in the near future. If not, a twelve-year-old double agent would be even more effective—who'd suspect him? Ape Face could spend *his* days in the Bronx tenement, serves him right for not springing me from camp when I told him to. . . .

Duck interrupted my reverie with "What's that big black thing up ahead?"

"Where?"

"In the middle of the road."

I swerved, not a minute too soon. "Wow, that's what I'd call a near moose!" Heh-heh.

"Very funny," said Duck, unamused. "I hope it's our last."

"You never can tell. They don't call it Moosehead Village for nothing, I imagine."

"Yeah, well, a moose head on a wall is one thing. A live head attached to a big black body is something else entirely," he complained.

"Grumble, grumble, grumble," I chided, making a right onto the main drag.

"Now where are we?" asked Duck.

"I 95, heading south."

"What'll we do when we run out of gas? We're pretty low now."

"Hitch."

"What if we get picked up by the cops?"

"We'll tell them we ran away from home but now we're sorry, so would they please deliver us back to our parents in New York."

"And if they know that's not true because Soonawissakit's already put out an alarm?"

"Then they'll take us back to Soonawissakit, where we'll get kicked out for running away from there, and the camp will have to deliver us to our parents in New York. Heads we win, tails they lose. Any other questions?"

"Not a one, Ape, not a one," he said, admiring me greatly, as well he might.

"Fine. Now it's my turn." I patted the CB radio resting on the transmission hump between the two front seats. "Do you know how to use one of these things?"

"Sure. The family I stayed with last summer when I was sing-ing with the Santa Fe Opera had one."

"See what you can find out about the cop situation on this road, will you? I don't mind being picked up for hitchhiking, but being remanded to some New York State correctional home for juvenile car thieves, dope fiends, and switchblade murderers doesn't hold quite the same appeal, as I'm sure you'll agree."

"Gotcha," said Duck, turning on the CB.

The ensuing exchange between The Squeaky Bird[1] and B.B.[2], in our four-wheeler[3], and Tough Tiddly[4] and the Jolly Green Grape[4], running shotgun[5], on a bounce around[6] to Nastyville[7] in their eighteen-legged pogo stick[8], ought to win the Gobbledy-gook Award of the Year:

The bears[9] were crawling on the big slab[10] (no City Kittys[11], Duck was relieved to learn), and one in the grass[12] at Exit 12.

"So unless you're hankering for a Christmas card[13], better hammer off[14], Squeaky Bird," said Tough Tiddly.

Duck translated. I slowed to a legit double nickel[15] and instructed him to find out if there was a more indirect route to New York than I 95.

[1] Duck's CB handle, i.e., code name
[2] my handle. Stands for Big Bill, the best I could come up with on such short notice
[3] just what it sounds like
[4] I never found out their real names. Tough Tiddly was the driver
[5] driving partner
[6] return trip
[7] Nashville
[8] eighteen-wheel tractor-trailer truck
[9] police switching from side to side of the expressway
[10] the expressway
[11] local police
[12] the median
[13] speeding ticket
[14] slow down
[15] I bet you can figure it out for yourself; I did. No? 55 M.P.H.

"What for an indirect route[16] to the Dirty Side[17], good buddy, you a skip shooter[18] or something?"

"10–4," affirmed Duck. "Plus we're almost out of motion lotion[19], entirely out of green stamps[20], we got a coupla slick tennis shoes[21], and lastly, me and B.B., running shotgun, are checkin' our eyes for pinholes[22]."

"That's real bad, Squeaky Bird," commiserated Tough Tiddly.

I took over the mike. "Tough Tiddly, B.B., here. If you're heading for the Dirty Side yourself by any chance, we sure would appreciate a lift, good buddy."

"Good thinking!" said Duck.

Tough Tiddly's reaction seemed encouraging. "How's about peeling off the slab at Exit 13 onto Route 201, hang a first right for Marty's Roadhouse, seven miles down the road, we can eyeball[23] it over some Kool-Aid."

"Fine, but nix the Kool-Aid," I told Duck. "I haven't had that stuff since I was a kid—a *small* kid—and I hated it then."

"Kool-Aid is liquor," explained Duck. "You'd hate that more[24]. Negatory on the Kool-Aid, Tough Tiddly."

"Coffee, coffee!" I prompted.

"—But a cup of mud would go down real good."

By them, this proposition (I use the word advisedly, as you'll soon see) was a definite 10–4—until they swaggered into Mar-

---

[16] there is apparently no code word for this—truckers don't use indirect routes
[17] New York City
[18] unlicensed CB user
[19] gas—true, too; the gauge read empty
[20] money—also true
[21] tire trouble—untrue
[22] tire*d* trouble—untrue, but sounded good
[23] meet
[24] that's what he thinks

ty's and discovered its sole occupants, other than the bartender, were not what they'd been mistakenly led to expect.

"Muskrats![25]" Tough Tiddly was disgusted.

"*Male* muskrats!" The Jolly Green Grape was even more so.

"You thought we were seat covers[26]?!" gasped Duck.

"With girlie voices and handles like Squeaky Bird and Bibi, what else would we think?" growled Tough Tiddly.

"Gosh *darn*!" I exclaimed, smacking the tabletop. "That never occurred to me."

(It probably should have, too, but when all your energy is going into acting like a twelve-year-old boy, it really never crosses your mind you might be taken for a seat cover.)

"Me either," said Duck, sheepishly.

"Well . . ." said the Jolly Green Grape with a look at Tough Tiddly.

"Yeah, well . . ." he agreed.

"Well what?" asked Duck, a bundle of nerves.

"Whaddya mean, what? What what? Adios is what," said the not-so-Jolly Green Grape. He turned to leave; Tough Tiddly did the same.

Duck darted in front of them and I did the same. Between us, we blocked their access to the door.

"But what about our lift to the Dirty Side?" pleaded Duck.

"Yes, you see, we ran away from home but now we're sorry, so we were hoping you could help us get back," I added.

Tough Tiddly said, "Let's get something straight. You musk-rats're running away *from* the Dirty Side or *to* the Dirty Side?"

[25] children
[26] attractive girls

"From," said I. "To" said Duck, both of us answering at once.

The Jolly Green Grape's response to this was either a stifled laugh or a belch—I couldn't tell which.

"What I mean is," I explained, "we *were* running away from there, now we're running *to* there."

"Then what's that four-wheeler with a Maine license plate doing parked out front?" asked Tough Tiddly.

Again, Duck and I both answered at once. "Um . . ."

"Uh-huh," said Tough Tiddly.

"Like I said before, adios," said the J.G.G.

Together, with humiliating ease, they broke through our pitiful phalanx and swaggered out. With sinking hearts, we heard the roar of the motor as they drove off in a huff.[27]

"What do we do now?" asked Duck, turning to me for help. As usual, and I wish he wouldn't because I take it all back. I do not think of everything. In fact, at this particular juncture—stranded as we were in a deserted roadhouse, seven miles from the nearest expressway entrance, almost out of motion lotion and completely out of green stamps—I couldn't think of anything we could do except call camp and ask them to come and get us.

Which is what we did, and I assure you, they were not pleased.

---

[27] an eighteen-legged pogo stick with two disgruntled truckers in it. Only kidding

11

"Fire you? Why should I do that?"

"So I can get my stock options and severance pay."

"Ah"—she laughed—"but suppose I don't want to fire you?"

"Well, I'm not quitting, that's for sure," I said, plunking myself on the couch. I was wobbly in the legs.

"Good. That's all settled then." She seemed relieved. "Let's get down to business."

What are you doing here? Is it really you? Yes, it is, just thinner, that's all, how did you get here—from Miss Moon the teacher to Stephanie . . . was that your first name, Stephanie? I never knew . . . Marshak, head of Galaxy? . . .

Her lips were moving but it was like watching television with the sound off. I only tuned in for the tail end.

". . . story meeting?"

"Uh, sorry, what did you say?" I asked.

"I said how did the story meeting go?"

"Fine thanks."

Why doesn't she recognize me? Oh. Because she never really met Dad—only once in the second grade, without a beard, and not at all in the third grade, too busy at the ad agency.

So if she never met him/me, that means I can't tell her I'm not just any old Mr. Andrews, I'm *the* Mr. Andrews who's Ben's father, because with a new name and a new job, how would I know she used to be Miss Moon Ben's teacher since I never really met her I couldn't know that I think I'm going in circles.

". . . trip out?" I heard, tuning in again.

"Fine thanks, and you?" I answered. Do I dare tell her who I really am? No, no, no—remember the little men! Pay attention, jerk!

". . . a trifle distracted today, aren't you, Mr. Andrews? I didn't go anywhere, you did. I was asking about your trip out—which seems to have been rather"—she raised her eyebrows—"eventful."

I sighed. "Miss Marshak, I guess there's nothing I can possibly say—"

"No-oo," she interrupted, "but there's something I'd like to say."

Here it finally comes. What took her so long?

"What," I said, knowing full well.

"Thank you," she said.

"What?" I couldn't believe my ears. She must be kidding, but she was smiling.

"Which word didn't you understand?"

It was Miss Moon of the good old days—funny, friendly, teasing. ("Ben Andrews, yours was the highest score in the spelling test, so you get to pass the juice and cookies." "Who, me?" "Which word didn't you understand?")

"Look, Mr. Andrews—or Bill, if I may, may I?"

Vigorously, I nodded yes.

"Stephanie," she said, tapping herself. "Look Bill, when you told Peggotty Horn I was a Killer Cream Puff—did you make that up, by the way? It's perfect—"

"You're not like that, I'm sure you're not, I *know* you're not!"

"No"—she appreciated the compliment, I could tell by her eyes—"but to make it in this job, I should be. Now, thanks to you, everybody thinks I am and will treat me accordingly—with a great deal of respect that I'm actually not entitled to at all."

She threw back her head and laughed. "If you knew what I was doing only five years ago, you'd never believe it."

It was irresistible. "Teaching?"

"Yes, teaching!" If I'd guessed her zodiac sign she couldn't have been more delighted. "That's incredible!— Or did Ty tell you?"

"Nuh-uh," I said modestly.

"Well, either I have Teacher written all over me or you're positively clairvoyant."

Happily, she recalled her past. "Yep, five years ago, I was teaching second and third graders in New York, and if I went to a movie more than once a month it was because someone else took me—I certainly couldn't afford it."

"Then what happened?"

"Then I married one of those someone elses—not a very nice one, I'm afraid"—she smiled ruefully—"and we moved to California, where he got a top job at Boeing Aircraft and I got a divorce."

Whew, that's good. Not that I could marry her anyway, I'm already married . . . to my MOTHER! Ye gods, I don't want to be married to my mother, I don't care what Freud says. I mean, I love her a lot, but I don't want to be married to her and I'm sure she won't want to be married to me either when she knows who I am, but if I tell her, here we go again with the little men in the white coats—

". . . boring the pants off you, I'm afraid," said Miss Moon.

"No! No, no, it's fascinating, go on, please, please go on," I begged her. Later, I'll worry about my wife later.

"Well," she said, "after the year teaching kid actors on location, I'd picked up enough to get myself hired as a script girl at Magno-International, and from there I wormed my way into the story department at Paragon, then they made me head of the story department at Paragon, and after that I went over to T.S.G. as Vice President in Charge of Production, and well—miracle of miracles, here I am."

"Just like that." I snapped my fingers.

"Just like that—oh, you know how it is," she said diffidently, "they have a funny way of doing things out here."

"So I've noticed," I said.

We both laughed, then there was an awkward silence, broken by her.

"Bill"—something about her voice made me suspect the Official Meeting had begun—"my spies tell me you have a wife and two children, that you're very ambitious," I am? "also very charming," that's nice, "and extremely good at your job." That's even nicer.

"So far, I can only attest to the charm element"—she grinned, I grinned back—"but assuming the rest of the information is accurate, how would you like to move your family and your charming ambitious self out here where you can be extremely good at an even better job—specifically, Vice President in Charge of Worldwide Production."

Pleased with her offering, she leaned back in her chair and concluded with "Oh, and you needn't feel you have to give me an immediate answer, Bill. Take all the time you want."

"Okay," I said.

There was another awkward silence.

"Naturally, you'll have all the concomitant increases and extras—that goes without saying," she added.

I waited.

Anxiously, now, she leaned forward in her chair. "Don't forget, the company will pay for the move, help you get a house, find schools for the kids, et cetera, et cetera—the lawyers will work out details later—if you're interested, that is, and I hope you are. I could use a fellow New Yorker."

"Which word didn't you understand?" Tit for tat, Miss Moon! "I already said okay."

"Oh!" she exhaled with relief; then, imitating me earlier, she snapped her fingers. "Just like that? You can make up your mind just like that?"

Wouldn't Dad? Of course he would. Besides, he wasn't there to ask. I'd just have to stand on my own two feet and make up my own two minds.

"Just like that," I said.

"What about your wife?" Her again! "After all, relocating to the West Coast—that's rather a big step to take without consulting her, isn't it?"

"Not at all," I said. "We have an old-fashioned marriage—wherever I go, she goes."

A flicker of disapproval crossed her face. "You're very fortunate."

"Or"—I made a generous concession—"if she and the kids are really miserable about living here, they can stay put and I can commute back and forth in my spare time."

There, that would take care of the wife/mother problem! And Annabel wouldn't care where we lived, she was at Yale, anyway. As for Dad, I absolutely didn't need him hanging over my shoulder all the time, monitoring my every move. I'd gotten this far without him, I could go the whole distance . . . which could be . . . *forever*, come to think of it! I'm not so sure I'd like forever. . . .

". . . awfully happy about this, Bill," said Miss Moon, ushering me to the door.

"Oh, me, too," I said, opening it. "Just one favor, can I borrow a—no, *may* I borrow a phone?"

"Ah," she exclaimed, "you're a man after my own heart, Bill Andrews. Nobody speaks decent English anymore."

"A lot depends on the teacher," I told her, "and mine was terrific."

12

The next morning (Tuesday) at breakfast, Letty "Ma Barker" Newsome, the camp nurse, stopped by our table to tell Duck and me we were wanted upstairs in the admin office as soon as we'd finished eating.

Duck, having just closed his lips around a spoonful of dank mucilage (oatmeal), removed the spoon, contents intact, and slapped it back in the bowl.

"I'm finished now," he said jauntily.

"Likewise," I said, shoving my bowl into the middle of the table.

Snorkel Bains shoved it back to me again. "You two are finished when I say you're finished and not a minute before."

Thor Swensen noted the look of revulsion on my face. "The condemned man ate a hearty meal," he snickered.

"That's right, Ape," encouraged Duck, zealously tucking into his mucilage, "the sooner we eat, the sooner we get condemned."

"And the sooner you get condemned, the sooner we get you two faggots out of my cabin, so eat up, Andrews," said Guess Who.

"Knock it off, Hitzigger," cautioned Bains.

"Yeah, Hitzigger, knock it off," said Woodruff Somebody-or-Other.

"Oh, that's okay," I said, scrupulously scraping minispecks from the bottom of my bowl, "we don't mind, do we, Duck."

"Not a bit," he said, winking at me.

I returned the wink, and rose from the table, as did he. And then, feature this, if you will, Duck Levine and the panty-hose queen, together again, walked the entire length of the dining room, hand in hand. What did we care—we were leaving anyway!

The problem was, we weren't.

"Not that you don't deserve to be kicked out . . ." Wilking scowled at us from behind his desk; Annabel and Terry Mallison stood dutifully to one side. "And not that Soonawissakit wouldn't be well rid a ya . . ." He scraped viciously at the inside of his pipe, then emptied it into a glass ashtray. "But Sis, here, tells me yer momma's gallavantin' around in the desert somewheres, unreachable by any means, be they telephone, telegraph, carrier pigeon, or Pony Express, and yer poppa's much too busy gettin' rich 'n' famous to take charge a ya hisself—"

"That's nonsense," I said.

93

"No, it's not," said Annabel, looking very·cat-that-swallowed-the-canary–ish. "Read this."

She stuck a Mailgram under my nose:

HAVE ACCEPTED GALAXY PROMOTION TO
VICE PRESIDENT OF WORLDWIDE PRO-
DUCTION. DETAILED LETTER FOLLOWS.
LOVE AND KISSES, SUPERDAD.

"Ohmigod, ohmigod, that's incredible!" I babbled.

"Watch that mouth!" thundered Wilking.

"Sorry, sir, sorry, sorry, sorry, a million pardons! Annabel, that is stupendously good news!"

"Fer yer poppa it is," said Wilking. "Fer us, it means we got no choice but to keep you here all summer. . . . Sh . . . oot!" He thwacked his pipe on the ashtray, cracking the ashtray and shearing the pipestem neatly in two.

"Aw, Ape, aw gee, Ape!" said Duck, devastated in my behalf.

"It's okay, Duck," I said bravely. "Now that I know Dad's all right, I don't mind staying." Until Ape's letter arrives and I can see what's what.

"As for Captain Wilking . . ." My eyes did a slow, disdainful crawl from the broken pipestem to his glowering, sour puss. "Well, sir, if I can put up with you, I guess you can somehow manage to put up with—"

"*Both* of you!" Wilking said angrily. "Not just one, but—"

"Both!" squealed Duck. "Why both? My parents aren't too busy to take me. I mean, they're busy, but not that busy. I can make myself very useful—typing Mom's book, assisting Dad—"

Annabel exploded with laughter. "In neurosurgery? His father's a neurosurgeon,'' she explained to Mallison and Wilking.

"In the office, stupid, in the office,'' shouted Duck, purple in the face. "Or I'll read the *Encyclopaedia Britannica*, or sing in the street for small change, I'll do anything, for crumb sake, but you have to kick me out, *please!*''

"Be reasonable, Arthur,'' urged Mallison. Arthur? Funny, he doesn't look like an Arthur. "We can't kick out one of you and not the other.''

"That's the stupidest thing I ever heard—we're not joined at the hip!'' said Duck.

"Just at the hands,'' snorted Wilking. "Forty years a Soona-wissakit, we never had a pair a sissies like you!''

"Right!'' I chimed in. "So split us up.''

"Just what we ought to do, Captain,'' said Mallison. "Andrews can stay in Mount Olympus and we can transfer Levine to High Ledge.''

"No, no, no!'' protested Duck. "I want to be kicked out. Come on, kick me out!''

"Oh, Arthur, look,'' said Mallison. "It's very simple. As I understood the facts from Ben last night on the phone, it was he who masterminded the whole hare-brained scheme, and he who drove the van—''

"Yes, but he doesn't get all the credit. I'm the one who used the CB radio. Illegally! I'm just as much a criminal as he is—every bit!''

"That may be,'' said Mallison doggedly, "but how would it look to your parents if we expelled you and kept him? They'd have a perfect right to sue.''

"We haven't had that happen in forty years, neither,'' said Wilking. "They're both stayin' and that's final.''

Something told me—the resolute look on der Führer's face, probably—that we were flogging a dead horse. Duck, on the verge of tears, evidently thought so too. I decided to salvage what I could from the situation.

"I guess Mr. Mallison's right, Duck," I said slyly. "Your parents might also sue for negligence—since it was insufficient supervision that led to the transgression in the first place."

"Wordy little kid, aren'tcha," said Wilking. He turned to Mallison. "What's he talkin' about—insufficient supervision? I thought you were asleep when they left."

"Well, actually . . ." I looked pointedly at Annabel and Mallison; mutely but eloquently they beseeched me to shut up. "Actually, I suppose being a heavy sleeper isn't exactly negligent . . ."

"Durn tootin' it's not," said Wilking, much relieved. But not as relieved as Annabel and Mallison.

To sum up the rest of the conversation, Mallison responded to my blackmail maneuver by suggesting that it wouldn't really be necessary to put Duck and me in separate cabins as long as he kept a careful eye on us. Wilking, after grumbling that one eye wasn't good enough, finally agreed—but warned us he didn't want any more of that sissy stuff, we should save it for Greenwich Village. Then it was case dismissed, and Mallison told us we were free to rejoin our friends in the scheduled morning activities.

"Friends? What friends?" groused Duck as we were macho-marching to the table we had optimistically vacated only ten minutes before. The hostility in that completely silent dining room was so thick you could choke on it.

"I think it's time we made some," I told him.

A lone, lewd whistle pierced the chilly still; within seconds, it had triggered a scene reminiscent of the one on the bus, but worse by a country mile. No mere aisleful, now, but an entire roomful of loathsomely like-minded little boys undulated and lisped through a full chorus of "Yeth, Thir, That'th My Baby" while Duck and I tried to shoulder our way to our seats.

"Who'd want us? How're we going to do it?" shouted Duck over the din.

"I don't know," I answered, "but it's got to be done, and soon!"

The time to act was now.

"Duck, where's Hitzigger?" I yelled.

Duck's eyes nearly popped out of his head.

"A hundred and fifty kids in this camp, and you want *Hitzigger* for a friend? You're insane!"

"I don't want him for a friend, I want him for an enemy. Where is he? Just lemme at him!" I snarled, starting off to find him.

Duck grabbed me by the shirt and hauled me back. "You've already *got* him for an enemy."

"Not a public enemy," I said, shaking myself loose, "and cut that out, I can take care of myself."

"But you're only going to get creamed!" howled Duck.

He was right, of course, and getting creamed wasn't exactly my idea of a fun Tuesday, but if by making a public enemy out of Hitzigger, I could make a public hero out of myself, it was well worth it, under the circs.

"Ape, Hitzigger weighs a ton and fights mean. At least let's punch him out together like we planned," pleaded Duck.

I hesitated. Considering what I was stuck with in terms of

external packaging, it was a tantalizing offer . . . but just then the kids launched into a second, even louder chorus of "Yeth, Thir," and I was more than ever determined to be the sole star of the creamation.

"Two against one is no way to make friends," I said, "and besides, from now on, it's every man for himself."

Duck cupped his hand behind his ear and leaned forward. "What?"

"Forget it," I shouted. Flexing a biceps and clenching a fist, I bellowed, "Where's Hitzigger? I wanna bust him one right in the chops! Hitz-ig-*ger?!*"

Suddenly it was as though there'd been a short circuit in the audio system—you could have heard a feather drop. Everyone stood stock-still, all eyes focused either on me or right behind me.

"Did I hear thomeone thay they wanted to butht me one?" asked Hitzigger, his voice a sinister combination of menacing and coy.

I froze in my tracks, clenched fist in midair. Hitzigger *behind* me I hadn't counted on!

"Here I am, thweetie," he taunted.

I could just picture him—hands on hips, simper on face, murderous, gay-baiting glint in eye . . . hands on hips, simper on face, murderous—oh, what the hell—

Quickly, I wheeled around . . . *and knocked him out cold on the floor!* It was easy—his hands were on his hips, he didn't have time to defend himself.

Chalk one up for our team!

13

Dear Dad,

Hold it! Duck and I are always reading over each other's shoulders—there are no secrets between him and me—and if Duck reads Dear Dad over Dad's shoulder . . .

I sighed. This would have to be our first secret. I changed "Dad." Good thing I had an erasable pen.

Dear Ape Face,

How would Dad sound in a letter, what would he say first? . . . Got it!

How's camp? Fine, I'll bet. That's good. I'm
sure you're going to have just as much fun
as I did when I was there.

How's the weather been? Today it's 94° and
sunny out here. I'm in my swimming trunks
at the pool

aw, who did that?!

as you can see by that splotchy
place in the corner.

I'd brought only one piece of stationery out with
me and was not about to make a marathon trek all
the way back to my room for another one. There was
probably stationery in the lobby, but since de Virgilio
took such a dim view of improper attire in his precious
lobby . . .

"I'm glad to see you here, Mr. Andrews."

Speak of the devil.

"No thanks to you, de V.," I said with a big grin
to show I was only kidding.

I forgot; in Hollywood, funnyness is not the way
to go.

"Please try to understand, sir, rules are rules" was
his sober reply.

"Mm-hm" was mine. I started back to my letter.

"Mr. Andrews." De V. had something more to say.
"Bob the Doorman wanted to have a word with you
in the lobby."

"How's right now?" I asked, hooking my thumbs
under my armpits and waggling my fingers at him.

He didn't take me seriously, but neither did he smile. "At your convenience, sir," he said with a business-like nod, then he clickety-clacked away in his shiny shoes.

I'm going to make that stiff laugh if it's the last thing I do!

Now, where was I? . . .

> I hope the news about my promotion put your mind at ease. I would've let you know sooner, but when I tried to phone you right after the meeting, all the circuits were busy, and then

I was having such a great time, it slipped my mind altogether until Monday when Mavis Ohler, who had been reassigned to me (all I had to do was request her and I got her—that's what I call power!), asked how Mrs. Andrews had taken my wonderful news.

I explained she hadn't heard it yet because there were no phones in the desert . . . phones! . . . Dad!—but my son Ben, at camp, would love to know; would Mavis take a Mailgram, I'd pay for it as soon as I could cash a check.

Oh, that wouldn't be necessary, laughed Mavis; for little things like that I was Galaxy's guest. Also, Galaxy would be glad to cash my check—if I'd make it out, she'd have the money for me by the end of the day.

Neat-o, I told her, and while she was up, could she buy (with my money) some transistor batteries and send them to my son's friend, Arthur Levine, same camp, same address as the one I was about to give her?

It would be her pleasure, said Mavis, and took care of the whole thing. Mavis is *terrific*!

Back to business . . . all the circuits were busy and then . . .

I was completely tied up

doing Disneyland, surfing at Malibu, roller-skating in Venice (California), and going on every roller coaster at Magic Mountain with good old Ray Ewald (it turned out when I thought he was shunning me on Friday, he was waiting for me in the executive dining room— I didn't know there was one—thinking I was shunning *him*).

Ray's wife was also away on a trip, so he was delighted to fool around all weekend doing kid things with me because "I have the soul of a kid myself." That's an exact quote! I could hardly keep a straight face. Ray is terrific, too. (More about that later.)

Let's see, how does it sound so far . . . all the circuits were busy and then I was completely tied up . . . tied up with . . . tied up with what? Ah!

with a ton of paperwork and business meetings—you know how that is.

"There is a telephone call for Mr. Andrews, telephone for Mr. William W. Andrews," boomed the loudspeaker.

"Where?" I said out loud.

"By the bar, where it always is," said the guy in the next cabana.

I thanked him and managed to make it without mishap to the phone. (Not as easy as it sounds. Even at twelve noon on a weekday, the poolside is jammed at the Bev Hills; picking your way through a minefield of oiled, baked bodies requires the skill of a seasoned Marine.)

"Bill Andrews here," I announced into the phone.

"Oh, Mr. Andrews, honey"—it was Mavis—"the bank just called. You made the funniest mistake—you put your son's signature on that check instead of your own!"

Funny once, not so funny twice, you bozo!

That was because he was so much on my mind, I told her; I'd make out a new check tomorrow if the bank could wait that long. She assured me the bank could; then, after exhorting each other to have a nice day, we both hung up.

I returned to my terry-toweled chaise, ordered a liquorless piña colada, and began practicing William W. Andrews on the back of the poolside menu.

Midway through the nineteenth signature—which was beginning to look quite legitimate—the loudspeaker announced a call for, of all people, Mr. Tyson Donovan.

Ty Donovan here? I took a furtive look around.

Yes, indeed, here: the guy in the next cabana who'd told me where the phone was (without even saying hello, Bill, how are you—he must be pretty mad; on the other hand, I didn't say hello to him either). He tossed aside his *Daily Variety*, jumped up, and sped to the phone.

When he reappeared, I exclaimed cordially, "Ty, I didn't recognize you!"

"I didn't expect you to," he said, settling himself back down with *Daily Variety*. "Now that I've been axed."

Zap.

"No, no, *no*, Ty, don't be silly! I didn't recognize you because—" quick, dummy, think of something! "—because you've lost so much weight—haven't you lost a lot of weight since the last time I saw you?"

Ty studied me carefully to see if I was bulling or not, and decided to believe me.

"Oh, about ten or twelve pounds, I guess." He put aside the *Daily Variety*—for good, I sensed. "Sorry about that, Bill," he said, referring apparently to the axed crack. "I'm suffering from a slight case of bruised feelings these days."

"Sure." I nodded to show I understood. "Listen, I'm sorry, too. About indie prod and stuff." Which I was. He seemed really nice.

"Yeah, well, it could be worse. Not that the phone's ringing off the hook yet or anything, but the money's okay for a while"—he knocked wood on the chaise—"and I've got a couple of genuinely exciting projects in the works."

The words were convincing, but the tone reminded me of Duck the day he told me he thought his voice was changing so fast he wouldn't be able to do the

Metropolitan Opera broadcast but I shouldn't worry, it wasn't the end of the world—when I knew it temporarily was.

"That's good," I said, answering him the same way I'd answered Duck.

Changing the subject abruptly, Ty reached out and slapped me on the knee. "Son of a gun, I almost forgot—congratulations on the executive stripes!" He shook his head admiringly. "Gotta hand it to you, fella, you've got more guts than I thought."

That's the second time. Why does he keep saying that?

"What do you mean by that, Ty?"

"Oh, you know," he said vaguely.

"No, I don't, and I wish you'd tell me," I said.

Ty cleared his throat and shifted position uneasily. "Well, frankly Bill, in spite of a reputation to the contrary, you've always struck me as a sort of second banana."

Dad a second banana?! I must've looked startled.

"Plenty smart and personable, and *likable*," he added quickly, "but not the male equivalent of a Killer Cream Puff, and certainly not someone who'd dare call *her* one on national television. Whew!"

He wiped imaginary sweat off his brow. "That was a bold, aggressive move, Billy boy, and politically savvy, but it could have backfired. Yes, sir, a big, gutsy gamble that could've backfired and didn't—more power to you."

He paused for reflection, then said wonderingly, "I

dunno, pal, I guess I just didn't realize you were capable of that kind of strategic one-upmanship."

"But I'm not!" I said, suddenly more worried about Ty's friendship than Dad's reputation. "It was all a weird accident. Believe me, when I talked to Peggotty Horn on the plane, I didn't even know who she was!"

"Bill, Bill," he said, raising a hand in protest, "spare me the lies, please! Look, it's all right. People do what they have to do. It's just that underneath the self-confident surface, I always figured you for a vulnerable type of guy—"

"But I am, Ty, I am! In fact, I'm so vulnerable I'm scared to death I'm going to get fired from this job before I start because, you know something? I'm in way over my head!"

Which was undoubtedly true and I just hadn't realized it until now.

"Well," said Ty quietly, "if that's really the case," and he finally seemed convinced I meant it, "I'd be careful who I admitted it to, if I were you. Actually, if I were you, I wouldn't even admit it to me."

What a crazy thing to say!

"Ty, that's ridiculous! If I can't trust you, who can I trust?—you're a good friend!"

And now for the zinger.

"No, I'm not," said Ty wearily. "I hate to disillusion you, sonny boy, but you don't have a good friend, and neither do I. Neither does anybody, not in *this* town."

He stood up, stretched, yawned, jammed his feet into his sandals, and said, "As for who you can trust, your wife is who, and be glad you have her. Mine walked out on me six months ago."

Having delivered this dour parting shot, he took off, leaving me with a whole bunch of thoughts that bugged me all day and half the night. Such as:

If you give the impression of being ambitious, aggressive, a strategic planner, in other words, a killer, it's as good as being one—better maybe, because you don't have to really *be* that way, you can remain a nice person who's just pretending. Like Miss Moon. Like Dad?

WHAT ABOUT DAD? Ty had him pegged as a second banana and acted disappointed and hurt when (thanks to Miss Moon's spies and my goof with Peggotty Horn) the company pegged him as a first banana and rewarded him accordingly. Is this because Ty is a deposed first banana himself, and jealous? I sort of don't think so—I stick by my first impression of Ty: a really nice guy . . . which would make him a second banana who got deposed—because he wasn't good enough at pretending? But if *this* is true, then Ty is disappointed in Dad because he thinks Dad was a first banana and a killer all along.

But was he, is he? Or is he just a terrifically successful pretender? When you come right down to it, what's the difference between the two? And who's to know which of the two you really are?

Only your wife, apparently, because according to Ty, you can't trust anyone else. Not even your kids, apparently, because why else would I be sitting in my Bev Hills hotel room at three in the morning asking myself

WHAT ABOUT DAD?

More to the point, *WHAT ABOUT ME?* On a banana scale of 1 to 2 (first banana and second banana being all there is), I'd have to rate myself at least a 14 in one of my rare assertive moods, and somewhere in the high 30's otherwise. With a personality like that, how long can I go on fooling all of the people all of the time? Even more to the point, how long do I want to?

I can't think about this anymore.

FURTHER LATE-NIGHT REFLECTIONS ON OTHER SUBJECTS

On Identity

Being first in line for a hit movie gets you a good seat. Being first in line in the school lunchroom gets you a good choice of sandwiches. Being first in line at the Bev Hills Polo Lounge gets you nowhere, because the captain won't give you a table unless he knows who you are.

"Right this way, Mr. So-and-So." He beckons to some late arrival Big Shot in the back of the line.

"Malcolm, you're a brick," says the Big Shot as he shoots past the rest of us peasants.

"Wait a minute, Malcolm, I've been here for twenty minutes," you complain.

"How's a table for two in the patio?" he asks.

"Great," you say, stepping forward.

But he's not talking to you, he's talking through you (transparent Plexiglas, that's what you are!) to a Miss

108

Big Shot who's been breathing down your neck from behind.

You step back in line again, she steps out and around you. A deep growl resonates in your cavernously empty stomach. There is a fierce ache in your salivary glands.

But now, ah-ha!, the phone on Malcolm's reservation desk rings. He answers it; he listens.

"Who? . . ." Bored, he scans the line. "I don't know. Never heard of him." He listens some more. "Oh . . . oh, really?" Impressed, he scans the line again. Then, setting the receiver down, inquires, "Is there a Mr. William Andrews here?"

Only since the day before yesterday, you turkey! would be a good answer. But you don't dare.

Instead, you settle for an understated raising of the hand and a subtle dig: "*A* Mr. William Andrews? How many of us are there?"

"*The* Mr. William Andrews, new Vice President of Galaxy, I should have said, sir," amends Malcolm with an unctuous smile.

He then goes on to say Bob the Doorman is most anxious to have a word with me (still! I forgot all about him). If I'd care to see him now, he'd have a lovely table in the patio waiting for me when I returned.

That's more like it!

On Power
Power is great for getting reservations, but when dealing with people like Bob the Doorman who's supposed

to cater to the whims of people like me, better watch your step.

My whim (if you've forgotten, go back to Page 66)— a navy-blue Mercedes 480-SL convertible—was parked smack in front of the hotel where, according to a reproachful Bob, it had been waiting for me all morning. Did I intend to drive it today? Because otherwise he'd have the parking attendant take it away till tomorrow.

But what would I do with it then? This car problem was going to have to be solved once and for all.

"I don't intend to drive it ever," I told him. "Didn't my secretary mention that either? I want a chauffeur."

"A *chauffeur*, sir?" He seemed surprised. Which word didn't he understand?

"Yes, a chauffeur. Available at all times, night or day, beginning with four o'clock this afternoon. As you may have heard, I'm in the market for a house here, and I want to check out some of the better neighborhoods, so could you please get me someone who really knows his way around," because I don't. It's all I can do to find my room.

Well, folks, at four o'clock on the dot, a nine-hundred-year-old Englishman in a black suit and tie, white shirt, leather gloves, peaked cap—the works—was waiting for me in front of my Mercedes.

I drew Bob aside. "Is that my *driver*?"

"No, sir," corrected Bob, pleased as punch at having catered to another of my whims on such short notice. "That's your *chauffeur*. His name is Barkham."

(*Barkham.* Can you believe it—*Barkham?!*)

A piece of incidental intelligence: In Hollywood, if

110

all you want is a plain, ordinary garden-variety driver who looks and acts like a regular person, don't ask for a chauffeur. A chauffeur is a driver with an idiotic name in an idiotic costume who makes you sit in the backseat—where you feel like a jerk—and is so stultifyingly boring and snobbish you fall asleep before you've seen even one third of Beverly Hills, let alone Brentwood, Westwood, Bel Air, or Pacific Palisades.

Conclusion: Power has its pitfalls.

More on HoJo's vs. the Bev Hills
I hate to keep harping on this, but in the food department, HoJo's wins again.

By the time I came back to my lovely table in the patio, I was so hungry I could've eaten the menu. Especially after I read it, because there was nothing on there I wanted to order.

"Couldn't I just have a peanut butter and jelly sandwich?" I asked the waiter.

"But of course, Mr. Andrews," he said, rushing off.

Ten minutes later, which even for HoJo's is the speed of light, he rushed back with a nine-dollar (!) Peanut Butter Platter: four dainty, crustless, toasted (I hate toasted, it's too runny) sandwich morsels surrounded—practically engulfed—by bushes of parsley, delicate carrot fronds and radish rosebuds. When I want a garden, I'll ask for a garden!

More on Identity
Meager as the edible part of my lunch was, I hardly had time to eat it, due to half the Polo Lounge coming

up to say hello and congratulate me on the great Galaxy news. It must have spread like wildfire while I was out negotiating for Barkham, because nobody but Malcolm knew me when I left, and now everybody knew me but I didn't know them.

With one exception—Peggotty Horn. She kissed me on both cheeks, plunked herself down at the table, systematically defoliated my garden—which was okay with me—and had to be introduced to all those anonymous fans—which was not okay at all.

For a while, I got away with Dad's Old Trick: When he and I run into someone he can't think of the name of, he says, "You know my son Ben, don't you?" to which the person usually says, "Hi, Ben," and Dad never has to come up with the name. (The first time he worked that scam though, after saying, "You know my son Ben, don't you?" *I* said no, and since he couldn't come up with the name, the man went away insulted. Dad acknowledged it wasn't my fault but warned me the next time, for Pete's sake, to keep my mouth shut.)

Well, I was doing nicely with "You know Peggotty Horn, don't you?"—because most people actually did and vice versa, but then a big fat man came along and said no, he didn't.

"Well, here she is," I said with a feeble smile.

"Harvey Godchaux," he said, shaking her hand. To me he said testily, "Your lawyer, remember me? We spoke on the phone only this morning about ironing out the final kinks on your Galaxy deal?"

"Good Lord, Harvey, I didn't recognize you!" because

you've *lost so much weight*! Pretty lame but it would have to do. "Haven't you lost a lot of weight lately?"

Godchaux sucked in his breath and gave his rotund tum a proud pat. "Nice of you to notice," he said. All was forgiven.

Henceforth, this weight-loss gambit shall be dubbed Ape's Old Trick. I used it frequently throughout my Hollywood stay and it never failed me.

One cautionary note, however. Don't use it in reverse—for example, "Millicent, I didn't recognize you, you've gained so much weight!" because Millicent will hate you forever, and if Millicent turns out to be Ray Ewald's wife just back from a health spa, you'll live to regret it. (More about that later.)

On Letter Writing

Don't try to finish a letter late at night when you're sleepy. Save it for later in the week when there's more to report anyway.

14

Tues., July 5th

Despite stunning victory over Hitzigger, was not carried out of dining room on shoulders of newfound admirers amidst cheers and huzzahs of exultant throng.

Instead, settled for dignified and Duck-less (my decision, not his) solo exit amidst discreet murmurs of praise and restrained back-pats from a scattered few. One triumph does not a hero make—this process would take time.

Volunteered for strenuous white-water canoe trip with de Menocal, Swensen, Biddle, Loring, and Hitzigger (!) with Snorkel Bains as leader. Duck didn't like the sound of it, elected not to come.

114

On short detour up Squangit River—which seemed vaguely familiar—Bains pointed out rope dangling from tree branch overhanging rushing river. Any takers? he challenged.

There were three possibilities: 1) Swing out far enough to dive safely into fathomless pool of glacially cold, clear water. 2) Swing out only far enough to dash yourself to death on jagged rocks protruding from turbulent water directly below. 3) Sit humiliated and shivering on bank while everybody else played Tarzan and called you chicken—which Bains pointed out was what my dad had done 30 years ago. (He didn't have to tell me—I suddenly remembered it all too well.)

This time, I was first to take plunge (glacially cold is an understatement), winning respect of all, even Hitz.

Chalk *two* up for our team.

That night after supper, snuck out of Group Sing (a practice session of camp songs and cheers led by Annabel), helped Garland, Beaty hoist canoe paddles up flagpole. A sudden sneezing attack (mine) alerted Mallison, who threatened to report us. Wouldn't if I were you, I told him. P.S., he didn't. Garland, Beaty impressed.

Wed., July 6th
Tried out for cross-country team . . . qualifiers to compete Sat. in Southern Maine Intercamp Track Meet, banking on Ape's pink, fresh lungs, my own occasional Central Park jogging, to see me through.

Made 3rd-fastest time with milliseconds to spare. Duck, overawed, said he'd never seen me run like that before. He'd never seen me try before, I told him. (True, obviously—jogging or no jogging, I was still in Ape's body.)

At Morning Swim, my buddy Roland de Berganza, heir appar-

ent to megabucks zinc fortune, was so condescendingly convinced waterskiing behind his family power launch on glassy
Gulf of Mexico had to be superior to waterskiing behind rented
speedboat (driven by Ellen) in choppy Long Island Sound, I
felt obliged to challenge him that afternoon.

Chalk another one up for our team. In spite of wind and
whitecaps on Soona Lake, passed Advanced status with swift
shallow-water start and stunning standing stool-on-disc 360°
turn; then topped off run by performing two requirements for
Expert—sideslides and 180° back and fronts, vaulting me into
top ten on ski ladder.

De Berganza, thanks to glassy Gulf of Mexico, nearly
drowned.

Returned to Mount Olympus to peel off wet suit, blow nose
(was this a cold coming on?), and accept congrats from all
bunkmates except Duck, whose only comment was "You told
me you hated waterskiing." (Is that so—how come he never
told his father?)

"This is the new me," I said.

"Mmn," was the noncommittal response.

"What's eating you?" I asked.

"Oh, stuff," he said despondently.

"Like what?"

"Like this, for one." He handed me a padded manila envelope
addressed to him from Galaxy.

I tipped it; out fell six transistor batteries.

"No accompanying letter or anything?" I asked, reaching
around inside.

"I don't need a letter; I know it's from your Dad."

"Well, I need a letter and I was supposed to get one, too,"

I complained. "The Mailgram said 'detailed letter follows.' Follows what, I'd like to know—Christmas? Easter? It's Wednesday already."

"Not only do I not need a letter, I don't even need the batteries," said Duck morosely. "What good are batteries without the Sony?"

"Jeeze, I want to know what's going on out there, Duck!"

"It's just like *The Gift of the Magi*, remember *The Gift of the Magi*?"

It was conversational gridlock.

"You're not listening to a word I say," I said.

"Ditto to you," he answered. "And if you really want to know what's eating me—"

"Not especially. I'm much more interested in what we're eating for dinner," I said, and took off for the dining hall with de Menocal and Swensen.

In game room after dinner, was beaten by Duck, 21–15 in Ping-Pong, marking first defeat for our team. Luckily, no one of importance was around to see.

Later, signed up for Soonawissaclimbers' 2-day Katahdin trip. (Not willingly. Was egged on by Wilking's scathing recollection of my old man "bein' too yellow-bellied to set one foot front a the other less'n it was on flat ground"—no fool he!)

Thurs., July 7th, Fri., July 8th
Katahdin is highest mountain in Maine. If afraid of heights, don't look behind you. Forget about lost canteen—death by dehydration is preferable to death by free fall. Besides, dehydration is impossible in Maine, it's The Land of the Summer Monsoon— a feature rarely disclosed in camp catalogues.

117

At 3 A.M., all eighteen of us abandoned floating pup tents, took refuge in hermetically sealed Reluctant Dragon, which normally seats twelve. No room, no air, no sleep.

Chalked up several more popularity points by regaling group with dirty jokes until dawn, when Wilking decided to cancel rest of trip and drove us back to camp. No fool he, either.

Spent rest of Fri. in infirmary with cold and low-grade fever, coughing up a storm, chalking up zilch. Still no mail. Day was total loss.

Sat., July 9th

Day was total triumph! Earned grudging respect from Wilking, gratitude from track team by demanding early release from infirmary in order to "win for Soonawissakit in the Intercamp Meet or die of pneumonia in the attempt."

Mission accomplished—a first in two out of three events, a tie for second in another!

Cough miraculously vanished—due, no doubt, to combination of youthful constitution and psychosomatic reaction to increasing popularity.

From here on in, could do no wrong, as evidenced by performance in late afternoon baseball game. I was 0 for 3 in the 7th (never was any good at that game), finally managed to connect with the ball—a rolling grounder straight to pitcher that should have made me 0 for 4 but pitcher made wild throw to first. Believe it or not, this was tactfully recorded as a base hit for me rather than an error for him!

After game, Swensen, #1 tennis player at camp, invited me to be his doubles partner in tourney semifinals the next day, substituting for #2 player, Gorsuch, who'd torn a ligament.

118

Said he'd been impressed with how I'd pulled Levine's chest-
nuts out of the fire for him in the quarterfinals last Sunday and
figured he and I would make a "ruhlly powerhouse combo."

I told him I'd like to, but was pretty much committed to Levine.

Swensen said he wouldn't want me to do anything scuzzy,
conscience-wise, but since I'd never win with Levine anyway,
if I could find some way to dump him, it would be ruhlly great.

Playing it ruhlly cool, I said I needed time to think about it
and would let him know later. Actually, I'd made my decision
the moment he asked me—it was only a question of implement-
ing some ruhlly crafty strategy already forming in my ruhlly
crafty mind.

After Dinner

"Hey, there, you two," I said to Annabel and Mallison at the
track-meet victory bonfire. "Making out okay?"

Annabel hastily disengaged Mallison's arm from around her
waist. "Is that your idea of sophisticated humor?" she said
disparagingly.

"Oh, no—" I began.

"Then wipe the leer off your face," she warned.

"—I just wondered how you were making out," I said, continuing to leer.

"Not too bad, considering the lack of privacy around here,"
said Mallison with a salacious twinkle at Annabel.

She gave him an affectionate dig in the ribs. My fatherly
blood began to boil. Clearly, they were making out just fine.

Stifling an impractical urge to tear Mallison apart with my
bare hands, I stifled an ostentatious yawn instead. "Golly, between the track meet and the ballgame, I'm gonna hit the sack

ruhlly early tonight. I bet our whole cabin will—except poor Duck, of course. He has one heckuva time falling asleep without that Sony. . . ."

Later That Night
Mallison, making his escape from the conked-out cabin, stopped by Duck's bed for a second.

"Enjoy," he whispered. Then he left.

"Enjoy what?" said Duck. "Another sleepless night?"

"This," I said, handing him the Sony. "And the batteries still work, Mallison said so."

"Ape, oh, Ape," he crooned ecstatically. "How did you get him to do it?"

"It was kind of a trade-off. My sister for your transistor, as it were." I sighed.

"Knowing how you feel about your sister, that was an incredible sacrifice."

"Knowing how you feel about your music, it was worth it." The moment was ripe. "Duck, I'm dumping you for Swensen in the semis tomorrow. I hope you don't mind."

No answer from Duck. So much for the ruhlly crafty strategy. I wasn't about to sacrifice my daughter for nothing, however.

"The thing is, with Swensen, I think I have a crack at winning the whole thing. I hope you don't mind," I said again.

"Under the circumstances, what can I say," said Duck in such a neutral tone I couldn't get an accurate reading on it.

"You could say I was a rat-fink deserter," I suggested humbly.

"No, I couldn't. I could never say that about you, Ape," said Duck loyally. "Go ahead, play with Swensen. It doesn't make that much difference to me. If it does to you . . . well . . ."

120

He clapped his beloved headphones on and rolled over. "Just make sure you win."

Sun., July 10th
We won all right. Wiped the court with them, in fact (6–2, 6–0), and since one of them was Roland de Berganza, born with a silver sneaker in his mouth, the victory was sweet indeed.

Sweeter still was the weekly awards ceremony after dinner, when I was presented with a plaque proclaiming me Soonawissacamper of the Week.

To the Greater Glory of Ape Face! I thought to myself as I raised the plaque high above my head. I did it for our team, rah-rah-rah!

But then, as I was being carried out of the dining room on the shoulders of my newfound friends and admirers amidst cheers and huzzahs from the exultant throng, a startling thought occurred to me:

I hadn't done it for our team and the Greater Glory of Ape Face. There *was* no our team; there was only my team and the Greater Glory of Me. Because Ape Face and I were probably never going to change back.

Or had I subconsciously suspected that all along? I wonder. . . .

15

(continued from July 5th)

Today, Sun., July 10th, it's 96° and so smoggy at the pool I can hardly see to write. I bet the air in Maine is much better—this stuff really burns your eyes.

Anyway, sorry for the delay, but the whole week has been a madhouse.

Wed. and Thurs. were full of meetings, screenings, and the usual dailies in the afternoon. Having to watch the same scene over and over again got pretty

interesting on Thursday when we had to watch a man and a woman take off all their clothes and make love in a wheat field over and over again.

boring after a
while, but don't worry, I didn't ho-hum any
more than anyone else.

Quite a lot less, in fact. In fact, being someone who
usually has to get a grown-up to walk me into an R-
rated flick, it was all I could do not to oh-wow! through
the whole thing.

Wed. night was the weekly dinner meeting
(catered at the studio) when all the top brass
sit around discussing their projects. I handled
it very well considering

considering what? . . . . Considering I didn't know what
any of my projects were and your friend Tony "The
Shunner" Crane kept pressing me on production details in order to show me up? I can't put that in, Duck
might read it. But I sure would like to know what
Dad ever did to him, the guy's a real snake. . . .

I'm new at the job.
Of course, it helps having Stephanie (Marshak—we're on a first-name basis, isn't everybody?) in my corner.
Speaking of Stephanie, guess what?! Remember that Miss Moon who taught you 2nd
and 3rd grade, the one you pretended not to
like because I didn't approve of her too much?
Well, that's *Stephanie!*—what a coincidence!
I certainly approve of her now, and not just
because she's my boss, either.

So there, Daddio!

Then, beginning on Thurs., late aft

Boy, was that only last Thursday? So much has happened since then; there's been a kind of real change in me since then—no, no, it's not what you think, I'm still 6'1" with a beard* and everything, it's nothing anyone looking at me could put a finger on, nothing physical, I mean, but since last Thursday . . .

I began looking at houses for us to live in.

I guess it was the houses that did it, the houses and the schools. Between Thursday and Saturday, I saw twenty-three rich houses†, eight schools, and every street, drive, boulevard, canyon, and hairpin curve in the greater Los Angeles area.

By Saturday night at Peggotty Horn's party—which was a combination Sweet Sixteen Come As Your Favorite Horror Film Hero/Heroine party for her daughter Melanie Sue and a Come As You Are party for everyone else in Hollywood—I was so confused and worried, all I could do was sit on a satin couch in front of the fireplace and stare into the fake flames (fueled by a gas jet underneath an asbestos log).

---

* I noticed this morning it's getting scraggly again but it's Sunday and the barber is closed. Maybe I'll shave the whole thing off—messing around with it's a royal pain.

† Harvey Godchaux told me on Wednesday the details of my deal were all worked out, and I should be thinking in the seven-fifty or slightly higher range.

"Dollars a month?" I asked.

"What are you, crazy? That'd get you a kennel for your keeshond!" (Everybody out here has dogs you never heard of.) "I'm talking about purchase price. In thou's." Gulp!

"Hey, chum, mind if I join you?"

I looked up. It was Ty Donovan.

"Heck, no, why should I mind? Sit down," I said, glad to see him. "How's it going?" Duck usually levels with me the second time around.

"Like I said, great," said Ty, still on automatic pilot.

I guess it was dumb of me to ask. What did I expect him to say? "Lousy? Everything's going lousy! Nothing good is ever going to happen to me ever again, I just know it!"—which is the way he looked. The big guys don't talk to each other like that.

"Well, if there's anything I can do . . ." I said vaguely, which was as personal as I thought I could get.

"Nothing. Unless you run across a hot property you want to shoot my way," he said.

"Sure thing," I said.

"How's by you?" he asked. "Feeling a little more on top of it than the last time I saw you?"

"Absolutely." I can play this stupid game, too, Ty baby. You're the one who taught me how. "Things absolutely couldn't be better."

". . . Because if you ever need a sympathetic ear . . ." He paused, studied the ice in his drink, jiggled it around, then looked up and straight at me. "Listen, Bill, about what I said the other day, forget it. I was just—you know, bruised-feelings department. I mean you really can trust me, I really am your friend."

"And I'm yours, Ty."

We both sounded so sincere, you'd certainly think we were friends.

Well maybe we are . . .

"Bill," said Ty, lowering his voice, "a word of warning, look out for Tony Crane."

. . . but maybe we aren't. For all I know, he's Tony *Crane's* friend.

"No kidding," I said cautiously. "I've only had a couple of meetings with him, but so far so good. He seems like a nifty guy."

All the warmth went out of Ty's face. "Okay, chum, I tried," he said, rising, "but if that's the way you want to play it, to each his own." He looked away from me.

But it isn't! I don't want to play anything. I feel like a rat chasing my own tail! "Wait a minute, Ty!"

"Ty who?" said a voice behind me.

I turned. It was Ray Ewald. "Ty Donovan," I said quickly, and turned back again but it was too late, he'd been swallowed up by the crowd.

"Is he a friend of yours?" asked Ray.

The moment of truth.

"He used to be," I said, "but I don't know if he still is."

"Just as well," said Ray. "He's a loser anyway."

"But I *hope* he still is," I said fiercely.

"Hanging out with losers isn't too swift an idea, Willy," said good old Ray.

"To each his own," I said. "What's your idea of a winner—him, I suppose?" I jerked a thumb at Tony

Crane making points with Peggotty Horn at the bar.

"Now you're talking," said Ray. "Or her," he said, waving at Miss Moon across the room.

I made a beeline for her. She seemed as pleased to see me as I was to see her.

"Bill! I didn't even know you were here!" She clutched my arm impulsively. "What a zoo!"

"You should see the children's zoo downstairs," I told her. "There was a girl standing around in a long white dress completely covered with blood all over her face and everything—very yuck—having a friendly conversation with a boy with an axe—presumably the one who did it to her.

" 'Boy,' I thought, 'if someone hacked me up like that, I sure wouldn't be standing around having a friendly chat, I'd be dead on the floor, and why wasn't she?'

"Then I found out she was Carrie from *Carrie*, which I never saw, and he was Jason from *Friday the 13th* Parts One and Two, which I also never saw because my mom wouldn't let me—" WATCH IT! "—take her (I have this nice old mom I take to the movies but she doesn't like the scary ones), and the two of them went together in real life."

"Real life," said Miss Moon as she surveyed the scene, "is pretty unreal sometimes."

Oh, Miss Moon, you don't know the half of it!

"Say, do you want to sit down somewhere with me?" I asked eagerly. "I need your advice on a few things."

She was willing, so we sat on the satin couch in

front of the fake fire and I told her about all the houses and how I couldn't decide among them.

Hadn't I been able to eliminate any of them? she asked. Weren't there one or two that shrieked, "Buy me! Buy me!" as soon as I walked through the door?

"That's the trouble, there are three like that," I told her. "There's the one in Pacific Palisades—top of San Remo Drive. A little expensive but a terrific view, huge swimming pool, *two* Jacuzzis, *and* a paddle-tennis court which Dad would love—"

The look on her face stopped me.

"—to play on when he comes to visit with my old mom."

"Remarkably spry, that old man of yours," said Miss Moon.

"Oh, yes, fit as anything," I agreed. What's the matter with me tonight!—I keep forgetting who I am! "Then there's a house on Mulholland. The price is right, and it has a great kitchen—built-in convertible microwave oven, compacter, white glass chopping-block counter, center island with top burners, charcoal grill—"

"Do you cook a lot?" she asked.

"No, but—"

"Your old mom does?" she suggested, grinning.

I nodded. "Yes, and so does my wife. My wife would like that Mulholland house very much. It even has an earthquake room."

"Ah, but how does your wife feel about earthquakes? Because Mulholland Drive . . ." she trailed off dubiously.

128

That was part of my problem, I explained. On account of my wife was still away and I couldn't check it out with her.

"But then there's the house in Westwood. I *love* Westwood. It's only twenty minutes from the beach, but it's like, I dunno, it's like . . ."

"New York," offered Miss Moon.

"Right! Record shops, pizza, movies, arcades, Adidas, ice-cream parlors—"

"I know, I know," laughed Miss Moon. "That's why I live there."

"No! Do you?"

"For now," she said. "But I'll have to move soon, I'm afraid. It's not"—she made a mocking face—"a suitable area for the president of Galaxy."

"According to the real-estate agent, it's not even a suitable area for a vice-president of Galaxy," I said.

"Supposedly not," said Miss Moon. "But if the house is nice, what do you care? How's the house?"

"Great! Great, *great* house. Not so jazzy kitchenwise or poolwise—postage-stamp pool, and no tennis court or paddle tennis, but a game room that won't quit. Giant wall TV, billiard table, pinball, jukebox, Space Invaders all included in the purchase price." CAREFUL! "My son would *love* that house."

There was never any point in trying to fool Miss Moon. "Your son, Bill, or you?" she said skeptically. "Come on, now, the truth."

So I gave it to her. "Me, I guess. Sounds silly, but I love those kid games."

"Then that's the house for you."

". . . But now that I think about it, my son might want something more status-y, Bev Hills maybe, or that Pacific Palisades house—"

"Oh, Bill, you make me impatient, honestly you do! You're so worried about what everybody else wants— what do *you* want?"

"What do *I* want?"

That all depends on who "I" is. If I'm Ape Face only temporarily in possession of Dad's body, then I have to make decisions he can live with when he repossesses himself—which isn't so easy because I don't know who he is either. (A first banana would go for status; a second banana posing as a first banana probably would, too. A regular, nonpretending second banana might care as much about pleasing his family as himself, but Mom likes kitchens and I like game rooms. . . . Knowing Dad, we'd end up on Mulholland with the microwave, and I really *love* that game room. . . .)

On the other hand, if "I" is Ape Face in permanent possession of Dad's body—

"Hello?" Miss Moon waved her hand in front of my face.

I came to.

"Good, you're still alive," she said, amused.

"Sorry. What do *I* want?"

"Yes, Bill." She smiled into my eyes. "What do you want?"

"I want . . ." My stomach turned over, I could hear my heart beating. "I want . . ." to kiss Miss Moon. I want Miss Moon to kiss me. I want, oh I want—

"Are we interrupting something?"

It was Millicent Ewald on the arm of Ray.

Without taking her eyes from mine, Miss Moon said gently, firmly, with a tiny shake of her head, "No."

Then she directed her attention to the Ewalds and talked about my housing dilemma. Or I guess that's what it was. You can hear words but it's hard to grasp their meaning when everything inside you has gone so suddenly still as death. There was talk about Ellen . . . ? Okay, I think I said. Talk about thought maybe we were separated? What? I said. . . . Separated? . . . Yes. No! She's in Window Rock, Arizona . . . for long? . . . I don't know, maybe. . . .

After a while I gave up. Said good night. Found Barkham. Went home to the hotel. Looked at myself in the mirror for a long, long time. Then reached out and touched the image of my face. Don't be sad, I told myself. At least now you know what it feels like—loving. That's something, anyway. And tomorrow, I lifted my chin, tomorrow . . .

I'm about to close a deal on a super house in Westwood because after looking at a bunch of them, I've decided it's definitely the one I want.

As for schools, I plan to sign you up for Wormley—it's very achievement oriented, you'll like it a lot, I'm sure, and you can be dropped off there on my way to the studio.

Gee whiz, Soonawissavisitors' Day is less
than a week away. I haven't talked to Mom,
but she can't be any more anxious to see you
than I am.

"Mr. Andrews? They just announced a telephone
call for you, Mr. Andrews. Didn't you hear?"

"No, but thanks," I said, looking up. It was the same
middle-aged bellboy with the paunch who'd delivered
my bags that first day.

"Hey, I've been looking for you ever since I arrived!"
I said, digging out a fiver from the toe of my Gucci.
"Here you go, and if you'll just wait a sec . . ."

I hastily scribbled Love, Dad, jammed the letter into
an already-addressed envelope, and handed it to him
with instructions to have it go out immediately.

Then I hippety-hopped my way over all the glistening bodies to the poolside phone.

"Hello?" I said.

"Hi, darling," said a very-long-distance voice.

"Mom!" I exclaimed happily. "Where are you?!"

Nowhere, apparently.

"Are you still there?" I asked.

I heard her clear her throat. Good. She was still there.

"This must be a horrible connection," she said. "I
thought you said, 'Hi, Mom.' "

"Oh-ho-ha-ha-ho-ho-ho-ho-ho-ho!" I laughed—
probably the longest laugh in history, also the phoni-
est, but it gave me time to think. "Not Mom, *Tom* is
what I said. Tom is a cute little kid I play with out
here at the pool.

"Not now, Tom," I said, off phone, shooing him away. "I'm talking long distance to my wife. Go play by yourself, g'wan, git!"

Two glistening bikini bods raised themselves up on oily elbows to look for Phantom Tom. Not finding him, they whispered to each other about me (not very subtly, either), then slid back down their elbows to broil themselves some more.

"Sorry about that, Ellen," I said. "Now tell me everything. How goes it in Window Rock, *are* you in Window Rock? I thought they didn't have phones on your reservation."

They didn't, said Mom. She wasn't there anymore, she was in Tucson because she was through, through, *through*—wasn't that exciting!—earlier than she'd expected. And how was I, darling?

Darling told her all about the promotion, and about the funny coincidence of *Ben's* teacher (this time I got it right) being my boss, and then, because I knew I couldn't put it off much longer, I tackled Topic A.

"I have great news for you," I said. "A wonderful house in Westwood."

"What wonderful house in Westwood?"

"A wonderful house for us. Or will be. The kitchen needs a small amount of fixing but there's a great ga—"

"Bill"—her voice had a sharp edge to it—"if you're saying what I think you're saying, you'd better not be."

"I was afraid of that," I groaned. "Well, there's another house on Mulholland that does have a great kitchen but I thought you weren't so interested in cooking now that you're working—"

"In New York!" she shouted. "I am working in New York, not in California. Are you out of your mind?!"

"But *Mom*," Jeeze! "*Tom*, will you cut that out, get away from me now, no more tickling!"

The bikini bods oozed upright, and watched me closely from under their pitch-black shades.

I covered the phone and explained myself. "It's dotty old Mom, she thinks my older brother's still alive—died years ago of—" what did people die of years ago? "diphtheria, poor Tom—but we have to keep pretending—"

Do I care what they think? Phooey on them. "Ellen," I said into the phone, "Ellen, listen to me—"

"Now he's calling her Ellen," observed Bikini Bod #1.

"Mad as a March hare," said B.B. #2.

Double phooey on them!

"No, you listen to me," she said, and for several fun-filled minutes, she let me have it right between the eyes about the scarcity of museum jobs and how hard she'd worked to get this one, and what did I think she was anyway that I could unplug her in one place and plug her in someplace else without even asking—a portable TV? I hadn't heard her that mad since the day I wouldn't eat Annabel's Sugar Coated Snappy Crackles because I didn't want to make *her* mad (you know how I am), and that was years ago. (Also a whole other story, which I won't tell now.)

But after I said I was sorry about twelve times, she finally calmed down. And then it got worse.

"Not as sorry as I am," she said in this lethally quiet voice. "You see, I thought we had a partnership going for us, but nowadays, I'm the kid in the mailroom and you're the chairman of the board—pardon me, Executive Vice President in Charge of Worldwide Production, *bucking* for chairman of the board—"

"Don't be mean!"

"Don't interrupt—and at the rate you're going, you'll probably make it, too, although I'm not sure I want to be around when it happens."

I let out a squawk of protest which she rode roughshod right over.

"—Because frankly, Bill, you're just not the same man I married."

I'm not? "What do you mean?"

"Aw, come on, Willy," she said angrily, "who needs a movie mogul? I want my nice, vulnerable," what's so great about vulnerable that everybody loves it so much? "struggling young writer back!"

Dad started as a writer? How about that!

"But aside from the writer part, you're describing me exactly," I said. Me and Dad both, I suddenly realized. Alike! The same! How about THAT! "That's exactly who I am. Exactly!"

"I don't think you know who you are," she said, sounding serious and sad and determined. "When you find out, I hope you'll let me know."

Was that a click?

"Mom . . . Tom? . . . Ellen?"

Definitely a click.

Oh Lord, now what?!

Behind my back, I heard the bikini bods discussing me.

"I think his girl friend just hung up on him"—B.B. #1.

"Why couldn't it be his wife just hung up on him?"—B.B. #2.

"If it was his wife, he wouldn't have tried to fool us in the beginning by calling her Mom"—B.B. #1.

"He didn't call her Mom, he called her Tom. Maybe it was a boyfriend just hung up on him"—B.B. #2.

"He also called her Ellen"—B.B. #1.

"If he called her Ellen, it was his wife—but not for long, honey, not for long. Splitsville, I hear"—B.B. #3(!!).

"Bull!" I said, facing them. "We're just having a few problems, that's all."

"I know," said B.B. #3, a.k.a. Millicent Ewald.

Just my luck!

16

". . . Sperling, de Menocal, Belknap, Loring . . ." Letty "Ma Barker" Newsome was handing out mail, "Von Volkening, Hitzigger . . ." to everyone but me, naturally—why should this day (Wednesday) be different from any other? ". . . Beaty, Levine . . ."

Duck's parents wrote constantly. If a neurosurgeon can find time, what's the matter with a film executive, he's got a secretary, hasn't he? What's the matter with "Hello, how are you?" dictated to a secretary? Fine father he's going to make!

". . . Swensen, Gorsuch, Andrews—"

Well, whaddya know! Finally! I leaped forward.

"*Annabel* Andrews," clarified Ma Barker.

I fell back—into Annabel, who elbowed me aside, quipping,

"Is your name Annabel?" (Ever since the day I made Soonawis-sacamper of the Week, or around about then, she'd begun being quite uncordial, I don't know why. Maybe she's the kind of foul-weather friend who only loves a loser.)

"A postcard from Mom," she announced smugly, whipping it under my nose too fast to read.

"O'Neal, e-a, O'Neill, e-i, Andrews, Ben . . ."

The A Group (Hitzigger, Swensen, Biddle, etc. plus Duck— a probationary member in on my coattails, so to speak), burst into happy applause for me.

"I suppose you got one, too," said Annabel, worried I was going to do her one better.

"A postcard from Mom *and* a fat letter from Dad!" I said, doing her one better.

"Bully for you," she said. (Annabel as a daughter is merely a continuing responsibility. Annabel as a sister stinks!)

I sat down on a stump and opened Dad's—my *son's* letter.

"What does he say?" asked Annabel, eagerly leaning over me.

I shifted positions so she couldn't see. "Is your name Ape Face?" Sibling rivalry is a two-way street, kiddo!

> Dear Ape Face,
> How's camp? Fine, I'll bet. That's good. I'm

"Boy, is he boring!" said Duck over my left shoulder.

I whipped around and glared at him. "Are you usually in the habit of reading other people's mail?"

"Yours, I am," he said, injured. "You always let me."

"Oh." In that case, there wouldn't be anything in this about Us, nothing that wasn't safe for Duck to read.

"Well, okay then," I told him. "But not you," I told Annabel.

While she stood by, seething with impatience, Duck and I skimmed the next few sentences about having fun at camp and California weather, blah, blah, blah.

"Boring isn't the word for it, it's the terminal big Z's," I complained to Duck.

"I guess he just writes the way he talks," said Duck.

"How do you know how he talks?" I said, highly offended. "You only met him once."

"Yes, but you told me a million times—"

"Told you what? What did I tell you?"

"Oh, you know," said Duck. "About how every day he asks you how was school? and you say fine, and he says that's good—don't you remember telling me that? And then one day you got so sick of the same dumb conversation, when he said how was school, you said fine except the tip of your finger got cut off in the jigsaw and you fed it to the guinea pig—"

Annabel let out a whoop of laughter. "Ape, you didn't! That's hysterical!"

"—and your father said that's good, because he wasn't even listening?" finished Duck.

Annabel's face fell. "Oh," she gasped. "Oh, no, that's awful!"

"Yes," I said, embarrassed. "It really is."

The realization that Ape's boring letter was actually a skillful parody of my own boringness made me blush all over.

Annabel put her arm around me. "Don't worry, Ape, he does things like that to me, too, sometimes. He means well, he just gets sort of—"

"Preoccupied," I suggested. "Very preoccupied with very demanding work."

139

"Yeah, right," she said loyally. Atta girl, Annabel! not such a bad sister/daughter/whichever, after all.

As a peace offering, I allowed her to read over my right shoulder while Duck continued reading over my left.

"Hey, listen to this!" Annabel snatched the letter away from me and read aloud the section on the Moon/Marshak revelation.

Learning that Moon was Marshak held no particular significance for me since I couldn't remember having met her in the first place. (School is Ellen's department—or was in those early days before she got involved in anthropology and I took over some of her responsibilities—well, I suppose they're partially my responsibilities, too. . . .)

"But I can't believe I'd pretend not to like someone just because Dad didn't approve of her," I said.

"*I* can!" said Annabel and Duck together.

"You're scared to death of Dad and you know it," said Annabel, adding complacently, "I don't know why."

"Neither do I." If true, though, it was a rather unsettling notion. As for the bit about "I certainly approve of her now, and not just because she's my boss, either"—was I being hypersensitive or was Ape Face, having already implied that I was a remote, uninterested and intimidating father, now zinging it to me for being an opportunistic *hypocrite*? If so, that was even more unsettling.

And you ain't heard nothing yet, folks!

"What's this about houses?" mumbled Annabel, reading on. "Whoop-de-doo-de-doo!" she hooted. "We're moving to California!"

I snatched the letter back, scanned it frantically. "Where does

140

it say that? Where, where, where?! I don't see anything about California."

Duck pointed to the sentence about Westwood. I read it once, then I read it again, and then I was outraged!

"How *dare* he! How does he know I want to move to California, maybe I do and maybe I don't! And what makes him think I want to live in Westwood, that's a ridiculous place for a vice-president to live, I'd rather live in Brentwood—"

"You're not vice-president, Dad is," said Annabel.

"Button up, missy, that's enough out of you!" I shouted.

"*Now* listen to him," she said to Duck scornfully. "He's even talking like Dad."

"That's right, that's right, I am! And I'm thinking like him, too, since he's too stupid and incompetent to think for himself—"

"Lawsy, *lawsy* me!" said Annabel. I wanted to wring her neck.

"—but if he could, let me tell you something, young lady, he wouldn't think much of your behavior this summer, you're an absolute disgrace, you and that goat Mallison sneaking around in the middle of the night doing heaven knows what—"

"It's none of your ever-loving business what we do, you little creep, but for your information, we don't do anything."

"Aw, gee," said Duck, "why not?"

"Another county heard from." Annabel rolled her eyes. "Because I've decided he's not my type, we're just friends."

"I don't believe a word of it," I declared. I didn't!

"I don't give a rat's ear *what* you believe, it's true!"

"And even if it *is* true," I went on, "between sneaking around in private and necking in public, you two are abrogating your responsibility to provide decent role models for impressionable

141

youngsters, which is something I certainly don't approve of, as you well know—so why are you looking at me like that Annabel"—she had a very peculiar expression on her face—"I've made myself clear on this issue many times before, have I not?"

"No, you have not," she said, narrowing her eyes in thought, "but Dad has."

"Annabel," said Duck, out of the side of his mouth, "I think he thinks he's your father."

This was getting a little too close for comfort.

"Don't be dumb. I know perfectly well who I am," I said, storking to prove it.

"You're sure?" Annabel was suspicious, I could tell.

"Sure, I'm sure," I said, losing my balance and crashing to the ground.

"Ape Face," she said tactfully as she helped me up again, "how would you like to go to the nice infirmary?"

"I wouldn't," I said. "I'm fine."

"Well," she said, linking her arm firmly through mine, "you seem a bit upset."

"Of *course* I'm upset," I said, shaking her arm loose. "Why wouldn't I be upset! Not one word out of that jerk for ten lousy days while I molder away in this crummy hole wondering what's going on, and suddenly it's Dear Ape Face, how are you, I'm fine, bingo, bango, guess what, we're moving to California, I bought a house in Westwood. *WESTWO-O-OD!*" I howled like a wolf. "He's got some bloody nerve. He can't make decisions like that without consulting me!"

After a second of strained silence, Duck ventured a timid question. "Why not?"

142

"Yes, why not?" Annabel chimed in. "Who *do* you think you are, might I ask?"

"That's beside the point!"

"No, it isn't, Ape. It's exactly the point," said Duck, hoping to get through to me with reason and logic. "After all, you're only a kid."

He couldn't possibly have said anything worse.

"Now *there*'s a clever observation!" I smirked.

"Cool it, Ape," said Annabel, protecting Duck.

She needn't have bothered. His response was to stare at me for so long and with such open hostility, I was forced to look away. Back I went to the letter, to another charming surprise.

"Now hear this," I said, attempting a reconciliation. "If you're interested, that is."

Annabel shrugged.

"Suit yourself," said Duck.

" 'As for schools, I plan to sign you up for Wormley—it's very achievement oriented, you'll like it a lot, I'm sure.' What makes him so sure?"

"Maybe he's heard about the New You," said Duck acidly, and walked away.

"Another foul-weather friend," I remarked, watching him go.

"Meaning?" asked Annabel.

"Meaning he liked me better when I was an oddball like him. And I suppose you did, too," I said accusingly.

"Ape," she said, evading the issue, "you haven't read your postcard from Mom. Here." She patted the stump, we both sat down, "give it over, I'll read it to you.

" 'Darling Ben, Work at Window Rock went wonderfully, completed research ahead of schedule and decided to stop off in L.A. to visit Dad for a few days—' ''

I slapped the postcard out of her hand. "She can't!" I brayed. "She was going to fly straight here, that was always the plan!"

"Well, now it isn't," said Annabel unflappably. "Now she's going to have an impromptu two-day honeymoon with Dad first."

"No honeymoon! That's out of the question!" I screamed. And I mean screamed. Alarmed birds flew out of the bushes, Ma Barker stuck her head out of the infirmary window to see what was going on. Annabel gave her a signal indicating scram, everything was under control, which it most decidedly was not.

"Brother mine," soothed Annabel, "you are a classic little-boy basket case in love with his mother—"

"I am *not* in love with my mother!"

"—which is a stage all little boys go through, just the way all little girls are in love with their fathers and I used to be in love with Dad—"

"—And now you're in love with Terry Mallison." I scowled at her.

"God almighty, Ape Face, you've got to be the only kid in the world in love with his mother *and* his sister! Sick, sick, sick!"

"Finish the postcard, will you please, doctor."

"Finish it yourself," she said, picking it up off the ground and tossing it in my lap. "I'm going for a walk."

. . . but the museum director wants me back in New
York, so there goes that!
Good!

Cannot *wait* for Saturday. I've missed you, love
you, Mom

Mom . . . Good-bye, Ellen, hello *Mom*?! *Forever*?! It was unthinkable. So unthinkable, I'd avoided thinking about it altogether.

But you really must, I told myself. You've got to begin at
the beginning and think it through, *all* through. From the beginning . . .

Well then: I have been given (by whom and for whatever
reasons I suppose I'll never know) a new lease on life, which
in my case means the chance to become what everybody, even
Ellen, already believes me to be: Willy Winner. Let's hear it
for Willy Winner!

"If I'd only known then what I know now," people are always
saying. Okay. For me, Then has become Now, and Now will
become thirty brand-new, born-again years to whip the world
into shape (funny word, whip—is that what I mean?)—how bad
can that be? I'm already number-one jock in the camp and I
betrayed my best friend in the bargain—congratulations, Willy,
you're on your way.

Another crack at Varsity track, another crack at college
boards, college interviews—Yale this time around. Do they still
have Freshman mixers?—poised, this time around. Do they
still have senior dances?—who this time around? Who do I
take? Anybody I want, they all want me. I want Ellen. Not this
time around.

But I want Ellen. To sit across the dinner table, to share the
little triumphs and sometimes little losses. To love me and to
love. *Not this time around.*

I want to walk my daughter down the aisle. But I'm not going to be the father of the bride. I'm going to be the brother of the bride, this time around.

I want to be a wiser, kinder father to my son. Too late, Willy Winner, too late . . .

I cried, then. Alone on a stump (in full view of nobody, thank God), the Soonawissacamper of the Week cried—isn't that something? Cried buckets for the thirty misbegotten years that lay ahead and the thirty irretrievably behind.

17

Every once in a while there's a day that starts off so badly, things can only get worse because one bad thing leads to another. I'm talking about Thursday, July 14th.

It started off with the *Today* show on in the bedroom and me in the bathroom, an English muffin on one side of the sink, o-juice on the other, trying to decide whether or not to shave off my beard.

On the basis of having nothing better to do at that moment, plus it was costing me a fortune at the barber, and I was bored with being told by everybody I met about the bit of this or that nesting in it (Frosted Flakes being the worst offender, bacon-cheddar cheeseburger remnants runner-up), I decided to go ahead.

I should have decided not to. Getting rid of a big tough beard with a puny electric razor is almost impossible. What you need is a machete, which I didn't happen to have. There was hair all over the bathroom, floating in the o-juice, sprinkled on the muffin—a surprising amount, really, when you consider how much of it was still on my face, looking as though rodents had nibbled at it during the night.

This is a gosh-darn mess, I said to myself. (Well, that's approximately it—what I actually said was a good deal shorter. One word, actually.)

From the bathroom phone, I rang the barber downstairs and humbly asked his advice. To go snip-snip with a nice sharp scissors first and *then* zippety-zap with the razor was his advice—why didn't I come in and let him do the job properly?

Because that would make me late for my 9:15 meeting at the studio with my boss, but thank you anyway, I told him—and tackled the job myself.

Bulletin: Scissors—the kind that come in the handy travel sewing kit your wife packs for you—are not nice and sharp; they are nice and blunt. Toenail clippers are nice and sharp, but short—only a half inch of cutting edge, and ever so slightly rounded downward at either end (so you won't get an ingrown toenail). This makes them perfect for toes but slow going for beards because after every half-inch snip, you then have to snip off the tufts the clippers missed at either end (but you won't get an ingrown beard).

By 8:40 (twenty-five infuriating minutes later), I was finally finished snipping and about to start zippety-zapping when Peggotty Horn began her daily hatchet job on—who would it be this morning? I wondered, razor poised in midair.

You'll never guess.

"A sorrowful little bird tells me that Galaxy's vice-prexy Bill Andrews and his lovely wife, Ellen, designer of Navajo jewelry," Mom'll love that! "are definitely splitsville."

"No, no, no!" I yelled and slammed the bathroom door.

In a rage, I picked up the electric razor, and imagining I was dismembering Piggotty Peggotty and her sorrowful little bird, a.k.a. Millicent the Buzzard, into itty-bitty bite-sized pieces to feed to the polar pears, I viciously whacked, hacked, pulled, tugged, yanked, and gouged away at myself until I was completely clean-shaven—and looked as though I'd been run over by a threshing machine.

For the next part of the day, on top of everything else, I suffered from an acute identity crisis, beginning in the hotel lobby.

Nobody down there knew me. De Virgilio passed me by completely, so did Malcolm the maitre d', Miss Vondermuhl, and even the middle-aged bellboy, who after my five-dollar tip had every reason to not only know me but love me. And at the front door, when I asked Doorman Bob if I could have my car, please, his answer was what car, sir?

149

"That car," I said pointing to Barkham and the Mercedes parked a few yards away.

"That is Mr. Andrews' car, sir," he said.

I started to tell him I was Mr. Andrews, but Doorman Bob, having already dismissed me as a nobody, was deep in conversation with a somebody. To heck with this, I thought, if Muhammad won't come to the mountain, et cetera, and marched to the car alone.

Barkham was engrossed in the London *Times*. I rapped on the window to get his attention and started to open the door, but after one quick glimpse of me he pushed the automatic door-lock button.

"Let me in, will you? I'm late already," I told him.

"This car is reserved for Mr. Andrews," he said in his hoity-toitiest voice, deliberately omitting the sir. (A chauffeur is never unintentionally rude.)

"Barkham, it's *me*," I said. "Minus the beard, that's all."

Barkham leaped out of the car and solicitously guided me in.

"Well, sir, I must say, sir," he said with a hollow cackle, "you look as though you'd had a bit of a run-in with the Demon Barber of Fleet Street."

"Very funny," I said, slumping in my seat.

Barkham eyed me edgily in the rearview mirror. "There are tissues right behind you, sir." He swerved to avoid collision with a Porsche. "Mind the upholstery!" Mind the upholstery! I'll kill him! (Or he'll kill me.)

"Forget the upholstery, mind the road!" I yelped,

150

trying to preserve what remained of my mutilated self in case Dad ever moved back in.

"As you wish, sir," replied Barkham stiffly—the last words he uttered until we reached the Galaxy gate, where he had to identify me to Miguel the guard, who also didn't recognize me, and neither did my very own secretary, Mavis Ohler. Honestly!

Frankly, the whole thing was getting to be incredibly ridiculous and humiliating; furthermore, my face hurt, and I was upset about Peggotty Horn and worried about my mother, and as for Betty Lou Bienenstock, she was the last straw.

"Excuse me, sir," she said as I headed for Miss Moon's office. "Sir! Where do you think you're going?"

"In," I said, my hand on the doorknob.

"Well, I'm very sorry," she said, not sounding sorry at all, "but Miss Marshak never sees anyone without a prior appointment—if you'd care to leave your name . . ."

"My name?! My name," I said, fighting for control, "is William," pause, "Waring," pause, "Andrews. And I *have* a prior appointment"—I tapped my watch impatiently—"which you are making me late for!"

Then, before there were any further protests, I barged right in and closed the door behind me.

"Sorry, I'm late," I said.

Miss Moon looked at me puzzled. "Don't I know you from somewhere?"

"Yes. I shaved off my beard."

"With a grapefruit spoon, evidently."

I forced a painful smile. "Might as well have been."

She was still looking at me puzzled, so I refreshed her memory. "Bill Andrews, V.P. in Charge of World-wide Production, fellow New Yorker."

She laughed. "Bill, I know who you are. But why do you suddenly look so familiar?"

Because among your other virtues, you are someone who *really* never forgets a face and you saw mine, unbearded, once in the second grade—but I don't want to get into that now.

"Beats me," I told her. "Listen, I know we're supposed to talk about future projects, but I want to talk about something else."

"Such as," said Miss Moon warily.

"Such as did you hear what Peggotty Horn said this morning on the *Today* show?"

"Oh, that," she said, breathing a sigh of relief. "According to Peggotty Horn, half the couples in L.A. are splitsville—I wouldn't be upset about that, if I were you."

"No? Well, I am. Very. Extremely."

She took off her aviator glasses. "Mm," she said thoughtfully. "Bill, if it's not too personal, would you mind telling me, are you upset because you and your wife *are* splitsville, or because you aren't?"

"Yes. No! I don't know. Both, I think. I'm all confused."

"That makes two of us," said Miss Moon. "Enlighten me. Have a seat." She pointed to the desk chair. "Take it from the top."

"Okay," I said, sitting, "but it's kind of a long story, do you have time?"

"No, but I'll make time," she said. That's Miss Moon for you—she always makes time when it's important, and miraculously, she always seems to sense when it will be.

Gratefully, I began. "Remember that first day when you asked didn't I want to check it out with my wife before I said yes to a West Coast job, and I said no, we had an old-fashioned marriage, she went where I went? Well, I should have said yes—I mean yes to the check-out, no to the job, because you see my wife has her own job—at the Museum of Natural History—"

"Which she doesn't want to leave, naturally." Miss Moon was not a bit surprised.

"No. In fact, when I talked to her on the phone in Tucson last Sunday, she was so mad at me for not taking her job into consideration, I think right now she'd rather leave me than it. And I don't know what to do."

Tell me what to do, Miss Moon, come on, tell me! But she wouldn't.

"Bill," she said, shaking her head, "here we go again, it's just like the houses. Granted, choosing between career and marriage is a slightly stickier wicket . . ." She briefly contemplated the problem, then made a suggestion. "What about your plan to commute back and forth?"

"I didn't even get a chance to suggest it—she hung

up on me! But she'd never go for that, I know she wouldn't. What am I going to do?"

Please, Miss Moon? Just one little hint.

"Friend," she said, folding her hands on the desk, "what do you *want* to do?"

Push, push, push! I can't take much more of this.

"It all depends," I said, squirming. Because if Dad and I aren't going to change back, even though I hate playing the Executive Banana Game, I want to stay here and marry Miss Moon—after all, I certainly can't stay married to Mom and I certainly do love Miss Moon. . . . I wonder if Miss Moon loves me—

"On what?" asked Miss Moon.

But suppose we do change back? Dad doesn't want to be married to Miss Moon, he wants to be married to Mom—hey, wait a minute—

"On what?" repeated Miss Moon, a little more insistently this time.

"Wait a minute, I'm thinking," I told her. This was important: Dad wants to be married to Mom, yes—but more than he wants to be chairman of the board? Mom doesn't think so, but I think so. I hope so. Better be so, because I definitely do not see myself as a child from a broken home. Should I resign from this job and ask for my old one back to save the marriage? But with my luck, it'll turn out we stay the way we are and I'm stuck in New York and—Oh, I dunno, I dunno, I dunno, I dunno, I dunno-o-o!

"On *what!*" said Miss Moon, pink in the face with exasperation. "Time's up, Bill, what does it depend on,

154

tell me—*what?!*" she begged, flinging her hands palm up under my nose.

Okay, Miss Moon, you asked for it!

"On how long I'm going to be stuck in the body of my father and he's going to be stuck in mine."

Miss Moon never missed a beat. In the same straightforward tone she might have used to discuss whose Magic Marker belonged to whom, she said, "This is not your body?"

"No, it's positively not."

"Right," she said calmly, her hand creeping casually toward the intercom box. "Now tell me again, where did you say your body was?"

"At camp in Maine with my father in it"—and here's where I noticed her finger pressing down the intercom button, and realized, too late, that except for the blood-red talons, we seemed to be enacting the very scenario I'd imagined the day I was waiting to be fired.

"Hey, what are you doing that for!" I exclaimed, and here's where she's going to whisper to Betty Lou about the little men in the white coats.

"Okay, okay, I'll go," I moaned, "but if Dad and I change bodies again while I'm in the cookie jar, will you give him his old job back?"

Tears were now cascading down my cheeks and stinging like fury in my shaving cuts. . . .

"Betty Lou," said Miss Moon, "Mr. Andrews and I would like not to be disturbed for a while, so cancel my ten-thirty meeting and hold all calls, please.

155

"Come"—she beckoned. "Everything's going to be all right, just come with me."

Obediently, I followed her to an inner-sanctum sitting room I didn't even know existed, where on request, I began with the body exchange in the Port Authority terminal and ended with, "So what you see before you is a twelve-year-old boy"—here's where I started to cry again—"who's very scared and homesick and Mom's mad at me and Dad probably is mad at me, too—well, anyway, now do you see the problem?"

"Yes, I do," she said gravely. "And I think I also see a solution."

"What is it?" I asked. "I'll do anything you say, just tell me what it is."

"A leave of absence, Bill, a good, long leave of absence."

She didn't believe me. I should have known.

"In the cookie jar, you mean."

"No, no." She patted my hand reassuringly. "Nothing like that. Just some time off to calm the nerves and mend the marriage. Maybe you and your wife would like to take a little trip together—"

"That is the last thing in the world we would like," I said, honking furiously into a Kleenex. I was so angry and disappointed with her I could hardly wait to leave. But first, "Where's your bathroom? I want to wash my face."

"Here," she said meekly, leading me to it and snapping on the light.

And there it was! Hanging on the wall just to the right of the sink. Framed and everything.

"Oh!" I marveled, standing practically in the shower to get a better view. "What a great stegosaurus!"

"Yes, isn't it," she agreed. "And how clever of you to know what it was." She cocked her head to one side and admired it fondly. "Most people are totally baffled."

"Listen, if I don't know what it is, who would?" I said, leading her on.

She refused to be led. "Mmn?" She gazed at the stegosaurus, lost in thought.

"After all, I'm the one who painted it."

Oblivious to this, too, she cocked her head on the other side and admired the stegosaurus from a different angle.

"A terrific little boy I once taught did it," she mused. "He didn't think it was any good, but I loved it." She smiled. "I loved him."

I could have melted in a puddle on the floor.

"It was mutual," I said, but I don't think she heard this either.

"His name was Ben . . ." She reached into her memory.

"Andrews," I said.

At last she woke up. "Right," she said, turning slowly to face me. "How did you— Oh!" She recognized me, finally. "Oh, no wonder you looked so familiar, Bill. You're Ben's father, aren't you! Ben Andrews' father! How *is* Ben?"

"I'm fine," I said.

"Yes, I can see that, Bill," she said briskly, "but how is Ben?"

I didn't know what to answer. I couldn't just keep on saying I'm fine, I'm fine, could I? What good would that do, she was never going to believe me anyway.

In silence, I let her steer me to the door.

"Good-bye for now," she said. "And when you see Ben, will you give him a kiss for me?"

I decided to make one last try. "Miss Moon, why won't you believe me?" I pleaded. "You always leveled with me, I always leveled with you, why would I lie to you now?"

There was a long, awkward pause, and then all of a sudden she lit up.

"You know what?" she said. "I think I do believe you. I'm probably out of my mind, and you're probably out of yours, but I really do believe you."

"You do?!" I whispered. "How come?"

"Because," she said, gurgling with laughter, "you haven't changed a bit. Look at you!"

I looked to see where she was looking. At my right leg. Storking on my left leg.

I destorked and grinned at her. "Okay, then, how about my kiss?"

She planted a lovely one right on my cheek. That's where you'd kiss a twelve-year-old boy, isn't it, on the cheek?

Good-bye, Miss Moon. I love you.

July 14th didn't turn out so badly after all.

18

"There she is," said Annabel, spotting Ellen among the Soona-wissavisitors waiting in front of the admin building.

I took off like a bat out of hell.

"Try not to make a complete jackass of yourself," she shouted after me. "She's only your mother!"

As if I needed reminding.

Even so, it wasn't easy. After being separated from your wife for over two weeks, a bear hug, a kiss on the forehead, and a comment on how much you've grown and how great you look is hardly a reunion to gladden the heart of the average man.

"You look great, too . . ." I might as well get used to saying it, "Mom," I managed to squeeze out.

"My sentiments exactly," said Annabel, with a kiss-kiss, a hug-hug, and an anxious "Where's Dad?"

"Dad?" said Ellen, stalling for time.

"Yeah, Dad—the one with the beard and the big blue eyes, remember him?" said Annabel.

Ellen usually responds to Annabel's teasing with some snappy comeback of her own. This time, her response was a deliberately vague "Uh, well . . ."

Annabel raised her eyebrows at me: Trouble in paradise? Ellen saw her and hurriedly continued. "I think he's coming directly from the Coast. I drove up with the Levines." Hm. "Aren't you going to say hello to them, Ben?" she added brightly.

"Sure." As soon as I figure out who they are. "Where are they?" I asked, hoping Ellen would pinpoint them in the group of parents I was pretending to squint at on the admin porch. "Any closer—"

"—we would have bitten you," said Duck's parents, who were standing right next to us. With half a brain, I could have figured that one out. Not only was Duck standing between them, all three were standing in fifth position. (Aren't genes extraordinary, or do we attribute this one to environmental influence?)

More hellos and hugs, and then Ellen put her foot in it.

"I assume you two guys are still thick as thieves," she said, affectionately rumpling Duck's hair.

Annabel nudged Ellen in the ribs.

"Not exactly," said Duck quietly. Then he turned on his heel and walked off, leaving the rest of us, including his parents, with egg on face and a large conversational void to fill.

"Kids," said Dr. Levine with an uneasy shrug.

"They'll work it out. Won't you," said Mrs. Levine, smiling

160

at me. (Nice woman, Mrs. Levine, a lot like Ellen, no wonder they get along.)

"Hope so," I answered.

"I'm sure," said Ellen.

More silence.

"Where's Dad?" I finally said.

"Yes, where *is* Dad?" echoed Annabel. "They're going to start the exhibition games in a minute, why isn't he here, Mom?"

"Annabel, how would I know," said Ellen irritably. "If he came straight from the Coast, he'd have to fly from Boston to Bangor and rent a car from there."

"No way!" I declared. After what I told him about driving, he wouldn't dare. "That means he's not coming."

"Oh no?" crowed Annabel triumphantly. "Then what is that?" she said, her sharp eyes riveted on the camp entrance.

Turning in was a Buick station wagon, driver in front, passenger in back. Over the rutted road it came, bumping and bouncing and all the while beeping and finally stopping a few feet away.

"What is that is right!" said Ellen in disgust, as the driver deferentially opened the door for a husband she seemed none too pleased to see.

"What *is* that?" I said under my breath after Ape Face and I had greeted each other publicly. "What have you done to my face, that face looks terrible, I almost didn't recognize it! Where's the beard?"

"It'll grow," said Ape complacently. I know where he got that from; it's my automatic rejoinder to his complaint about a too-short haircut.

"Oh well, why should I care, it's not my face," I said.

"Daddy, Daddy, Daddy, what happened to your poor little

161

self!'' lamented Annabel, caressing a Band-Aid on his chin. What a disgusting display—if she knew that was her *brother* inside there! . . .

"Hello, Bill," said Ellen, keeping her distance.

With a hesitant "hi," Ape Face approached and kissed her gingerly on the cheek.

"Is that the best you can do?" said Annabel. "What's the matter with you guys!"

"Mind your own business," I told her, although privately I agreed. Ape Face's reticence was understandable, but after being separated from your husband for over two weeks, he merits more than a cool hello. In other words, something was definitely the matter with Ellen.

"Oh!" enthused Ape Face, sighting the Levines.

He bounded over to say hello, I bounded after him, but too late. He was already into "Hi, Dr. Levine, hi, Mrs. Levine!" cordially pumping the doctor's hand and kissing the doctor's wife more heartily than he'd kissed his own mother.

The Levines, glassy-eyed with nonrecognition, tried to cover with the usual nice to see you again's, and I tried to intervene.

"Dad—" I began.

"I get it!" said Ape Face, thinking he knew what was wrong. "You two don't know me without my—"

"Dad, they don't know you at all," I reminded him.

"Well, you do now," he said with a giggle. "Bill Andrews here, great to meet you after all these years!" More hand pumping and cheek kissing, followed by "Where's Duck?"

"Well," said Mrs. Levine, "I think he's—"

"Never mind, I see him, hey Duck!" he yelled, "How are you?"

Duck, undoubtedly torn between wanting to avoid me and greet my nice father who'd sent him batteries, waved tentatively, but stayed put.

"Duck!" yelled Ape again. "C'mere! C'mon over here!"

Duck reluctantly did. "Hello, Mr. Andrews. Thanks loads for the batteries."

"Sure, Duck. Oh, wow, Duck, am I glad to see you! Wow!" rejoiced Ape Face.

"When did you two get so clubby?" said Annabel, arriving on the scene with Ellen.

"At the Port Authority terminal, love at first sight," said Ape Face, on the ball this time. "Like father like son, right, Son?" he asked me. "Right, Duck?"

Duck licked his lips nervously. Ape Face picked up on it immediately. "You two okay?" he asked, his eyes zigzagging back and forth from one of us to the other.

"Bill, I'd leave it alone if I were you," quietly cautioned Ellen.

Ape Face ignored her. "Still best friends and everything?" he asked us.

"Oh, yes," said I.

"No," said Duck coldly. "Ben's best friend is Brian Hitzigger now."

"Brian Hitzigger!" Ape Face roared at me. "Brian *Hitzigger*?!"

"Attila the Hun," Annabel explained to Ellen.

"So I've heard," said Ellen.

"Oh, dear," said Mrs. Levine, commiserating eye-wise with her husband. They, too, had obviously heard of Brian Hitzigger.

Ape Face simply couldn't get over it. "What did you have

163

to do to get *him* on your team?'' he said in a tone of blistering contempt.

''Nothing! He was making fun of me in the dining room so I knocked him out cold on the floor—''

''You *did*?!'' He was momentarily diverted by this bit of news.

''Yes I did, and he's been crazy about me every since. But that's not my fault, is it? *Is* it?'' I asked Duck.

''Maybe not,'' acknowledged Duck, ''but you're also best friends with Baker Biddle, Sandy de Menocal—''

''Never heard of them,'' said Ape Face.

''Superjocks,'' said Duck, plunging the dagger in deeper, ''with nothing in the noodle. The last of the fetal pigs.''

''Not to mention Roland de Berganza, son of the Marquesa de Berganza y Santa Lopez,'' suggested Annabel snidely. Whose team is she on, I'd like to know.

''He's not a friend, he's a rich wimp!'' I said but nobody paid any attention.

''And best, *best* friends with Thor Swensen,'' said Duck, giving the dagger a final twist.

''The hell I am!'' I shouted. ''Duck, listen to me. I have one best friend and one only, and that's *you*.''

''Oh, yeah? Prove it!'' said Duck, blinking back the tears.

Ape Face tried to defuse the issue. ''Duck, who's Thor Swensen?''

''Number-One tennis player, your son is number two,'' said Duck. ''Any minute you can see for yourself.''

''Now listen up, all you Soonawissafolk,'' bellowed Wilking through the bullhorn.

''Like right now,'' said Duck bitterly.

164

"For the next hour, it's our pleasure to present to you Soona-wissakit's finest solo athletes as they demonstrate their prowess in exhibition waterskiin', archery, riflery, rock climbin', wrestlin', tennis—"

"Starring Swensen and Andrews," said Duck.

"—and track," concluded Wilking. "Last but not least"—his voice implying quite the opposite—"there's Ping-Pong for the kids not doin' anythin' else, cuz after all, what's good enough for the Chinese is good enough for us."

Laughter and applause from the parents.

"Excuse me, everybody," I whispered as Wilking started reading out the names of Soonawissakit's finest solo athletes. "I'll be right back"—which I was, in time to hear his pseudo-gracious concession to Soonawissakit's nonathletes.

"Also durin' this hour's gonna be exhibitions of arts 'n' crafts—which includes loom weavin', metalwork, tie-dyin', and suchlike, plus nature studies pertainin' to various flora and fauna indigenous to the Maine terrain, plus a photography and water-color exhibit in the dinin' hall for folks whose kids've been fan-cyin' that kinda activity." God help 'em!

"Now after that's gonna be exhibition team sports of lacrosse, soccer, and baseball; and for the kids not participatin' in any a them, we got a tug-a-war with a rope, and a three-legged race, followed by a picnic lunch on the grass, such as it is—more like pebbles and pine needles, heh-heh-heh—for every-dang-body in the place!

"So go to it, Soonawissafolk, and have yourselves a real nice day."

Applause, applause, applause.

Then, just as the Andrews/Levine contingent was about to

165

disperse, Swensen appeared, sparkling white from teeth to toe, and rarin' to go.

"Ready, partner?" he asked me, taking a few impeccable backhand swipes at an imaginary ball with his graphite racket.

"Golly, Swensen, you're going to think this is ruhlly scuzzy of me, but I've decided to play Ping-Pong with Levine instead."

For probably the first and the last time ever, Duck and Swensen reacted identically. Both their mouths dropped open.

Swensen recovered first. "You're dumping me for Levine?"

"Why not? I dumped Levine for you once. Maybe this'll even up the score," I said, looking first at Ape Face, then at Duck, then back to Swensen. "Don't sweat it, pal, I've already fixed you up with Gorsuch. He's number three, and ruhlly dying to take you on.

"Ready, partner?" I asked Duck as Swensen stalked off in a snit.*

"How do you know I want to play?" said Duck. "Maybe you dumped Swensen for nothing."

"Seeing as I dumped you for less, Duck, that's the chance I took."

"He's better, he'll beat you," warned Ape Face. He was testing, testing.

"I'll take that chance, too," I said, passing the test. . . .

And losing the match. Not on purpose, either. In full view of all the Andrews, Levines, and assorted others, he beat me fair and square—he happens to be a better player.

But not a better runner! After Ping-Pong, we paired up for the three-legged race and came in—well, let me describe it this way: When one person is running straight ahead and the

* Somewhat akin to a huff but minus the wheels

other person is running due left because that's the direction his free foot is facing, it's extremely difficult to progress.

We not only didn't come in first, we didn't even come in last; about halfway to the finish line, we fell flat on our faces and just sat there laughing and scratching and hooting and hollering—Duck Levine and the panty-hose queen, joined at the hip forever (metaphorically speaking)—we never came in at all.

At the awards ceremony before lunch, when amidst cheers and huzzahs and humorous catcalls from all the other losers in the camp* Duck and I received the Soonawissabooby Prize, I don't know who was the most delighted—Duck, me, Ape Face . . . or Swensen!

* Who seemed like a nice gang—I made a mental note to get to know them better

19

The picnic lunch (soggy paper plates of lukewarm whole wheat spaghetti with "meat" sauce, gritty lettuce, fruit, cookies, milk) was pretty bad. Not that it mattered. The four of us weren't hungry anyway. And the atmosphere was awful. Annabel and I tried to make cheerful conversation but we kept running into trouble.

"Wasn't that three-legged race the funniest thing you've ever seen in your life, Mom? Dad?" she said.

"Mm-hm, oh, yes," said Mom, making a valiant effort to be jolly. "And I'm sure Duck appreciated your entering it with him, darling." She patted Dad on the shoulder.

"Right you are!" I said. "Making up with Duck is

168

worth a booby prize any old day, don't you think, Ellen?"

"Yes, I think," she said with a slight emphasis on the "I," meaning "that's what *I* think but I'm surprised it's what the future chairman of the board thinks."

"Me, too!" said Annabel. "Besides, Ape Face can afford a booby prize after what happened last Sunday. Ape, tell them what happened on Sunday."

"I was named Soonawissacamper of the Week," said Dad. "No big deal," he added modestly.

"Nonsense, it means you were the best," said Mom with another shoulder pat for him and a sarcastic crack for me. "Dad must be very proud of you."

"Well I am—very. Aren't you?" I asked her.

"I thought I'd already indicated as much," she said. Thunk. Silence.

A look of alarm shot from Annabel to Dad to me.

I looked down at my plate and carved tic-tac-toe marks on it with my plastic knife until I could see pine needles coming through the bottom.

Annabel made a second attempt. "Say," she said animatedly, "how does everybody like Dad without a beard?"

"It's a little hard to tell right now," said Dad, tactfully referring to the scabs and the Band-Aid, "but I think I liked him better with it."

"It'll grow," I said again. "It's got some stubbly stuff already, see, Annabel?"

Annabel ran her fingers against the grain on my

169

cheek. "Grr," she growled to show approval. In a pinch, she's a real trouper.

"And you, Mom," she asked. "How do *you* like Dad without the beard?"

"About as much as I liked him with it." Mom smiled sweetly at nobody in particular but especially not me.

"Okay!" Annabel blew up. "I've had enough of this—absolutely enough!" She snapped her fork in half. "What's going on here! Mom, Dad, did you two have a fight or something?"

"No. Absolutely no!" I declared.

Mom cleared her throat delicately, meaning "he's a great big liar!"

"Then what's she so mad at?" said Annabel, nodding at Mom.

"That's what I'd like to know," said Dad, glaring at me.

"Well," I sighed, "because of the move, I guess. See, when I got offered the California job, Mom wasn't around to discuss it with, so I said yes, forgetting all about her job in New York—"

"You didn't!" said Dad. "That's appalling!"

"I know, I know," I said, distractedly twirling spaghetti strands around my plate with my finger.

"Bill, stop playing with your food, you're worse than Ben," said Mom crossly. At least she was still talking to me.

I licked my finger and looked pleadingly at her. "But I thought you had . . . we had a different kind of marriage than we do. I thought . . . I thought . . ." I surrendered. "I didn't think, period. I'm really sorry."

"Well," said Mom, relenting somewhat.

"Well, nothing!" said Dad. "It's just the most inconsiderate thing I ever heard in my life!"

"Listen, Mr. Holier Than Thou," said Annabel to Dad, "what are you trying to do—make things worse? If I remember correctly, when that letter arrived, you never gave a thought to Mom's job either—all you were concerned about was having to live in Westwood!"

Dad looked as though he'd been punched in the stomach. "True," he admitted, hanging his head, "I'm afraid that's true."

"Sweetie," Mom reminded Annabel, "he's only a child."

"That makes two of us," I said to Dad.

"No wonder you're upset," said Dad to Mom.

"Oh, I'm not all that upset," she said, back to nice and normal. "Just a little ticked off. And a little worried." She frowned. "What *are* we going to do, Bill?"

"I've been given a leave of absence to think it over, if that's anything," I told her.

"Swell," she said. "But after the leave of absence, what then?"

"I don't know," I said. "I just don't know. Could you and the kids maybe stay in New York, and I could commute back and forth?"

"Commute!" shrieked Annabel. "That's some commute! I don't understand. Don't you two love each other anymore?"

"Yes, we do," said Mom and Dad together.

Annabel scowled at Dad. "Not you, dummy, *you*," she said to me.

"Yes!" I said. "But . . ."

"Could you . . . uh, you could . . . quit," suggested Dad tentatively.

"Not in a million years," said Mom, turning to me for confirmation. "Would you. I know you."

"No, because I'd lose my stock options and severance pay," I said, showing off for Dad. "But I could make them fire me."

"Would you?" Mom looked at me with surprise mixed with what—excitement? hope?—both?

I had an idea. "Ape Face," I said, "if you had to choose between your wife and your job, which would you choose?"

"Oh for heaven's sake, what are you asking him for?" said Annabel. "What would he know about it?"

"More than you think," said Dad. He gave me a decisive nod. "I'd choose my wife."

"That's good to know," I said. "And so would I."

"Oh, Willy!" Mom squeezed my hand.

"Would?" said Annabel. "What do you mean, would?" She's got bat's ears, my sister.

"It's not so simple," I said.

"Oh." Mom withdrew her hand.

"Dad, can I talk to you alone? I've got to talk to you alone!" said Dad.

"Excuse us," I said, and we went for a walk in the woods.

20

Now that we were alone, I didn't know where to begin. We went quite a long way in silence.

He said he wanted to talk, why doesn't he talk! And he'd better have some answers, because my brain is on strike.

"You go first."

He probed a scab on his chin.

"Would you mind leaving my face alone?" Great beginning, Bill, just great. Sounds positively hostile. It was meant to be funny—

"It's not your face anymore, remember? You said so yourself."

—but naturally, he didn't take it that way.

173

I aimed my foot at a toadstool and kicked it to smithereens.

"I can do anything I want to with this face," he said, glowering down at me. "I might even get it lifted!"

Now that *is* funny. When he gets mad he's really funny.

"What are you laughing at?"

"Nothing, sport." I didn't know he ever got mad. Good for him. He's human after all.

I reached up to touch him.

"Quit it," he said, ducking out of the way.

I don't know why I did that. He was only trying to be nice.

This kid isn't just mad, this kid is about to self-destruct—*do* something! I don't know how. Do *any*thing.

"Hey, Ben? Benjie? Listen, we're in this together, we've got to solve it together. I need your help."

His voice was so . . . different, gentle sort of, it took me by surprise. For a second, I couldn't say anything.

Come on, kid, aren't you even going to meet me halfway?

"Yeah, I know, Dad. I'm sorry."

"It's okay."

"You want to sit down? Here's a flat place."

"Why not?" I got partway down.

"Or would you rather keep walking till we come to a rock so I won't get pine tar on your pants?"

"They're your pants now. And it doesn't matter anyway—here is fine, but whatever you want to do."

Why are people always asking me what *I* want to do? I don't know what I want to do, I *never* know what I want to do, I'm sick of it!

"Sit, I guess."

"Fine." I went the rest of the way down.

I think I'm going to jump out of my skin. . . . Better not, who knows whose skin you'll jump into next—could be Millicent Ewald—uch! or Hitzigger. Oh, sit down and think of something to say, it's your turn and he's waiting. I can't think of anything. I *can't*.

He sighed heavily and looked away.

"I guess it's been rough these last couple of weeks—yes? . . . No?"

He wouldn't look at me and he wouldn't answer, just stared vacantly into the Maine woods. Poor little guy, what in God's name was he thinking now?

I can't stand it when he's nice to me! He's being *so* nice to me . . . I think I'm going to cry.

Ah. So that was it.

"I haven't got much of a shoulder these days, but you're welcome to what there is of it."

I must've been making a terrible face because he asked, "What's the matter now?"

"It stings in the cuts."

I wiped the tears away with my hand. "Where? Which one?"

"This one," he said, pointing—just like when he was three.

He kissed it. "Better?" he wanted to know, just like when I was little.

"Yes," he whispered. "Are you crying, too? You look as though you're crying, too."

"What do you want from me?" he said, scrambling to his feet. "I'm only a little kid."

I laughed, and got to my feet, too.

The tension was gone, now, but not the sadness.

"Yeah, well, I wish you weren't," he said ruefully. "I want to be the little kid and you be the grown-up. I'm not ready. It's too hard," he said, storking on my pants—*his* pants! "Much too hard."

"Oh, no it's not," he said, trying to cheer me up. "You've already missed the hard part. What's ahead is all downhill sledding. I'm the one you ought to feel sorry for. I've got to live through all that rotten stuff all over again.

"I'd much rather be you,"   "I'd much rather be you," we both said at once, and for the second time in one week, I crashed to the ground. Storking is simply not one of my talents.

"Jeeze Louise, Ape Face, look what you made me do to my pants!" I said, examining a colossal triangular rip in the knee. I must have been in shock. I mean, after enduring two hideous weeks of imprisonment in your son's body, not to mention his world, when you finally get your own body back, you don't complain about pants!

Ape Face had a firmer grip on reality. "Better yours than mine," he said with a wild and wicked guffaw. "Boy, am I glad that's over!"

Then he fell into my outstretched arms and snuggled there cosily while we

1) Exchanged factual information about our experiences in L.A. and Soonawissakit—not in any great detail, just hitting the highlights—at the end of which, Ape said, "Say, Dad, you know that composition they always make us write in the fall—'How I Spent My Summer Vacation'? Well?" He wiggled his eyebrows up and down rapidly like Groucho Marx. "What do you think?"

What I thought I won't disclose now. What I said was "I wouldn't, if I were you."

"Ha-ha-ha, but you're not!" he said gleefully. I'm telling you, once this kid gets started, there's no stopping him—he was full of beans.

He also knows when enough is enough. "Because of the little men, you mean?" he asked, sobering up.

"Partly," I told him. "Mostly, I'd just rather you didn't. But there's always the rest of the summer. . . ."

A fleeting cloud crossed his face. "I can hardly wait," he said. "Is this place as bad as it seems?"

"The pits."

"It must have changed since your day, huh, Dad?"

"Not one iota."

"*No?!* Then how come you loved it so much?"

"I didn't. But over the years, I guess I managed to block out the worst of it, so when you wanted to go—"

"But only because I thought it would make you happy!"

"And guess why I wanted to go?"

"To make Grandpa happy?"

I nodded. "And if you send any kid of yours here, I'll break every bone in your body!"

"Poor Duck," said Ape,

which led to

2) A discussion on jocks vs. nonjocks, in which we agreed that being a Soonawissacamper of the Week, i.e. a fabulous superjock, was maybe sixty percent motivation and will, and only forty percent native athletic ability.

"You probably could have done it yourself, Dad," observed Ape.

177

"What do you mean? I did do it myself!" I said, briefly succumbing to a residual attack of pride.

"In my body," he reminded me.

"With my motivation and will," I reminded him. "If you'd been here, would you have been Soonawissacamper of the Week? No." A sudden, searing insight: "Because aside from motivation and will, it also requires ruthless aggression, and you're too nice."

which led to

3) My admitting that his extraordinary niceness had always awed me to the point where I didn't know how to communicate with him, resulting in all the vapid "how was school?" conversations, including the quintessential feeding-the-fingertip-to-the-guinea-pig incident, for which I humbly begged his forgiveness. He then admitted to me that the guinea pig incident had never actually happened, he'd invented it for Duck in a moment of extreme self-pity, for which he humbly begged *my* forgiveness. I was only too happy to give it.

More important was his admission that what I'd taken to be extraordinary niceness was nothing but Yellow-Jell-O cowardice because he was scared of making people mad at him, in fact he was scared of quite a few things—

"And scared to death of me, I gather."

"I used to be," he said, "but not anymore."

"Well, well, well! And why not?"

"Because it turns out we're so much alike."

"I consider that a compliment," I told him.

"To me or to you?" he said with an impish grin. Cocky kid! I rubbed his face in pine needles till he yelled uncle.

"Ape Face," I said when we'd stopped horsing around, "I'm afraid of things, too. Everybody is."

"Like not having a job?" he asked.

"Yes, just like."

"But you know," he said, "aside from the problem of Mom, from what I've seen of your job, I'm not sure it doesn't take more guts to keep it than to quit."

which led to

4) An indignant monologue from Ape Face on the subject of executive game players like Tony Crane and Ray Ewald; the loneliness of men like Ty Donovan who couldn't afford to trust anybody but their wives—if you didn't have a wife, you were really up the creek (it was phenomenal how much he'd picked up in only a couple of weeks!); and then some juicy philosophizing about how to survive in a business where the thing that counts is not what you are but what people think you are—as evidenced by Miss Moon's Killer Cream Puff coup which worked vs. Ty's indie prod pretense which didn't—

leading finally to

5) Ape's Bottom Line: What kind of banana was I anyway? This was very important for him to know, he said.

I considered myself only a second banana, I told him. Would this be satisfactory?

Quite, he assured me. Actually, it was the only kind he liked.

So, with all that settled, we returned to camp, where we received a somewhat reserved greeting from Ellen and an overly effusive one from Annabel, who had the sleaze bag in tow.

"Daddy! I'd like you to meet my good friend and co-worker, Terry Mallison."

"Sir," said Mallison politely.

Ape Face, being the soul of generosity, was overjoyed to learn that Annabel had found a friend to call her own in this

179

godforsaken place (he had Duck, after all). "Any friend of Anna-bel's," he said pleasantly.

Annabel, still smarting from the tirade delivered by her little brat brother earlier in the week, misinterpreted this altogether, and countered with an ominous threat. "One more word out of you, Ape! . . ."

"What did I do?" whispered poor bewildered Ape.

"Later," I muttered, "I'll explain later."

"Well," said Ellen to Ape and me, "you two were gone long enough—did you solve the problem?"

Mallison, realizing he was an interloper, slipped away, leaving just the four of us.

"Which one?" said Ape, cheery as a bird dog. "We solved tons of them." Light dawned. "Oh, you mean did we solve *The* Problem. Dad!" he turned to me in a panic.

"Don't worry, sport, it's not your problem anymore," I said.

"But it is yours, Willy—ours," said Ellen wistfully. "Didn't you come up with anything in all that time?" She looked at the rip in my pants. "Or were you just fooling around."

I sat down beside her on the grass; Ape and Annabel sat, too.

"Now, here's what," I said, putting my arm around her. "One: you are going to keep your job. Two: I am going to accept that leave of absence. Three: we—meaning just us," I said to Ellen, "are going to fly to L.A. tomorrow to tie up a few loose business ends, and after that comes Number Four. . . ." I kissed her (it's been a long time).

"Which is?" prompted Ellen, kissing me back.

"Malibu or Pebble Beach or somewhere for a nice, long hon-eymoo—"

180

"Dad!" said Annabel, gesticulating madly at Ape Face behind his back. "Certain people are allergic to that word, ahem, ahem."

Ape Face, he's no dope, turned around and caught her at it.

"Who me? What's wrong with a honeymoon?" he asked.

"Nothing!" said Ellen.

"I think it's a great idea," said Ape.

"You do? Oh. Well, fine then," said Annabel, understandably nonplussed. "You didn't think it was so great on Wednesday."

"I've had a complete change of mind," he said serenely.

I couldn't have put it nicelier myself.

21

Maybe it was just because I was feeling so good about Dad and me, or maybe because I was expecting so much worse, or maybe a combination of the two, but camp turned out to be not so terrible after all.

In fact, between the jocks continuing to like me (although I wasn't quite the athlete Dad had been, owing to lack of motivation and will, I suppose) because I'd once made Soonawissacamper of the Week, and the nonjocks liking me (which they apparently hadn't before) because I'd stuck by Duck on Soonawissavisitors Day, I was getting along just fine with everybody except Swensen, Hitzigger, and Splasher Wilking—them I'm *never* going to like. Duck was getting along fine with everybody, too; not that peer approval is all that important to him anyway—he's perfectly contented with one good friend and a Sony in good, working condition.

In *fact*—this you're going to find hard to believe—since Duck's parents were pretty tied up in New York and mine were still in California, they gladly gave us permission to sign on for the Soonawissakit second session, and we ended up spending a total of eight weeks in the place. (To be accurate, eight for Duck, only six for me.)

A few days before camp was over, I got a letter from Dad.

> Dear Ape Face,
>
> I know Mom has written you and I'm sorry I haven't, but I've been extremely busy with some writing of my own—a screenplay, finished last week (untitled as yet), which Ty Donovan considers a hot property and is going to produce in association with Galaxy. Everybody is thrilled and loves it, especially your wonderful Miss Moon.
>
> And what is it about? You may well ask! It's the story of a twelve-year-old boy and his father who spend two weeks in each other's bodies, etc., etc.—you know how it all comes out. (You also know now why I didn't want you to write your "How I Spent My Summer Vacation" composition on this subject. Hope you understand and forgive—after all, it's your story too, but as a full-time

writer, which is what I've decided to be, with Mom's blessing, I figured my need for material superseded yours!)

Incidentally, Ty is floored by what he calls my "uncanny ability to crawl into the mind of a kid," and wonders how I managed to do it. Mom, though she's crazy about the screenplay, seems to take this aspect of it for granted; she says I might be amused by a composition Annabel wrote years ago called "Freaky Friday"—she'll dig it out for me when we get home.

Tell Duck more batteries are on the way, and if you could come up with a good title for me, it would be tremendously appreciated. I can't seem to think of anything.

I love you,
Dad.

22

This morning I got a Mailgram saying

HOW ABOUT SUMMER SWITCH?
I LOVE YOU, TOO. APE FACE.

THE END   **THE END**

185